Jilian bent down suddenly, pretending to pick up an object from the ground, pulling her knife from her boot instead. Holding her blade before her, she rose and spun in one move. The knife caught on her cape. She yanked it free just as he ran to meet her.

Running so hard that he could not stop.

Arms flung wide in an attempt to slow before he went over the cliff, the man impaled himself on her blade. He grunted once and slid to the ground.

'I was only trying to warn you,' he gasped out. 'He won't let you live. He dares not.'

She bent over him. 'Who?'

'The . . . prince.'

'The prince! That's absurd! How dare you accuse Nikolis of such a thing?'

But the man was beyond listening.

*Also by Amy Stout*

The Sacred Seven

*About the author*

Amy Stout has worked in magazine and book publishing since 1983. Besides being the author of two novels and several short stories, she is also an editor with Del Rey, the American publisher of fantasy and science fiction. She lives in Oregon with her husband, author Alan Rodgers, and their three children.

# The Royal Four

Amy Stout

**NEW ENGLISH LIBRARY**
Hodder and Stoughton

Copyright © 1997 by Amy Stout

First published in Great Britain in 1997
by Hodder and Stoughton
A division of Hodder Headline PLC
First published in paperback in 1997
by Hodder and Stoughton

A New English Library Paperback

The right of Amy Stout to be identified as the Author of
the Work has been asserted by her in accordance with the
Copyright, Designs and Patents Act 1988.

10 9 8 7 6 5 4 3 2 1

A CIP catalogue record for this title is available
from the British Library

ISBN 0 340 65363 9

Typeset by Palimpsest Book Production Limited,
Polmont, Stirlingshire
Printed and bound in Great Britain by
Caledonian International Book Manufacturing Ltd, Glasgow

Hodder and Stoughton
A division of Hodder Headline PLC
338 Euston Road
London NW1 3BH

This one's for the kids – Alex, Andrea, and Abe – who never let me forget what's important and always remind me why it's worth the struggle.

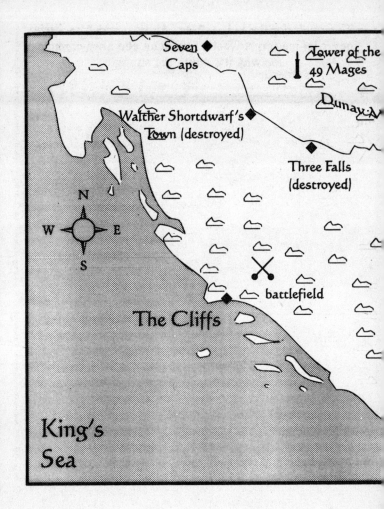

Seven Caps

Tower of the 49 Mages

Dunay-N

Walther Shortdwarf's Town (destroyed)

Three Falls (destroyed)

N
W    E
S

battlefield

The Cliffs

King's Sea

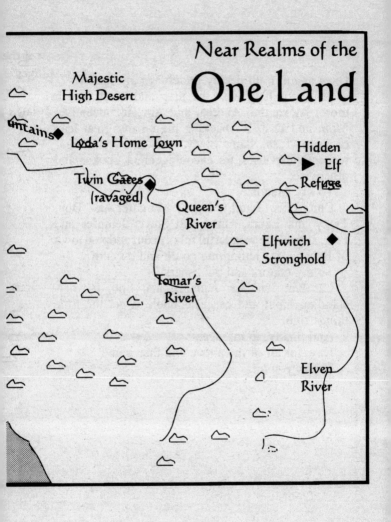

# Near Realms of the
# One Land

Majestic
High Desert

untains◆

Lyda's Home Town

Twin Gates
(ravaged)

Queen's
River

Hidden
▶ Elf
Refuge

Elfwitch
Stronghold

Tomar's
River

Elven
River

## Acknowledgements

Once again, I am deeply grateful to my family:

Alan, for help with the map and much, much more; Alexandra, Andrea, and Abe, for incentive; Mom and Dad, for backing me on my great leap of faith; Lisa, Sam, Stacy, and Luci, and their respective spouses, for encouragement, spoken and otherwise.

To my friends:

Dan, Lois, Jenni, Megan, Margaret and Don, Tracy and Laura, Jamie and Steve, Jennifer and Pete, and all the wonderful folks in our adopted town of Eugene, for letting me go on and on and . . .

To my editors and publishers:

Carolyn, Jennifer, Jennifer, and Lou, for outstanding input and caring enough to get the little things right.

And finally, to my agent:

Kay, for all of the above and then some.

Thank you all.

# DRAMATIS PERSONAE

## Humans

Princess Jilian – Twin to Prince Nikolis and co-heir to the ruling throne of the One Land; spent her childhood and most of her adulthood unaware of her parentage or of her brother's true nature as a human rather than a dragon.

Prince Nikolis (Nik) – Fraternal twin to Princess Jilian and co-heir to the ruling throne of the One Land; due to a spell gone awry, until very recently his body was in the shape of a malformed dragon named Mut.

King Tomar (deceased) – known as the Great King for re-uniting the seven realms into the One Land; his success was short-lived.

Sir Maarcus the Sixth – A native Shoreman; formerly King Tomar's personal physician and currently advisor to the royal twins.

Master Abadan – The royal magician (known throughout the One Land as the Magician).

Sir Maarcus the Seventh – Loyal grandson of Maarcus the Sixth, who serves the One Land in whatever capacity his grandfather or Prince Nikolis suggests, be it as a statesman or a spy or any role in between.

Wanton Tom – Mercenary known to travel in the company of the dragon, Grosik; former consort to the mage, Roslin; father of the mage, Ginni.

Ginni – Forbidden offspring of Roslin the mage and Wanton Tom the mercenary; extremely talented but untrained witch who possesses unusual ability with fire; highly skilled in the art of disguise.

Roslin (deceased) – Witch exiled from the Tower of the Forty-nine Mages; only slightly less powerful in magic than her daughter.

Lyda – Wife of Willam; a common shopkeeper's wife who rose to lead legions of refugees to safety.

Willam – Husband of Lyda, a former shopkeeper.

Revered Mother Caronn – Current leader of the Tower of Forty-nine Mages.

Revered Sister Dita – One of the seemingly favored witches in the Tower of the Forty-nine Mages.

Revered Sister Masha – One of the seemingly favored witches in the Tower of the Forty-nine Mages.

Lyam – A jailor.

Ivan – A jailor.

Prince Hadrian – King Tomar's fifth child.


## Elves

Alvaria – Daughter of Zera; mother of Jilian and Nikolis; evil and extremely powerful elfwitch known as the One.

Zera (deceased) – Alvaria's mother and the royal twins' grandmother; tutor in the arcane arts.

Notti – A goatherd whose mother was exiled; tended a sick Nikolis when the prince was still in his form as the dragon Mut; also known as 'Goatboy.'

Harmon – Zera's former apprentice now studying under Abadan.

Tabor – Brother of Theron; one of Alvaria's messengers.

Theron – Brother of Tabor; one of Alvaria's messengers.

Jedrek – Leader of the elves who were exiled for challenging Alvaria; also known as 'the Elder.'

# THE ROYAL FOUR

Lilith – An exiled elf.
Paly – Jedrek's captain of the guard; an exiled elf.
Ingaret – Notti's mother; an exiled elf.


## Dwarves

Walther Shortdwarf – Celia Sailclan's uncle; one of two
known survivors of village massacre; possesses unusual
magical sight and ability to produce visions.

Celia (Ceeley) Sailclan – Walther Shortdwarf's niece;
adoptive niece of Sir Maarcus the Sixth and Princess
Jilian; an orphaned dwarf.


## Dragons

Grosik – Known traveling companion of Wanton Tom
the mercenary. One-time consort to Barik.

Barik – Mother of twin adolescents, Ezrek and Nadik.

Ezrek – Female adolescent twin to Nadik.

Nadik – Male adolescent twin to Ezrek.

'Grandpa Maarcs?' A child squeezed the royal physician's arm. 'Grandpa Maarcs!'

Ceeley's insistent prodding dragged Sir Maarcus back from the place his mind always wandered whenever he remembered Zera's body beneath the mob of elves.

'What happened after that?' she asked.

Sir Maarcus the Sixth shook himself and gave the young dwarf a stern look. 'Celia Sailclan, you know the story as well as I do. You were there.'

The girl put on her best smile, but not even she could warm the physician on this cold morning.

'It was very smoky,' she said. 'I couldn't see much.'

'None of us could, Ceeley. It's why the elfwitch could get away so easily. Here now, why don't we turn to more pleasant tales?'

The dwarf child bit her lip and considered. 'You look a little tired, Grandpa Maarcs. Are you sure you wouldn't rather rest? My da always said old folks need as much sleep as babies.'

She's slowly healing, Maarcus thought. She can actually talk about her dead family without the words catching in her throat. He sighed and wished he could say the same for himself. 'No, no,' he said aloud. 'You know we all like doing our duty and taking turns watching you.'

Maarcus winced inwardly. That wasn't what he'd meant exactly – though sometimes the child could exhaust him in a way that his own grandson never had. Of course, the younger Maarcus had had nannies and tutors and protectors. Celia Sailclan only had a makeshift family of orphaned humans and dwarves.

Celia paid his gaffe no mind. She simply settled back into her oversized seat and reminded him to begin. 'Tell me about the Great King!'

Maarcus still missed the boyhood friend who had become king. The effects of his premature death rattled around the bleak castle now more than ever, though two generations had gone by. But for all that, the memory had never held the sharp pain of seeing Zera stoned at the hands of her own people.

The royal physician nodded. 'All right,' he said, 'a tale of the Great King. Which one?'

'Oh, you know,' she said.

'True enough, I do.' She nearly always wanted the same one. 'Well,' he began, 'not so very long ago before you were born but when I was already a full-grown man, there lived a magnificent king. His name was Tomar and he forged the greatest truce the One Land had known since the days before any of the magicians took to recording their spells and chronologies.

'But Tomar . . .' His voice cracked. Perhaps he wouldn't

14

be able to tell this story after all. He paused and glanced around the cavernous room Ceeley had claimed as her play area. The child deserved better than this. They all did.

He cleared his throat and continued. 'Tomar had an unfortunate tendency to spoil his children. You won't spoil your children, will you Ceeley?'

'No, Grandpa Maarcs. I promise.' She shook her head impatiently. 'So what about the twins?'

'Ah yes, the twins. I'm getting to them. When Tomar was something of an old man—'

'As old as you are today?' she asked, as if she had not already questioned their ages countless times.

'No, not by some years. You see I was younger then and that was many years ago.'

She cocked her head and stared at him as she always did, apparently trying to imagine him twenty or twenty-five years younger.

He waited until her brow unfurrowed before going on. 'Now Tomar was the father of the twins. Their mother was an elf he hoped would raise them well, but she was evil.'

'Evil, evil,' Ceeley echoed. 'Because she was Alvaria the elfwitch!'

'Right you are. And even though Alvaria had a very good mommy—'

'That was your poor friend Zera,' Ceeley put in sadly. 'She was nice to me, you know.'

'Right again,' Maarcus said, swallowing hard. 'Well sometimes there's only so much one person can do. Zera couldn't make Alvaria be good because Alvaria was a grown-up who had to choose to be good herself.'

'So the elfwitch ran away and the king died . . .' Ceeley prompted, rushing him to her favorite part.

'But there were still the twins, Princess Jilian and Prince Nikolis.'

'Aunt Jilly and Uncle Nik! I get to call 'em that because we're practically family.'

'Agreed again.' Maarcus was losing his patience for telling this story. He should have been able to get through the entire tale in minutes but the girl couldn't keep from interrupting. 'Jilian and Nikolis were sent to live with some wonderful foster-parents. Then the border wars started and no one could find them for a long time.'

'But one question, Grandpa Maarcs?'

He smothered his impatience under a stiff grin. The child had no one else. Her entire village lay beneath ash covered in winter's deepsnows. 'What's that?'

'Why didn't anyone think Uncle Nik was strange when he looked like a dragon?'

'That is an excellent question,' he said with nearly as much sincerity as he had when she'd first asked it on their journey back from the elven lands weeks ago.

She beamed at the compliment.

'I guess they were a little bit afraid of him. Not too many people have got close to dragons and lived.' Maarcus stifled a yawn.

No longer able to sit, Celia jumped up and circled her chair. She stopped suddenly and stared at the family crest engraved on the chair-back. 'It's a dragon! King Tomar knew his son would be a dragon!'

'I doubt that,' Maarcus said softly. 'When he chose the crest, he could not have foreseen what would happen to Nikolis. He merely picked an emblem he felt would be strong and unifying.'

Her brow wrinkled again in thought. Maarcus supposed he'd spoken over the child's head yet he couldn't bear another explanation. He was simply too utterly worn down.

'I bet he was a nice dragon,' Ceeley offered.

'He was very protective of Jilian even before either of them realized he was her brother,' the physician said, not quite agreeing with the dwarf.

'The elfwitch did one good thing,' Celia said.

'What's that?' Maarcus asked, only half listening.

'She turned Prince Nikolis from a dragon back into a man. That was a good thing.'

'Well, yes, I guess it was.' At least he hoped so. It was a difficult thing to know. Was Nikolis bitter over having been a misshapen beast for all but the past few months of his life? Did he mind losing the carefree lifestyle of a four-footed creature? Did he resent the host of duties thrust into his arms with so few companions to help him carry the load?

'It's okay if you go take a nap, Grandpa Maarcs. I'll be fine.'

'Thank you, my dear.' He gave her a hug and left the room without stopping to worry over who would watch her once he left. In a daze, he roamed the halls toward his own chambers.

Celia Sailclan anchored Sir Maarcus the Sixth in the present only sporadically. The scene that lingered in his mind always was of Zera's funeral – his darkest moment, a moment from which he no longer expected he would recover.

. . . Sir Maarcus had lit the flame and stepped back from the funeral pyre to stand between his grandson and Abadan the magician. Jilian, Nikolis, Walther and the others had fanned out to either side.

'Grandfather, come away from here,' the younger Maarcus said. Then more quietly, he added, 'Don't torture yourself. Zera chose loyalty to the elven people above the One Land.'

The royal physician didn't answer right away. What mother had the strength to destroy her own child – even one as barbarous as Alvaria? It would have been unnatural for Zera to do differently from what she had. She had been a good woman. His grandson would learn the truth of this soon enough. 'No,' Maarcus told his namesake at last. 'She deserved a better end and a heroine's funeral.'

'She will be remembered for sacrifices as great as King Tomar's,' the magician added.

'Greater,' Jilian amended.

Maarcus the Seventh wiped tears from his eyes but remained silent.

'Peace of the Seven Sisters,' the physician whispered.

'Peace,' echoed the group one by one.

Next to Zera's smoking ashes, a second pyre burned. It was a small fire even though nearly every troll had died in the battle. The poor creatures had steamed and fallen in on themselves before the first scrap of kindling caught, the elfwitch's magic consuming them before the flames did. As always, the physician's stomach tightened at just the thought of those unseen powers.

The smell was overpowering. This had been the same dreadful scent which washed through Abadan's magic chamber not so long ago. Maarcus turned away and coughed into his handkerchief.

'Grandfather, please come,' the younger Maarcus repeated.

The senior nodded. He couldn't manage to utter good-bye. 'Peace,' he said again, and moved away.

There were no prisoners. The elves had all fled into the night. Maarcus and his companions had been simply too few and too spent to give chase.

With so little to pack, they were ready to begin the journey as soon as the fires burned down. Still Maarcus lingered, reluctant to leave.

A child's high-pitched voice cut through his grief. 'Are you sure you're a dragon, Prince Nikolis?'

Her companions laughed. 'It's a long story, Ceeley,' answered one.

'It is? Did you hear that, Uncle Maarcs? You know, Prince, I really love long stories.'

'Well, I'm not sure . . . That is . . .' The prince had fumbled for words. 'Perhaps your uncle knows more than I do.'

Maarcus the younger had smiled and wrapped an arm around his grieving grandfather. 'I do indeed, but here's just the man who can tell you everything.'

The old physician had sighed, secretly grateful for the task. This would keep them all occupied on the way home. In his best storytelling voice, he began, 'It started many years ago, before any of us was born.'

# Chapter 1

## HARD LESSONS

Wanton Tom the mercenary brushed the hair off Ginni's troubled brow, a move he no longer dared when his daughter was awake. He kissed her forehead and tried to smooth the wrinkles with his hand. His rough skin against her unscarred flesh only reminded him how completely he'd failed to protect her from the arcane powers of witches. 'Maybe a cool, damp—'

Grosik snorted. 'She's not feverish. She's poi – um, she's unwell.'

This was the closest the dragon had come to admitting the truth about Ginni's run-in with the elfwitch, but Tom checked his urge to pounce. His daughter was a difficult subject for them both.

Although days upon weeks had passed since Roslin had died by the elfwitch's hand, the human mage still seemed to rule her daughter more often than not. Ginni's new obsession with the Dragon Prince consumed her remaining hours. She had lost all interest in mercenary work either on behalf of the One Land or their own empty stomachs.

Tom sadly shook his head. He never thought he'd see the day. She'd never been overfond of going hungry – but more, she loved her disguises and trickery.

He hadn't let her out of his sight in nearly a month. He couldn't even bring himself to leave her in Grosik's care for fear she'd somehow bewitch the dragon. Unable to labor at their usual trade, coin had deteriorated to credit which in turn quickly fell to 'pay up or find yourself on the street.' His was always a harsh livelihood in the best of years, and now the Elfwitch's Autumn had cured most merchants from extending a hand further than the middle finger.

Tom reasoned a change to simpler living might just clear his daughter's mind of whatever demons harried her. Last week they'd retreated to the dragon's favorite cave, expecting Ginni's talents with fire to guarantee cooked game and warm shelter at the least.

'A fool's hope on all counts,' the dragon had predicted and Ginni had proved him right. Her eyes yet shone with the wild, untamed look they'd held the night Tom and Grosik had rescued her from the elfwitch, and her fires remained as uncontrolled as everything else. Finally, the dragon had ordered a stop to her play tonight when she'd unmindfully singed his tail.

Tom went to join the dragon some steps back from the fire they'd allowed against their better judgment.

Grosik sat gingerly. His tail barely brushed the floor rather than resting heavily as it normally did. 'We've got to do something about that girl,' he told Tom in as quiet a growl as the mercenary had ever heard from him. His expression showed more regret than annoyance.

'Agreed,' Tom answered, as if he hadn't already tried

to say as much enough times to call down all Seven Sisters. Again he looked at Ginni, curled near the puny fire. Even in sleep, her face held Roslin's fierceness. It was as if all the worst aspects of her dead mother had buried the better parts of both mages – and left the survivor less than either.

'First thing in the morning,' Grosik continued.

'Now,' Tom argued, knowing how the dragon hadn't quite accepted the inescapable and might well change his mind come morning when he couldn't face her.

'I will not discomfort the child any more than I must. We will be in the Shoremen's capital by nightfall.'

'The Cliffs? Why there? I thought we were taking her to the Tower of the Forty-nine Mages.'

Grosik snorted. 'You would abandon your only off-spring to the hags who rejected her mother when they learned she carried this very child.' The dragon's tail twitched reflexively against the ground. He winced but refused to admit the depth of his pain. 'I think you are lacking in sleep.'

Tom shoved his numb hands into his pockets and wished they didn't need to conduct this argument so far from the fire. 'The latter I don't deny, but I've never known it to affect my judgment.'

'You were younger then.'

'Hmph.' Tom had received more than his share of remarks about his age lately. He'd have thought no one had ever heard of a man living to forty-two with his wits and muscle intact. 'As for the Forty-nine "hags" as you call them, where else would one take an unschooled and unfettered witch?'

The dragon gave Tom his dirtiest 'are-you-bereft-of-your-senses?' look. 'Have you forgotten Abadan?'

'Have you forgotten she tried to kill him?'

The dragon approximated a shrug. 'The old gas-bag wasn't harmed . . . much. He can survive this.'

'But will Ginni?'

'Of course.' Grosik moved closer to Tom. 'Abadan will know what to do with the girl and he will perform in a trustworthy manner. The Forty-nine will have their own aims. Better we throw her off the ledge than risk her to those, those . . . vipers.'

An odd description coming from a dragon, Tom thought, but kept it to himself. 'We'll do it your way,' he said at last, without any confidence.

His sleep that night was restless. He kept rolling over to check on Ginni. Seeing her form in the darkness didn't ease his mind. Come morning he knew why.

Ginni was gone, her shape just another shadowed outline under the blanket.

Maarcus the Seventh rested the tip of the rapier against his opponent's ribs and pushed just hard enough to draw a drop of blood.

Prince Nikolis looked down at the dragon-shaped birthmark under the blade, then into the other's eyes. He waited to see what the Shoreman would do next.

Maarcus lowered his sword and spat on the solarium floor in disgust. 'You can do better than this, Nik! So you've lost your sword. You've still got your dagger.' When the prince didn't answer, he raised the rapier in challenge. 'Come on, man. Move!'

That was just it. Being a man took getting used to. Mut hadn't expected that. Even his name needed constant vigilance. Often as not, he thought of himself as Mut the mercenary's dragon rather than Prince Nikolis, heir to the throne of the fractured One Land.

Nor had the prince foreseen the unending weeks of

swordplay. The old physician did all his teaching from the perimeter while Nik thrusted and parried with Maarcus the Seventh. The grandson wasn't half bad at wielding a blade when he concentrated on the purpose instead of Nik's sister Jilian – not that the prince could blame his slow progress on anyone other than himself.

Nikolis couldn't repress a smile. 'Sorry, I keep wanting to use my teeth.'

Maarcus tried to remain stern and failed. His face broke into a grin as wide as the prince's. 'What do you say we speak with the cook about a proper midday meal?'

'Oh come now,' the elder Maarcus called from a safe distance. 'Neither one of you has begun to breathe hard yet.'

'Grandfather, can't you see our breath steaming above us?'

'I can see my own, equally well,' the older man countered. 'It's unseemly for a man of your training to complain about the cold.'

'I enjoy the frigid wind and the rise of gooseflesh,' Maarcus joked. 'But it's the blue lips and stiff fingers I look forward to each morning.'

The elder man shook his head at the two of them. 'This is serious business.'

'Indeed it is, Grandfather. Nonetheless, I could drill the prince for another hour and his chest wouldn't rise any quicker than it is now. You'll need to come up with a better measurement than that.'

The physician scowled and waved his hand in acquiescence. 'I have matters to attend to,' he said, as if the call to halt had been his idea. 'I'll expect both of you back here working a twin-time this afternoon.'

The two younger men stood in mock solemnity until their tutor reached the far end of the solarium.

Nikolis rubbed the circulation back into his arms. Today the sun was bright outside, but this morning the high windowed shutters had once again scraped against deep-packed snow. No question a hard winter had arrived in The Cliffs, a season made worse by the Elfwitch's Autumn – as the past three deadly months had come to be known.

Of necessity, this winter had become a time of healing. Snow settled on the ashes of the villages that had not withstood Alvaria's onslaught and wiped those towns from memory. In each of the remaining ones, people had buried their dead and now looked to the spring.

Most survivors hoped to forget the elfwitch and her unnatural trolls. In the darkest hours of deepnight, Nikolis wished he could share in their reprieve. Come daylight, he knew he couldn't abandon the One Land to chance when fresh rumors of new terrors already floated around the capital. Nikolis gave a mental shrug. Whether true tales or not, the elfwitch wasn't idle and therefore the resistance couldn't rest. Their wounds would mend or they must learn to ignore them.

'Your teeth,' Maarcus repeated, bringing the prince back to the present. 'You will never be a swordsman, my liege.'

'No, but I'll make an uncommonly dangerous dancer.' He performed a two-step that one of the chambermaids had taught him.

Maarcus appeared impressed. 'Your feet hardly seemed to touch the ground. Next you'll be trying to fly.'

'No,' Nikolis answered. 'I gave that up years ago. The wings wouldn't hold me.'

'Pity,' Maarcus said. 'It would have been a useful talent against the elfwitch.'

Nikolis looked at the flawless skin on his arms and

abdomen. Only the dragon birthmark over his ribs marred the flesh. 'Yes, well, so you've told me a time or seven.' He exhaled, trying to make smoke rings in the frigid air then giving up. It had all been easier in the days when he looked liked a malformed dragon, when he and Jilian had believed he'd been abandoned by the great beasts because of his useless wings. The prince moved to stare out at the snow mounds and beyond them to the hastily patched stable which housed scores of refugees. Turning the talk to less personal issues, he asked, 'How fare the newest round of incoming?'

Maarcus shook his head. 'Food, shelter, discontent over who gets what. All of it wearies me and leads me no closer to a solution. How can there be a fair answer when more people arrive every other day despite the deepsnows?'

Nikolis put his hand on the man's shoulder in a fatherly gesture he never would have imagined himself using only weeks ago. 'You do as well as you can, Maarcus. Neither of us was really meant to spend our days settling disputes over supplies.'

Maarcus made a strange face. 'Some of us were intended—'

'Done so soon?' called out a woman's voice from across the room. 'I was hoping to take him on once you'd worn him out.'

Nikolis turned to watch his sister striding purposefully across the stone floor. Though her voice had been light, her tight expression suggested something troubled her. No point in asking about it now. She'd be in a more talkative mood after a good work-out at her brother's expense. 'Which him?' he asked. 'Maarcus is always game.'

Jilian lifted one shoulder and let it fall in a careless gesture. 'Whichever. I'm not picky. Especially since I can whip either of you one-handed.'

Maarcus jumped up and raised his sword in a formal challenge. 'What say you, fair princess, to whipping us both two-handed?'

The princess bowed low. When had she learned to do that? Nikolis thought.

'I accept your feeble show of defiance. Prepare yourselves, gentlemen.' Jilian chose a well-balanced sword from the wall-rack and raised it in jaunty salute. 'Any time.'

Maarcus nodded to Nikolis and the two advanced. They recognized this trick for their tutor employed it several times a week. Whenever practice broke down, the physician plucked Jilian from her sessions with Abadan and sent her in to goad them into proper exertion. She was quite skilled with both heavy and light swords, having learned from some of the finest outlaws in the One Land in the days when the prince still ran free on four feet.

Nik had been more useful to his sister then. He shook off the thought and concentrated on the fencing exercise arranged for his benefit.

The men went easy on the princess at first, giving her a chance to warm up. Before long, the trio was engaged in fierce combat. Jilian and Maarcus were evenly matched, though either could have killed Nikolis without risking personal harm.

Suddenly needing to prove his worth, the prince settled into his task. He got off a lucky thrust, surprising all three.

'Not just a pretty face, after all,' Jilian teased and went after him in earnest. In moments, he was cornered, only to be rescued by Maarcus.

The Shoreman held his sword to Jilian's back. 'Rule number one, princess. Destroy the stronger before the weaker. Else you will always be outmatched.'

Jilian lowered her blade and winked at Nikolis. Once Maarcus lowered his rapier, she spun about with her brother beside her. 'Rule number two, Sir Maarcus. Always know which side your companion is on.'

Together the twins took on the Shoreman until he bowed in surrender. When at last he called a halt, all three were breathing hard and well covered in sweat.

'Excellent, my prince.' Maarcus tipped his head. 'We might make you a swordsman yet.'

Nikolis shook his head. 'Passable perhaps, but I wouldn't rush to trust your life to my arm.'

Maarcus, the statesman-spy, laughed. 'Not to worry, sire.'

Jilian returned her sword to the wall-rack and brushed her hands together. 'Now that we've done our duty . . .' She trailed off, confirming the prince's suspicion that the elder Maarcus had sent her.

'Supper?' Maarcus asked.

The others agreed and all three strode toward the dining hall.

Lyda wound her way through the old, oversized stable on her morning circuit. As always, the youngest and the oldest needed the most healing while those in between required the most talk.

The first group of refugees had been in the capital for weeks now, but peace was as far away for them as if they still trudged through snow-clogged valleys. The men were growing restless. They wanted to fight but feared meeting a fate similar to that which had befallen a number of their friends. Instead, they let anger mask the unspoken self-reproach for their perceived cowardice. The women tiptoed around their men, trying to comfort them and being scorned for their trouble.

Lyda looked down the rows of sleeping-pallets and bit her lip. Something would have to change soon.

She patted heads on her way past the new arrivals and whispered prayers to the Sisters, prayers that she had invented herself and was beginning to doubt anyone heard. That so many travellers had endured the Elfwitch's Autumn and now the deepsnows of winter was a wonder which even yet astounded her.

Beyond that, her self-proclaimed role here in The Cliffs was to welcome the spent voyagers and see them settled comfortably among the dozens of others, while at the same time steering them away from dividing into elves, dwarves, or humans. The three races naturally gravitated toward those they considered their own, no matter that they were from different towns. Lyda took advantage of their exhaustion and disorientation to anchor them among a group already rooted to her satisfaction.

Perhaps it was a small contribution, perhaps a large one. She wasn't sure. When she'd fled the elves' wrath and abandoned poor Willam that bright fall morning, she never would have guessed the road would find her leading this quiet sort of revolution.

By the time Lyda reached her own private corner, she half wished she could keep going right out the door. She looked at Willam, his chest rising and falling in regular waves after working long into the night. No, she had left him once; she wouldn't do it again. She wouldn't succumb to the temptation to escape without him.

Still, she needed air. Lyda gently kissed her husband on the forehead and whispered, 'Take your rest while you can. I'll be back as soon as I visit the privy.' He smiled in his sleep, looking as content as any man alive despite sleeping on the floor amidst hundreds of half-frozen strangers.

The snow seemed deeper than it had on her previous trip outside though she couldn't remember a fresh snowfall since last night. Was it her own exhaustion or the elfwitch's magic? Lyda didn't know, but she hoped Alvaria wouldn't waste her strength when fatigue and hunger were likely to cut down half the evacuees who managed the treacherous journey through the mountains.

Lyda tightened her scarf and headed away from the privy. She wanted a few moments alone and hoped to avoid chance meetings, especially at this well-travelled hour. She topped a rise and let out a strangely contented sigh. From here, the world seemed pure. It replaced her fears with faith.

The great stone palace and the surrounding near buildings loomed large yet welcoming. Her gaze rested there, where within a Sisters' week she would be meeting the prince for the second time. Another odd gathering to be sure. She doubted he would be any more certain of his place in this new order than was she, and both would pretend to the contrary.

She smiled to herself and the very air seemed to warm. A chill she'd forgotten she felt lifted from her bones. 'Thank you,' she whispered to the Sisters for her moment of respite, and turned to go back inside.

'You're welcome,' someone answered.

'Who's there?' Lyda asked, startled out of her restored calm.

The elves showed themselves as if materializing from a dream, just as they had a few months and so many more footsteps ago. Their formerly shimmering, multi-colored cloaks had been transformed into a dazzling white, though the cloth maintained its bizarre power to stun the senses into not quite seeing what one thought. The elves' features were nearly lost amidst the blinding light, but surely these were the same elves who had spared her life and settled the turmoil in her soul.

'You've done well, better than anyone had a right to expect,' the tallest said.

'Thank you,' she answered, although it seemed a curious sort of praise at best.

'You deserve a proper rest and to be soothed in your soul.' But his voice let her know they asked more of her.

Lyda wanted to collapse from the weight of his unspoken task, but she instinctively suppressed a plea for mercy and pulled herself up to full height. 'Yes?' she said, neither wholly inviting him to continue nor denying the oath which she had willingly pledged to him and his elven brothers in return for the great gifts they had given her.

'You have gathered the people to you and done the best you can. It is time for you to let these unfortunates heal themselves while you embark on another trip.'

Lyda was confused. 'Are there others who need my help to find the paths beneath the deepsnows?'

'No, no,' said the elf in a calming voice. 'The message has been spread. All but the unredeemable already make their way here – or will be once the snows melt. No. We have a secret, urgent quest for you.'

Something about the elf's request turned her knees to jelly. To her shame, she feared where they would send her. Lyda looked down at the snow. Every snowflake seemed stained with the blood of her cowardice.

Nonsense, Lyda told herself. She had led tens of starving exiles through the early deepsnows to The Cliffs. She could go wherever these elves directed her. She stiffened her resolve.

Even so, her voice quavered when she asked, 'Must I find the bracelet? As the one who sold it against your instructions, I owe you that much at least.'

The elf smiled, the first smile she'd seen. But Lyda thought she saw a hint of torment, as if these somber beings had looked into the abyss and barely flinched.

'Thank you, no. You have already repaid that debt.'

'Not to mention we already know the bracelet's whereabouts despite those who tried to keep it from us,' added the elf standing off to the right.

'I'm pleased to hear it.' She paused, took a breath to gather her courage, and said, 'And what of Willam?'

'He is here with you, is he not?'

Lyda nodded. 'Indeed . . .'

'But?' prodded the elf.

'But something happened. A mage perhaps . . .' She could ask no more of these three who had given her so much.

'Be at peace. He will heal. The Sisters have taken him into account.'

Taken him into account? What did that mean? Once more Lyda had misgivings and once more she blamed her own reluctance to face a journey that was likely to be more harrowing than the long trek which had brought her to the capital.

'Your shopkeeper is a stalwart and steady man.' Another grin with the hint of darkness. 'He has been chosen to serve as your compass in this difficult task. You must both leave within a twin-day.'

Lyda's shoulders loosened with relief. She'd sworn and sworn against abandoning him ever again and the Sisters seemed to have heard this one prayer if not any others. 'But he can barely find his way across a new town. How will he direct me?'

'The Sisters guide us all. Be at peace,' said the elves and dissolved into the night.

Lyda hoped it was true, for only after she made her way back from the privy did she realize they had not told her where she ventured or why.

Walther Shortdwarf's lessons with Abadan progressed, but he still couldn't fathom how he'd come to be taking them from the Magician in the first place. What was more, to be learning alongside the princess Jilian – who was seemingly less talented than he – struck the dwarf as bordering on the absurd.

Sometimes he couldn't decide if this were a blessed dream or a cursed nightmare, especially when Jilian's studies went poorly. The princess had no patience for her own errors and there was no being around the woman when her anger ruled. She listened to no one but herself – and at times he wasn't sure she heard that. Better she unleashed her wrath in swordplay.

Walther felt no regret when Jilian left to join the men in the solarium. Her departure didn't improve Abadan's mood, however, and the dwarf was relieved when the magician ended the session shortly thereafter.

After twin doses of Abadan and the princess, the best antidote was Ceeley. The only other survivor of his village, his young niece had a way of reminding him of what was truly important.

He headed for her favorite spot, the indoor play-yard. Abandoned a generation ago and only recently reopened, the place still hung heavy with an air of disuse. Ceeley had thrown herself into attempting everything a six-year-old could to revive it.

Childsize practice swords were stacked along one wall, small to big, freshly dusted. Scraps of wood gathered from the Sisters knew where were called into service as blocks and doll-houses. Ceeley stood amidst these, her lips pursed in thought.

The elder Maarcus was nowhere to be found. Perhaps he'd been called away. There was altogether too much of that these days and the girl often got the short end of everyone's attention as a result. Seeing his niece alone made him doubly glad he'd decided to visit her.

Celia smiled and lifted her cheek for a polite kiss. 'Hello, Uncle Walther.' The child's welcome was edged with the formality she'd never quite lost after she'd discovered him with one of the elfwitch's dragon coins.

He'd rather she'd held out her arms for a hug, but it was a grand improvement over screaming and running away every time she saw him. He pecked the cheek and ruffled her hair for good measure. 'How goes the furniture moving, Curly-top?'

'Well,' she said, very seriously, 'I think this room needs to be completely redone.' She shook her head. 'I've tried and I've tried, Uncle Walther, but it just doesn't seem like . . . like home.' Her voice broke on 'home' and silent tears trickled down her cheeks.

Walther gathered the girl into his arms, feeling selfish for having wished for just such an excuse. He held her until her crying calmed. 'What would make it feel like home?' he asked, afraid to hear the answer.

She sniffed. 'Some dollies would be nice. I haven't had a dolly in a very long time and the house is lonely without them.' She pointed to the makeshift doll-house. 'I don't think Uncle Maarcs had dollies when he played here,' she added. Then in a very quiet voice she said, 'Some other children would also be nice.'

Walther stared, not knowing what to say. 'I'd like to, Ceeley, but there aren't any other children in the palace.'

'I know. Just old men and Aunt Jilly.' She skipped to the window and pointed toward the converted stable. 'What about the kids out there? Can't I play with them?'

The dwarf's mouth fell open. How did she know about them? 'It's just that . . . um . . .'

'Just what?'

He tried to speak, but words refused to come.

'Uncle Walther, is something wrong with me?'

'With you? Of course not, Ceeley.' He recovered enough to add, 'To be honest, Curly-top, I don't think any of the grown-ups have thought about it. You see, we don't know those people very well and we haven't had a chance to get to know them. And we wouldn't want you to . . .' Not wanting to alarm her, he trailed off.

'To what?' Celia asked.

How could he finish that? 'I'll talk to the others,' he said, returning to her original subject. 'We'll think of something. And maybe send in some dollies too. What do you say?'

She clapped her hands. 'Hear that, house? Dollies. Lots and lots of dollies, hurrah!'

Walther laughed aloud. Even though Ceeley brought him new challenges, she always made him feel better – just as he'd known she would. 'Why don't we practise swordfighting?'

Ceeley stopped and stared. 'You promise not to get bored?'

'Well, not for a while.'

'Even if I win and win and win?'

Walther flushed and stuttered out, 'Don't be silly.'

She shook her finger at him. 'It's bad to lie, you know. The Seven Sisters always know when someone doesn't tell the truth.'

36

Too smart for her own good, Walther thought. Or maybe just too smart for my own good.

'I think we should play horsie until you get tired. You won't have time to get bored then.' She held out her hand. 'Deal?'

Thinking, definitely too smart for my own good, Walther took the pudgy palm and gave it one good shake. 'Deal.'

Jilian scraped a chair back from the dark oak table and slumped into it. Elbows in the spot where her plate should be, she cradled her head in her hands. The swagger from their swordplay seemed to have fled back to the solarium. Nikolis knew all the signs. She was ready to talk.

'Something wrong?'

'Not if you don't mind a royal sister who's been thrown out of court.'

Maarcus laughed, not understanding or ignoring the depth of Jilian's black mood. 'Around here, that's hardly unique.'

She scowled at him. 'I mean Abadan,' she explained. 'I've offended him so badly I don't know if I'll ever . . .'

Nikolis tried to draw her out without making her feel worse. 'You're not known for your humble nature, but—'

'Very true,' Maarcus interjected. 'But then neither is he.'

The prince continued, ignoring the Shoreman. 'It couldn't have been so terrible that you can't apologize with grace.'

'And then stand still while he berates me. I can't bear it.' She slammed her hand down on the wood. 'I didn't spend all those years as a mercenary just to have an old man treat me like a child.'

Nikolis smiled. 'It's no worse than what I endure with the physician. Be glad Abadan never forgets the task at . . . um . . . hand. That is . . .' The prince swallowed his words. He'd meant to cheer up his sister, not bring up another difficult subject. 'I think you're making more of this than you need to,' he added softly.

Her anger deflated by the mention of Sir Maarcus's worsening condition, Jilian idly traced circles on the table. 'I don't know. You didn't see the magician's face.'

'He looks good in purple,' the prince joked. His sister scowled. 'Anyway, he'll calm down and then you can make it up to him.'

'Don't do it,' Maarcus advised, as if he hadn't heard the comment regarding his grandfather. 'It'll only make him more demanding.'

'Don't drag Jilian into your feud.'

'He and I have proclaimed our truce,' Maarcus said loftily. 'Regardless, we don't have to coddle the arrogant old trickster.'

'Yes, we do,' Nikolis argued. 'He's the strongest ally we have against the elfwitch. And as for arrogance, there's plenty to go around, don't you think, Maarcus?'

'Where's the food?' the Shoreman answered, without missing a beat. 'I'm starved.'

Jilian and Nikolis both laughed. 'Go ahead, change the subject.'

'A full stomach is a soldier's best defense.' Maarcus kept his face straight. Only the light in his eyes suggested otherwise.

The prince let the jest slide by. They deserved a few minutes to relax, however brief.

Maarcus was right that the three had waited an unusually long time for their meal to be served. 'Maybe they're working on a new recipe to entice me to try another sort of disgusting meat.' He made a face at the thought. It had taken a good bit of doing to train the cook to prepare meals suitable to his peculiar palate, which had somehow carried over from his dragon days. Maarcus's grandfather assured the prince he could eat anything Jilian could, but only fish and vegetables appealed to him. Pity about the alcohol, though. Abadan had an excellent wine cellar.

'More likely they're trying to stretch the dwindling stores into something edible,' Jilian grumped.

'Ah, here's the food,' Maarcus said with more enthusiasm than the paltry dishes warranted.

Nikolis glanced at his sister to let her know he wanted to arrange a private conversation later. She stared past him without acknowledging his signal until he finally turned his attention to the arriving food.

A servant entered pushing a wheeled cart and quickly slammed a bowl in front of each of the three. His arm shook as he set down the prince's portion and a bit of stew sloshed onto the table. The man made no move to clean up the spill. Instead, he silently disappeared without waiting to be dismissed, neglecting to place the serving-pot on the sideboard in his haste.

'He might at least have made certain we didn't require more drink before going,' the Shoreman commented. He held up his empty goblet.

'New man?' Nikolis asked.

Maarcus shook his head. 'So many in and out these days, it's hard to say.' He speared a hunk of meat and took a bite. Around his food, he said, 'I don't recall seeing him before.'

Nikolis felt a warning chill run up his spine. He examined his bowl. The stew smelled more vile than usual, but that was probably his typical aversion. He turned to Jilian. She too was poking at the bits of meat.

Across the table, Maarcus spat his food into his napkin. 'Did they change the cook?'

'Not that I'd been informed.'

A man came running in. Nikolis recognized the physician's livery. 'Don't eat it! Don't eat—' He stopped to regain his composure when he saw all three staring at him, their meals virtually untouched. He straightened his jacket, then calmly announced, 'We found the cook with his throat cut.'

# Chapter 2

## HUMBLING ENCOUNTERS

Ginni finally stopped to rest when the sun shone strong in the valley. The world was wrapped in white, broken only by evergreens which were themselves dotted with snow. From here she could see Widow's Peak. On its opposite face, her father was already awake in the cave and deciding what he would do about her.

Last night she had lain on her side, listening as Tom tossed on the hard cave floor. Though he was so close she could have touched his shoulder, she kept her hands tucked between her knees. There would be no comfort for either of them until she found a way to rein in her newly unpredictable talents.

Eventually Wanton Tom's thrashing calmed and his breathing slowed. He would sleep well and soundly for a few hours. The last of Roslin's special potion secretly mixed into his dinner had seen to it.

She glanced at Grosik. There was nothing she could do about the dragon other than put her faith in his ability to sleep through a mountain-slide if he chose.

Ginni sat up and pulled on her boots. Silently, she stood and took her pack from its place in the corner. She hated to leave her cloak behind, but it would serve the illusion of her presence and therefore soothe her father should he wake before morning. With her talent for fire, however unruly it had become, the young mage knew she wouldn't freeze.

As she slipped past the careworn man and then the motionless dragon, it did not escape her that Tom had done the same to Roslin before Ginni's birth. She'd heard the story many times from her mother – Roslin's resentment growing in each retelling – but even Roslin had ultimately admitted that he hadn't fully realized what he'd abandoned until years later.

Ginni had stood at the cave mouth, peering into the darkness where she knew her father lay. She had wanted to let Tom take her to Abadan. In her gut, she felt sure the magician wished her no ill. Nonetheless, Roslin's mandate ruled.

In the deepdark hours of countless nights, Ginni had felt her mother scowling at her. Before Roslin's death the goading had come from without. Ginni had learned to close doors, open books, or stare out windows when her mother prodded. But now the taunting came from within. Awake or asleep, daytime or night, the memories of their many clashes seemed to merge and transform.

Ginni no longer knew what, or who, directed her thoughts and actions. For the first time since she'd been a child, her magic sporadically overtook her in the midst of the simplest acts. She couldn't trust herself around enemies any more, and so she pretended to lose interest in her father's usual trade. She seemed not to notice their dwindling coin and growling stomachs. She appeared not to care that they were reduced to huddling in a cave.

Privately she had hoped they might safely wait out the winter in the cave. That wish died within days of their arrival, at the very moment she accidentally set Grosik's tail afire. The young mage knew she was getting worse. She couldn't continue to endanger her family.

She needed help – or further training.

Roslin's murder had freed stray thoughts and random wisps of sorcery without giving them order. It was as if she never expected Ginni to control them – as if she had assumed she herself would always command her daughter's muscle, wits, and magic. Ginni needed someone else to look into her mind and guide her through all the forgotten bits magically locked inside. Someone else must teach Ginni which notions were her own.

Until she understood her mother's legacy and bowed it to her own will, she could not put herself in the hands of any man. Thus, she had faced into the wind and begun her descent down the mountain with only stars and her own magic to light her way.

Now the afternoon shadows grew long. Ginni must move or risk dying from the cold. The proud (some said 'stubborn') daughter of a powerful mage and an extraordinary mercenary resumed her urgent journey. She would travel through the deepsnows of the high mountain pass as quickly as she could until she reached the one place Grosik had wished to avoid because the witches had rejected her mother for her rebelliousness. It seemed to make no sense, but she was compelled to go to the valley which protected the Tower of the Forty-nine Mages.

Walther was still trying to get the horseback riding kinks out of his neck when he settled Ceeley in the main hall and hobbled in to join the royal twins and Maarcus for lunch.

All three had pushed away their food as if distance could make it more palatable. Then the dwarf noticed the physician's man standing at attention in the corner. 'Something wrong?'

'Nothing fasting won't cure,' the prince said.

'Nikolis!' his sister admonished.

'What would you have me do? Jump up and down, hollering "assassin" for all the palace to hear?'

The servant blushed.

'Not your fault,' he told the man. 'Under the circumstances, a little ruckus was a good thing.' He turned to Maarcus. 'We're losing too many who are loyal to us. Jilian's chambermaid, your valet, now the cook. It's time we do something about these pretenders.'

'We could always go back to being mercenaries,' Jilian suggested. 'It was safer when we only worried about protecting other people from assassination.'

Nikolis locked eyes with her for a moment. 'Yes, well . . .' was all he said but the dwarf would swear it meant more. 'Too bad you missed the first course, Walther,' the prince explained. He waved at the full plate. 'It was laced with an unusual spice.'

'Poison?'

The prince nodded.

'And the cook?' the dwarf asked.

'He sure isn't sleeping with an extra smile in his neck,' the Shoreman snapped.

'Maarcus! No need to shout at Walther.'

'Why wasn't he here?'

'Don't be ridiculous. Why weren't your grandfather and the magician here?'

'Sorry, Walther.' The Shoreman's apology was immediate and seemed sincere.

The dwarf tipped his head in acknowledgment, but he

wasn't altogether ready to forgive him. His temper was too hot for a man come of age in such dangerous times.

'I feel responsible,' Maarcus said, by way of defending his rudeness. 'This happened on my watch. I've known the cook since childhood and knew he was incorruptible. I got lazy and forgot that others wouldn't consider his loyalty to their benefit.'

'Maarcus, no one blames you for this—' Jilian started.

'I do.'

'Nik!'

'It's not personal, Jilian. His oversight endangered us all equally.' The prince offered a sad smile, then he added, 'And I doubt Maarcus is looking for an untimely retirement from his current duties any more than we are.' He paused, his grim look holding their attention. 'But Jilian, Maarcus is right. He should have expected this sort of thing and taken steps to avoid it.'

The Shoreman stood and bowed formally as he spoke to the floor. 'Prince, I've failed you. I give my life into your hands.'

A shocked silence fell over the room.

Nikolis glared at Maarcus while the others gaped at the prince.

Voices shouted over clanging dishes in the adjoining hall. Time hung suspended inside the small room and no one moved.

He is the reigning prince, Walther thought. He could sacrifice the man if he chose.

Finally, Nikolis slapped the man on the back. 'Oh, get up. Now you're being ridiculous. I'm merely pointing out the stakes. We are all too casual with our safeguards. The physician and Abadan cannot carry on the fight without us.'

Red-faced with shame, Maarcus returned to his seat.

Walther felt a new respect for Prince Nikolis. Just as the dwarf's own encounter with the elfwitch had aged him, so had the prince's. Alvaria had destroyed their reckless wanderlust; they had become more settled, more directed in their actions. In contrast, Jilian and Maarcus still approached the elfwitch's onslaught as if it a were minor skirmish to be thrown off whenever they chose.

'The prince is right,' Walther said. 'It's time we formed a plan.'

'Any ideas?' Nikolis asked, but no one answered.

Ceeley wasn't one to wait on grown-ups. These days, they were all too busy fighting the war to remember their promises. First she thought she might follow Uncle Walther to the private dining-hall. She could see how Aunt Jilly and Uncle Maarcs were faring without her, and help Uncle Walther make her case for a new playmate at the same time. Then loud shouts coming from that end of the hallway changed her mind. She just wasn't in the mood for arguing. It made her stomach hurt.

She decided right then to bundle up and go visit the new people herself. The guard tipped his plumed helmet to her and saw her out. She started to tell him where she was bound and reconsidered. After all, his job was scrutinizing arriving strangers, not worrying over the departure of a familiar child. Anyway, she'd be back before anyone knew she was gone.

The wind hit her square in the face, but she concentrated on finding someone her age to play with. She wouldn't even mind if it was a boy maybe, or someone older or younger – just as long as they were nice.

The snow was so deep that it was a struggle for Ceeley to get across. She thought of the drifts, taller than an adult dwarf, and shuddered. Her short legs and stout body were no match for that. She kept to the main path, well marked by brightly colored sticks.

Halfway there, alone under a steel-grey sky threatening yet another storm, she belatedly wished she'd remembered to put on snowshoes. She tsked at herself. Daddy'd always said her 'pulsiveness would get her in trouble one day.

Her leg was stuck again. She lifted with all her strength but only managed to lose her balance and fall back into the bank. Ceeley felt completely drained. Her way seemed lost between the harsh white and darkening grey. 'You were right, Daddy. I'm sorry. You were right.' She repeated it over and over as if it were a mantra, the words slowing to match a mournful rhythm. Tears streamed into the cloth covering her face.

''Ere now, what's the matter? Do you need 'elp?'

Ceeley looked up, but didn't recognize the speaker. He seemed tall, but nearly everyone seemed tall to her. She should have been afraid, but she had mostly stopped being scared after the battle of the elfwitch.

The man bent down, pulled her out of the snow and brushed her off. Much warmer now, she realized how cold she must have been and wondered what might have happened to her if he hadn't come along.

'Tell me, child. What calls you out when it's freezin' like this and a storm's comin'?' His voice was kind, but he held her arm as if he wouldn't let go until she gave him an answer.

'I didn't mean to sneak out. It was an accident. I couldn't help myself.' The words came unbidden. She didn't know if she meant now or her misbehavior months ago in her home village. 'And now I'm the only one left – 'cept for Uncle Walther. But I'm really all by myself a lot of the time. Oh, I am so sorry. So sorry.' She broke off in sobs.

'Go with the Lady, child. Lyda will see to you.' The

man turned her around and she realized the entrance lay just ahead of her. She looked back but no one was there.

A woman opened the door before Ceeley knocked. She smiled and the girl knew she was home. 'Mama,' Ceeley breathed, though the woman wasn't her mother, wasn't even a dwarf.

'Daughter,' the woman answered and bent to take her into her arms. She lifted Ceeley up.

Over her newfound mother's shoulders, Ceeley saw a soft glow that had to be a trick of the dim lamps.

'Who is it, Lyda?' a man called.

'Our daughter, Willam,' she answered. 'The one we've always wanted, and here she is alone on our doorstep.'

The man tried to look stern and failed. He said, 'I'll check to be sure no one's lookin' for her. What's your name, 'oney?'

'Celia Sailclan, but my friends call me Ceeley.'

'A pleasure, Miss Sailclan. Welcome.' A gust of wind banged the door against the wall and he stepped forward to close and bolt the door.

Lyda turned to follow his movements.

'Storm's kickin' up.' His eyes grew wide. 'She was outside!'

Ceeley felt Lyda's nod.

'By the Sis—' he cut off in mid-oath. 'The Sisters must be watchin' over 'er.'

'They are indeed,' Lyda answered with complete assurance. 'They are indeed.'

Abadan entered the study chamber, with more than the usual banging. He slammed a heavy book down on the table he'd claimed as his teaching podium. Empty-handed, he thudded the door closed and let the newly installed wooden bar crash into place.

'You're both here. Good.'

As if this were unusual, Jilian thought. She bit her lip to keep from muttering aloud.

The magician stood with his back to them, flipping the stiff pages of his tome. 'Ah, here it is.' He bent closer and began to read silently.

Jilian fidgeted. She shuffled her feet. She leaned forward in her chair, and back. She put first one elbow on the tabletop, then the other, and finally both.

She worried over her brother. He seemed odder and odder with each passing day. They were all nervous about the battle they knew must come. Yet Nik's behavior grew more and more grave, as if the carefree Mut had never existed.

Beside her, Walther was the picture of the calm acolyte awaiting his master's bidding.

Abadan's imperious manner was common enough for him, but the princess couldn't see why he needed it. When he faced away from them more often than not, she could only think he did not really wish to pass along his knowledge.

She closed her eyes and pretended patience.

'Finally, Jilian, you understand.'

She straightened abruptly. Had he been waiting on her? She would not ask and he said no more on the subject.

'Let's see how you've done.'

Abadan scraped at the poultice on Jilian's arm, examining it and her arm in the process. 'Good enough for an apprentice healer,' he grunted. 'You've done this before.'

'You know I have. Guarding against assassins can take many forms.' She strove to keep her voice even. The need for apology from the morning session hung heavy between them.

'Arrogant girl,' he muttered. 'From me you will learn

49

to do it properly.' He took apart the poultice. 'Now begin again. The herb paste must be of thick enough consistency to stay together. The poultice needs heat to work. Where is your wet cloth to set on top and keep the warmth in? Why have you not placed the poultice in suitable gauze so that it can be freshened more easily?'

He snapped the questions off, giving her no time to answer. Jilian looked down at the crumbled mess he'd made of her work rather than into his face. She'd grant that he had his point, but she wished he'd make some effort to leaven his harsh criticism.

Slowly she slid a look to Walther, who was busily rebuilding his own poultice. Beneath his full white beard, his face was red to the ears.

When Abadan returned to his magics on the high counter behind them, Jilian tapped the table gently to get Walther's attention. The startled dwarf jumped. 'Sorry,' she mouthed when he refocused on her. 'Don't fret so,' she whispered. 'Yours will be fine. It's just me.'

At that the magician leaned over to study the dwarf's labor. 'Fine, Walther. You listen well.'

Abadan shot another glare at Jilian. 'How is your nettle tincture progressing?'

'Three more days by my count and I will be ready to separate the fluid from the herbs.'

He frowned for no reason that Jilian could discern. She put her hand beneath the table and tightened it into a fist then relaxed. Tightened and relaxed until she barely heard him say, 'It will have to do.'

What difference could this lesson make with everyone across the One Land trapped beneath mounds of snow? Jilian's hand stopped in mid-flex. Abadan did not speak lightly. There was purpose behind his words. 'Has something happened?'

He ignored her at first. 'How is your tincture coming, Walther?'

'The same as the princess's. We set the nettle to soak on the same day.' Walther paused. 'Master Abadan, *has* something happened?'

The magician's glance passed over Jilian to look into the dwarf's eyes. Perhaps he was easier to face than the presumed princess of the realm. 'How can either of you ask that after so recent an attack on your persons? The entire One Land is in peril and you ask that.' He shook his head. 'Sometimes I wonder why I bother.'

Jilian had had enough. Weary of insults, bored from the exercises, tense from the attempted poisoning, and hungry besides – all combined to rip apart what little thread of patience she possessed. 'Why do you?' she asked. 'While the elfwitch moves ever closer, we follow your silly routines that are as binding and useless as ill-fitting boots.'

Abadan didn't answer her right away. 'Walther, you've come so far.' His mouth curled into a smile. 'Who would have ever thought I'd be tutoring such a talented dwarf? Sometimes the Sisters amaze even me.'

'Thank you,' Walther whispered in embarrassment.

The magician faced Jilian and clapped his hands together. The room echoed with a boom not entirely human-made. 'You!' he scolded her.

She opened her mouth to reply, but he cut her off. 'You didn't learn a killer's tricks in a handful of hours. You didn't come to know poisons and their remedies or the ways of sword and knife by ignoring the masters. Why do you take this so lightly?'

It wasn't the first lecture. She should have held her tongue.

She did not. 'Master Abadan,' she started as respectfully

as she could manage. 'Those other skills were a matter of survival. Mut – that is, Nikolis and I would likely have starved without the training.'

Abadan's face went purple-red. 'And your survival—' the word sounded base as he said it '—is more important than that of the entire One Land! How dare you show such selfishness in my presence? You know the evil we face and you are one of the few who might have the talent to overcome it.'

He raised an arm as if to strike her, then caught himself. 'Leave now, Princess. Do not return until you have learned to see beyond your own dinner plate!'

The reference to her recent close call stung, yet Jilian's foolish stubbornness bowed before his anger. Princess or not, how could she miss the folly of her towering arrogance? She desperately searched for the right words.

'You're still here!' Abadan shouted. 'No one remains in my chambers but on my sufferance. Get out now before I remove you myself.'

'But Master . . .' She swallowed hard. 'I . . . I'm sorry.' There, she'd said it.

'Don't you dare "sorry, master" me. You must regain the privilege of my time. Talented or no. Royal or no. I teach only those who are ready to learn.'

Behind him, Walther was motioning her out. 'I'll talk to him,' he mouthed.

'Go now!'

Jilian looked at the magician. The unhealthy color in his face was spreading to neck and hands. He wouldn't be calm enough to speak with for hours. Slowly she pushed back her chair and rose in retreat.

He turned to face the dwarf, dismissing her completely without another word. 'Let's try something different, Walther. Imagine yourself . . .'

She closed the door and the silence of her failure enveloped her.

Somewhere during their long journey home from elven territory, Nik had realized his sister had lost heart for the battle against the elfwitch. In the weeks since they'd reached The Cliffs, she had grown ever more reckless and shown ever less interest. Her body went through the motions whether with swordplay or mage lessons, but her mind rebelled. She put in the least effort a task required and she fought Abadan's training at every turn.

All of which meant an additional burden to the prince. It was not enough to be preoccupied with his unfamiliar human form, but now he must worry over Jilian while struggling to fathom their next move.

It was this last thought which led him to dodge his afternoon exercises with Sir Maarcus the Sixth. Instead, he wandered the castle seemingly aimlessly while having his goal in mind all the while.

When he was sure no one dogged his steps, he headed for a little-used wing where he settled himself in a tiny room which overlooked the sea. For some reason he did not quite understand, this view drew him. South of The Cliffs, the beachfront had long since given way to fortification. It was not a place one went for comfort and solitude.

But to the north, the wide beach was deserted at this time of year. He could walk northward for miles and find no one. He imagined he had happened upon an enchanted land, one where his wings could reach beyond his imagination into the true realm of bone and sinew.

Snow swirled and fell into the waves. Debris littered the white sand. Small bits of driftwood, weathered clean, jabbed through the snow. Entire tree-trunks stood upright as if expecting to bloom come spring though the branches had broken off.

Nikolis looked out to sea, at the vibrating colors where water met sky. Blues, greens, greys melded into a mass that knew no boundaries.

The prince reached out with mind and flesh to this edge of non-boundary. In this barren no man's land, he might achieve what he could not in the ordinary places of rock and air. He held out his arms and let a strangely warming wind rush over him. His body rose of its own accord.

Staring over the devastation with new eyes, his binocular vision separated into two images. Not right and left as he might have expected, but ghost images of each other. Even a life spent as a dragon had not produced this sort of eyesight.

As Prince Nikolis watched, the scenes diverged. The one extended into the future when strange buildings crowded the ocean-front. The other reversed to a time when people in animal skins camped during the warm months and dug for clams along the shore. A woman walked between the two worlds, seemingly at home in both.

Neither vision made sense. Nikolis closed his eyes to shut out the optical chatter. He instantly fell like a loose stone. In panic, he opened his eyes again and the freefall halted. Close open close open. Fall halt fall halt. Strange but exhilarating.

The dragon prince folded his wings.

And was jolted awake at the castle window, jailed in his own man-flesh.

Ceeley nestled into Lyda's warmth and fell asleep. Later, she woke to the welcome scent of soup.

'You should eat,' Lyda told her.

Ceeley's stomach growled. She smiled. 'Excuse me,' she said as she'd been taught. 'I think I missed lunch.'

'Probably more than that.'

Ceeley wasn't sure what Mama-Lyda meant unless she'd slept through dinner too. Not wanting to disagree with her, she smiled again and sat up. 'The soup smells yummy. I think I'm ready to eat.'

The woman set the bowl beside the dwarf on a low makeshift table. 'Every drop now,' she encouraged.

'I'll try.' It wasn't so hard. She really was very hungry.

While Ceeley sipped the soup, Willam gently asked after the girl's family.

'Dead,' she told them. 'All dead.' And she tried not to cry.

''ave you no one at all?' he asked again.

Ceeley set down the soup spoon and looked into the empty bowl.

'It's important to be sure. We wouldn't want them to miss you.'

'She has us, Willam. Who else does she need?'

'I do have an uncle,' Ceeley offered, knowing it was important to be truthful. 'But Uncle Walther is very busy. He's going to fight the elfwitch.'

'There now, that's enough, child. Don't you worry about that one. We'll speak to your uncle Walther.'

Jilian returned to her rooms. She sat, she stood, she paced like a newly caged beast. Had she been caught outside in this weather, she would have paid dearly to find shelter. As it was, she could barely contain her fitful yearning to escape. At last she settled for throwing wide the shutters and staring out the window.

Late in the afternoon, she was still standing transfixed when a knock sounded on the heavy wood. 'Princess?

Jilian? Are you in there? It's Walther.' He pounded again.

She considered sending him away, but her mouth spoke before her mind was made up. 'I'm here, Walther. Come on in.' As the chamber door opened, she closed the shutters and turned to face him.

He hesitated in the doorway. 'Storm blew itself out quickly enough. The snow's already stopped.'

'I wish you were greeting me with news of the same for Abadan.'

The dwarf sighed. He seemed reluctant to approach her. 'Princess Jilian . . .' he began.

She waved him forward. 'Do step in and shut the door. If you're going to lecture me, I'd just as soon keep it between us.'

'I didn't exactly plan to give a speech,' he said as he closed the door behind him.

'Not exactly.' Suddenly exhausted, she sat down on a stiff-backed chair. 'I tell you, Walther, one more session with Abadan and I'm likely to do the man physical harm. His insults are only a matter of degree. His most considerate comment is to call me competent as an apprentice healer!'

Walther spoke softly. 'We are apprentices.'

'I've been preparing poultices for ten years and no one's died yet.'

'And how horrible it would've been for you if someone had.'

Jilian gave him her nastiest scowl.

'My mother always told me my face would stay that way if I frowned often enough.' He shrugged. 'Then again, maybe it's different for humans.'

Jilian almost laughed. 'I'd bet we're more similar than you might think. As for your mother, you can tell her . . .' She winced in sympathy at the man who'd lost his entire clan to the elfwitch. 'I guess you can't. Sorry, Walther.'

'Not your fault,' he said. 'Have you ever noticed how often you apologize to people?'

'Well, pardon my manners.'

'See what I mean?'

She didn't answer.

He looked down at the floor and said quietly, 'It might be easier to try not to do things you'll have to be sorry about.' He glanced up and smiled shyly. 'Just a thought.'

His embarrassment took the sting out of his words, but she felt the criticism all the same.

'Now I'm off to apologize myself. I promised Ceeley I'd talk to someone about finding playmates for her, but I didn't get a chance with everything else that's going on. Want to come?'

'No, thanks. I doubt I'd cheer her up.'

'You know she misses seeing you more often.'

'I think I need to be alone for a while.' She followed the dwarf to the door and stood watching him until he reached the corner. 'Walther, tell her I miss her too.'

'I will, princess, I will.' His voice echoed sadly down the hallway.

Jilian went back inside, but the dwarf's visit had made her more edgy than before. Her brother accused her of being reckless these days and perhaps he was right. She didn't understand how he could have changed so much. He had transformed from a dragon without a care to a man full of worries – and he muttered fewer complaints than she did when breaking in a pair of new boots.

Such as those in the corner.

The unfamiliar luxury of extra clothing and fine bedding did not offset her own loss of liberty. She chafed under the constant requests for her presence. Requests, my left eye,

Jilian thought. A demand known by any other name smells just as foul.

That her lessons with Abadan were going so badly only added to her frustration. She was not used to accepting a charge she could not fulfil. Yet she'd found herself working tirelessly to develop her dubious magical talents. She felt like a river fish suddenly thrown into the sea with no hope of learning to breathe salt water.

She'd been indoors for too many days. She needed air, wind, to hear snow crunching underfoot. Jilian yanked off the soft shoes Abadan had insisted she wear and threw them under the bed. She found the goatfleece-lined winter boots Maarcus had given her, thrust her feet in, and tightened the knee-high leather lacing. She stomped the stiff boots harder than she needed to be sure she'd tied them well. Satisfied she was capable of managing at least one small chore, Jilian slowly straightened to work the tense knot out of her back. She snatched the new felt cape – another gift from Maarcus – from its peg by the door and headed outside without stopping to inform anyone.

It was full dark and the wind was up. The few palace guards stationed outside had found a nook to protect themselves from the weather. They did not expect anyone to be out on such a night and behaved accordingly. Jilian slipped by them with no effort at all and went down into the streets of The Cliffs.

The cape took some getting used to. It kept her warm, but she was unaccustomed to the way it swirled about her legs and entrapped her arms. It distracted her and might have been a true hindrance if she'd known where she was bound. In the end, she decided to ignore it and hope it settled around her the way proper boots stopped pinching after a few weeks' wear.

No one was about and Jilian preferred it that way. She

ached for solitude. She had never in her life been around so many people for such an extended period of time.

Or if she must have company, let it be no more than a drunken mercenary shouting tales of glory to all the denizens of the Crisscross Inn while she swallowed a mug of ale.

A foolish wish. That was behind her. The Crisscross was gone. Most of the city of Twin Gates surrounding the inn was gone, surrendered to the elfwitch.

The elfwitch. Always and ever after, the cursed elfwitch.

Jilian let her feet take her to the cliff overlooking the sea. Since moving into the castle, the water called to her in a way she had not expected. It was in her blood no less than the mountains always had been. She strolled the path along the edge. The wind moaned in her ears and seemed to warn of death.

Snow crunched behind her, giving away someone stalking her.

She measured her steps carefully and listened as the other's faltered to match the pace. She hurried forward while coming in from the cliff's edge. Again her pursuer echoed her moves.

She bent down suddenly, pretending to pick up an object from the ground, pulling her knife from her boot instead. Holding her blade before her, she rose and spun in one move. The knife caught on her cape. She yanked it free just as he ran to meet her.

Running so hard that he could not stop.

Arms flung wide in an attempt to slow before he went over the cliff, the man impaled himself on her blade. He grunted once and slid to the ground.

'I was only trying to warn you,' he gasped out. 'He won't let you live. He dares not.'

She bent over him. 'He . . . who?'

'The . . . prince.'

'The prince! That's absurd! How dare you accuse Nikolis of such a thing?'

But the man was beyond listening. Blood gushed from his mouth and his glassy stare could only be seen on the dead.

Jilian checked for a pulse and warm breath to be sure. Nothing.

She closed his eyes and studied his unlined face. He seemed very young. Finally she patted his pockets in hopes of finding anything to tell her who he was. She came up empty until she noted the ring on his right hand. It bore the royal crest.

Had it belonged to her brother?

Jilian didn't remember having noticed it before. Then again, what better way for Nik to deny any connection than to avoid wearing it?

Confused and genuinely frightened, she slipped the ring off the corpse's hand and into her pocket.

She considered wrapping her cape around him as a burial shroud but decided it could be too easily recognized as hers. Instead she whispered, 'May the Sisters keep you,' and shoved him off the cliff.

Princess Jilian shivered as the body bounced against the rocks below. 'And may the Sisters forgive me.'

# Chapter 3

## GONE MISSING

No ordinary elf notices when the clan's goatboy shivers in the depth of winter or loses fingers to frostbite. One Goatboy in particular had just a little tent to block the wind and his animals to provide warmth.

He did not despair. He only needed to recall 'Notti,' his long forgotten private name, and his mind conjured his exiled mother's face.

He thought the expression meant something like 'precious', 'adored' and 'mischievous' all braided into one. He'd never be sure, though, because no elven clan wove tales about goatboys.

Long before the child became Goatboy, his father had voiced his impatience over the kind pet names that spawned soft men. With waving fists and crashing pottery, he swore at the faithless woman who shamed him by using such frivolous terms when she thought he couldn't hear. The second time he caught her tending the boy with hushed giggling and conspiratorial whispers, he turned her over to the elfwitch. His wife's banishment grieved him no more than a fisherman might mourn a rejected minnow.

His wrath he saved for his son.

The child was sentenced to look after the goats. To the man's disgust, the boy defiled them both by perverting the punishment into his personal indulgence – or so Notti's father spat between gritted teeth. 'Any toddler understands that the People are above such loud and smelly beasts. She—' meaning his expelled mother '—has done this. You are no flesh of mine!'

He left the boy to his debauchery, thereby formally disowning him – all because the child had wondered aloud why the goats were each as different as the elves themselves.

Whereas the father settled on ignoring his son, the man's second wife took her pleasure in degrading him. Goatboy endured. He let her jeers blow in the right ear and out the left; his bruises healed. She dared no more for no one else would watch over the goats so well.

No, the worst part to this day was the guilt over his mother's exile. Each glimpse of his father's stiff-jawed profile wrenched Goatboy to the core. Years had passed without word. No one knew how she and the other banished elves fared. None but Goatboy cared.

And yet, he was not unhappy among the goats.

Huddled on the edge of the forest behind a windbreak, he patted his old friend's flank. They were all good fellows, who never caused him harm. Goatboy sighed and wished he could say the same. Death comes to all, elf and beast, but the boy hated to choose the time. This one's end would come in the morning.

With the winter so harsh and some near starvation, the camp was forcing him to sacrifice more goats than was wise. He was down to only a Sister's handful now, and Goatboy sometimes worried whether any would live come Spring. For tonight, they would keep each other warm and the boy would tell stories until he fell asleep.

His favorite was the ongoing saga of Dragon, inspired by the Dragon Prince himself. The tales always began and ended the same way, but the adventures in between were marvelous. The boy cleared his throat. 'I once knew a Dragon. He was a small, malformed creature, but he had the bravery of a bear and the wiles of a fox. No animal could best him for long.' In a conspiratorial whisper, he informed his audience, 'Some said he was a prince in disguise, but I don't think we'll ever know for sure.'

In full voice once again, he said, 'As it happened, Dragon had broken a wing when he tangled with that giant falcon. And remember, he was not big himself. His enemies thought, "Now is the time to show that misshapen thing its place." But Dragon knew just what to do . . .'

As Goatboy spoke, he ignored his own poorly mended hand. Thin bones had shattered in the beating he received last fall and he'd had to splint it himself. He ran his twisted fingers through the coarse fur and went on with the story until the close breath of the goat lulled him to shut his eyes. He forgot what happened next. 'And remember,' he finally said through a yawn, 'the dragon always wins.'

Away from the sea and back in the streets of The Cliffs proper, the wind spit snow into Jilian's face. She pushed on. Another storm threatened to be one of the worst of the winter and she couldn't risk waiting it out among strangers. She had to get home, unwelcome as it was.

The lady's maid, the cook, the near poisoning, the dead

man at the cliff's edge. Now this biting, bitter snowstorm. It seemed even the Sisters conspired against her.

Jilian no longer knew how to ward off danger. Despite her years outwitting assassins, no one had ever bothered to make her a target except as a way of getting at the person she'd been paid to guard. Now common folk died for standing in her service.

Distracted and blinded by snow, Jilian lost her way. She studied the buildings. They all seemed constructed of massive stone and she had trouble telling one from the other. There was a statue not far ahead, so she must be in one of the city's many plazas. She moved closer to see if she might distinguish this from others and thereby divine the right direction.

Close up, this one might have been the Great King himself with his sword raised high overhead. She tried to brush snow from the base to read the legend. Maarcus had once told her all the statues were originally laden with ornamental gems. Since then each set of corrupt twin-rulers had chipped away until the monuments freed their treasures.

The idea of defacing the statues offended Jilian. To pilfer such precious stones was criminal, but worse was the attitude of the so-called kings who would parade such pettiness and need before the very people they were sworn to watch over.

For each brush she gave the inscription, the wind returned snow seven-fold. Jilian gave up trying to clear it. Assume it is the Great King and choose your road from there, she told herself. East, the castle will be east. She strode across the square, praying to the Sisters she headed east.

Exhausted from struggling against the wind and preoccupied with her own thoughts, Jilian had forgotten to monitor her surroundings. When someone abruptly separated from the shadows and came at her hissing obscenities, the dead man's warning suddenly came back to her.

A stray light glistened off the attacker's raised hand. He held a dagger aimed at her. Jillian's reflexes took over. The cape which had seemed such an annoyance served excellent duty as a soft shield. She swirled it about her to make herself a larger quarry while at the same time making it harder for the assassin to reach her vitals.

'Princess, my right eye,' muttered the man. 'I'll send you to the Sisters and let them decide your claim.'

He moved in close and swung wildly with the blade. She felt the sting as it scraped her cheek but ignored it as she retaliated with a knee to his groin. As the man doubled over she brought her fist under to meet his chin. He tried to get in another swipe and sliced air instead. Jilian hammered the back of his neck with the side of her hand and the man went down.

'They had one thing right,' he groaned. 'You sure don't fight like a princess.'

She kicked him in the gut for good measure. He grunted and lay quiet, watching her.

Jilian pulled her own knife from her boot, the very knife she'd won from Maarcus on their first meeting. Waving it before his eyes, she said, 'You'll find I'm not afraid to use this.' She smiled with a hint of self-satisfaction. 'And you would do well to note that I'm much more skilful with it than you've demonstrated thus far.'

The man raised up at the insult and she instantly brought the knife to his throat. 'Go ahead,' she offered, 'test my skills. I've been looking for a good sparring partner.'

He collapsed back to the ground.

'Who sent you?'

No answer.

'Come now, don't make this difficult. Give me the proper information and you might not spend the rest of your days in a dank prison cell.'

More silence.

Jilian shrugged. 'Have it your way. Get up.'

He looked in her eyes. 'We deserve a true prince.' He made no motion to rise.

'You know,' she said casually, comfortable in her old mercenary role, 'I like a challenge. Thing is, though, I never lose. Are you sure you want to die tonight?'

Slowly he began to get off the ground, looking for another chance – and found it.

The wind whipped snow into her eyes. As she blinked, the man yanked her feet out from under her and fled into the storm.

Ceeley went back to sleep once she finished her soup. Secure in Mama-Lyda's care, she didn't stir again until deepnight. When she woke, her new Mama and Papa were sitting not far away and talking so low she couldn't make out the words. The dwarf lay on her pallet, content to wait until they noticed her. She tapped her fingers on her blanket for a while and silently played counting games with herself after that. Maybe they needed a polite hint.

She sat up. 'Good morning, Mama-Lyda and Papa-Willam.'

The two looked up in surprise and came to crouch next to her.

'Shh,' said Papa, with his finger to his lips. 'It's very early.'

'I didn't know you were awake.' Mama's face had worry lines all over it.

'Only just now. Is it time to get up?'

'No, child. The sun hasn't even considered rising yet.'

'Oh.' She thought a minute. 'Then why are you up?'

'We had to talk.'

Ceeley nodded. 'My other mama and papa used to do that sometimes too.'

Mama-Lyda smiled. 'I imagine they did. Celia?'

Mama looked as if she had something serious to say. The girl sat very still with her hands in her lap and waited to let her say it in her own way.

'Celia,' she began, 'we couldn't find your Uncle Walther.'

'Oh.' Ceeley didn't know how to feel about that. He tried hard, but he didn't know how to be a full-day papa. He was just too busy. 'I guess he's getting ready to face the elfwitch. She's coming here, you know.'

'Shh, daughter of my heart. You're safe here.'

Mama-Lyda didn't understand how much Ceeley knew and the child didn't suppose this was the best time to explain it to her. The dwarf just smiled and said, 'I know.'

No one spoke for a long moment.

'Is there something else you wanted to tell me?' the girl finally asked.

'Celia, I've been asked to undergo a long journey. I'll need to leave before first light.'

Ceeley tried not to let her disappointment show. She only had her new mama for a few hours and she was already leaving.

Mama-Lyda wrapped her arms around her in a big hug that felt so good the child could almost forget this was goodbye. She let go and leaned back.

'Take me with you,' Ceeley was saying before she thought about it.

Mama-Lyda shook her head. 'It will be hard going. We couldn't ask it of you.' Her eyes filled with tears.

Beside her, Papa-Willam held her hand and looked at the floor.

'It'll be okay,' Ceeley promised. She pulled herself straight with pride. 'I am of the Sailclan. We are all travellers.'

'But you've come so far already.'

'It was good practice.'

'Well . . .'

Willam spoke softly without looking at Ceeley. 'Come now, Lyda. The child must belong to someone here.'

'Look at her, Willam. Could it be any plainer that the Sisters sent her to us?'

She jumped into the other's arms. 'Great! Where are we going?'

Mama-Lyda's eyes went big at the question. Something haunted lurked there. She spoke into the girl's hair. 'I don't quite know.'

The girl shrugged. 'It doesn't matter where. I've survived the elfwitch twice. I can do it again.'

'See, Willam?' Mama-Lyda pleaded. 'She was meant to be with us.'

'All right, all right. Who am I to deny the Sisters?'

Ceeley looked around the room of sleeping people. 'What about them, Mama-Lyda?'

Mama-Lyda squeezed the child tight. 'I wish I could protect every one of them,' she said, 'but I have been called elsewhere. I've sent word to the prince to watch over them in my absence. It's all I can do.' She stared beyond the child into the room. Her voice went distant and she seemed to be assuring herself as much as Ceeley.

'They will be defended here in the capital. The Cliffs are dangerous too, but it is of a different sort which won't likely affect the refugees.'

'The prince is a nice man and so is the princess,' Ceeley assured her. 'You'd like them.'

'Yes, I'm sure you're right,' not sounding sure in the least. 'I hope I'll meet them again one day.'

'We'd best be off,' Willam reminded them. 'Don't want to be 'ere when they wake or we'll be 'ere all day.'

'Yes, yes.'

Together the three stood to pull on their coats and gather up their few belongings. They bolted the door against the rising wind just as the dawn birds cracked the crisp air with song. With the King's Sea to the west and deserted country directly north and south, their one possible heading was east – toward the elfwitch.

Abadan stared at Walther's most recent attempt to master the fusing potions and shook his head. 'This doesn't seem to be your talent.'

Walther tried not to feel shame. 'No, it doesn't.'

'Surely a mage is not equally proficient in all things.' Jilian's speech went stiff with formality as she rose to the dwarf's defense.

Walther looked into the basin of failed magic and wished she would let the magician's annoyance pass.

'Surely not,' Abadan mocked her. 'But one hopes a modest level of competence would not become over-taxing.' He seemed to point at Jilian's flaws rather than the dwarf's.

She flushed angrily.

Stay silent, Walther thought. Just be still.

She would not. 'I would say he has achieved a modest level.'

'You would say. You who are more able to judge than I?' The volume rose with each word so that his voice boomed out and echoed off the walls by the time he paused. When he spoke again, he barely whispered. 'Princess, I allowed you to return to your lessons this morning because I promised someone long ago. But sometimes I wonder that you don't have more of your mother than your father in you. Zera told me to be wary, that one of her rare dreams warned of birthing both the deliverer and the destroyer of our people.' He stared hard at her. 'I am not so sure she was wrong.'

Jilian's expression warred between outrage and grief. Tears welled in her eyes. Without another sound, she unbarred the door and ran from the room.

When Sir Maarcus met Abadan in the great hall, the magician was still fuming over Jilian's most recent offense. Instead of coming out with it, he swore at his tasteless food and at the new cook.

Maarcus wasn't fooled. He'd heard about yesterday's incident not an hour after it happened. 'What were you expecting? We both know she's got a stubborn streak at least as wide as her father's. And who knows what influence her mother had?'

Abadan frowned, but made no effort to pretend he didn't know of whom the physician spoke. Like Maarcus, he didn't name her for fear someone might be listening. 'That's precisely the problem. If she can't learn to be more self-disciplined, she'll never stand a chance against the elfwitch.'

'She's withstood her more than once. You should stop looking for trouble three towns out when there is plenty under your nose.'

'Resisting her is not the same as overcoming her.'

'Well, no . . .' Maarcus let it hang. Abadan always had a way of cutting to the heart of a matter – and leaving the physician feeling utterly demoralized in the process. It seemed Abadan needed precisely this reaction to fuel his own thoughts into creative paths. Maarcus didn't enjoy his role, but he'd quit fighting it long ago.

A man came into the hall, shaking snow from his cape before joining the food line where portions were carefully ladled from the communal pot. Maarcus pictured Alvaria somewhere beyond the Dunavs where deepsnows seldom reigned. He doubted she would wait until the spring thaws to plot her return.

'Her power to compel others to do her will means she can act any time,' said Abadan echoing the physician's own thoughts. 'She—' meaning Jilian '—must understand the urgency.'

The click of a courier's footsteps echoed on the stone floor as he came to a stop behind them.

'Why don't they let me finish a meal once in a while?' muttered Abadan. He quickly began to spoon in the thin stew.

'Sirs, a man requests an audience at your earliest opportunity.'

The magician spoke with his mouth full. 'Tell him we're eating.'

'With your permission, sir. He says to tell you his name is Tom and he is sometimes known as Wanton Tom the mercenary.'

Abadan leaned toward Maarcus and whispered around his food, 'His daughter is up to something. I know it.' He didn't wait for the physician's answer before telling the man, 'We'll meet him in the library.'

The messenger dipped a quick bow and left.

Abadan tossed his spoon into the empty bowl. 'Dreadful stew, but that Wanton Tom has always had annoying timing just the same.'

Nikolis sheathed his sword. 'Another session like that and I might as well exercise with the recently departed cook.'

Maarcus gave him a sour grin. 'There's an idea.'

The prince didn't excuse the Shoreman's performance as much as he would have liked to. The bleak certainty that the witch was drawing ever nearer meant none of them could afford the luxury of wasting a few hours. 'Maarcus, though we all have reason to be distracted, it's no cause to permit lesser problems to rule us.'

'Sorry,' he said, doing his best to sound contrite. 'My mind is elsewhere.'

'I know. Is it Ceeley?'

Maarcus leaned against the wall. All his bluster escaped in a whuff of breath. 'I've known that girl since she was an infant. Her father had a premonition, nothing more than a feeling really. He feared a coming war and with good reason.' He looked past the prince to something only he could see. 'Nik, he left her care to me if anything should happen to his near kin. I've failed both him and myself.' His voice cracked. 'Most of all I've let down Ceeley.'

'Do you want to go find her?'

'Out of the question. You need me here.'

'If I gave you leave?'

'You yourself just said we can't allow our personal concerns to take priority. No, I belong here.'

'Doing what? Teaching me poor technique? Your grandfather could do me more good shouting from the next room.'

The other blushed.

'Listen, Maarcus, you've got a skill. I know you detest skulking about, but I could use you out there. Just this morning, I received news of trolls heading toward The Cliffs.'

'If that's so, then I'm one of the Seven Sisters.'

'I agree. Then again . . .' Nikolis spoke in earnest now. 'I can't imagine how it's possible to stage a troop movement in this weather, but I'd like someone reliable to verify or deny the rumors. If they're true, we've got to act before they reach us. We're too vulnerable here. No one is prepared.'

'Are you sure this isn't chasing after shadows?'

'No, no I'm not. I'll tell you this, however. I can smell the witch is up to something. My skin crawls with it. We need to have someone who can quickly ferret out her plans and live long enough to pass along what he's learned. You're my best hope, Maarcus. If using Ceeley as your cover allows you to actually find the child in the process, no one will be more pleased than I.'

'I might be useful at that.'

'You'll need to go soon if we hope to learn anything in time to prepare our defenses.'

Last of the four to arrive at their private noonday meal as usual, Walther noted a shift in seating since yesterday. Now Nikolis claimed the head which had been vacant. Jilian sat to one side and Maarcus the other. Despite the changes, a funeral wake would have been more lively. Everyone silently picked at the food, examining it for signs of poison and tossing out anything suspect. With Ceeley so much on his mind, Walther wasn't inclined to improve their spirits.

'Why didn't you alert us sooner?' Maarcus asked before Walther had settled into his chair.

'Why didn't you check in on her once in a while!' Walther blasted back.

'Shut up, both of you. Accusations don't help.' Jilian's pained voice broke through the bickering. 'We're having the entire castle searched. We'll find Ceeley.'

Walther glared at Maarcus but held his tongue. The Shoreman did the same.

'Thank you, gentlemen. Please—' She motioned to the sideboard laden with stale bread and more of the morning's stew.

Walther rose to serve himself. 'Are you sure it's safe?'

The prince speared a bit of potato. 'I scooped it from the common pot myself.'

Jilian laughed in spite of the dire situation. 'I'll wager that got them talking.'

'No worse than the murdered cook.'

Walther looked down at his food. What little appetite he'd had fled. Nonetheless, the dwarf forced himself to swallow the tasteless broth.

'Maybe we should just give over the kitchen to the refugees,' Maarcus said. Though his bowl was full, his spoon and fork still lay clean on the table.

'And poison them!' Jilian was appalled.

'No, that's not what I meant. I was thinking someone should be eating this and they might as well since they're on such short rations already.'

Walther dropped his spoon. 'That's it!'

'What? You've decided to give up food?'

'No, that's where Ceeley went! She wanted someone to play with and I promised I'd ask about it. When I found her gone, I completely forgot.'

'Walther, are you saying she's gone out to look for other children?'

The dwarf nodded at the princess. 'I'm sure of it. We spoke about the refugees just yesterday. Their leader, Lyda? I hear she keeps a record of all the comings and goings there. She'll know where Ceeley is.'

The prince looked stricken. 'I received word this morning that Lyda was called away on an urgent mission. The place is in complete turmoil, with different factions arguing over who's best suited to claim her role.'

'Any more good news?' Jilian asked.

'Someone broke into the store room during last night's storm. We caught the traitor, but not before some of his fellows made off with several barrels of flour. We can all expect the soup to get thinner.'

'Thanks for that cheery bit, Maarcus.'

'Ceeley was probably outside during the st—'

'No, I won't hear it.' Jilian cut him off. 'We will find her and she will be fine.' She clipped each word precisely and no one wanted to argue with her.

Nikolis went to the sideboard for a second serving, then returned to his place. Walther and Jilian followed him. Finally Maarcus picked up his spoon and began to eat.

Walther shut out his worries and used all his concentration to keep the soup down. Silence was so thick he nearly dropped his spoon when the prince spoke.

'I've been thinking we could use better reconnaissance, so I've asked Maarcus to go out on an assignment for me.'

Maarcus pushed away his meal with obvious relief. 'Grandfather confirmed your report of a massive group of trolls moving our way. A mercenary by the name of Wanton Tom brought the news this morning.'

'Wanton Tom, huh? I wonder what he's doing here?'

'You know him, Jilian?' the prince asked.

'Never really met him, but he's gathered something of

a reputation over the years. You remember, Nik. He's the one who travels with a dragon. Has a daughter who briefly attempted your rescue . . .'

'Yes, right, of course.' Nikolis was tight-lipped.

Walther wondered again why the young mage had risked her life to help an uncrowned prince, then abandoned him in the midst of battle. It seemed that she and the prince himself were the only ones who would ever know.

'Maarcus, you might want to talk with this man before you leave.'

The Shoreman nodded.

'I'd like to go as well,' the princess announced.

'By all means, see what you can find out from him.'

Jilian shook her head. 'That, too, but I mean I want to go with Maarcus.'

'Absolutely not!'

'What's the matter? Can't bear my company?'

'It's not safe.'

'As if poisoning is. If it comes to it, I'd prefer to die at the end of a blade. Anyway,' Jilian continued. 'I can't stay here.'

'Now don't start that again.' The wrinkles formed in Nikolis's brow. 'If I can bear the transformation from lap-dragon to prince, you can certainly manage—'

'That's not it. Abadan and I . . .'

'Again? I thought you were going to apologize.'

The princess gripped her fork like a weapon. 'So did I. Apparently I remind him of someone else, someone he doesn't like.'

The prince's frown deepened. 'That's ridiculous. You're the one he's been seeking for more than a generation.'

'I don't think he's altogether pleased with what he found. I'd like to go,' she repeated.

Maarcus said, 'Go or stay, let's get back to the topic. Trolls have been sighted at least twice and it seems they're coming in our direction.' He spoke with assurance, in his element now. 'I need to leave directly, today if possible. You'll tell any who notice that I'm looking for Ceeley.'

'We,' Jilian stressed, '*we* need to leave soon.'

'Jilian . . .' Maarcus turned to the prince for help.

'She's never listened to me. You're on your own here. Besides, I think you'll have better odds of surviving together.'

'Maarcus, this is what I'm good at.' A trace of her old confidence shone through.

'Sneaking around you mean.'

'If you want to put it that way, yes.'

They're like soldiers, Walther realized. Both the Shoreman and the princess needed to be moving. The waiting was sapping their strength more than the poor food and bad weather. The dwarf spoke up. 'I agree that it makes sense for Jilian to go. The elfwitch is behind this and we need to know what it is. She'll be able to detect things you can't, Maarcus.'

'If you're alluding to my lack of talent with things magical, I've survived perfectly well without it this long.'

'Maarcus, Walther is right. My sister can cover your back with her understanding of the enemy as well as with a sword. I depended on it for years.' The prince's honesty seemed to convince the Shoreman where simple logic could not.

'As you wish. We travel together.'

'Thank you,' Prince Nikolis answered sincerely.

To Walther, the man's skill and style appeared very kingly indeed.

\* \* \*

Tom felt like an idiot. Grosik wasn't helping – gung-ho to drop Ginni at Abadan's feet one minute and all but unwilling to come within firing range of the capital in the next.

The mercenary sat at their pleasure, awaiting the chance to repeat his story for the very princeling Ginni had tried to rescue. Tom kept his mind on his empty belly and sore feet. Better to think about commonplace body gripes than worry over his daughter or give in to his rising impatience. 'The Old Grouch could've at least tried to find a more hospitable trail to set me down,' he grumbled to the empty room.

Finally a whole crowd arrived to stuff themselves into the tiny room. Seeing Maarcus the Sixth and the magician for the second time in one day lessened his surprise at their decline. It wasn't just that they were both a little more grey and wrinkled. It was the trace of defeat creeping into the physician's posture and the look of suspicion that replaced the air of command in Abadan's gaze.

By contrast, the prince moved like a man meant to rule. Apparently he'd shed his doubts along with the elven robe when they battled with the elfwitch. He led the others into the room and took up position where he could see the door.

The younger Maarcus followed his grandfather. The eternal Shoreman's chip remained fixed on his shoulder but his smile held less cockiness than Tom remembered. Loss comes to us all, Tom thought.

The way the woman carried herself, she seemed the perfect mate for Maarcus. At first Tom thought her no more than that until he caught how closely her features mirrored those of the prince. She'd be the mercenary turned princess then. Tom would bet she kept at least one knife hidden in her clothing. Plainly she preferred her former profession over the current calling.

The last of the group was a dwarf. The man's shock-white hair suggested someone much older, yet the dwarf's walk and skin both held the springiness of youth. Ginni would have been able to uncover this one's role, but Tom settled for knowing better than to dismiss anyone so soon in the game. He nodded a respectful greeting to the dwarf, just as he had with the others.

No one bothered to make introductions.

'My advisors tell me you've seen something I should know about.'

Sisters spare him from smug young upstarts. These 'advisors' had been piloting the whole leaking boat for nearly two generations. Tom said nothing for a minute, watched the way even the old men took their cues from the prince. Uncomfortable as new fathers they were, but willing to stand back and let the kid risk a bloody knee. Tom swallowed bile. He spoke more formally than he had in a decade. 'Yes, I have.'

'We'd like to hear it,' Prince Nikolis said. It could have been an order, but it felt like a request.

'Well,' the mercenary began, 'I was astride Grosik—'

'His dragon,' Maarcus the Sixth explained. 'He travels with—'

The prince held up his hand for silence. 'I think it'll go more quickly if we let him say it his way.' Again, he seemed closer to asking a favor than stating a directive.

Okay, Tom thought, not just another smooth-skinned face. 'We were looking for my daughter Ginni. You might remember her.' He paused then said without a hint of venom, 'She tried to help you escape the elfwitch.'

'I remember.' His face and voice went blank with the effort to mask his feelings.

Tom lost track of the others in the room. Suddenly he was just a father addressing the man who'd spurned his daughter. He couldn't resist twisting the knife. 'She's not been herself since Roslin died. Last night, hours before we'd planned to bring her here, she disappeared.'

'With all due respect, Nik, what has this got to do with the trolls?'

'Patience, Maarcus. You're as bad as your grandfather.' He glanced toward the Shoreman and softened his words with a genuine smile.

His attention returned to Tom. 'Kidnapped?'

'Unlikely.'

'Then what?'

'I think she's gone to the Tower of the Forty-nine Mages.'

'What can we do about it and why should we?' The question could have been harsh, but wasn't.

'She's alone in the worst winter anyone can remember on her way to a place she's never been with equal odds of being welcomed and destroyed.'

'I see.'

'No matter what, you can bet your boots she will not come out the same girl she went in.'

The prince sounded age-old. 'None of us do, Tom. None of us.' The last three words seemed to hang in the air. 'Tell me about the trolls.'

'That's it? No "we'll think about it, see what we can do."?'

'We'll do more than either, but first the trolls.'

Tom doubted they'd give him another chance to discuss Ginni, but he let it go. Years of turmoil didn't change much. When the king nods, subjects scurry to obey. Make that 'prince,' he thought. 'We were looking for my daughter, north and a touch east of The Cliffs,

80

'bout halfway between here and what's left of Three Falls. Weirdest sight I ever saw. Must've been a couple hun'erd of 'em, all stumbling this way like they had an appointment with the king.'

Nikolis frowned.

'Sorry about that.' The oddness of the scene had shaken him and he'd let his usual loose language slip in despite his best intentions.

'Not important.'

'They just kept going. Nothing stopped them.'

'They'll rest at night,' the prince said, as if he'd seen them in action. 'But nothing will stop them by day if the elfwitch has set them a task.'

'I was still hoping to speak with Sir Maarcus and Master Abadan about Ginni,' he continued, 'so I was trying to talk Grosik into heading this way. After that, even he agreed we had to alert you.'

'We appreciate it. Any idea how fast they're moving?'

Tom considered the terrain. 'I'd say they'll be here within a couple seven-days, maybe less if the weather holds.'

Nikolis turned to his sister.

They said as one voice, 'For them, it'll hold.'

# Chapter 4

## LEAVING HOME

Jilian hummed to herself as she cinched her pack tight. She was getting out of this treacherous town and couldn't leave fast enough. She had just one task left to help put her mind at ease and only her twin could help her there.

She waited in the doorway of Nik's office while he gave his man instructions. 'Move the gentleman into the east wing. It's warmer. And be sure he has a view of the mountains if you can.'

'Very good, sire.' He nodded and left.

'Kind of you to find Tom a better room.'

'I don't imagine he likes it indoors any better than you do.'

'But not you?' Jilian asked, wondering if there really were a dragon buried down inside him somewhere.

'I could use fresh air now and again, but I've got Maarcus Senior and his swordplay to keep my blood flowing.'

'Be honest, Nik. Aren't you aching to put a long day's hike between you and civilization?'

Nikolis smiled sadly. He glanced toward the shutter closed against yesterday's storm and back to his sister. 'Well one of us has to stay put and I seem the more likely candidate.'

Jilian went to stand by the fire. 'Why is that, do you suppose?'

She'd planned to gauge his reaction to the incident on the ridge and the other in the plaza. As the silence stretched she found herself wondering, Had he sent someone to kill her? Could he have known about the poison? He never touched the tainted food.

In the fireplace a log burned in two, falling with a loud crack and sending flames high.

'I wish you'd told someone you were going out last night. I was up until all hours waiting for word. And when my man came back and said he couldn't find you . . .'

'Sorry to make you worry, Nikolis. I just needed—'

'Air,' he finished for her.

He still knew her mind, but should she presume the same? So much conversation about the very thing that bothered her made her feel more penned in. Was he merely showing he understood? Or did he hope to make his sister more eager to leave, by purposely reminding her of her aversion to cities with their ever-present buildings stuffed overfull with people?

'Well,' she said cheerfully, 'I'm ready to go. My room's so tidy the chambermaid will be hard-pressed to find anything left of mine.'

He brightened as if he hadn't heard such good news in weeks. 'That's splendid!'

'If I didn't know better, I'd say you're glad to be rid of me.' She hoped she sounded carefree behind her tense smile, but found herself thinking, Do I know better? It was less trouble to grasp his reasoning when he couldn't speak.

As if to prove her suspicions right, her twin gave her a look she couldn't read. 'You'll be safe,' he said. 'I'm not certain what makes me believe it, but you will be. Even if, Sisters forbid, you get caught, the elfwitch has different plans for you. Her primary goal with me was to demonstrate her power before her people.'

'But what about her—'

'Armies? Leading them would have been useful to her, but she never counted on it. She could dispense with me without a second thought.'

'Ah, Nik, don't say that.'

'You know it's true.'

Jilian looked past him to the shuttered window. He was right – the elfwitch had risked killing him in the transformation. 'But what if you'd died in front of the crowd?'

'So, she hammers home her control over life and death. Jilian, you are the daughter she couldn't raise and the mother she rejected all in one. She won't turn against you so easily.'

She folded her arms across her chest. 'Great. She'll simply torture me endlessly hoping I bow to her will. That's something to look forward to.'

'There's the old spirit.' His smile was genuine and infectious.

It blew away her suspicions like a spider-web in a strong wind. She responded with a grin of her own. They stood chuckling at each other for absolutely no reason at all, but she still couldn't bring herself to tell him about the night before.

'I'd like you to take something with you.' Nikolis

crossed the room to the fireplace. He slid open the corner of the mantelpiece to reveal a small secret chamber. 'I found this and the dagger within not long after I decided to use this room as an office. It was the only thing that lay inside it. I've come to think of it as my own good luck charm.'

He stepped over to her to hand her a hilted dagger wrought in sterling silver. It shone as if it would never tarnish. On the pommel's round tip was a deep engraving of the royal crest.

'It matches your dragon coin. It must have been our father's. King Tomar, that is.'

The princess nodded. Odd to hear the Great King referred to that way. Jilian pulled her own smaller dagger from her boot. 'You remember this one. It's the blade Maarcus left behind when he hired us to guard the elfwitch. Take it.'

'But won't you need it?'

'Trolls won't appreciate the subtleties of a concealed knife and Alvaria no doubt already knows where I keep it. Besides I'll have Maarcus to watch my back.'

'Well, all right then.' Nikolis reluctantly accepted the gift. He examined the blade, balancing it in his hand. Suddenly he gripped the handle and threw the dagger. It whipped past Jilian to bury itself in the mantel at the exact spot where the larger dagger had been hidden. The prince nodded. 'A fine knife. Thank you.'

She silently watched him as he retrieved the blade. Her heart pounded in her ears and her throat was tight. 'You're welcome,' she managed. I'm being foolish, she told herself. I've just seen the wrong end of too many knives lately. But she couldn't fully convince herself he hadn't meant the dagger for her. Jilian gave him a weak smile. 'Maybe you shouldn't bother Sir Maarcus to further your sword-fighting. I think you've found your weapon.'

Maarcus the Sixth glanced at the two at his side. Abadan hurried along, stiff and serious. Walther, though much shorter, calmly kept pace. Nearly out of breath himself, the physician asked, 'Can't we do this in your rooms instead?'

Abadan glared at him. 'No.' His face was grim, grimmer than Maarcus expected.

The physician hated Abadan's magic chamber. The concentrated magicks seemed to press all around him here, though the sorcery could not influence him for good or ill. Just one in a lengthy family line of men who had no talent for deciphering any of the magician's work, Maarcus longed to prod and poke these as he would the tangible realm of his medicines. Barring that and try as he might to do otherwise, he could only fear it.

As always Abadan ignored the physician's reluctance. The wards in his chamber made it the safest place to go to address any matter of import. Maarcus let out a sigh, and the three proceeded down the hall without speaking.

Once inside with the door bolted shut, the physician did his best to dismiss his misgivings. The magicks were not intended to bedevil him.

'The elfwitch must be resting today,' he ventured in a light tone. 'I don't smell any rotting flesh.'

'Be quiet, fool. How can you suggest such a thing when the trolls even now are massing for attack?'

'Sorry.'

Abadan scolded the physician as if he were a child, but he didn't take offense. Since Zera's death, he seemed more and more unable to focus beyond his own small needs.

'I've never seen the phenomenon up close before,' Abadan was saying. 'It would have been interesting to . . .'

Maarcus stared at his friend. 'I'd think the girl's situation is rather more serious than hollow experiments,' he said primly.

'Baah, pay attention, you old f—' Abadan leaned in to get a closer look at the physician's eyes. 'You need more sleep,' he said, but Maarcus was sure he was thinking something else. 'I'm not talking about idle curiosity,' he continued. 'This is critical. Roslin could have been a powerful ally and ultimately became a dreadful enemy. If her daughter knows even a portion of what she knew, we . . .'

He let the sentence hang. Maarcus imagined the words struggling for an ending and vainly trailing into open space.

Walther spelled it out. 'If she fell back into Alvaria's hands, she could do us more harm than Roslin herself.'

'Exactly,' Abadan said. 'The girl is less disciplined, less predictable – and apparently also possesses far stronger magic than her mother's considerable gift.'

There the magician went again, enlightening Maarcus when he should have grasped the matter intuitively. Walther, too, saw the physician's weakness. Maarcus could interpret politics and the ambitions of men, but even a simple overlay of magic clouded his thinking. A sinking in his gut told him it would be his downfall someday – and soon. 'Of course,' he said, pretending he'd understood all along. 'But what do we do about it?'

'Send Tom after her.' Walther spoke as if it were obvious, then blushed. 'Beg your pardon. I didn't mean to overstep.'

'Nonsense,' Abadan said. 'What do you have in mind?'

Walther paused. 'Well, obviously he knows something about his daughter and we know something about the Tower of the Forty-nine Mages. We can—'

'We do?' Abadan asked.

'We do,' Walther stated forcefully.

'How is that?'

'My people have traded with them for generations.'

'You have?' Abadan asked. He seemed utterly surprised.

Walther shrugged. 'Even they can't do everything themselves. We're never admitted beyond the outer gate, but we've had many occasions to study the stone wall while we waited on Revered Mother or one of the Revered Sisters to approve our wares. I think I could at least get Wanton Tom – and maybe his dragon – onto the main grounds.'

'Is that so?'

'Yes, to the east of the central entrance is a much smaller, little-used gate. It's never completely overgrown, so I'd venture one of the mages uses it for her own private purposes now and again, but . . .'

Maarcus lost track of the dwarf's plan. He was too busy trying to shake the sense of grasping fingers trailing his every move. He strolled about the magician's study, picking up bottles and examining salves as if he'd never seen them before. He thought someone might be calling his name, but it really didn't seem vital just then.

When Goatboy rose in the morning, he felt a change in the air. He crawled from his tent, stood, and stretched the stiffness from his joints. Flexing his aching hand, he looked east over the meadow.

Her tent was pitched in its accustomed place beside the lake just as it always had been – except men now guarded the entrance flap. The One had arrived without warning sometime during the night.

In the still morning air, people hurried about preparing a feast to celebrate her return. He looked at the last few of his goats and hoped the revelry wouldn't claim more than one today. Ultimately they would each be butchered, chosen with the elfwitch's unerring skill at picking his favorite while he silently grieved.

In the months of the One's absence, the elves had not kept up her dwelling. They had excused themselves by conjuring wild tales of her death – predicting she had been ripped limb from limb at the hands of her own trolls, or perhaps bitten in two by the fearsome dragon, had been a commonplace pastime this winter.

The boy patted his goat's flank. 'She'll know,' he told the animal. 'It will come to no good.'

Indeed the two who had invented the most ghastly stories now labored to sweep out debris and mend every tear in the tent canvas. As if they felt Goatboy watching them, the boys abandoned their chores and headed his way.

He turned away and occupied himself with needlessly checking over his own tent. 'You'd think the terror of her punishment would keep them so busy they wouldn't have time to make a special trip just to torment me.' He shrugged, accepting the inevitable. 'I guess I'm simply such a tasty target they can't resist.' He thought he knew how the goats must feel just before the mortal blow.

Tabor surprised him by speaking with near politeness. 'The One wants you.'

Goatboy twisted to be sure there was no one behind him. 'Me?' he asked, feeling altogether foolish.

'Yes, you.'

'Probably wants your help in spicing the goat stew,' suggested Theron mildly.

His fellow elbowed him in the ribs. 'Not now,' he hissed.

Goatboy held his face calm. Theron could well be right. 'I'm ready.'

He followed quietly behind the two, maintaining enough distance to keep out of their reach. He needn't have worried. The usual whispered insults and clever guffaws were as damped down as his own spirits. The mood weighed heavier and heavier the closer they grew to her tent.

All the elves seemed subdued as they went about their tasks. With hunger and cold a constant in the aftermath of the battle, it could only be fear of the One's outrage that caused this new wariness.

They stopped before two heavily-muscled guards, one elf, one troll. They raised their shining swords to bar the entrance.

'The One requests this boy's presence,' said Tabor, with more gentility than Goatboy would have imagined possible.

Swords were lowered and the three entered the elf-witch's private domain.

A lowly goatboy, he had never been inside before – and those who had been so honored dared not tell of it. Where he'd expected luxury, he found spare conditions and a harshness that called up war epics. In contrast to the many pillows strewn about his father's wife's tent, here were simply fine carpetings and stiff camp stools. The furnishings suggested richness without comfort.

Two more sentinels, twins to those outside, stood watch within. The elfwitch ignored them, though Goatboy felt sure they could recount her every movement.

She favored him with a warm smile. 'Ah, you're here. Good.' She turned to the two boys and her face and voice went icy. 'Why are you still here? Leave us.'

Goatboy swallowed hard as the boys scurried out of the tent. She could have discarded him just as quickly – and probably would sometime soon.

She faced the guards. 'Go.'

The sentinels bowed with dignity and left.

'Notti, come forward.'

Had he heard correctly? How could she know that name when he doubted anyone including his own father remembered it? Did the One listen to his dreams?

He gulped again and walked toward her as carefully as though he teetered on the edge of a sheer mountain path. 'Y-yes, M-ma'am.'

'There's no need to fear me. Move along, child.'

He forced himself to take the few remaining steps at a normal pace. He stopped an arm's length away from her and kneeled, keeping his eyes to the ground. The scene on the carpet beneath him depicted a bloody transformation of man to beast and back again. Repulsed, he abruptly pulled away. She moved in, her gaze inches from his.

'You have endured much,' she said ignoring his discomfort. 'I think you understand the rigors of discipline . . . unlike those outside.' Her arm swept wide as if to encompass the entire One Land. 'I need elves like you.'

Goatboy held himself rigid lest he give away any hint of his contrary emotions. He didn't feel brave enough to withstand her attention.

'Get up,' she said. 'There is no need for that here alone with me. I know your true heart, Notti.' She repeated his name with complete casualness as if it were used every day.

But no one knew it, no one except his mother.

Goatboy rose, utterly confused. Was this a new trick, one he hadn't considered possible? Or could she be genuine? He smiled tentatively. 'How may I please

you?' The words seemed to escape his lips of their
own will. He couldn't imagine wanting to please her,
could he?

'You already do,' she answered, in an intimate voice
he assumed she reserved for those closest to her. Certainly
he had never heard it when she addressed the whole camp.
'But there is something more—'

She let the word hang until he felt compelled to say,
'Suggest how I may serve you and I will gladly do so.'
Again she seemed to pull from him words he would not
have thought existed.

She favored him with a radiant smile that lit her face
and warmed his soul.

Goatboy waited, transfixed by the eyes. 'Yes?' he
whispered.

'Continue your work with the goats for the moment,
but I will make that work easier. Soon there will be a task
only you can perform. A journey you must undertake. I
will tell you when the time comes. Be ready.'

A chance to flee this place without disgrace? He could
hardly contain his joy. Goatboy allowed himself to answer
her smile. 'I will be.'

The Tower of the Forty-nine Mages was in fact a
collection of large, squat, attached huts circling seven
middling-high towers. A fence barely taller than an
average woman encompassed the grounds. The entire
arrangement appeared so haphazard and flimsy that Ginni
would have mistaken it for an eccentric farmer's home
and out buildings if she hadn't known what to look for.

Likewise the mage at the gate seemed unremarkable.
Her looks were ordinary, her dress and carriage even more
so. Ginni, master of disguises in her own right, recognized
it in others. The eyes almost always gave away a person's

true worth. This one's were deep-set, brown – and sharp with attention.

A simple address was best. They would already know who she was well before she arrived at the rough-hewn door. 'I am Ginni, daughter of Roslin.'

'Forbidden daughter of Roslin.'

Ginni bowed without humility. 'Paternity has never been a concern of yours. I see no reason it should start with me.'

The woman's eyes darkened.

'You enter on the sufferance of the Forty-nine. Everything you have ever known means less than nothing to us.' Ginni nodded without hesitation. The mage stepped back to allow the new apprentice to pass inside.

Inwardly, Ginni breathed a sigh of relief. She had never really believed she would get this far. Now that she had arrived, her mind felt clearer than it had since before Roslin's death. Not for the first time, she wondered whether her mother had guided this action. Roslin had never approved any of Ginni's doings; this could be worse than most, crawling back to ask help from those who had rejected both mother and daughter.

If not Roslin, who had called her to this place?

The mage escorted Ginni along a packed-dirt path shoveled clear of snow. A barren, uninviting entry opened into a narrow hallway, which in turn led to a richly carpeted room with a brazier set at the foot of each of three upholstered chairs. The woman ushered her inside. 'At your pleasure.'

Ginni took several steps into the room and turned to face the witch, who had not followed her guest. Instead she waited in the hall until she saw the young mage settle into one of the chairs and was now closing the door. Ginni didn't bother rising to test the lock. Witches such as these would only allow her to go where they wished.

They left her unattended long enough to try her patience, but Ginni did not yield. Thus far the tests had been easy. She had learned exceptional patience as a toddler in Roslin's care. She could amuse herself for hours, even days, without food or human companionship if necessary. Only extreme thirst would drive her from the room and this wouldn't be for at least seven fold seven hours yet.

Ginni studied the room. Simple carpetings covered the walls. Their geometric designs suggested the hangings were more for warmth than idle decoration, though there was something reminiscent of the rug Roslin had used to magically silence tavern noises.

She brooded over what had become of Roslin's magicks. The rug, her potions, the scrying bowl, Abadan's babble-box, and the map – all had disappeared with Roslin. Did the elfwitch have them now?

As she examined the room, she realized for at least this one moment that anxiety sat lightly on her shoulders and the shouting in her ears had diminished to a whisper. Maybe Roslin concurred with her after all – or maybe the witches had induced calm. Regardless, it was welcome respite and Ginni was exhausted enough to allow herself to savor it.

She sat back and relaxed into the chair. She let her eyes close and her breath even out. If the witches wanted to harm her, they would. So be it. She'd come to them, and for the moment Ginni was content to put herself at their mercy.

Willam strengthened Lyda just as she had always supported him. As a new bride, she had faithfully followed him halfway across the One Land. Now they reversed the journey and their roles. The weather had been mild then; so now they must endure it at its most severe.

They stopped behind a tree and watched the snow whip past. Willam wrapped his arms around her. 'Lyda, I promised m'self. We'll come through okay. Even if we have to cross the Dunavs.'

She looked into his eyes then down at the child huddled against her knees. 'Her lips are blue.'

'We'll find shelter.'

He spoke as if he believed it.

This new mission of hers was so very different from her trial during the Elfwitch's Autumn. That journey had begun in anger and given way to serenity. This one started where the other left off and the Sisters only knew where it would lead.

And yet to travel with a family gave her a feeling of completeness she had never expected to glimpse.

And yet—

And yet they suffered.

She had not completed the test.

The elves had given her a quest and a will to see it through. They had not promised she would survive it; only that she was worthy of the journey and it was worthy of her. It was up to her to complete it.

'Yes, we will find shelter,' she echoed.

Together the three turned and walked into the blinding storm.

Jilian sat her chestnut mount uneasily. Her every bone and muscle ached already. 'I hate horses. They're stupid, smelly beasts.'

'Would you prefer to run along beside mine?' Maarcus asked.

'We'd likely move as quickly.'

The Shoreman laughed. 'Care to place a wager?'

'Don't be ridiculous. We haven't time for such non-sense.'

'What's put a crimp in your riding-pants? I'd've thought you couldn't wait to be away from all that.'

What could Jilian tell him? Last night someone tried yet again to kill me and he may have been ordered by my brother? Or, I dumped a dead body over a cliff rather than see him discovered? Or, gee Maarcus, have you ever slain a man by accident?

In her mind's eye, she saw only an anonymous body falling over a cliff. His final words floated up behind him. 'The prince won't let you live. He dares not.' Echoes drowned out by the crashing waves.

Jilian could barely stomach thoughts of the evening's other encounter. Could that meeting have been simple happenstance? Had he stalked her on Nik's order? Her brother had said he sent someone looking for her. Could Nik have changed so much since his transformation from that poor furry dragon? Had the elfwitch found a way to command his soul?

'Jilian!'

The shout jolted her so that she nearly fell out of her saddle. 'What?'

'I was saying—'

'I hate horses,' she muttered again.

'So you've said. What's the matter with you? It's perfect riding weather. A cloudless, afternoon sky as stunning blue as any I've ever seen.'

'You're facing north. That's a witch-cursed storm coming from the east.'

He glanced over his shoulder. 'So we're in for a little wind and snow.'

97

'Maarcus, I'm serious. There will be more than just a delicate sprinkling of snowflakes.'

'What have you got against horses?'

'You'll do anything rather than discuss magic. Fine, I'll humor you. Just remember, magic hovers all around you whether you realize it or not.' And whether I confront it or not, she thought. She patted her mount's neck, but it didn't soothe either of them. 'Horses always shied away from my brother when he was a dragon,' she said, answering his question. 'I never got much of a chance to master them.'

'They aren't dogs, Jilian.'

'Says you, horse-lover. We'll debate the Sisters' beasts and creatures later. I've got trolls to chase and a blizzard to outrun. In case you haven't noticed, it's closing fast.' She dug her heels into the chestnut's haunches and shot ahead.

Abadan shook his head sadly. 'It's a waste. Jilian could be a great asset if she had the discipline.'

'But . . .' Walther wanted to say. But what? The magician was right. Jilian would have to find things her own way.

'We begin again. Tell me the healing properties of dragon's claw, both leaf and stem.'

'It serves as a strong purgative and therefore should be used with caution,' Walther recited. 'It was given to women to cleanse the body for conception but seemed just as likely to harm the child.' He slowed. 'However, old hags' tales claim it induces twins in those the Sisters deem worthy . . .' He trailed off. 'Do the prince and princess know?'

'Know what?' Abadan looked down to fuss with the magicks set out for the day's lesson.

'Do they know their mother was given dragon's claw?'

The magician didn't answer the question directly. 'What of it?'

'You manipulated events to fit the prophecies.'

'Again, what of it?'

'They are not true.'

'That they were influenced has no bearing on truth,' the magician snapped. 'Are you less alive because your village has been destroyed?'

Walther felt a rising anger he had not allowed himself in many weeks. He spoke through gritted teeth. 'Do not mock me.'

'Any more than you mock me. The Forty-nine Witches predicted twins. The seers mention parentage not at all. The two could as well be dragons as humans. They could be dwarves. It matters not at all so long as our twins seek to reunite the One Land.'

Abadan's smug expression dared Walther to argue. The dwarf tried and found himself tongue-tied by the magician's logic.

In her sleep, Ginni could feel the pull and tug of the three witches. They were seated around a scrying bowl. Their conversation came to her as clearly as if she stood in the room with them.

'She's perfect!' said the one who'd admitted Ginni at the gate.

The second woman looked up at her, annoyance plain in her features. 'Premature, don't you think, Dita?'

'No, no, I'm sure of it. She won't need much work at all. All of her mother's talent as well as a more proper dose of humility.'

The other pushed her chair away from the scrying bowl with a loud scrape of wood on wood. 'Nothing worthwhile is that effortless. She came to us. We did not summon her. She will have her own expectations, ambitions which likely have nothing to do with our plans.'

The third sat between her companions and let them argue. 'You are each partially right, partially wrong. You speak more from your own hopes than from any true knowledge.'

The two reddened as if slapped, seeming to shrink in on themselves.

'Yes, of course, Revered Mother.'

'My apologies, Revered Mother.'

Their meek voices did not mask their mutual dislike as they fidgeted and glared at each other over their leader's bent form.

She ignored their discomfort and continued to peer into her sorcery.

Ginni had the startling sensation of watching her own dreaming face flicker with flashes of emotion. But I thought it was forbidden to study current time, she thought.

'An interesting case, no question,' said Revered Mother. She smiled into the bowl where no one could see save the young mage herself. Her expression suggested kitchen vermin might be equally valuable.

'A mage and a mouse are both animals of the Sisters' making to be used as best we can.'

Had the Revered Mother spoken aloud or were her words for Ginni alone?

She didn't wait for the answer. Ginni fled back into herself.

She woke immediately, still trembling at the vision. True or not – and her dreams never lied – she would stay until she got what she came for. Revered Mother had yet to decide what to do with her. In the meanwhile, Ginni would learn what she could and then she would leave.

They could not keep her against her wishes. No one could.

# Chapter 5

## MAKING FRIENDS

The euphoria from Notti's audience with the One passed quickly. He spent his day watching over the goats and occasionally poking under the snow for a blade of grass. They would all starve if they stayed where they were. First the goats, then the elves.

Absorbed in his misery, he didn't notice Tabor and Theron until they dropped a wood-handled brazier at his feet. Notti stared as the hot metal hit the frozen ground with a heavy thud, which immediately became the hiss of melting snow.

'Th-thank you.' He was so startled that his stutter surfaced.

'Don't th-thank us, Goatboy,' mocked Tabor. 'The One said to give you this.'

'And this.' Theron dropped a thick quilt atop the smoking brazier.

Notti snatched up the blanket and inspected it to be sure it hadn't caught fire. When he looked up again, the boys were halfway back to the main camp. For once, the wind carried their ridicule away from him.

He carried the brazier into his tent and carefully placed it two hand-widths' from the canvas wall. Next he brought in the blanket and set it down close enough to let it gather in some of the heater's warmth. Finally, unable to resist, he pulled off his gloves and held his palms over the coals.

Notti hadn't felt so serene since he'd first met the malformed dragon. Perhaps his desire to escape was misguided. Perhaps it was only the need for intelligent companionship which drove him to plot a route across the Dunavs during the deadly time of deepsnows.

At last he thrust his fingers back into the worn gloves and returned to his dwindling herd.

This night he did not tell himself stories of small, courageous dragons. Instead, he climbed into the cozy tent, checked the brazier, and wrapped himself in blankets. He was warm, oh he was the most wonderfully warm he'd been in weeks.

Notti instantly fell asleep with a rare smile parting his lips. Heat wound through his dreams. A tall, calm elf called him by his true name – not Goatboy, not even his mother's secret petname, but the name his father had given him on his birth, the name he would have built upon during his manhood ceremony had he been allowed such last autumn.

He tossed and turned until he became knotted in the unfamiliar bedding. This man might wish Goatboy well, but his stares to the very core of the boy's soul frightened him. The elf would discover Notti's plans for escape. He would—

'Be still,' said the voice. 'What I know, I keep to myself. When you are freed of those here, the Sisters will call to you to travel far. If you are brave and deserve to live through your crossing of the Dunavian Mountains, you will find me. I will teach you more than how to tend goats.'

Even in his sleep, Notti's heart sank. The elder could teach him, but there would always be the diminishing of himself, of having had the weakness of enjoying the chores of an outcast. This elf offered more than most, and he had seemed less severe than his father.

But when would the boy be called upon to be simply as he was?

Then it struck him, this elf had come to him in his dreams! Did he need any more proof than this that he was worthy? That he had something that merited cherishing?

Notti had never been through the Dunavs, had never ranged past the patch of ground where his goats grazed. In his dreams, he ran through a checklist. He would need as much food and clothing as he could carry. The brazier he would keep so long as he had coals, and then discard it. The goats would help him. He would pick his finest and together they would find the pass in the mountains and cross it.

Notti would prove his worth. He would show them all.

Jedrek collapsed against the carved straight-back with a 'whuff' of exhaled air. Whatever the benefit of contacting the goatboy, disembodied travel over such long distances took a lot out of him; and he wasn't getting any younger. Soon he would need to name a successor. The elf absent-mindedly drummed three fingers on the chair-arm. None of his students would do. They simply lacked the boldness of vision to go beyond their prescribed duties.

The goatboy, Notti, did seem encouraging. He'd have

to give the child's mother credit there. However, his talent was far from proven. He lacked experience. He was young, so very, very young. And he lived in Alvaria's shadow where she would taint him with barren promises.

'Master, are you well?' The timid voice grated like a crow's caw, dragging his mind more fully into the room. Reluctantly, Jedrek returned his attention to the bracelet. The other matter would not be solved today.

It was odd how the bracelet had returned to his possession. Hidden for years with Lyda and Willam, only to be sold against all instruction to the mage-child, Ginni, and then to woo it away from her father. Jedrek shook his head. The Sisters had ways he did not understand even now after years of study,

As ever, the bracelet rejected his touch. Only by steeling himself with his strongest magic could he tolerate it at all. Most often, he preferred to handle the thing with a polished wood knife-point.

The six other mages closed in a semi-circle around the table though none dared to reach within the bracelet's sphere. 'You all know why we've gathered today.' The elfpriest looked at each of them in turn. 'We must debate whether the time has come to restore this sacred object to its rightful owner.'

'The One will have our heads.'

Jedrek snorted. 'The One. Since when has she deserved her self-appointed title?' He stared hard at the elf. Was this the betrayer – or simply a coward? The woman flinched but held her ground. 'Alvaria would have our heads in any case. Her actions do not rule ours. Anyone else?'

The rest stood mute. Worse than a pack of traitors, they feared to venture any opinion at all. Jedrek felt like a schoolmaster seated before a group of chastened students. 'No one else has anything to offer?'

Still no response from the small crowd.

'Am I the only one here who has considered the signs?'

A mumbled chorus of 'no's' and 'of course not's'.

'Well then?'

'I agree with Lilith. We risk our lives,' one began.

'And did you think you were doing any less when you joined me?'

'That was years ago. I had nowhere else to go and nothing to lo—' He began hotly, but trailed off embarrassed.

'Nothing to lose,' Jedrek finished for him, 'because you were already outcasts. But now that you're comfortable and have made new lives for yourselves, you are loath to sacrifice that which you promised me years ago.' As the elf spoke, his voice rose and with it his body so that he boomed out and towered over them when he finished. 'Good, bow your heads. Show proper respect, but not a nerve among you!'

He waited, hoping to be defied openly rather than in a darkened hallway. His heart pounded in his ears when he finally broke the silence. 'Though we are seven, plainly it is my decision alone. Therefore, I say we take it to the dragon prince so that he might make use of it while he's able.'

Three of them rushed him then – no, not him, the bracelet. He almost smiled. At least they weren't all spineless.

Lilith reached out, then yanked her arm back. Her shout of pain was genuine.

'It will heal,' he told her. Between the enchanted treasure's own defenses and those Jedrek had added, none of them would be able to challenge it.

The elfpriest settled back into his chair. 'Well now that

that's settled . . .' He clapped his hands and his personal sentries came running in. 'It's as we expected,' he said to the chief guard. 'Take them.'

Jilian thought she hated rain until now. Through all the autumn with the floods and the droughts, she had wished for the rain to be elsewhere and hoped she didn't call down a shortage in its place. It had never occurred to her once – despite a life spent primarily under the trees and stars – that the bewitched autumn downpours would likely become mage-cursed winter snows. In their turn, snow-showers became deepsnows, and the deepsnows blizzarded upon them one after another.

She had wished to be out of the castle and her brother had granted her petition. Now, as she pulled her horse forward through driving snows, she cursed her wishes and her luck.

'Ah, stop your complaining,' Maarcus snapped. 'You've been grumbling since you got to The Cliffs that you missed the mountains. Well, by the Sisters, we are on our way to your twice-cursed mountains.'

Jilian shook the snow off her hat and out of her hair. Hat in hands, she spoke with forced politeness to his back. 'I don't believe I requested your learned opinion.'

He answered her sarcasm with a barb of his own that struck closer to home. 'Told you you should have brought the cape.'

'So you did.' She slammed the hat back on her head. She didn't want to tell him she'd torn it fighting off an assassin, or that she'd left the wrap behind because she considered it bad luck. 'Any other useful advice I should have heeded but didn't?'

Maarcus stopped and turned to face her. His smile was

full of mischief. 'Well,' he said slowly, 'if you're sure you'd like to hear the list . . .'

Something about his sly look tugged at Jilian. Split between wanting to hit him and hug him, she settled for a noncommittal grunt. 'What say we find some decent shelter tonight?'

'Have you any idea where we are?'

'Have you always answered with unrelated questions – or is this just a new habit you've acquired under the strain of war?'

'I was merely suggesting that the nearest inn is some days walk from here.'

'There you go again, not answering the question put to you.'

Maarcus laughed. 'Oh, that. Sorry. Most people don't notice it.'

'Well, I do and it's both distracting and annoying.'

'You would and I agree it is. I find it dissuades casual questions from strangers when I'm not of a mind to attend to their concerns. Generally it works quite well.'

'And no one's stabbed you yet? You must have the Sisters' luck.'

He shrugged. 'As I said, few notice it. They're too busy asking questions to hear answers.'

Interesting point. Jilian would take it to heart. 'Now that we've established you don't mean to drive me to wanton butchery, can we return to my original question? You know, sleep?'

'We're nowhere near an inn. Most of the wayside inns closed up with the witch's campaigns.'

'Even this far in country? She hasn't been anywhere near this close to the capital yet.'

'No, but fear advances well ahead of her troops.'

'Poor Ceeley. It's as if they simply vanished.'

'Now who's wandering off the subject. Jilian, don't worry. I have a feeling she's warm and dry wherever she is. That child has good instincts.'

'When she's not haunted by the elfwitch.'

'Is this the monthly lower-than-low day?'

'I feel culpable,' she explained. 'I should have kept a better eye on her.'

'So should we all. Besides, her father trusted her to my care should anything ever happen to him.'

'Only because he didn't know any better.' Jilian meant it as a tease, but her words struck deep as they often did when she least meant them to.

Maarcus winced. 'Anybody ever tell you you're as sharp as a fishing-knife and just as savage?'

'Not in so many words, but I have gutted my share of highwaymen.'

'Time to get moving,' Maarcus said, apparently no longer in the mood for a battle of wit. 'We'll freeze to death if we don't.'

'Likely freeze to death if we do, too. I think it's time we built shelter if there's none to be found. No caves around here at all?' she asked, expecting the worst.

'Not that I recall . . .' Maarcus stood quietly in thought.

Jilian waited, feeling oddly patient, knowing without knowing why that he would think of something.

His face brightened. 'There is a small cave. It was a tight entrance when I was a boy, but I think we'll fit. Very cozy inside. It's about an hour's walk from here.'

The princess suppressed another groan. 'Lead the way.'

It took closer to three hours to find it and the burrow was even smaller than Maarcus remembered.

Jilian stood outside, dubious that she could wiggle through the hole.

'Look on the bright side,' Maarcus offered. 'There won't be anything in there big enough to eat us.'

'If we're lucky, we can eat it.' She cocked her head to the side and studied the opening then walked around to assure herself there wasn't an easier way – for her or another animal. 'You're sure it's bigger inside?'

'It was the last time I was here.'

'And when was that?' She held up a hand to forestall his answer. 'Never mind I don't want to know. If I'm going in anyway, I'd just as soon not rush the disappointment.' She removed her pack and shoved it into the gap. 'No growling. That's encouraging.' She placed a knife between her teeth then lay flat on her stomach. 'Here goes.'

Maarcus put a hand on her shoulder. 'Let me go first.'

She sat up and scooted out of the way. 'By all means.'

Maarcus took off his pack and pushed it in behind hers. It met resistance, but there were no animal sounds of protest. He lay flat and crawled through. There was a long moment as she peered into the darkness, then he called, 'Come on in. Nobody here but us fox furs.'

Jilian didn't hesitate. She'd do almost anything to get out of the wind. The walls scraped her shoulders and face as she wriggled in. Strong arms pulled her the rest of the way.

'We'll have to sleep rather close. It's smaller than I remember,' he apologized.

'Bits from childhood memories often are. I don't mind, Maarcus. At least it'll keep the snow out of my eyes for a few hours.' She slid away from the opening and squeezed next to him against the opposite wall.

'Watch yourself. There's my best dinner-jacket and a six-course meal in the corner.'

Jilian laughed. 'And they say the King's Own aren't generous.'

'Who says?' sounding slightly hurt in the close darkness.

'No one,' Jilian mumbled already half asleep against his shoulder. 'Pleasant dreams, Sir Maarcus.'

Though the candles had burned themselves out, Ginni made no effort to rekindle them. To control the Sisters' flame meant she welcomed shadows as easily as light. She would sit in darkness.

Sometime late in the night, the mage who Ginni now knew to be named Dita came for her. Silently she led her down a dimly lit hallway to another room. 'Your training begins in the morning.'

The chamber was more sparsely furnished than the first – a bed, a cane chair, a bureau, a throw rug. Nonetheless, a fire blazed in the hearth. Apparently, the witches did not follow the deprivations Roslin had practiced.

Buried within the larger hive of huts, the interior room gave her no view to the outside. Ginni would forget the cycles of sun and moon if she weren't careful. She began to get an inkling of how her mother had worked for days without rest.

Ginni stayed awake long enough to remove her wet boots and pants. Along with her sodden cape, she hung the clothing near the fire. Spent from her travels, she finally climbed beneath the heap of blankets. Comfortably warm, Ginni was more aware than ever of the danger here in the Tower. She could allow herself to sleep, but she'd have to return to the unsettling dreamlessness her mother had often imposed. She could not accept untainted rest until she could fully trust herself to block their powers.

A knock at the door sounded before she was fully disrobed. 'Come,' said a female.

Ginni used her most respectful tone. 'May I dress?'

A rustle of clothing suggested a shrug. 'Revered Sister will not wait long.' Already the voice was fading.

She snatched her boots and ran into the hall. Hobbling as she pulled them on over her still-damp stockings, she hurried after the receding woman.

She eventually found herself in another bare-bones room without windows. Revered Sister and Dita and the mage at the gate turned out to be one and the same. 'I understand you control the Sister's fire,' Dita said. 'Show me.' She remained seated behind a broad desk, her manner as stiff as Roslin's at her most severe.

Ginni looked into the mage's eyes, then closed her own. The flame responded sluggishly to her call. It had always been second nature, but this moment held so much more import than whether she might fool others or cook the dragon a hot meal. How had she ever thought she could be satisfied with such trivialities?

'No, concentrate!' shouted Revered Sister.

Ginni opened her eyes. She had scorched the mage's tight-cropped hair. This wouldn't go down well.

'You must maintain discipline, Ginni. The Sisters have gifted you a great talent and you are squandering it with foolish mind-fur!'

The apprentice suppressed a giggle. 'Mind-fur' described most of her life.

Her tutor made no effort to restrain her scowl. 'You find the situation amusing?'

'No, Revered Sister.'

'You find me amusing?'

'No, Revered Sister.'

'I think maybe you do. Recite the Principals from start

to finish.' Dita looked down at a scroll on her desk as if to verify her pupil's answer.

Ginni accepted the task without complaint. Roslin's punishments had been so much harsher and more demeaning. She shuddered inwardly at the number of men she'd had to approach and entice. Though none of them had managed their ultimate goal, a few had come close. The violation had been more her mother's than the men's. They drunkenly followed their natures while she had intentionally established Ginni as prey.

She took a deep breath and exhaled. Though she looked at Dita, she saw only the ancient parchment Roslin had copied in secret. 'For each of the Seven Sisters, there exists a charge which she maintains. The four elements form the quadrangle of the major Sisters and the three races form the triangle of the minor Sisters.

'Of the four elements, fire is the most rare and most difficult to control. It can easily annihilate that which it was meant to aid before the wielder has grasped the degree of devastation. Water seldom races unchecked across the mountainside, but be wary if it should leave its boundaries. Air surrounds us and will ever do so. Earth can be tamed but it will rebel if not properly respected; therefore, it is the most deceptive.

'The three races survive only at the sufferance of the great elements. So too do the little Sisters bow to their great Sisters.' This simple statement had surprised Ginni more than all her other lessons combined when she initially stumbled across it. It seemed only the mages thought to divide the Sisters thus. She'd never heard the common people refer to them this way.

Ginni paused to see if Dita would challenge this assertion, but the woman showed no reaction. So, it was the mages' belief, just as Roslin had taught her.

As Revered Sister continued to study the flattened scroll, Ginni wondered, Could all witch's logic be this forthright? Was it possible that its arcane nature was more in the presentation than in the fact?

Revered Sister looked up at her continued silence. 'Yes?'

'Should I proceed to the Rule of the Races?'

'No need,' said Dita, slightly mollified. 'We will return to the matter at hand. Fire.'

Once more Ginni concentrated, and watched as the flame ran unchecked from her hand to one of the tapestries.

Dita scoffed. 'This is all you've learned in so many years.'

Blood ran hot in Ginni's face. Her heart pounded. 'No, of course not, Revered Sister. I—'

'Quiet. I did not ask for your excuses. I will speak to Revered Mother.'

And denounce me as a failure, she thought. She could not bear it. 'Please give me another chance. I will prove myself to you.' She sounded whiny and pathetic even to her own ears.

Dita looked hard at Ginni. 'I'm certain you will prove yourself.'

The statement seemed more threat than promise. The young mage shuddered. 'Yes, yes, I will,' she answered, suddenly afraid of achieving her purpose.

Blinded by darkness and snow, Lyda chanted to keep them moving. 'The Sisters' will. The Sisters' will. We do the Sisters' will.' The words held no comfort, only a rhythm for their feet. To stop in this cold meant death.

Hours crawled by; they could have been days in this land of white on white. Involuntary whimpers threaded their way underneath the howling wind. Pain surrounded her as it had not since she had stumbled through the graveyard of a once lively village. No joy endured in the wake of the elfwitch.

Could this blizzard be her doing? No matter, Lyda told herself. She did the Sisters' will.

'We do the Sisters' will!' she shouted into the storm, daring it to break her. 'We do the Sisters' will!'

Her numb hands and feet began to tingle with warmth. She shook Willam and Ceeley out of their frozen stares until they too took up the chant.

For one brief instant the moon shone clear, bright, and round. In that moment a shadow crossed their path. Lyda followed it without question through the close-packed trees. Uphill or down, she had lost the ability to judge. If it directed her over a cliff, that too was the Sisters' will.

It led into the ground. Lyda trod after, pulling her charges along. Warm air struck her face.

The child cried out. 'We're saved!'

They had found a cavern. Not far off slept a bear, a bear as big as a shadow-guide.

Tears streamed down Willam's face.

Ceeley put her stubby arms around him. 'It's okay, Papa-Wil. It's okay. We're here now.'

'I know,' he said. He tried to smile but the muscles barely responded.

'We can make it to the ends of the world if we have to!'

Willam went pale. ''ope we don't have to go that far,' he whispered. 'It's a long, long way.'

'I've been from the Three Falls to Twin Gates to The Cliffs to here,' Ceeley declared. 'I can go anywhere I have to, even over the Dunavs.'

The girl's delirious, Lyda thought. Or Sister-blessed. She nodded. 'We might just have to at that.'

Prince Nikolis looked out at the assembled crowd from a safe corner before stepping onto the parapet. He missed Jilian more than ever. She and Maarcus would have checked the crowd, the square, all their old contacts. No one could insure against a lone assassin, but he didn't worry as much about that. The Cliffs was a city of conspiracies, of groups huddled in corners making plans. Nikolis sighed. Just like me and my advisors, he thought.

Already the rumors had spread. Bad enough in truth, the trolls became more terrible in the retellings. All the city's inhabitants could see the wave of refugees. Even now, some few straggled in whenever the weather broke. They were all mobilized, fearing he would rally them to war.

Fearing he would not.

Nik's back itched. Lately, he'd been feeling conjured wounds again. His non-existent wings ached to stretch and soar. Fully a man in form now, he was still a half-breed beast haunted by his past as a misshapen dragon. Unlike Jilian, Nikolis felt no longings to return to his old life. He simply wanted to fly, truly fly just once.

'Feet on the ground now, Prince Nikolis.' Abadan's voice broke into the man's thoughts.

'Oh, so you read minds too, do you?'

The magician had the good grace not to act surprised at the suggestion though his words denied it. 'It's seldom necessary when the subject of my observation is staring into the sky as if he'd like to be there.'

'Here I thought I was checking over the crowd.'

Abadan laughed. 'Unless they're seated among the

Sisters, I'd have to say you were staring into the roiling grey clouds overhead.'

There was never any use in arguing with a magician, most especially the royal one. 'Do you think we could fly some day?' he found himself asking as if he were a small child.

Abadan shrugged. 'I've seen my share of strangeness and the Sisters have been known to start men down unusual paths when it suits them. Don't let it distract you. Other matters are more pressing.' He nodded toward the window. 'There's our man's signal. Do your father proud.'

He ignored the longing in his shoulders. Images of flying dragons fell away. When the prince stepped forward, the others saw only the regalness he was born to. 'Thank you all for gathering here,' he began with just a touch of the everyman accent. 'I call you here today to rally you to battle.'

''Bout bloody time,' a heckler yelled, and Nikolis was unsure whether the man was on his side or not. He could have been one of the hastily arranged seeds strewn throughout the group to insure the people swayed in his direction.

'I do not undertake this war lightly. Nor do I ask for each and every one of you to take up your swords with a casual heart. Some, perhaps many, of you will die. Still, we will all surely perish if we remain as we are. The elfwitch and her trolls won't stop until she reaches the sea – if then. We cannot allow this.' He paused and licked his lips. Fist raised to the sky, he shouted, 'And so I say, let's march!'

The crowd cheered and waved their weapons. They seemed perilously close to becoming a mob.

'Now, let's do it now!' yelled the heckler.

'Today we prepare. We train. We strengthen our skills.'

Men moaned. 'Let her attack us in our sleep you mean!'

'No!' Nikolis shouted. 'No! But we will confront her on our terms. Within the seven-day, the elfqueen Alvaria will know our strength.'

'Hear, hear,' yelled someone.

'We'll show 'er,' echoed another.

The entire group thundered its assent.

Nikolis raised both arms triumphantly then bowed low. He rose and looked out without seeing the crowd, only the slaughter many of them would know. Before the vision could show on his face, he stepped back inside.

He was sweating and breathing hard. Somehow he hadn't expected it to take so much out of him. Rallying men to die was not what he'd meant to do, yet he knew with complete certainty he had done exactly that. Little more.

# Chapter 6

# MANIPULATION

Jilian didn't know how to feel, waking up wrapped in Maarcus' arms. Oh, she knew how she felt, but she'd been quite able to avoid these situations. On the rare occasion when she'd been tempted to touch actual flesh, Mut had conveniently stepped in with teeth showing. No man would test that, not if he valued his future.

But there was no Mut. Indeed, the Dragon Prince had sent them off on this mission without him.

She cuddled deeper against Maarcus' shoulder and he tightened his hold.

'Better?' he asked.

'I miss Mut.'

'Oh, well, you are, uh, close.' He sounded hurt.

'Sorry. I didn't mean it like that.'

He pulled away from her to sit up straighter against the wall. 'How did you mean it?'

'He's been my travelling companion my whole life.'

'Jilian, he's your brother.'

She nodded into the darkness. 'I know but we've shared so much.'

'Would you like me better with fur and fleas?'

The princess laughed and broke the growing tension. 'No, I don't think fur would do a thing for you. Funny, though, I don't think Mut ever had fleas not even in summer.'

'I can name a few soldiers who'd like that secret.'

'He's definitely a man with hidden talents.' Too much hidden these days, Jilian thought.

'Could we talk about something else?'

'I thought you liked him.'

'He's okay for a prince. Swings his sword like a girl, though.'

'Like me?'

'No, you fight like a man.'

'Thank you, I think.'

He wasn't making this easy for her. She longed to tell him of the attacks, but couldn't bear to accuse her own twin – especially when Maarcus ridiculed the entire conversation. Jilian sat up, took a breath and let it out, then tried one last time. 'You do believe he's all right? Without us, I mean?'

Maarcus took her shoulders and gently pulled her back against his chest. 'Jilian, he's fine. He's nice and warm in the palace. We're freezing inside a cave too small for a mid-size bear.'

His breath was hot against her neck, but it sent chills down her spine. If she didn't move soon, she'd be choosing her consort, a princess's suitor. 'Maarcus?'

'Hmm?' he whispered, lips lightly brushing her jawbone.

'Do you think we can do this?'

'Oh, I know I can.' His voice was a deep rumble. He shifted beneath her to kiss her cheek.

'I've no doubt of it,' she said, still not really trying to stop him. 'But a lot of people are depending on us. It makes us more vulnerable to the elfwitch.'

'I promise not to tell her if you don't.' His hands began to massage and press. His fingers found the pouch where she'd hidden the coin.

'Touch that again and you're a dead man.' The words were out before she considered them.

His hands paused. 'Pardon me, princess, but I assure you I am not interested in material wealth.' He tried to sound amused, but each word was clipped with annoyance.

'Sorry. I didn't mean . . .'

'Oh, just forget it. I think I hear nature calling anyway.'

Jilian bent forward to let him scoot past. 'Just make sure it doesn't have fur and fangs.' Judging by his noncommittal grunt as he crawled back out, the joke fell flat.

'The wind's died down,' he called back. 'We might as well get moving while the light's good. Your highness.' The sound of splashing followed.

Jilian waited a discreet moment after the water stopped then shoved the packs outside. She headed out next.

A hand roughly yanked her to her feet.

'Maarc—' Maarcus was leaning against a tree, hog-tied and gagged.

'Glad you could join us, princess,' said a man she'd never seen before. He quickly roped her arms behind her back. 'The prince sends his regards.'

'Pruns? Wha' pruns?' The Shoreman tried to speak around the cloth.

Jilian wanted to feel surprise, but this thug only confirmed her worst fears about Nikolis.

'I hear the elfwitch does as well. Come along.'

'The prince does the elfwitch's bidding?' Jilian asked, hoping against hope that she was wrong.

'Just say they've got an agreement – nothin' you need to worry about till we get where we goin'. Now move.' He shoved Jilian ahead of him.

The princess tripped a step forward, then recovered her balance and stayed rooted where she was. 'You can't just leave him here. He'll freeze to death!'

The man whipped out another filthy rag and flapped it in her face. His smile showed blackened and missing teeth. His breath smelled of rotten meat. 'My orders are to deliver you unhurt. These aren't gen'rally harmful. Do we understand each other?'

She eyed the disgusting shred of fabric. 'Yes.'

'Good. Now hand over that knife you always carry.'

'Knife?'

The man calmly walked to where Maarcus sat and booted him in the stomach. The Shoreman cried out and doubled over in pain.

'Your knife.'

Jilian looked through tear-filled eyes at the groaning Maarcus. Mechanically she offered up her knife. 'I keep a second in my pack.'

He gave her another gap-toothed grin. 'Never know when you might need a spare weapon,' he said reasonably, as he accepted her blade. He hefted the knife. 'Nice piece o' workmanship.' He grasped the handle and aimed for Maarcus.

Jilian flinched but tried to regain her usual air of indifference. She shrugged. 'It was a gift from the pr—'

'The prince. Isn't that fine.' He stowed the knife. 'Don't worry. I'll see that it finds its way back to its proper owner.' He dug around in her pack and pulled out the ring she'd taken from the dead man. 'Well look at this! I guess we know what happened to our runner, don't we?'

Jilian stared past him as she remembered pushing the body over the dreadful cliff only two nights ago.

'As for your friend here, I'll send for him as soon as I deliver you. You don't co-operate, he dies. He isn't here when I get back . . .' The ruffian spread his hands as if the outcome were beyond his control. 'You won't die, but let's just say my prince won't be happy.'

'Whi' pruns?' Maarcus insisted. 'Whi' 'un?'

The man kicked his prisoner again, brutally connecting on the side of the Shoreman's head.

Maarcus fell over without a sound.

The cut-throat spat on the unconscious body. 'There's only one true prince. The rest 're pretenders. Hangers-on like you 'd do well to remember that.' His face lit up with a nasty expression, then the heel of his boot met his helpless victim's nose with a sickening crunch. 'Didn't say he had to be in prime shape,' he explained to no one in particular.

The man turned to Jilian, grabbed her elbow and squeezed hard. 'Let's go, princess.'

Stunned by her captor's vicious treatment of Maarcus and completely disheartened by her brother's betrayal, Jilian silently went to meet her fate.

Despite Ginni's pleas for one more attempt, Revered Sister sent her back to her room. She followed the guide quietly, too preoccupied to pay much attention to their route. The way seemed longer, but she dismissed that as an offshoot of her distress.

The bedchamber appeared darker and damper. Each footfall on the wood floor sounded with a flat thud rather than a sharp tap. These too, Ginni assumed, only reflected her mood.

Ginni pulled off the boots and soggy stockings again, and left them where they landed. She threw herself atop the covers and sulked. Knowing she acted like a child didn't change her behavior. She hadn't been this disappointed since she'd been a child.

If she could not prove her value to the Forty-nine, she had no business here. They would not teach her and she would come out the worse for their bedeviling her. She would rest and gather her strength today. Tonight would be soon enough to find her way out.

She had not meant to dream. The Revered Sisters had already shown her the threat. Yet she did dream.

Children haunted her: an elf boy tortured by his foster-parents, a dwarf girl taken in but still in terrible danger.

Ginni never gave thought to bearing children of her own, but she always felt a special affinity for orphans. Not one herself, but oh so very close at times, so very close.

Unease yielded to short-lived relief when the vision gave way to the witches.

Revered Mother leaned back in her chair and set her feet on a padded stool. 'Roslin's essence must be explored. The girl has absorbed more than I would have thought. Perhaps Roslin prepared her in advance.'

'No one in living memory has ever succeeded in transferring a complete essence. She is at great risk and must be told,' said Dita.

'Eventually,' argued the other woman, whom Ginni had yet to hear named.

'Sisters.' Revered Mother slapped her hand on the nearby table-top. 'Since the girl will be our guest for many days to come, there will be plenty of opportunities to talk with her about Roslin's legacy – this apparent possession. Meantime, there's no cause to quarrel over such trivia.'

From the smug triumph in Revered Mother's eyes, it

seemed to Ginni that the elder mage was already speaking for her captive student's benefit; and Ginni didn't like what she was hearing.

Revered Mother turned her full attention to the second sister. 'Masha?'

So that was her name.

'Yes, Revered Mother?'

'We have been inhospitable hosts. I don't believe the girl has been fed since her arrival. She must be hungry.'

'Yes, Revered Mother.'

'And Masha.'

'Yes?'

'See that she is properly accompanied. We wouldn't want her to tire herself wandering the halls in search of that which we should have provided.'

Masha bowed, understanding just as Ginni did the veiled command for a guard to be stationed outside the locked door. 'Yes, Revered Mother. Caronn?' she continued.

Revered Mother's eyes flashed. 'Excuse me?'

'I beg your pardon. Revered Mother.' Masha corrected herself. Her voice was contrite, but held a tinge of resentment.

'We enter an era where carelessness can be deadly,' warned Caronn.

'Yes, Revered Mother.' Masha paused, glanced at the tight-lipped Dita and back to their leader. 'Don't you find her talent fascinating?'

'How so?'

'You just hope to . . .' Dita broke in, then trailed off.

'To what?' Masha asked, daring her to speak.

The mage bit her lip and kept quiet.

'Dita, you must learn not to blurt out ill-considered thoughts.'

The chastened mage looked toward the smiling Masha and back to Caronn. 'Yes, Revered Mother.'

'Masha, you have duties.'

'Yes, Revered Mother.'

Ginni frowned in her sleep. The entire conversation felt stiff and false, as if it had been arranged just for her. Her dream twisted back to the elf boy, huddled among his goats and the dwarf girl, shivering beneath her thick woolens.

The mage tossed on her bed, knocking her pillows to the floor.

The One stood among the elves with a small smile playing at her lips. Notti tried to see her as the dragon might have, but each time he made the effort he found himself thinking of thick blankets and warm braziers.

'My people.' Her soft voice commanded the crowd to be still lest they miss her next words. 'Tonight's feast will be a poor celebration of our greatness.'

A wave of grumbling discontent flowed from the group.

'But,' she said, just a little more loudly, 'but I commend your efforts. Know that you are not to blame for your plight.'

'Glad to see that trouncing we got last fall didn't cloud her reasoning,' said an elf who'd been harder hit than most. Having lost his brother to battle wounds and his wife to starvation, he was quickly becoming the focus of the camp's unhappiness.

'Know that the Dragon Prince, who sits on the Shoremen's crumbling throne, fights us at every turn. Know that he seeks to re-join us into the so-called One Land even if there is nothing left but our corpses. Know that our sole recourse is to strike before he brings the battle to us.'

Notti listened spellbound. One by one the complaints transformed to cheers.

The elfwitch raised her arms. Her hands were clenched in fists, but it was the silver bracelets that caught the goatboy's attention. Her wide sleeves slid down to reveal gleaming metal, ringing her flesh to the elbows like exotic chain-mail. He would have sworn that the bangles writhed to shadow her every movement.

Fixed on the fluid silver, Notti chanted and shouted along with the rest.

For a fleeting moment, he recalled that the Dragon Prince would still be a lowly beast were it not for her.

Such a vulgar thought was unworthy of him.

Unworthy of her.

Measured against the prince's evil intent, the human's grand essence faded to a trivial matter. To defy the elfwitch over such trifles was sacrilege when doing so gambled their homeland.

Their way of life.

Their very lives.

Joyfully, Notti lifted his fists in salute to their leader and let his voice echo the roar of 'War before death! War before death!'

Prince Nikolis stared across the rough-hewn table at his two most experienced advisors. 'Master Abadan, are you saying we have no idea where they are? That Jilian and Maarcus have vanished?'

'Yes, that's what I'm telling you.'

'How can we lose them so quickly? I thought you gave them a magical device to keep them in communication.'

The magician's constant frown deepened. 'So I did. However, the babble-box does not prevent mishaps. It merely allows us to speak with each other. It cannot tell me where they are unless they speak into it.'

'Well, by the bloody Ladies, contact them!'

'This is what I'm telling you. They don't respond.'

Nik slammed his hand down and embedded a splinter in his palm. 'By the Sisters,' he cursed, more annoyed than in pain. 'Doesn't anyone sand or polish the furniture around here?'

Abadan didn't bother to answer. Sir Maarcus seemed not to notice. In fact, Sir Maarcus appeared oddly untroubled by the news – or the conversation in general.

'What about your scrying bowl?'

'I have no means to track your sister as you well know. The protections we set on you both as infants will likely last until your deaths . . . or mine. Had I been able to find her, I would not be sitting here now, watching you impale yourself.'

Nikolis felt his gut clench. His shoulders itched. 'I do not need this sort of bad omen on my way to the battlefield.'

'Welcome to war with the elfwitch,' Maarcus said. 'The door to death is always open.'

'Sir Maarcus? Are you feeling well?' the prince asked.

The man's attention was fixed on a mouse in the corner. 'We need a cat. They've cooked all the cats.'

Nikolis shook his shoulder. 'Maarcus!'

The elder turned to him with cloudy eyes. 'My grandson is missing. I think I lost him. Perhaps he's playing hide-and-sneak. It's always been one of his favorite games.'

'Yes, that must be it,' Abadan said gently, too gently. 'We'll find him.'

'Well, son, thank you for hearing us out.' Sir Maarcus rose to depart. 'You will let us know when you've found him, won't you.' It was an order, politely put though unmistakably not to be ignored.

Nikolis played along. 'Yes. I'll notify you just as soon as I hear anything.'

The old physician leaned down and whispered, 'We must keep him safe from the court. He's a very special child.'

'I know,' the prince said. 'Don't worry, sir. We'll find him.'

Maarcus left, closing the door behind him. Abadan made no motion to follow.

That man's going to wander into a snow bank and forget his way home, Nikolis thought. He dug at the splinter with the knife Jilian had given him only yesterday. 'How long has he been this way? He seemed fine a few weeks ago. Didn't he?'

Abadan pursed his lips. 'I'm not so sure. I thought so then, but Zera's death hit him hard. I don't think he'll ever really get over it.'

'He's got to. We can't spare another good man to watch him.'

The magician said wryly, 'Thank you for your concern, your highness.'

'Sorry. We can't spare him either.' He poked at his hand. 'They're falling like game-birds and we've yet to take up arms.'

'As the learned man said, "The door to death is always open."'

'You don't think he actually knew what he was saying?'

'It's true that his mind has a longer rope mooring it to the dock these days. Nonetheless, the knots are still tight.'

'Just so a storm doesn't bash the boat against the landing.' He was beginning to sound like Jilian.

'May I?' Abadan asked, pointing to the prince's palm.

Before Nikolis could grant his permission, the magician bent nearer. He reached out and pinched the skin. 'Ah, got it!' He held up a sliver of wood, dotted with blood. 'You should show more caution. Men have been known to die from such slight wounds.'

At last the shadows lengthened with the late afternoon sun. The One released the elves to attend to their duties. Freed from the frenzy of the shouting mob, the drained goatboy returned to his dwindling herd. He walked among them, patting flanks and scratching behind ears. As always, the animals listened to his ramblings, yet not a one possessed enough brains to respond.

The dragon would have understood, but the dragon couldn't talk either.

Notti wanted conversation. He wanted to be regarded as part of his own people. He wanted to heal the ugly old wound caused by his mother's exile, the same wound that was ripped open and left exposed to the raw air when the Dragon Prince escaped.

A sliver of daylight pierced the barren trees. Full dark was nearly an hour off. The goatboy double-checked the feed buckets. Against common sense in these times of shortage, he shoveled in grain to the brim to be sure the animals wouldn't disturb him.

He collapsed inside his tent, where no one could see his shoulders shake and nobody would hear his muffled sobs in the rising wind.

The soft wailing didn't take long. The older he got, the less it comforted him and the more it seemed he'd cried out his grief years ago. If he wanted the elves' acceptance, he would have to act. The camp had denied him his manhood ceremony. Nonetheless, he was becoming a man.

He wiped the tear tracks from his face and lifted the tent flap.

Tabor and Theron waited in the meadow prodding a goat with a heavy branch. The animal stood her ground. She'd endured worse from this pair.

'You two! Stop that.'

'Stop that!' they mimicked, though the surprise at his sharp tone showed on their faces. Goatboy felt a rare wisp of satisfaction as they dropped the stick.

'What's your business here? I can't imagine you've come to tend to the beasts.' He let his annoyance show plainly. Notti had had all he cared to take from the likes of these.

'The One,' said Tabor.

'Now,' said Theron, trying to look smug and failing.

'Very well.' He straightened his jacket and smoothed his hair. 'I'm ready.'

Once again the three trooped across the meadow. This time, Notti led and the brothers trailed. He held his head up, refusing to flinch from such a vulnerable position. To be in front dared others to stare at him as they passed, yet none did. The entire camp was busy with their delayed chores. Not a one set aside his own task to hinder the goatboy.

The guards let him through with a stiff nod. Notti entered the elfwitch's tent as the last ray of light faded behind him.

The One casually put away the scroll and coins she'd been studying when the goatboy walked in. Notti stood respectfully just inside the flap and waited. He assumed she proceeded slowly for his benefit. So be it. She would have him see what she wished and he would note her movements without letting curiosity overwhelm him. He fixed his eyes on the opposite tent wall to keep himself from unseemly attention.

She straightened and turned to receive him. 'Thank you for coming so promptly,' she said with such gracious sincerity that he almost believed this was an uncommon occurrence.

He blushed and felt foolish for letting her affect him this way. 'My pleasure, Highness.'

'Come.' She motioned him forward.

Goatboy's chest tightened. He steadily closed the gap between them, using small steps so as not to insult her with his boldness.

'Come now, you needn't be so timid. You are here by my invitation.' Her hands beckoned him. Beneath the long sleeves her bracelets jangled.

He stared at her arms and found he was walking toward her, not altogether of his own will. He stopped inches from her face. Her brown-yellow eyes captivated him. How much more expressive than the goats' deep brown they were.

'Notti, I have an important task for you before you undertake your journey.'

'Yes, Highness?' Enthralled beyond words, he would agree to anything.

'There are two boys not much older than you, who have a tendency toward savagery. I'm sure you know the brothers I mean.'

Oh, he knew them, all right. He was their favorite prey.

'I do not condone anything other than civility. They need to be taught a lesson.'

A tiny voice screamed inside Goatboy. Anything he did to them would come back to him sevenfold. It was the Sisters' way. They would find a way to punish him.

The elfwitch seemed to read his thoughts. She set cool hands against his cheeks. Her silver bracelets whispered. 'Have no fear of reprisals. They will be beyond such desires once you've shown them their errors. Won't you like that?'

Would the Sisters endorse his deeds? His gut wrenched while Goatboy smiled and nodded agreement.

'Excellent.' She flung her arms wide, full of enthusiasm. 'Here's what I'd like you to do.' She began a complicated plan, which must have been at least part incantation. Afterward, he could remember only the barest sketch – and that piece alone filled him with dread.

He left her tent feeling fuzzy-headed and overwarm. The cold air slapped him in the face and cleared his mind. He began to head toward the goats when he saw the troublemaking brothers slip under the elfqueen's tent.

This made no sense. Where were her guards?

He felt conflicting desires. Should he shout out the intrusion and betray Tabor and Theron? Should he run as far as he could to escape their fate?

Notti could do neither. His loyalty to the elfwitch was stronger than that to himself. He must risk himself for her safety. He turned back toward the tent opening.

The elf re-entered the tent—

And found no one there.

No witch, no boys, no sentinels. No one.

But on the floor was one of the strange medallions and next to it the map he'd seen her putting away. The goatboy began to back out of the tent, his eyes fixed to the artifacts in front of him.

Suddenly Tabor and Theron jumped out at him from behind the One's chair. 'Robber, thief!' they called. 'We caught him trying to steal the map.'

'No,' said the elfwitch.

He thought, Had she been there all along?

'None but you two knew the map existed,' she accused.

The surprise on their faces no doubt mirrored his own.

Outside a crowd gathered. 'Stone him!' someone shouted.

'No,' answered his father. 'He deserves punishment. The flaming stake is too good for that corrupt creature!'

The enraged elfwitch stormed out of the tent. 'Who dares to presume more than I? Tabor and Theron are the thieves.'

The crowd mumbled, confused. 'Tabor? Theron?'

'But they never mean any harm.'

'Take them away.'

'No!' came an anguished lament that could only belong to their mother.

The goatboy watched the elves' bewilderment turned to shock and fear as two sentinels dragged them away.

Ceeley woke before Mama-Lyda and Papa-Wil. In the close warmth of the bear cave she lay motionless with eyes closed and pretended she'd always been a part of this family. They were explorers, setting out to map the One Land. They had braved many great adventures in her short life and countless more waited just ahead. When they finished their travels, they would settle near a nice inn without too many roughneck types. Mama-Lyda and Papa-Wil could while away their old age telling the tales of their adventures.

Ceeley liked stories. When she grew white-haired, she would spin the most spellbinding tales for all the little children orphaned by war.

Now if one thing got her feeling sad or maybe mad, it was this struggle to fight the elfwitch. Little children shouldn't have to be without their real families. Little children should always have someone to hug them and kiss them goodnight – even if sometimes they had to go to bed too early.

Celia knew this kind of thinking wasn't good for her. It made her cry and 'rum'nate', as her Da used to say. Then she thought she might give up.

But her Da also said the Sailclan never quit. Whenever she'd been frustrated over learning something new, like tying her boots by herself or writing her letters, he'd told her all about the exploits of her forebears. If those courageous dwarves could keep going against blizzards and bear attacks, she could face another try at bootlaces.

Only now she was the one battling blizzards and bears.

She opened her right eye.

No big furry bear.

She opened her left.

No big furry bear.

Was he part of a dream? Well, better that than the horrifying recall of her burning village.

Ceeley sighed. It was going to be one of those times when she couldn't escape. Every stray thought led her back to how much she missed her family and her home. She turned away from her new parents and let the tears run quietly, oh so quietly, so as not to wake Mama-Lyda and Papa-Wil. She didn't want to anger them.

They might decide she was too much trouble and leave her behind.

Someone groaned and rolled over.

Ceeley fought to control her crying.

'Ouch! So 'zat's what's been nestled in my backbone all night,' said Papa-Wil. A stone clattered against the cave wall.

'Careful, Willam. You'll wake the bear – or the child.'

'Bear. Right. Thought I'd 'magined that.'

So did I, Ceeley thought.

'No,' Lyda said softly. 'Not unless I did too.'

'Stranger things have 'appened these last months.'

'Willam?' Mama-Lyda lowered her voice to a whisper that caught Ceeley's attention.

Silently, silently, like in a game of hide-and-sneak, she struggled to hear.

'I'm worried about the child.'

'You're doin' the best you can, Lyda. We both are.'

Gravel scraped the cave floor as they moved closer together.

'I know, Willam. But she sleeps so poorly. Last night I watched for near an hour as she tossed and rolled. If we'd had any sheets to offer her, I would've worried she'd strangle herself the way she was twisting. I tried to tell myself it was just the hard day behind us and the hard ground beneath her.'

'Now, Lyda. Don't go blamin' yourself. 'Ere you go. Dry those tears.'

Mama-Lyda sniffed. 'But it breaks my heart to hear what she says in her sleep. How can anyone subject a child to such horror? How?'

'Evil is a hard thing for good folks to understand,' he told her and Ceeley thought that was true. 'Won't 'elp to tear yourself to pieces over it. All we can do is try to face it square on and stop it when we can.'

'But what'll we do about Celia? She's a fine child that deserves better than this.'

'Most kids do . . . at the start anyway. I don't see there's much we can do. We couldn't send her back when we've come so far even if we wanted to.'

No, don't send me back, Celia prayed.

'And we don't want to in the first place.'

'No, we don't,' Mama-Lyda agreed.

Oh, thank you, Sisters. Thank you, thank you, the dwarf thought.

'She's got no one but us.'

'True, Willam.'

Not quite true, but nearly. Ceeley squirmed with guilt then forced herself to be still.

'I'm sorry, Willam.' Mama-Lyda sounded very sad, almost as sad as Ceeley felt.

'Whatever for, Lyda?'

'For the bracelet, for leaving, for . . . this.'

'What's done is done. 'Bout time someone else got to watch after that elf-cursed jewelry anyway.'

'Don't say that.'

'It's certain. Even the elves themselves said so.'

'No, I mean "elf-cursed".'

'Honey,' he said gently but matter-of-factly, 'some things are cursed. The elves are not immune. Look what they did to me. Look what they did to Ceeley!'

'Shh, she'll hear you.'

'Anyway,' he said, quieter now, 'we came of our own choice. You aren't at fault for what 'appens along the way.'

'But it's so hard, Willam. I didn't think it would be. It wasn't before, not even when I walked through a dead town. There was always hope somewhere pushing me on, making me believe . . .'

'You can believe,' Papa-Wil whispered. 'As long as we're all together, you can believe.' He kissed her. She sighed into the kiss and there was only the sound of breathing for a long minute.

Yuck, Ceeley thought. I don't want to listen to this. She made a show of standing up to stretch and yawn. 'Good morning Mama-Lyda. Good morning, Papa-Wil.'

'Good morning,' they mumbled, their faces caught somewhere between annoyed and sheepish.

'Did you sleep well?' Mama asked, as if she didn't know.

'Okay,' Ceeley answered, continuing the charade. 'But you know, I dreamed there was a bear in here. A big, brown, furry bear. Or maybe he was black. Did you see him, Papa-Wil?'

He sat up and extended both arms over his head. 'Yes, yes I did, my darling dwarf.' He grunted as he bent and straightened the stiff limbs. 'I say it's time we get moving before the old boy comes back from wherever he's gone.'

Ceeley put her hand on her chin, doing her best to appear grown-up and thoughtful. 'I don't know if that bear is coming back, Papa-Wil, but it seems to me we've got a job to do.'

'Right. Absolutely. Come on, Lyda. You too.'

'I'm coming,' but she made no move to rise.

Ceeley smiled her biggest smile at Mama-Lyda. 'Sailclans never give up, you know. My other Da always said so.'

'He would be very proud of you,' Papa-Wil said.

'And my new parents, too.' She took hold of one of Mama-Lyda and Papa-Wil's hands in each of hers. 'So I hereby make you honorary members of the Sailclan.' She pulled on Mama-Lyda until the woman finally stood. 'Now you won't ever give up either!'

# Chapter 7

## FRIENDLY FIRE

Prince Nikolis roamed the castle without purpose. With Jilian gone and the call to arms behind him, he should have been spending every spare moment on strategy. He should have been picking the brains of any soldier who remembered how to fight – not that he expected it to do much good against the elfwitch.

Instead he seemed to inherit his sister's restlessness. The royal mantle hadn't taught her a thing about dignity and his own poise appeared to be slipping. His shoulders itched horribly though his skin remained unblemished. Maybe he was reverting to his previous form.

He paused in his wandering. He'd been assuming his human shape was permanent. What if it wasn't? He needed to speak with Abadan about this unexpected possibility.

Soon. He didn't want to clutter his mind with yet another obstacle to overcome.

The prince resumed his stroll. As he moved down the

hallways, he still considered it strange that others bowed and catered to him even though he himself felt no sense of honest ownership. He wanted to shout, 'I'm an imposter – a defective dragon in man's clothing!' He'd do well to avoid the attention before he lost control – along with what tenuous loyalty he'd earned.

Nikolis chose a darkened passage despite the recent attempts on his life. He reasoned that no one would expect to find him in such a deserted section of the castle; therefore, an ambitious murderer would not likely be lurking for him here.

Dust lay heavy on the floor and sconces. The hangings had not been cleaned in many months, maybe years. Under the disuse and neglect, Nikolis noted a finer quality of woodworking, a higher caliber of smithing and weaving. Unlike most of the other halls and rooms, the materials remained wondrously intact. That some of the exquisite carpets remained in public view at all was remarkable since at least as many thieves as assassins claimed these grey stones for their home.

Something momentous must have happened here, something so important that no one had possessed the courage to challenge the aura left behind.

Prince Nikolis proceeded cautiously, each step bringing him closer to his own destiny. He peered in at the occasional doorway, but no, whatever he sought was not there.

Near the end of the hall, he found two massive doors made from rare cedarwood. The one on the right stood ajar, its brass catch slightly askew. He pushed on the door and it swung open with the piercing screech of unused metal. Before he could enter the cavernous room, the door's upper hinge snapped. The heavy wood thudded to the floor.

Careful to avoid brushing against the decrepit door lest he dislodge it and crack the lower hinge, Nikolis walked into an enormous bedchamber. As in the preceding hallway, thick dust covered the carpets and furniture. He ranged around the room, feeling the need to touch each and every item as if a piece of his past were imbedded in the cloth and metal.

Marvelous weavings hung askew on the walls. He moved to right one and was surprised by a familiar voice.

'In all these years, I have never straightened them.'

Nikolis spun about to face Sir Maarcus the Sixth. He reached for the rapier he'd worn since the failed poisoning and let his hand rest on the undrawn hilt. The prince stifled an embarrassed laugh. Could he actually kill this man?

Could this man kill him?

Suspicion gnawed at the prince. How much did he really know about the physician, especially his state of mind of late?

'Sir Maarcus, my apologies.' He nodded at his sword and dropped his hand.

'Not at all, sire. I owe you the apology. I didn't mean to startle you.' He sounded in control of his faculties.

For the moment.

What was he doing here?

The prince struggled for suitable wording to expose the other's purpose. 'In these uncertain times, I should have been listening for anyone trailing me – not that you meant me harm of course.'

The physician looked briefly hurt and shocked at the suggestion. He quickly composed his expression and nodded sadly. 'It's true. One does well not to trust any but those he has known since birth. More's the pity.'

It's the only way I've ever known, Nikolis thought. I don't think I'd be comfortable if it were different.

Maarcus glanced around. 'Actually I wasn't following you. I come here every so often to remind myself of why we continue to fight.' His gaze fell on the rumpled bed which commanded an imposing spot. 'This was your father's chamber. He spent his last months here.' In a quieter voice the physician said, 'He died here.'

'How could you let it fall into such disrepair? This room is a disgrace.'

'I agree. It is a shame.'

'Well then?'

'I've left it as he lived it. Abadan and I tried to impose order on your father, but he chose his own path. The last weeks of his life, people crowded this room as if they attended a coming-out party rather than his impending funeral. He allowed it and thus was the room a humiliation to any who honored the Great King.' The physician's hand shook as he reached up to smooth the bedsheets. 'I miss him. Tomar was a great man.'

His face suddenly hard, Maarcus looked up into the prince's eyes. Nikolis braced for an attack.

His elder had other things in mind apparently. He didn't seem to notice Nik's change of posture as he said, 'But the Great King was fallible as all men are. He made grave mistakes, errors which may well have cost him everything he achieved. You and your sister were his last hope. See that you don't dishonor his memory.'

Prince Nikolis didn't know how to respond. Here stood a man who'd probably forgotten more than he himself would ever learn about the One Land. The prince could learn much from him. Yet something stood in the way.

Was it his own hesitation or the scientist's?

Nikolis willed himself to take advantage of this moment before the man's clear head deserted him forever. 'Would you tell me about him?'

Maarcus began to pace. 'Which man do you want to hear of – the one who forged a peace that united peoples long forsworn to war, or the over-indulgent father? Or perhaps you'd like to know how you came to exist?' The royal physician sounded surprisingly bitter.

'I've no need to tear him down,' Nikolis said gently. Thinking, *I've already lost him*, he added, 'Though there may come a time when I might learn from his failings, I'd prefer to leave those between the king and the Sisters for now. His strengths are what united the One Land and these are the lessons I would study under you.'

Maarcus stopped in mid-stride and again stared into the younger man's eyes. 'There's where you're wrong. I cannot teach you anything useful about his strengths.' He paused. 'Well, maybe this. Because Tomar didn't believe others when they warned him against the impossible, he made the inconceivable happen. Thus was the One Land born on the one hand.' He extended an open palm, inviting with possibility. 'Thus did it die on the other.'

He curled the hand into a fist and shook it at the prince. 'You and your sister must learn to embrace the two halves into a proper whole.' All ten fingers intertwined and wiggled at him as if Maarcus played a child's game. 'This is your legacy as the king's twin offspring.'

His hands fell to his sides as his focus dropped to his feet. He looked like a boy about to be scolded. 'Forgive me, sire. I'm not normally given to pronouncements or prophecies.'

Nikolis's chance had passed. 'Quite all right, Maarcus.' Thinking over the vague advice he'd been offered, the prince circled the vast room. He caressed the tapestries, the bed, the floor coverings. Beneath the dirt and disarray, his father spoke. Nikolis would find a way to reach through the murky layers of time until he discovered what lay buried in this room.

A hand rested on his shoulder then pulled away. Footsteps echoed on the stone floor and into the hallway. Nikolis dismissed the distractions.

He checked behind every hanging, underneath every carpet. Finally he went to the writing desk in the corner. If anything it seemed even more mistreated than the rest. He opened the lid and checked through the papers. Interesting only as archives now, these were merely ledgers of the times.

Nikolis knocked on the wood top, bottom and sides. He flipped the desk over and pulled and twisted at the legs one by one. On the third leg, he found what he'd been searching for. It twisted out neatly. At the base where the leg joined the table, a dragon coin rested neatly in a pouch.

Jilian's captor led her at a quick clip. With nothing but piercing blue sky in the wake of the previous day's storm, they made good time. Expecting to be shepherded to a deserted route where he hoped to kill her, the princess was surprised by his course. They were plainly heading back to the capital.

Rather than entering the city under the blackness of a starless night, they passed through the gates in full daylight. In better days the traffic would have been at its height.

A large, heavy-set guard came out of his tower and shouted, 'State your business.'

'The prince.'

'You'll be heading toward the palace then.'

'No. There's a house near the water the prince is partial to.'

'Ah, the house on the water. I see.' He raised his sword in salute. 'Do go directly. The streets are dangerous even here.'

'We will. Thank you.'

Familiar with more than her share of corruption, Jilian instantly recognized a conversation spoken in code. Odd that they never referred to her brother by name. In fact, her keeper had yet to use so much as the common title of Dragon Prince.

The princess shrugged it off. Every conspiracy had its quirks. Perhaps Nikolis himself or the elfwitch insisted on this foolish 'anonymity' of the prince, as if there were any other princes in The Cliffs.

Later, the thought would gnaw at her along with Alvaria's many other eccentricities, and she would remember Maarcus repeatedly asking, 'which prince?'.

As the iron gate swung open, the watch signalled another man, who immediately ran off toward the sea. Preparing the way for new arrivals, Jilian thought glumly.

No one noticed her. Dressed in sturdy but ordinary traveling clothes, she did not look like a princess. In the tense battle-charged atmosphere, residents did not stop to gossip as they encountered each other on the street. With the town flooded with starving refugees, they did not meet a stranger's eyes. Only a beggar seemed to note her passing.

'Coin, mistress, for a hungry man?'

A yank on her arm and a whispered reminder of Maarcus kept Jilian from saying more than a tight-lipped, 'I'm very sorry. Sisters' peace.'

Having so recently craved her own return to obscurity,

the princess was horrifed at how easily and quickly it was accomplished. Perhaps in a city of ever-changing factions, no one dared to publicly acknowledge her for fear it might cost them their lives.

She gave up looking for help and settled for studying their approach in preparation for later escape. The buildings on this side of The Cliffs weren't much different from those in the mountain towns she had known her entire life. Tiny houses stood packed shoulder to shoulder. Beneath the smell of salt from the nearby ocean lurked rot and sewage. It was a nauseating mix that made Jilian's empty stomach roll.

For all that this was the nominal capital of the One Land, sections were almost as devastated as the villages hardest hit by the elfwitch's campaign. A generation of warfare left pockmarked buildings and piles of brick rubble poking through filthy snow and ice. The road was in such poor repair that it barely deserved the designation. Men were more likely to lead their horses than sit them lest the animals trip and break a leg. When finally peace settled here, it would be hard to tell from war.

Her captor took her down a cramped alley Jilian couldn't distinguish from its fellows. Her confusion wasn't unexpected really; she hadn't had much of a chance to explore the city in recent months and she had tended to avoid it completely in her previous profession.

He knocked on a door that was a mate to all the others they'd passed – weathered wood with a heavy catch meant to hinder intruders. The brass knocker was molded into a dragon's head. Neither was this particularly unusual. Many humans felt nostalgic for the calmer years under the Great King's rule.

On second glance, the dragon held a strong resemblance to the imperial crest. The metal was not polished to bring attention to itself. Nonetheless, the comparison seemed undeniable if one knew where to look – the tilt to the head, the flaring of nostrils. Could this be an old hideaway of royals past . . . and present?

A soldier met them at the door with sword drawn.

'You can go now,' he told the kidnapper.

'But what about my money?'

'You'll get it.'

The scoundrel puffed up his chest. He stared up at the man nearly a head taller. 'When?'

'What about Maarcus?' Jilian asked, taking advantage of the rift between them.

He tapped the tip of his blade against the man's gut. 'She's right. Job's not done 'til we have 'em both.'

'Should've given me some help if you were in such a hurry.'

The soldier smiled. 'I'm in no rush. I've got plenty of wood to keep me warm and cook my food. As for the prince, I think he would've been just as happy if they'd both been eaten by trolls.'

'But the prince—'

'The prince is rethinking his position. He's not so sure you're doing us any favors by bringing them here.'

The man's face fell. 'I wanted to help the prince claim the throne.' His disappointment seemed genuine. 'I'm not in this for that elfwitch.'

The soldier's expression softened slightly. He sheathed his sword. 'See that Maarcus the Seventh arrives safely and you'll get your coin.'

'Good enough.' He released Jilian into the other's control. 'You mind your manners now,' he told her, 'if you value your friend.'

The princess didn't bother with a backward glance. Nothing could save either of them if her own brother wanted her dead.

Ginni did not leave that night or the next morning or the morning after that. Curiosity overruled the common sense her father had labored hard to teach her. Instead, she pushed the Sisters' luck beyond all prudent barriers and stayed to learn what secrets she could.

She dressed in the plain homespun they gave her. Forbidden a mirror, she let her hands check for a missed button on the blouse or an off-kilter bow on the apron. This took no great effort on Ginni's part, as skilled as she was at disguises.

Minute by minute, she grew more confident and her explorations gradually took her farther and farther from the room she'd been assigned. Despite Revered Mother's warning in Ginni's dream-vision, no one commented as she took up a mop or dust-rag to excuse her wandering the Forty-nine's maze of huts. No one rifled her things while she was out or barred her exit. Food appeared on schedule.

Ginni accepted it as her due. She was simply more inventive than they were. The mages had grown stale in the towers.

Even so, she chose the early hours when the hallways were empty. The witches had yet to be called to the morning meal and most were in their rooms. Casual listening told her which doors might open onto private chambers and she avoided these.

On the third day after her arrival at the Tower, Ginni found a store-room stacked to the ceiling with wooden crates. Those at the bottom had crumbled from weight and rot. Other boxes still smelled of fresh pine. Her every instinct rang with knowing. She was meant to discover this closet.

Quickly, Ginni closed the door behind her. A flame sprouted in the darkness. Ginni smiled. Her talents were intact after all. Quietly, as quietly as Wanton Tom had trained her, she dug through the piles. Dusty scroll upon dusty scroll lay inside each crate. She smothered her sneezes and kept searching.

She stopped when she came across an old parchment annotated in her mother's own hand. Ginni's hand shook as she read through Roslin's evidence of the coming battles with the elfwitch. All the great mage's seeings had been ignored, yet they had shown themselves true and had come to pass nonetheless. Here were her predictions tossed away like so many old mouse droppings – or buried like so much unwanted news.

Ginni sucked in her breath, held it, then let it out, thinking what to do. The Seven Sisters might have inspired her quest, but Revered Mother would surely hold a different view.

Frenzied now, she burrowed into the piles. Each box was filled to the brim with dire warnings of this time, yet all of it was left to rot. She ran across a letter from the Revered Mother one generation back. Addressed to her successor, it said only what Ginni had already surmised.

Dear Caronn,

I hesitate long and hard over passing down our predecessor's policy. As I grow toward twilight, it strikes me as foolhardy in the extreme for the elder mages to lead the Forty-nine in blissful ignorance, doing no more than what we've always done and leaving knowledge of the locked room only to the next Revered Mother. To continue our traditions without imparting true understanding will likely be our doom.

Yet knowing all this I suddenly lack the strength to fight the others. Daughter of my heart, I pray the Seven will grant you the courage to take on in your earlier years what I delayed until too late.

The letter was unsigned but for the seal of a dragon, as incongruous a mark as Ginni could imagine a mage might use. Apparently, the woman's wish had gone unheeded. Caronn had been as short-sighted or power-mad as the others. Else Roslin would not have remained exiled from the Tower, nor would the elfwitch have continued to expand her reign never once to be denounced by the Forty-nine.

A voice broke into her thoughts. 'She's in there.' A door across the hall creaked open. 'I'll call Revered Mother Caronn.'

She was caught. Her curiosity had damned her as surely as her mother's arrogance.

Notti slept in the elfwitch's tent that night. He knew it was a great honor but he couldn't dispel the uneasiness. He missed his smelly goats. It was too warm and too bright and too noisy.

She roused him before dawn and he was almost relieved that he needn't feign sleep any longer. 'You will stand witness to their treachery.'

'What treachery?' he asked, head still muddled from poor rest.

She smiled. 'You are generous and noble for withstanding their assaults, but there is no need to protect Tabor and Theron.'

'Assaults?' he echoed stupidly.

She bowed low and loosely as if drunk. '"The elfqueen calls Sir Goatboy to her tent"', said the One in a perfect imitation of Tabor.

'"Indeed she does"', copying Theron now. Her voice grew loud and imperious. '"Bring me the Goatboy!"' Again she bowed low and straightened.

'"You dare ridicule the One here within range of her hearing?"'

Notti listened aghast as his own words and voice rang through the tent.

'"You dare ridicule the One,"' mimicked Alvaria as Tabor. '"Keep your admonishments for your goats. They won't save you from your fate."'

Alvaria shrugged and all notion of the boys was gone. 'You may dismiss their mistreatment of you if you wish,' she said, wholly herself once more. 'However, you must not deny it. They. Have. Scorned. Me.'

It was true. Were it not, Alvaria's speaking the thought aloud would have made it so. Goatboy looked at the rich red carpetings on the floor, the walls, the ceiling. Everywhere was the color of blood.

She laughed in a boy's falsetto-just-turned-to-adult pitch. Notti would have sworn on his life that Theron stood in the tent with him.

Alvaria's face held Tabor's expression. '"And she had to get the guard to make him bow"',' she said, falling back into character. '"Who looked more foolish then?"'

She tsked sadly. '"No manners in those goat-humans, no manners at all."'

'"What do you suppose she wants with him?"'

'"Who knows? Probably enjoys watching a mighty prince begging to save his pitiful village."'

'"Or his own skin."'

She lifted her chin and abruptly returned to herself. 'I seldom go to such trouble to make my point. See that my effort wasn't wasted.'

Goatboy nodded, afraid to speak.

'I warn you, Notti, just as I warned those two. My business is mine alone. What you see here is not to be discussed outside. With anyone.'

'Yes, mistress.'

'And Notti,' she continued. 'I will not be mocked, not by children nor grown men.'

A sentinel appeared before the goatboy could respond. 'The prince at your request, mistress.'

She sprinkled incense in the brazier and lit another far more pungent burner at the entrance. 'What are you waiting for?' she asked the guard. 'Don't leave him out there for the entire camp to see. Bring him in, bring him in.'

'The One will see you now,' he told the prince.

The prince reeked of human scent, which overpowered the delicate elven spices and clogged the air nearly to unbreathability.

The One showed no sign of discomfort as she motioned the man forward. 'Quickly. We haven't much time before the rest awaken.'

Notti rubbed his watering eyes to get a better look. He saw only the back of a bulky, dark-haired human dressed in armor.

'What about him?'

Notti caught a glimpse of the man's face as he glanced toward the boy then returned his attention to the One. Oddly, he reminded Notti of someone he knew. The goatboy had the vaguest impression he knew this man though he'd never met a human in his life.

'The boy is mine,' the elfwitch said, 'and therefore no concern of yours.'

'See that he doesn't become one.' This human was not easily cowed.

'Let's go on to important matters, prince,' she said in not quite deferential tones. 'The potion must be prepared exactly. If not, it is likely to be deadly to the recipient.' She paused. 'As well as the one who composed it.'

'Yes, yes, I understand.' The man was too impatient, too dismissive. He did not understand at all, Goatboy thought.

'I want her alive.'

'I've agreed to your terms already. Shall I bring the Shoreman as well?'

The elfwitch considered, looked down at the service-berries in the bowl behind her. With her thumb she flattened several and licked the juice, toxic to most people in such concentration. 'Yes, do,' she said. 'I'm sure I can find a use for him.'

Goatboy's gut tightened at the human's chuckle. It reminded him of Tabor and Theron. And their fate.

'Do take care. I won't grant you or your men passage without them.'

'I know my business. I would not have survived this long otherwise. Good morn'.'

The tent flap dropped behind him.

'Notti, tend to your beasts. I will call you when I need you.'

The elf boy followed the human into the frigid dawn. A brisk wind and cold looks met him outside, but there was no sign the prince had ever been there.

Though the camp was beginning to stir with elves at their morning chores, it was unnaturally quiet as Goatboy trudged uphill to the meadow and his animals. He felt the people watching his passage, none willing to risk speaking words to displease the One. He braved their glares only once when he turned to look where her tent stood apart from the others. As stifling as it had been, it seemed a snug haven now.

# Chapter 8

## APPROACHING OBLIVION

Walther missed Jilian more than he'd expected. Between
her bluster and Ceeley's charm, he hadn't had much
chance to brood on his own problems.

Despite Abadan's training, his visions still came when
they willed. If anything, they seemed more unpredictable.
Certainly they arrived more often. Abadan was delighted,
but Walther couldn't share his enthusiasm. They gripped
him by his vitals and shook him until he was exhausted.
Sometimes he had more than one a day, when he'd barely
had time to recover from the previous episode.

Thinking of Ceeley brought a sad smile. Once they'd
thought to check among the refugees and word came back
that she'd adopted the humans Lyda and Willam, he felt
sure she was fine. Any woman capable of bringing so
many of the dispossessed to The Cliffs could surely
look after one little girl. He should have done better
by her, though. He'd sworn it before her parents and all
their village.

Worry took him back to her old play-room already converted to a soldier's indoor training-ground. He walked across the polished floor, his footsteps echoing in the emptiness. Her toys were shoved into a jumbled pile in a corner to make space for sparring. She had placed them so carefully that it tore at his heart to see them so carelessly treated.

Walther began righting the furniture to stack it neatly until the girl's return. He picked up her toy sword and suddenly his body went rigid with fear. He forced his arm to raise the sword into view. Turning it over and over, he struggled to read something in the wood grain and met only his own unstable shortcomings.

He put down the sword, but his misgivings couldn't be set aside so easily. He took up the toy once more and resolved to keep it with him until he understood the feeling well enough to speak of it to Abadan.

He couldn't shake his anxiety the rest of the day or the next or the next. But on the fourth day, as he sat taking his noon meal with Abadan and Maarcus, his disquiet suddenly magnified to unreasoning terror. He yanked the wooden blade out of its makeshift scabbard and stared at it for long moments.

He saw his village destroyed as intimately as the others his visions had shown him. But he knew each of these victims. He knew their names, their birthdays, their occupations, their children.

It happened in a matter of moments just as Ceeley had said. He saw the elfwitch through the trees, just as Ceeley had described. The trolls ran rampant, setting everything afire until no wood could withstand the heat. They stood guard at the cages, which were placed at the only way out where his friends were forced to endure dreadful if short-lived torture. In his horrified fascination, he saw it all and registered it as he had not that bleak afternoon he'd returned home to a graveyard.

And he confronted, as he had not been ready to face in those dark hours, that there were not nearly enough dead. He didn't need to count the fallen; he joined the dwarves as they were force-marched past dying relatives. Grief-stricken and guilt-ridden for the few extra hours of life, none of them dared to hope they might meet a kinder end.

Joined by rope noosed at their necks, they trudged away from the flames engulfing their homes. Only the last dwarf in line could twist freely enough to look back and mourn what they'd lost.

Walther watched his family and friends fade into the greenery and felt his heart go with them.

But where was Ceeley? Had she hidden from the beginning? What was she doing away from her clan? Had someone known this was coming and protected her? How could anyone have foreseen it when not even the sight of the Shortdwarf clan had saved a single soul.

Walther tried to direct the vision to look for Ceeley on the docks where he'd later found her or through the trees to follow the hostages. Control was not his to yield or aim. The image rested squarely on the burning village until the homes collapsed in on themselves and every stick was but a charred cinder. When nothing moved but tendrils of smoke on the fetid wind, the vision let him go.

Tears ran down the dwarf's face when he finally rejoined his fellows.

Maarcus studied him strangely. Poor man, Walther thought. Bad enough he can't see the vision. Now he doesn't even understand what he's missing.

'Master Abadan, they took hostages. Why?'

The magician nodded his head. 'Yes, why. Walther,

you need to redouble your efforts. We must find out where they've gone and exactly what she's done with them.'

Walther stared down at the untouched plate of food. 'It's useless. No matter what I seek to do, the sight has a will of its own. Sometimes I don't even think the visions are mine.'

'Maybe they aren't yours.'

'How can he own another man's vision?' Maarcus asked. 'Does not each see what the Sisters mean him to behold?'

Walther jumped at the voice, eerily reminiscent of a dying man.

'Well, yes, certainly,' Abadan answered. 'But perhaps he is able to intercept—'

'Please, old friend, don't try to convince me with your magical musings. I'm too tired to follow the logic. Perhaps another day.' He pushed his chair back from the table. 'I think I'll go rest a bit.' Instead of retiring to his chambers, he remained seated and closed his eyes.

Walther felt as old and lost as Maarcus looked. Whether or not the two elders debated, the dwarf's fate wafted between them with no more self-direction than the train behind a royal robe.

It was time Walther spoke up to reclaim his destiny. While sifting through the ashes of his village, he had sworn to find those who'd done such evil and avenge the victims. He had begun that journey only to let subsequent events distract him. Now that he knew there might yet be survivors, he needed to resurrect his oath and take on a further purpose. 'We have to save them.'

'Save who?' Abadan asked.

'My village.'

The magician stared at him as if he'd sprouted a new –

and absurd – vision. 'Walther, they're dead. It's dreadful, I know, but—'

'No, you don't know. I assumed they were all gone, but in the back of my thoughts I realized there weren't enough bodies on the pyre. Ceeley was right. The elfwitch is doing something with them. We must rescue them!' He slammed his fist on the table.

'You're right. She is doing something with them,' said Abadan softly. 'We have suspected as much for months.'

'I think Zera knew but couldn't bear to speak it aloud,' said Maarcus, suddenly awake. 'She's converting them one by one into her army.'

'Are you out of your mind?' Walther asked.

Maarcus turned to gaze at him with rheumy eyes. He considered the question. 'No, I don't believe I am. However, you are an ill-mannered young dwarf.'

'My apologies, Sir Maarcus.' Why am I arguing with this man? he thought. His mind has wandered into a forest so deep no one can follow his tracks. 'With all due respect, sir, it seemed a ridiculous notion to me.'

'When you are as old as I am, you will find very little is as preposterous as it might first appear.'

'Nonetheless . . .'

'Nonetheless, nothing.' His voice held no rancor, only complete assurance of his position.

Desperate not to lose the substance of the conversation, Walther turned to the magician. 'Master Abadan, you can't believe such an absurd idea. My people would never execute such treachery.'

'Under ordinary circumstances, that's true.' He looked serious as he added, 'Need I remind you the elfwitch is a good deal more than extraordinary?'

Walther felt the blood rush to his face. 'She could

torture them all, Sisters forbid, and they would not join her.'

'Torture is only part of it,' Abadan said. His mouth twisted as if he'd eaten foul meat. 'We believe . . .' He swallowed and licked his lips.

'Now who's stalling?' Maarcus asked him.

The dwarf didn't understand the reference. In the physician's current state, it could have been something that happened this morning, last year, or a generation ago.

'We think the elfwitch is transforming her prisoners into trolls.' His voice rose above Walther's protests and echoed throughout the room. 'I do not make such statements lightly. Never, never underestimate the elfwitch.'

Walther glanced at the physician, who was idly drawing patterns on the table with his fork. 'How can you sit there scribbling, Sir Maarcus? Aren't you terribly bothered by this?' It was a petty jab, he knew, but the enormity of the elfwitch's deeds had reduced him to less than a mere man.

'Being troubled robs me of what little I have left to fight her with.'

He seemed to be separating into two men. Where the first grew ever more unflinchingly clear-eyed and plain-spoken, the second meandered between whimsical notions and their fanciful explanations.

'If what you say is true, this does not change my intent. It only makes it all the more urgent that I rescue them before it's too late.'

Abadan reached out and put a hand on his shoulder. 'Walther, if she has them, it is too late. Of this we are sure.'

'No.' The dwarf shook his head in vigorous denial. 'No, I won't accept that.'

'There's nothing you can do to save them,' Maarcus

sounded like catastrophe itself given voice. 'You can only fight to prevent it from happening to others.'

'I will not relegate them to such a walking death. They can be saved and I will find a way!'

'Perhaps you will, Walther. But it will cost you all you have and more.' Maarcus did not face the dwarf as he spoke but rather stared into a future only he could perceive.

'I will gladly offer up everything for them – just as they would for me.' Walther spoke boldly, but he was no fool. The Shortdwarfs had a talent for stumbling across prophecies as if they were so many stray boulders strewn about the One Land. Like its brothers, this prediction might well change the dwarf's path, but it would not protect him from the deadly wound-snake hiding beneath the rock.

'Are you sure?'

'I have no doubts about myself.' *That I am willing to speak aloud at any rate*, he finished silently.

Sir Maarcus turned his watery eyes to Walther. 'Do not forget that any prisoners who still live do so because they have already yielded to Alvaria. There will be nothing left for them to give you, no way for them to aid their own release.'

Ceeley did her best to keep her spirits up. She noticed that Mama-Lyda and Papa-Wil didn't frown so much when she pretended to treat the long, hard trip like another grand adventure. When they were happy, she didn't have to think about the horror of her six-year birthday party.

She just wished her dreams would behave too.

Ceeley began to wonder about her choice of guardians once they got above the tree-line. Mama-Lyda seemed sad and confused. What if she couldn't shepherd their way across the mountain? They would all be lost. Forever.

She would never have a chance to make something beautiful to pass down to her children and her children's children. It would be as if she never lived, for a dwarf measures her life by what she can build out of Sister-given creation. Her dada told her so the day she turned six at their private family celebration before the big party. Before the witch ruined everything.

Curse that elfwitch, curse her! Ceeley thought. She didn't want to ruminate, but she couldn't help it. It was better to look in toward her memories than out toward the icy landscape. When she saw the snowy cold mountaintops, she couldn't stay cheerful – and Mama-Lyda needed her to try hard. She didn't say anything, but Ceeley could tell. Mama-Lyda's face was creased with lines that got deeper and deeper the farther they walked.

She snuck a peek at Papa-Willam. Something bothered him and that worried her. Sometimes he walked as if he'd been hurt and the pain never quite went away. She didn't think his body ached; she thought it was in his heart. Prob'ly something bad had happened to him.

She wasn't sure she wanted to know what it was.

Oh, she liked him fine and she trusted him all right. She knew what she was doing when she chose him to be her papa. But she couldn't bring herself to find out what was eating at him. She was too afraid it might be worse than what she'd already seen from the elfwitch, and then where would she be? Swimming in nightmares day and night. There's only so much a six-year-old can take, after all.

She felt like stamping her feet and having a tantrum. Her mama said she was too old for tantrums and maybe she was right. Mama never really understood, though.

Tantrums were just like thunderstorms. They built and built and then they broke. Later the air got clear and easier to breathe. Tantrums did the same thing. Afterwards her blood stopped pounding in her head and she could think again.

She supposed she wouldn't get to have tantrums when she grew up. It's very silly for big people to stamp their feet and scream. She imagined she'd miss them, though, and she wondered if she'd be able to think as well without a sporadic squall.

Right now wasn't the time for one anyhow. She was too tired. She was used to hiking on rounded, gentler hills. These were sharp and craggy. And the trees, she missed the trees. Green leaves in winter made her smile. There was always something to watch in a forest – a bird flitting from branch to branch, a squirrel nibbling on nuts. Chirps and barks filled the air and made a dwarf forget her troubles. Dada said that too.

She missed her da. She missed her mama, too, but it was Da at times like these who could tease her out of anything. He had a special 'no smiling' trick that always did the reverse in no time flat. She could do with a no-smiling-smile about now.

Tears began to trickle down her cheeks. She let them run, feeling too gloomy to wipe them away. Her feet were moving, but she was falling behind. She'd catch up in a minute.

An unfamiliar finger gently rubbed her face. She looked up at Papa-Willam.

He squatted to her height. 'What's the matter, Pumpkin?'

'Pumpkin? Nobody's ever called me pumpkin before. Pumpkin, pumpkin,' she repeated, trying it out like tasting a new vegetable.

'Well then,' Papa-Wil said very seriously, 'would you like it t' be our special name?'

'Pumpkin,' Ceeley said again. 'I like it.' She nodded her approval.

He smiled at her then and for just a moment he reminded her of Da. That thought made her sad, but a little happy too. It felt good to have a proper da. Uncle Walther and Uncle Maarcus just didn't know how to be one yet. They got too busy and forgot to keep their promises.

He straightened up and offered her a gloved hand. She put hers in his and he clasped it tight. 'It occurs to me,' he said conversationally, 'that you might be frettin' over where we are. You're a smart little girl, so I won't lie to you. Mama-Lyda and I aren't quite sure ourselves.'

I'm going to die, Ceeley thought. After all this, I'm going to die and no one will even know about it until the snow melts in the spring.

Papa-Wil squeezed her hand. 'It doesn't mean we're done for. I swear to you, like I did with Lyda, we're going to get through this.' He paused. 'And, Pumpkin, I always keep my promises. Always.'

One glance at the well-worn steps leading down to cells girded by sturdy iron bars made Jilian's predicament plain. The prince's hideaway had obviously housed its share of prisoners before her. Only a fool would bet that she wasn't simply the most recent in a succession of hostages secretly kept and tortured. She wouldn't take the wager on dying here either; she'd already used more than her share of Sisters' luck on living.

Some hours after she was locked in, footsteps sounded in the narrow, twisting stair-well. She sat up and prepared to face her captor.

Her brother. Her oldest friend.

Two soldiers marched past her without so much as a sideways look. Between them strutted Maarcus, his characteristic cocky grin shining through the dim lighting.

Wonder of wonders. The elfwitch and the Dragon Prince walking arm-in-arm would have been less astounding.

By keeping their word, they'd caught her off-balance. Not good, that. She needed to keep her wits intact if she had a chance of survival.

The men installed Maarcus a few cells down and across from hers. 'We seem to be the only guests at the inn,' the Shoreman remarked as they slammed the door. 'Must be the lovely dank decor. A pity, though, when so many refugees are looking for shelter.'

'Quiet,' the guard said. 'The prince may yet decide you're too much trouble alive.'

'Oh, he can count on it,' Maarcus answered. 'Count on it with . . . uh . . . with dragon-bells.' She couldn't see him from her cell, but the pain amidst the swagger in his voice was unmistakable.

'Don't push y'ur luck,' the second one growled.

'Maarcus, don't,' Jilian pleaded. She had the barest hope for herself, but her brother might let Maarcus go if he'd behave himself. If. Right now these two weren't taking kindly to his mockery. 'Please?'

'That's right. Listen to the princess,' said the guard.

'For now,' Maarcus said. His footsteps echoed on the stone floor. Wood creaked as he settled on the bed.

The soldier nodded.

Jilian released a breath she hadn't realized she was holding.

'No talkin'.'

'Got it, no talkin',' Maarcus parroted in a fair approximation of the other's voice.

'I'm warnin' you.'

Maarcus remained silent a long moment as the men considered their options then finally went to confer at the jail entrance.

'You take first watch. I'll be down in four hours.'

'Be sure you're on time. Four has a funny way of becomin' six with you.'

'Yeah, yeah.' He proceeded up while the second settled into a chair.

Jilian's next shock came at shift-change.

The guard was an hour overdue and his fellow had long since resorted to muttered threats by the time he arrived.

'Prince said I had to feed 'em,' he explained.

'Took you an hour to make that! Get the cook to do it next time.'

'Cook refused. Anyway, you going t' dish it out or wait here while I do it?'

'What I'm going t' do is leave.'

'But the prince said—'

'I don't care. Next time, don't be late.' He was halfway up the stairwell before his companion gently kicked the food under the bottom bar of Jilian's cell.

She expected a hunk of stale bread and a rusty cup of water. He surprised her by serving a thick stew and half-decent ale in portions only marginally smaller than she'd been eating at the palace. It wasn't good, but she'd gone hungrier between mercenary jobs. Jilian forced it down without comment and could hear Maarcus doing the same.

The guard went back to his chair.

Maybe her brother would let her live a while, say long enough to escape and kill him.

Princess Jilian began to plan.

'Parade rest.'

Fully a third of the company fell out before realizing they weren't dismissed. Most scrambled to reclaim their places. A few kept going despite urgent whispers from the others.

Prince Nikolis ignored the deserters as he strode through the ranks. With Marcus the Seventh missing and the physician so seldom of sound mind that he might as well be, the prince was alone in trying to prepare his dwindling army to confront the elfwitch. Hour by hour, one by one, soldiers fooled themselves into believing they were safe or that someone else could better serve the crown.

Certainly someone else would be better suited to leading them. Short on strategy and tactics, long on inconceivable knowledge, the prince didn't contribute much.

What had the elfwitch actually intended he do when she'd made her long-ago suggestion that he head up her forces? Lag behind and watch as the trolls wreaked havoc? Charge in front and hope they didn't kill him in the chaos?

In good conscience, he couldn't send out this ragtag corps to be slaughtered.

He couldn't not send them either.

Nikolis inspected the threadbare clothing and shabby boots. It was easier than looking in their faces.

'Where's your sword?' he asked a tall soldier on the end of an uneven row.

'Don't have one. Don't need it either. I can whip those trolls with my eyes closed. Strangle 'em with my bare hands.' He lifted his arms to demonstrate choking the air.

'That may well be true of ordinary men. However, these are anything but.'

The man's eyes lost focus as he concentrated on digesting the words. Sisters! the prince thought. I need to keep the language simple if I expect half these addle-brains to know what I'm saying.

'Don't you fret,' the soldier assured him. 'I can handle myself.' He lowered his voice. ''Sides, wouldn't you rather save the swords for some of these little guys?' He winced as if he didn't hold out much hope for them.

Odd the way the man echoed the prince's own bleak thinking. 'Don't you worry about them. We've got weapons enough for everybody.'

The soldier blushed and offered a gap-toothed smile. ''Course. I should've knowed there were plenty of top-drawer swords to go around.'

'Absolutely.' Not that many or that fine, Nikolis thought, but they'll have to do. 'Archers,' he called out. 'Present arms.'

Three young men held out their bows.

Nikolis forced pride into his voice. 'Excellent men, excellent.' Silently he offered a soldier's plea to the Sisters, for as sure as they stood on this training-ground today they would not be standing at all a week from now.

Willam never doubted Lyda. Himself, that was another thing. He stood at the top of the highest mountain in the world (so far as he knew anyway) and looked beyond at the plains. He felt dizzy, but not from the height. It was all that flat land rolling before him. The view made him as ill as the ocean had the one time he went to The Cliffs. Green grasslands in the dead of winter unnerved him, they did.

Ceeley was another matter just as terrifying. The child

hopped about so unpredictably that he expected her to fly off the mountain at any second. He felt the blood drain from his face as he watched her skipping along, no more than a palm's width from open air. Stones clattered down the hillside.

He wrapped his arms around himself, holding tight and telling himself that children would be children. Finally he could stand it no more and shouted out, 'Ceeley, come 'way from t'ere!'

She turned around, confused and a little frightened. 'Yes, Papa-Wil? Something wrong?'

'No, no, nothin's wrong. I just, well, um . . .'

Ceeley looked at him, studying his colorless face. She came back from the ledge and took his hand. 'You're very cold.' Her little face scrunched up in a sorrow so deep it melted his heart. 'Oh, Papa-Wil. I scared you. I'm sorry.'

'It's okay, honey. Gave me a start, was all. It's a long drop and you aren't as sturdy as those big boulders.' He puffed out his cheeks to imitate a fat rock and the child laughed.

'Papa?' her voice was very grave.

'Yes?' He was still getting used to the way she could switch from utter frivolity to complete seriousness.

'How long do you think those elves will keep Mama-Lyda?'

He stooped down to her height. 'Hard to say, Pumpkin. They've been real good to her and she owes 'em a debt she might never be able to pay back.'

'I thought they were only going to talk with her a *short* while.'

'Sure, honey. But you know how long grown-ups can talk.' He closed his eyes, put his head on folded hands, snored twice, then opened his eyes once more.

Ceeley laughed again then immediately sobered. 'Papa-Wil?'

'Yes?'

'Do you ever have nightmares?'

Here it comes, he thought, and I'm not ready. I need Lyda. He looked over his shoulder, as if thinking of his wife might summon her back from her audience with the elves. 'Sometimes,' he said.

'Then it doesn't mean I'm a bad girl? My aunt used to say that only naughty kids had scarey dreams.'

'Well, shame on your aunt!' Willam said. 'Even grown-ups, good ones, get nightmares now and then.'

'I don't like 'em one bit. They make me tired in the morning and I feel like a fly's buzzing in my brain so I can't think straight.'

'Sounds more like magic than nightmares,' Willam said without thinking.

'Huh,' Celia answered, hands on hips. She let that sink in and didn't speak for a moment. Finally she cocked her head sideways and asked, 'Do flies live on the tops of mountains? I thought they only lived down by where the river runs into the sea.'

'Honey, there are all kinds of flies. I wouldn't be surprised if one of 'em liked it way up here in thin air.'

'Oh.' She thought some more. 'Papa-Wil, does Mama-Lyda get nightmares too?'

They were bothering her more than she wanted to admit. 'Celia, everybody has bad dreams now and again. Even someone as pure as your Mama-Lyda.'

'When will she be back?'

'Soon.' Willam didn't want to go through that again. 'Let's play a game while we wait.'

She ran behind a bush. 'How about Hide and Sneak?'

'How 'bout somethin' easier on the old man here?'

Her curly-haired head popped above the bush. 'You mean a word contest or a counting match, so you don't have to run too much?'

No, he meant something where *she* didn't have to run too much or too close to the edge. 'Uh, huh,' he said.

'Well, why don't we try the Tale of the Three Dwarves and the Big Bad Troll. I'll start and you have to tell me what comes next.'

The door opened. Masha and Dita stood facing Ginni wearing identical expressions of patience tried beyond the limits but held nonetheless. Candlelight shown through the doorway behind them, lighting their faces in almost sacred fashion.

'By the Sisters,' Ginni thought to keep from laughing at the image.

'Sorry to interrupt your roaming,' said Masha, sounding more pleased than annoyed. Worse and worse. This one enjoyed her superior position far too well.

Ginni kept her eyes on their shoes. She framed her response carefully, wrapping the words in humility. 'I meant no harm. I would do your bidding gladly.'

'I should expect you would,' the Sister said, rustling her skirt. 'You'd be out in the deepsnow if it weren't for our generosity.'

'Yes, and I thank the Sisters every day for it.'

'It appears you have yet to lose the dreadful arrogance your mother seems to have instilled in you.'

Ginni braced herself. This was the first time they'd mentioned Roslin to her since her arrival. Given their mutual opinions of each other . . . Better not to finish that thought.

'We were hoping you'd learn by our example,' said Dita.

'Unfortunately this hasn't been the case,' said Masha.

'We may have been imperfect in our teachings.' Dita's voice was smooth and comforting.

'More likely, you have been remiss in your studies.'

'But I've been given no lessons,' Ginni answered, genuinely confused.

'Perhaps if you spent more time in your room, you would notice the materials placed there for your instruction.'

Ginni recognized the shake-down. She had seen government thieves employ it any number of times on the road. She had even played the part of the soother while Wanton Tom posed as the bully on a few hungry occasions. She could not win through argument. 'How may I better serve you?'

'That's just it,' said Dita, sadly. 'We're not sure that you can.'

Ginni wasn't ready to be thrown out . . . yet. That they might do worse she wouldn't consider. It's just another role, she reminded herself. She'd seen tougher spots. 'But I do so want to. Serve you, I mean. I'll redouble my efforts.'

'We've given your problem a great deal of thought.' Dita gently lifted Ginni's head so that she looked into the other's eyes. 'We've decided you'll need some help.'

The young mage let her relief show while hiding her genuine fear at their scheme. She didn't have to wait long.

A third woman returned with a fourth, who Ginni recognized from her dream.

'Revered Mother Caronn,' said Masha, 'I believe you know Ginni, the forbidden daughter of Roslin and Wanton Tom.'

'Yes,' said Caronn.

Ginni curtseyed. 'I'm honored, ma'am.'

The woman was all business. 'Enough of that. We both know who leads the Forty-nine. Don't we.'

It was not a question. 'Yes, Revered Mother.'

'I'm glad to hear it. Your mother did not. It was her downfall.'

Ginni waited.

'If you are to reach any level of profiency, you'll need to forget everything Roslin taught you – and I do mean everything. You'll likely be as helpless as a baby for some time until we can retrain you.'

Imposed amnesia? Ginni had done so for isolated moments at Roslin's insistence, but this seemed much more far-reaching. Much more crippling.

'We begin today. Return to your room. Now.'

Masha and Dita insured that she went – and that she stayed within.

The lock was beyond her ability. She saw only an ordinary keyhole. She detected no magic. Yet the knob did not turn and the door would not open from inside.

They soundlessly delivered several fine meals that day. Somewhere in the bowels of the compound, a cook worked wonders with the very few fresh supplies delivered during such a harsh winter following a poor growing season. As the young mage ate the food, she hoped the witches rewarded the chef for her trouble.

Hunger, thirst, bodily functions were each addressed to her comfort. No one saw to her mind. Boredom and brooding were her enemies. Her impotent bungling enveloped her. The witches let her stew.

She examined her room's every nook, cranny, and crack to keep occupied. She found nothing noteworthy, nothing engaging. If waiting on her mother had been unbearable, this reached a new tier of excruciating.

Dreams flooded her night. The adversities of people she'd never met disturbed her rest.

Exhausted past thinking, it came to her that they would not feed and house a failure. 'I'm ready,' she said to the empty room. 'I'm ready to learn whatever you will teach.'

Revered Sisters Masha and Dita arrived together. They flanked her on each side, but Ginni had the impression their positioning had more to do with keeping each other honest than preventing her flight. They went down the hall to yet another interior room. Were there none with windows in this maze?

Though it shared identical dimensions with the previous rooms she'd seen, this one was less inviting. No blazing fire warmed the hearth. Unpadded ladder-backs rather than over-stuffed chairs discouraged rapport.

Ginni was beginning to think of the home of the Forty-nine as a mouse warren, jammed full of little rooms. Oddly the interior didn't match the view from outside. Perhaps most of the compound was built below ground.

'What's the difference between a decoction and an infusion?' asked Masha, without preamble.

The woman's abrupt style reminded Ginni of Roslin. She answered automatically before they could dismiss her as dull-witted or worse. 'An infusion is as simple as brewing tea. A decoction is made from the woodiest parts of the plant and therefore must be simmered a while to attain full strength.'

'How long?' asked Dita in gentler tones.

'The length of time depends on the plant. A Sisters' twin watch – that is, what's commonly counted as ten to fifteen minutes – is generally enough.'

'Sea-holly decoction,' said Masha.

What did she want to know? Remembering her mother's stiff phrasing, Ginni said, 'Helpful in afflictions related to eliminating liquid wastes. It can also be taken in as a tincture.'

'Huh,' grunted Masha. 'Your cockiness is unwarranted. Milk-thistle.'

'A simple infusion drunk three times a day to help stimulate mother's milk. It too can be prepared as a tincture.'

'Good,' murmured Dita, ignoring the other's scowl.

So began the drill. Bittersweet, skull cap, poke root, wormwood. Common and obscure. Each herb spat at her in Masha's gruff voice. Each answer praised by Dita.

Ginni knew a set-up when she saw it. She didn't care. There was no other way to escape the Tower but through the very heart of it.

# Chapter 9

## ENEMY CAMP

With Abadan's blessing, Walther paged through tome after tome, unwrapped scroll after scroll. Nothing told him what he needed to know. Either the lore of transformation had been so thoroughly hidden that no mage, including well-meaning ones, might find it – or it had been stolen.

'I warned you that you would not find it,' Abadan said over the dwarf's shoulder.

'Then why did you let me look?'

'I hoped I might be wrong. Fresh eyes often find what old ones miss.'

'Alvaria has them, doesn't she?'

'Almost certainly.'

'And you let her keep them?'

'How were we to stop her?'

'She was but a single woman!' Walther accused.

'All the better to slip in and out unnoticed. And who would have held the capital while we chased after her shadow?'

'Never mind,' Walther said, defeated in more ways than just this. He could not help Jilian. He could not find Ceeley. He could not defeat the elfwitch. He was a tired, worn-out dwarf, though he'd barely come of age among his people. 'What's the use?'

'Because,' hissed Abadan, 'we cannot win if we do not fight.' Veins stood out on the magician's face. He seemed as angry as Walther had ever seen him, yet his anger was shot through with a truth Walther could not deny.

'All right, Master Abadan. All right.' The dwarf crossed the chamber and settled back into his chair.

'Now, the Three Great Sisters from the beginning please.'

'The Three Great Sisters guard over the races of people – human, elven and dwarven. Unlike mortals, they do not fight amongst themselves for glory or territory or petty—'

A knock sounded on the door.

'In!' shouted Abadan.

The knob turned. The door swung open. An elf walked in and closed the door.

'You two will remember each other, yes?'

The elf tipped his head to Walther and the dwarf nodded in response. He was Harmon, Zera's apprentice. Where had the man been these last months since her death? Secluded in mourning?

'Harmon will be joining us until Jilian returns.'

Why? Walther dared not voice his question aloud.

'We'll need every magician we can find,' Abadan continued smoothly, answering the unasked. 'And Harmon has trained under one of the best.'

Meaning Zera, of course.

'Your talents will complement each other.' He waved at the chair claimed by Jilian until days ago. 'No need to wait for an invitation, man. Sit.'

Harmon glared at the magician, but did as he was told. 'We were drilling. Do you know the Doctrine of the Great Sisters?'

'Yes,' Harmon answered in clipped tones.

'Well, go on then.'

Harmon let out a pained sigh and began the recitation.

Maybe it's the chair, Walther thought. No one who occupies it seems able to abide the magician who rules over it.

As Harmon spoke, his cadence lulled Walther into a waking trance. As always, the vision gripped him and held him as the veils dropped from Alvaria's absolute evil.

Atop twin altars lay two young elves – apparently male though it was hard to tell from the faces misshapen in agony – elves in the process of becoming trolls.

'No, don't!' Walther shouted. 'Please, Sacred Sisters, stop it. I don't want to see.'

There was never any rescue, never a release from the elfwitch's horror.


For Goatboy, the next hours moved as slowly as an old man, but their end arrived as abrupt and unwelcome as a newborn's death. Throughout the day, he could hear the mournful wails of Tabor and Theron's mother. Silently, the rest of the camp went about preparing for a ceremony. No one dared to speak aloud the word 'transformation' though most feared it just the same. Had not the elfwitch threatened to exact such a punishment when she converted the dragon into a human?

Goatboy was as cursed as the brothers. He dreaded nightfall with all his heart. He hated his part in the proceedings with all his soul.

A sentinel summoned him into the One's tent at sunset. The boy shivered uncontrollably from having spent the day outdoors in the unusually frigid winds, yet he couldn't recall his earlier sense of comfort amidst the heat of the braziers. Endure, he told himself. You can only endure.

The elfwitch had changed into stunning red robes rimmed in gold. 'Attend me, Notti.' She held out a large, empty ceremonial bowl. 'Carry this and bring it near when I tell you.'

Goatboy didn't answer.

'Do you understand?' Her voice was harsh.

'Yes, I understand,' he answered in a monotone.

'Don't disappoint me,' she hissed just as she led him out into the eerily quiet camp.

She stopped behind the central altar to take in the sun's last rays glistening off the lake. A fire blazed in front of the dais between the elfwitch and her subjects. With the sun down, it provided a strange orange light made from more than birch-wood.

Tabor and Theron were bound, gagged, and strapped to altars on either side of the elfwitch.

'My people,' Alvaria began. 'I warned against this months ago.' She shook her head. 'But some doubted my word. Some questioned my power.' She pointed into a crowd so silent that only their swaying torches gave away their presence. 'Many of you expected me to sit idly among you, each and every day, though I had other duties, other burdens.' She looked down at the captive elves. 'Two of you dared to mock me as if I were no more than a lucky troll come into her own!'

'Have mercy!' shouted their mother. 'Please. They are only high-spirited boys.'

'Mercy.' Alvaria spat into Tabor's and Theron's eyes. 'Boys who commit treason will be repaid sevenfold for the agony they hoped to inflict on me.' The woman moaned but the One ignored her. 'Tonight you will see that my power is limitless. Tonight you will learn that I always keep my word.'

She glanced to the goatboy and he stepped forward with the bowl.

'It's all his fault. Goatboy's the one that did it!' shouted the woman. 'You all know it's true.'

Through Notti's tears, he witnessed her imploring and tugging on her neighbors. All stood stiff as statues. Not one came to her aid.

'Here.' The elfwitch pointed and the goatboy moved to place his bowl where she'd indicated.

He knew without knowing what came next. He attempted to close his eyes to keep from watching, but unseen fingers held them open.

Alvaria raised a finely-wrought silver knife and plunged it into Theron's heart. The elf jerked once and was still. Blood ran down the grooves carved into the altar and into the vessel in Notti's hands.

'Now you will see,' the elfwitch shouted at the hushed gathering. 'Now you will know!'

The One strode across to the captive Tabor. Notti's footsteps echoed hers. She began to chant.

He tried to follow her words. He found he barely had strength and concentration enough to remain standing.

At some point, she pried the bowl from between his fingers. Blood splashed in his face and on the face of the prone elf. Screams rang everywhere. He was surrounded by the agonized cries of legions of elves.

They are out there, he thought. Seven upon seven upon seven of them . . . and they are coming for me.

Notti wiped the burning blood from his eyes. On the altar lay what had once been Tabor, an elf not much older than he was himself – an elf, now hideously transformed into one of the largest trolls ever seen.

The goatboy gasped. He'd expected a human or a dwarf, or at worst a four-legged beast such as a lowly goat.

But a troll? A troll destined to fight and die for the elfwitch in a war it could no longer comprehend. Notti couldn't imagine a more abhorrent fate.

For one long moment, goatboy and troll stared into each other's anguished faces. Understanding dropped away from the troll and the eyes went dead. Yet the creature breathed. The monster lived.

A shriek tore itself from Goatboy's throat. He looked into the angry crowd, brandishing their torchlights, and he ran.

Ginni shook herself awake and stretched in the chair where she'd fallen asleep against her best efforts. Now she understood her mother's obsession with the arcane, for she had slipped into its passionate embrace as easily as a lover's nightwear.

Captivated by the lore Roslin had rarely explained, the young mage joyfully studied around the clock. She barely slept or ate or stirred from the chair behind the desk. To think that the Revered Sisters contrived this rigorous torture as punishment almost made her laugh aloud. She chose it for herself the moment she saw what they could teach.

Masha or Dita – she wasn't sure which – stood over her. The Sister's raised arm slowly fell back to her side as if she fought moving water.

Ginni glanced at the Sister's face and dredged up a shadow of her old demeanor. ''Morning, Ma . . . Dit . . .' She tried to mumble a name. Her mouth was dry and fought the sound; her memory choked on extraneous details. Was it morning? It could just as well be night in this windowless room.

Her eyes fell to the scroll on the desk. To waste energy in recognizing individuals diverted her from her goal. The two mages merely drew the carriage by which she approached her magic. Ginni decided the niceties of a greeting weren't worth the effort. She concentrated on the strangely familiar symbols.

'You progress well, novice.'

Novice. As if she didn't have more talent lodged in one fiery finger than the Revered Sister had touched in her lifetime. 'Thank you,' she whispered, keeping her annoyance damped. It too could distract her from more significant tasks.

'Revered Mother Caronn will be observing you today.'

Savage glee tainted the Sister's voice as if she thought the apprentice might not enjoy the examination as thoroughly as her tutors. Ginni ignored the woman's malice. Her words were what carried import.

She noted her place on the scroll and looked up at the Sister. 'Oh?' she asked politely. 'Have I pleased Revered Mother?'

'That remains to be proven.' She spoke with more reserve now that she realized she commanded Ginni's full attention.

'But I'm sure you will,' put in the other mage from across the room.

'And so I shall,' Ginni said. She forced a genial smile. These two tried to yank her about by using their foolish parlor games of granting and withdrawing approval. Any child could see through the charade. 'How would you have me prepare for Revered Mother?'

'Rest,' said the one she now remembered as Dita.

'Today you will eat, sleep, and relax.' She pushed aside the scroll and set down a tray.

The aroma of fresh-baked bread wafted up. Bacon surrounded perfectly shaped egg-yolks. Ginni's mouth watered. Her stomach grumbled. 'I guess I am a bit hungry.' Left hand still on the scroll, she took up the fork in her right. 'Maybe just a few bites.'

Dita smiled and settled back in a chair to watch her.

The meal was as delicious as her first one here had been some days ago. Physical hunger overwhelmed her diligence and she let go of the scroll. Moments later when she thought to study it while she ate, it had been removed. The mage shrugged. There would be other chances.

Ginni finished the food, sopping up the last of the egg with the bread. She stretched and yawned like a cat in the sun. 'My compliments to the chef.'

'We'll pass them along,' Masha said stiffly.

'Come, dear. Time to rest.' Dita came around the desk and took her by the elbow.

'I am rather tired.' She rose from the chair.

'Your room is just next door.'

Panic gripped Ginni. She didn't want to be locked in again.

Her body didn't respond. It belonged to the Sisters.

They led her sluggish form into another bedchamber, identical to the previous one, and sat her on the bed. Dita gently pushed her shoulders until she lay on her back. Masha removed her shoes and stowed them where Ginni couldn't see.

Dita tugged on the blanket and brought it up to her chin. 'Don't you worry. Revered Mother will be very glad indeed.' She patted her arm through the quilt. 'Rest now. We'll return after you've had a nice nap.' The Revered Sisters left the room and closed the door behind them.

'Nap,' Ginni repeated. She might just as easily be entering her death dream. At the least she'd ingested poisoned herbs cleverly disguised amidst a flavorful meal. At the worst, well, from toxic to deadly is only a matter of degree.

With her last shred of strength, Ginni conjured her mental box. Quickly and carefully, she laid in all that she had learned in the past frenzied hours. Finally without a slice of hesitation, she put her very soul in the box. She could not protect her body from the Hags, as Grosik called them. But she could guard her essence from their misuse. Ginni smiled in her sleep. Indeed, Roslin had taught her well.

Prince Nikolis flipped through the ledgers for the third time and rolled up the scroll. No matter how many times he reviewed the numbers, they still didn't balance. So much food; so much drink; so many refugees.

People were going to start starving soon. He'd have revolution on his hands then, but not the one he'd stumbled into leading. Nikolis affixed a seal to the parchment and gave it back to Sir Maarcus. 'Any other good news in that bag of yours?'

Beside him, the physician stood at attention, mercifully clear-eyed and even-voiced. 'No, sire, I think that's all I have.'

'So what are my choices?' He ticked them off on his fingers. 'One, let the army starve. Two, let the refugees starve. Three, let everyone starve albeit more slowly?'

'I wouldn't word it so harshly . . .'

'No, you wouldn't and I appreciate it.' He sighed. 'Who else knows how low we are on supplies?'

'Only Abadan. I've divided the duties so that no one sergeant fully realizes our desperation.'

So much for putting the best face on the situation, Nikolis thought.

Maarcus shifted his weight and continued. 'However, three or four of my best are beginning to reach obvious conclusions. Another dozen will know as soon as these few begin to speculate aloud.'

'At which point, pandemonium won't be far behind.' The prince didn't need to see the physician's sour expression for confirmation. 'I'm inclined to cut all rations from two-thirds down to half. We've got to have an army, but there's no point to it if the people we're trying to save are dead.'

'I agree. It's the only way.'

'How long will we have on half-rations?'

'Six to ten weeks at the current population.' He paused to put the ledgers back in their leather casing. 'But we might not need more than that. The spring thaws . . .'

'Will undoubtedly be late in coming this year if the elfwitch has any say in it. And the exiles still arrive almost daily.' The prince drummed his fingers on the desk. 'This is as effective as resetting a soldier's broken arm while he bleeds to death from a gut wound. We must win this battle against the trolls and reverse Alvaria's death-tide. Once men see it can be done, we'll be able to gather an army strong enough to defeat the elfwitch herself.' Rather than think about the shabby state of his diminishing troops or the starving citizens, he switched to an equally dismal topic. 'I don't suppose we've received word of Jilian and Maarcus within the last few hours?'

A look of confusion crossed the physician's face. 'Are they ill? No one's mentioned it to me.'

Sisters preserve me, Nikolis thought. Do I remind him again or simply assure him all is well? No, he needs to have a grasp of the facts, however painful. 'You know of course that we sent them on reconnaissance duty,' he said casually, 'and we haven't heard from them in some days now.'

'Oh, yes, that,' Maarcus said, seemingly relieved. 'Don't worry, sire. My grandson has been in tough spots before, but he always pulls through.'

'No doubt. Jilian too.' The prince didn't have the heart to push the torture of the specifics on the man, but he couldn't refrain from brooding himself. 'I don't know, though. There's something about the two of them together that I should have considered before I suggested this mission.'

'What's that?'

He shook his head, part in awe, part in dread. 'When they're pleased with one another, they're too wrapped in joy to note potential threats. When they're squabbling, they're too angry to see any dangers outside their own petty insults. This strong bond might well make for a lifelong union, but only if Jilian and Maarcus live long enough to make the wedding.'

The senior Maarcus kept his eyes downcast and didn't comment.

'Tell Abadan to try harder. Tell him to enlist more magicians if he needs. Anything he wants, give it to him.'

'Yes, sire. I will, sire. Anything else, sire?'

'No, that's all.'

The physician never once raised his view from the scuffed oak floor as he crossed to the door and closed it behind him.

Wondering how much longer he could risk depending on the man's failing judgment, Nikolis pulled his sister's knife from the desk drawer. 'It won't do any good,' he whispered to the empty room. 'None of us have the power to defeat her.' Angry beyond words, he stood and threw the knife. It spun tip over pommel and buried itself in the door inches from where Maarcus had just passed.

Jilian quietly inspected every crack and crevice of her cell. She found a loose brick here and there and plenty of spiders. She logged it all out of habit, though there was nothing unexpected and nothing likely to aid her escape. Through it all, Maarcus remained unnaturally silent. Was he well?

When she heard the guard descending with their food, she paused in her scrutiny so that she appeared to have nothing more on her mind than calmly awaiting her meal.

'All that deep thinkin' won't get you out of here,' snapped the guard, who like most jailors enjoyed harrassing his prisoners.

'All that fine talk won't save you from the trolls,' Jilian retorted.

He laughed. 'You believe that nonsense? You're dumber than the usual half-breed.'

'Seen 'em with my own eyes.' She sized him up. 'I'd say they could take on three or four of you.'

He snorted. 'You think you can talk your way out of here, you keep right on tryin'. Don't matter to me.' He slid her tray under the barred door. 'Oughta know, though, the prince isn't much for hearing anybody but himself.'

She listened to his footsteps as he delivered Maarcus' tray and went back to the guard station at the entrance to the prison. Once he'd settled down next to his partner, she attempted to focus on her food. But her mind was on trolls and her brother and . . .

Transformations.

Zera had told her the trolls were like her brother.

So they must have been transformed – from humans. Probably dwarves and the odd defiant elf as well.

All of them reshaped by the elfwitch's will. All of them controlled by that same hand. All of them doomed to fight their own.

She let that thought sink in as she finally dug into her food. 'Hey, what happened to the stew?' she called to the guard. 'There's barely a good-sized spoonful covering the bottom of the bowl.'

'You'll have to take that up with the prince. Seems to be having a bit of trouble gettin' supplies.' He lowered his voice. 'Word to the wise, half-breed. Just let him know how much you enjoyed the soup.'

'You talk too much, Ivan,' muttered his companion. 'Next you'll be telling her about his run-in with the cook.'

'Don't need to, Lyam,' said the other. 'You just did.'

They can't truly be this inept, Jilian thought. Still, she was never one to miss an opportunity. She joined in the conversation as if they were all comrades. 'I know a thing or two about my brother's odd eating habits. Come on, I'll trade you one for one.'

The same guard who'd brought the food came back to stand by her cell. 'There you go again, trying to prattle your way free of here. I'm tellin' you it won't work.' He crossed his arms across his chest. 'But I'm willin' to listen to a good story.'

'You know he only eats fish?' Jilian asked.

'Go on,' Ivan said, not admitting to what he did and didn't know.

'The head cook had a terrible time finding something he'd eat. Poor Dragon Prince couldn't manage to keep the food down.' She laughed and it seemed genuinely funny to her.

'That's nothin',' said the guard.

'I'll wager you can't do better.'

'What've you got to bet?' A nasty grin spread across his face.

'Watch yourself, Ivan,' the other guard warned. 'The prince won't want her damaged.'

'Mind your own business, Lyam.'

'Just so's I don't have to cover your hind end, friend, when the prince comes hollerin'.'

Ivan puffed up his chest. 'Never mind him,' he told Jilian. 'Let's just say you and I have a private understanding.'

The princess gave him an enigmatic smile. 'So what's your tale?'

'Fish isn't the half of it. Won't eat soup either.'

Are we talking about the same man? Jilian thought. 'Why not?' she asked aloud.

The guard cocked his head sideways. 'He's your brother. Something to do with an incident twenty years ago. Poured soup all over the king.'

We can't be talking about the same man – can we?

'Anyway, now we're low on supplies like I mentioned and the cook tries to stretch the food a little.' He chuckled. 'Picture this. The prince has a terrible temper, right?'

'Right,' said Jilian, meanwhile thinking, he does?

'The cook's afraid he's going to lose his head, but he figures it's better than slow starvation while no one eats – 'ceptin' the prince, of course.'

'Of course.'

'So he wants to apologize by puttin' this note on the silver dinner-tray. Figures he'll soften up the prince before he eats.'

'Your shift, Ivan,' Lyam called from the alcove.

'Yeah, I know. Go warm up a wench for me.'

'Find your own, you lazy bugger.' He turned, climbed a few stairs, and stopped. 'Ivan, you're going too far. Don't come ask me for protection later.'

'You worry more than my mother, Lyam.' The warning must have bothered him though because he frowned and lowered his voice. 'There's the prince sittin' in his padded chair doin' some princely thing. I'm just inside the door, protectin' his highness. Along comes the dinner-tray.'

'"Over there",' he says and waves a hand without looking up.

'The cook clanks the dishes when he sets them down. Poor fool freezes stiff as a dead bird 'cause he knows the prince don't abide clumsiness either.'

'Another one of those long-ago incidents with the king,' Jilian said, as if she had any inkling of what this man was referring to.

'Right, you got it. So the prince must've been in a good mood. All he does is let out one of those tolerant, put-upon sighs and he says, "One of the worst things about this absurd war is I keep losing my help. Go away before I have your hand chopped off." The cook heaves a relieved breath and starts to leave.

'And then the prince sees the tureen of soup with a note. He picks it up and reads it aloud just to be sure everyone knows why the cook is going to die.'

'He's going to die for a few words on paper?' Jilian asked. However, she realized that sort of thing happened often in the capital.

'No, for the soup. We were discussin' eating habits, remember? By the Sisters, half-breed, are you really that slow-witted?'

'Only when I'm hungry.'

'Huh,' Ivan grunted.

'What'd the letter say?'

'Nothing much.' The guard stood a bit straighter and added a haughty note to his voice. 'It went something like this. "My humblest apologies for serving you my finest soup. With The Cliffs on half-rations, I have been unable to secure supplies and therefore have had to concoct what I could from diminishing private sources."

'Well, the prince does not live as the rest of us do. He threw the bowl at the wall. "That's what I think of your soup!" he shouts. "I do not eat soup. Ever! See that you find supplies or next time it will be your head that shatters."

'The cook meanwhile stands in the doorway with his eyes as big as royal coins. The instant he hears the words "next time" he figures he's safe and backs into the hall.

'After the cook's gone, the prince is still ravin'. "No one puts me on half-rations!" he yells. "I pay plenty for the best food in the capital." This goes on, but he calms down after a time. Finally, he looks up and says to me, 'Find me something I can chew on.'

'As I'm digging around in the kitchen, I'm thinkin' the prince's connections must be dryin' up if the cook is desperate enough to risk his wrath. That spells trouble for you, me, your friend down there, mine upstairs. Everyone.' He pointed at Jilian and himself, then spread his hands to encompass the others. 'I'm thinkin' you might be able to help me. And I could help you,' he added meaningfully.

'I see,' Jilian said, but she was less and less sure that she did.

Lyda had lived in mountains all her life, but she'd never seen anything like the high plateau where she now stood. Peaks rose in the far distance on either side. In between the air was thin and the vegetation sparse.

She should have been happy to be so close to the Sacred Sisters. Instead despair weighed her down. She missed the lush greenery of her home moutains. She dreaded what she must ultimately face at the end of this seemingly luckless journey.

Here was not harsh beauty. It was desolation and want laid bare. This was not a mission of healing. It was a voyage through pain which led to agony.

And Ceeley . . . What could she do for the girl? As the child's night-time mumblings grew more fierce, Lyda's resolve to struggle toward an unnamed goal weakened. Something ate at the girl, something beyond the gruesome destruction of all her kinfolk, something beyond Lyda's ability to cure. Ceeley needed comfort and tranquillity, not further hardship.

And now this summons to leave the others behind. Lyda had hugged Ceeley and Willam as if she might never see them again. She berated herself for alarming them, but was powerless to squelch her own rising panic.

It seemed the elves had taught her to be at peace with herself and now they would do the opposite. Even their opening words, spoken in soothing tones, chilled her soul.

'We have brought you here to show you a terrible thing.'

Her heart pounded in her ears. 'And what must I do about this terrible thing?'

'You will know once you have seen it.'

The elf was gone, replaced by images too dreadful to remember in their entirety. Before this moment, Lyda had seen only the aftermath of Alvaria's devastation. She had aided the refugees who lived to flee, rather than stood by helplessly watching the ill-fated casualties.

Here were men, women, children, all re-formed and

molded into something so much larger but so much less than themselves. Giant monsters emerged from the essence of living breathing flesh. Their will was that of the elfwitch; their minds were lost in alchemy. They came from all races and towns, suffering the one constant. Their new shape was born in misery and maintained through suffering.

Lyda couldn't keep the particulars in her mind. It was not important to remember which individual had been twisted to which troll. Rather, she understood that it was critical to return them to their rightful form if she could, but she must release them from the elfwitch at all costs.

She was alone when the vision ended.

Lyda went down from her barren place of solitude.

Willam and Celia looked up from their game, their faces anxious. Ceeley rose first and ran to meet her with arms outstretched. 'Mama-Lyda, Mama-Lyda. You're safe!'

Lyda smoothed the child's curls while smiling over her head at Willam. 'Yes, I'm safe.' And very lucky to be alive, she thought. 'We must go. There's work to be done.'

Silently, her husband and daughter resumed their journey.


The wall around the Tower of the Forty-nine halted Wanton Tom as effectively as if it were an army of archers sending down a rain of arrows. He looked from the ordinary-seeming wood, to Grosik, and back to the barrier, then simply lost himself in wool-gathering.

He wasn't considered friendly by human standards – and he was downright antisocial by dwarven reckoning – so keeping company with Grosik had suited him just fine for years. The dragon offered occasional conversation and steady transportation. What else did a mercenary need that he couldn't tend to himself?

Tom had never asked Grosik's reasons for putting up with him. As dragons went, the Old Grouch was atypical. That much was obvious. Dragons were solitary beasts who seldom tolerated shared quarters with their own kind, let alone humans. A dragon didn't need anyone (unless you counted mating . . . for which another male of any species would be useless) or anything.

So how had the Old Grouch come to be here risking his life for an inferior man and his daughter?

'Tom?'

How had the dragon come to feeling so much affection for Ginni that he would willingly risk his freedom for her?

'Tom.'

Maybe it was like the legendary relationship between virgins and unicorns.

'Tom!'

The mercenary jumped. 'What are you shouting about?' he whispered. 'I thought we were trying to pull this off by way of stealth?'

The dragon snorted. 'Then why have you been standing there staring at the wall? Did you expect Ginni to come running out, cloak in hand?'

'Well, it's a thought,' Tom answered, in an attempt to cover his confusion. What was he doing? Oh, yeah, considering the angles. Their information was good, coming from Abadan himself. There'd be a pay-back, but Tom would handle that later. In its way this rescue was going to be even tougher than challenging the elfwitch. Powerful as she was, there was only one of her. The witches had their weak spots, but they were smart enough to recognize the strength of numbers.

Tom bent down to yank a stray twig out of the snow-covered ground and began chewing.

'Tom.'

The mercenary thought back to Roslin's curse the night he left her. He wondered if she'd twisted his fate ever since to bring him to this moment, or whether it was just the inborn result of what a man did for a daughter in a fix.

'Tom, you're doing it again.'

Either way, he'd have the brief remainder of his life to manage whatever new curses the Forty-nine were about to shower upon him.

Someone yanked the twig out of Tom's mouth. He spat on the ground. 'What was that bitter—'

'Probably mugwort,' said Grosik. 'If you keep letting your mind wander away, I'm going to have to retire you to a rocking-chair and a roaring fire.'

'Huh?'

'Has the maiden taken your tongue along with your trousers?'

'What maiden?'

'That's better.' The dragon sounded satisfied. 'There's no maiden, Tom. Just you, staring at that wall as if you expect to burn a hole in it.' He tsked quietly. 'You've got to scale it. No other way. And Tom, your sword-arm's usually your strength, but you've got to remember to hold onto your wits. The magic out here is child's play compared to what's on the inside. *These* wards are meant to confuse *everyone*. In there, the hags will be looking for *you*.'

Tom grunted as if he'd been hit in the gut. 'Thanks for the reminder. Any other jolly thoughts?'

'It'll be just like the grand opening of a whorehouse, more pretty ladies than you can service.'

He thought of Forty-nine witches dressed in sheer lace veils and grimaced. 'Strike that. Don't give me any more thoughts. Just let me run the plan through. I climb the wall, cross the grounds, find where they're keeping her. You circle overhead, come down wnen you see us outside, and swoop us away.'

Grosik nodded. 'That's it.'

'Sounds like it's got a beggar's chance in a grave-yard.'

'I'm aware that you prefer not to skulk around.'

'Sure, but this is Ginni and these are witches.'

'Got anything better?'

Wanton Tom stared hard at the dragon. 'You know I haven't. But this is Ginni and she hasn't exactly been her-self lately. And that's not even mentioning the witches.'

'You're repeating yourself, Tom. Don't worry,' the dragon assured him in a voice meant to do the reverse. 'They should love you after all you've done for them in the past.'

'Oh, you mean corrupt the best apprentice to wander their way in generations. Yeah, they've always appreci-ated that. Why is it that every time I talk to you these days I end up feeling worse? Just wish me luck.'

'What kind? Dragon or human?'

'Never mind.' Before he could lose his nerve, Tom threw the rope over the top of the wall. He made sure the grappling-hook caught securely and began to climb. Behind him bare branches rattled in the wind as the great beast took flight.

# Chapter 10

## CANNON FODDER

There was no sane reason for anyone (let alone a runaway goatboy) to climb the mountain at the top of the world. Only those seeking divine inspiration would dare move so close to the Sisters. Few made the hard journey in summer; none but the arrogant and the desperate made it in winter.

Goatboy thought he was the latter and feared he might be the former.

Up here the very air could kill. Light winds could suddenly whip into gales that snatched grown men from the steep trails – and Sister help the insolent fool trapped among the iced and treeless crags when a true storm blew in. Even for people accustomed to living far above the sea, ordinary breathing became shallow and fast.

The horror of the trolls' transformation wiped all else from Goatboy's mind. He came to the foothills and began the ascent. He who had lived all his life in the gentle valley now struggled to succeed where many failed.

Corpses left to spend eternity exposed to the primal elements warned him away.

Still he climbed. He needed pardon for his part in the transformation. He had not willed their punishment. Yet he had stood by afraid and made no move to stop it. That Tabor and Theron would have rejoiced in his torture made no difference. The rightness of a situation lay not in what others would do, but in what one did oneself.

He had wrapped himself in layers of clothing, leathers and furs, goat-hair knitted tight to block the wind, goat-hide cured well to repel the snow. Hands and feet he covered once, then twice, then a third time to honor the three Great Sisters.

More likely to pay homage to the twenty great fingers and toes, Notti thought, giddy with exhaustion. This was no attitude with which to approach the Sisters. He might as well jump from the nearest precipice into a snow-bank and lie down for death as ask forgiveness with such lack of piety. He forced his mind into a properly somber state and stepped forward into the wind.

His shoes were not suited to the terrain. They were meant for striding across deep snow in flat plains, not hardened ice. He slipped and slid his way up the approach. Again and again he was saved by frantically thrusting his stolen knife into the mountainside.

Notti lost sight of the trail. Somewhere, somewhen the wind had picked up. The snow blew horizontally now and he could not see his hand spread wide-fingered before his face.

He took a dispirited step. Goatboy didn't know whether he headed up or down. It suddenly didn't matter, for he'd fallen on his rear and was tumbling. Downhill? He must be moving down. There was nothing to grab onto. No trees grew this high up. He'd dropped the knife.

The Sisters had rejected him.

He slammed against the mountain and stopped moving. Slowly his mind grappled with the need to do something. Walk or die. It was the byword of all who climbed the Great Peak. Forgiveness had no part in it. Atonement was irrelevant to the wind and rock.

Without life there could be no atonement. He must live.

Clumsily, he rose to stand. There was no pain, only numbness. Fingers, toes, legs, arms, all responded as if another master pulled the strings.

The Sisters may well have spurned him, but he had not given up. He would triumph.

In the meanwhile, Goatboy carefully picked his way. He told himself stories as he had always done and he spoke to his one-time friend the dragon so that he might put order to his world.

'Just as there are no plants on the Great Peak, there are no animals. Why struggle to dig roots into frozen rock? Why fight to cling to a mountain where the winds can topple away even the most determined of beasts?

'There are many more hospitable climates,' he told his dragon friend. 'Droughts and fires, floods and rock-slides are of little moment against the trials of the Great Peak.'

So did Goatboy endure, traveling down toward the place where he had left his favorite goat. As the surrounding seemed more familiar, he sought out the refuge he had prepared before the ascent. It was a tiny cave, barely more than an indentation to block the wind.

He expected to find it around this bend. Or was it the next? He turned again. The slope wasn't as flat as he remembered. Should it be this steep?

He circled and circled, assuming any motion might at least keep him alive. The wind still bit at his cheeks and nose.

Someone screamed in agony. A plaintive bleating echoed in response. His goat? Notti peered through the blinding snow. The goat should be in the cave. How could she be out here, hobbled as she was?

The goat breathed warm, fetid breath across his face. It was the most wonderful scent he'd ever smelled. His useless hands patted her face. She nibbled at his fingertips, pulling him forward.

He half fell, half crawled into the cave and she settled in after him to take the brunt of the wind. Why hadn't he found a way to block the entrance? Hubris – he had not thought he would need it.

Notti lay curled against the goat until he began to shiver uncontrollably. If his body knew enough to manage this, he would live. He leeched the animal's warmth the same way the elfwitch drained the essence from her victims.

Later when he woke in the cave with the storm quieted and the night clear, feeling and reason had returned. He recognized the recurrent cries of pain for his own. Fingers, toes, and face were blackened by exposure. Likely he had been stingy in cloaking his extremities and should have honored not a mere three but all seven Sisters.

He breathed in and out, in and out. Pain and frostbite would not kill him . . . yet.

Notti patted his goat in thanks. She was as stiff as a statue.

Dead.

Instantly he doubted his newfound faith that he would survive. With quavering voice and shaking hands, he stuttered his goodbyes and smoothed the goat's fur. His fingers hit hard wood. The block he used to hobble her and keep her safe inside the cave was still attached to her leg.

Perhaps the Sisters blessed him after all.

\*     \*     \*

Jilian awoke to keys clanging in a cell door. 'Let's go, man. Time for a visit with the prince,' said the guard.

'Huh, wha . . . ?' Maarcus sounded sick or drugged.

'Lyam, come over 'ere in case he's up to mischief.'

I should be so lucky, Jilian thought, but knew otherwise.

'All right, all right, Ivan. Keep your pants on.' He joined his companion and together they tried to get Maarcus to stand and walk.

'Guess the food doesn't agree with him,' said Lyam.

'Maybe we should ask cook for the recipe?'

'Maybe.'

Laughter echoed off the cell walls.

Slapping his face got no reaction, so they tried letting him stand on his own. He collapsed in a boneless heap.

'He's out,' said Lyam. 'We gotta carry him.'

The Shoreman's face was bloodless and his body limp as they dragged him past.

Ivan paused and gave Jilian the grin that made her bile rise. 'Be back for you soon, princess.'

'I won't stop thinking of you the whole time you're gone,' she told him – and she meant it.

Feet thudded on the stairs as they climbed. 'Bangin' his shins pretty bad, don't you think, Lyam?'

'Yep,' he agreed. 'Magine we are.' They continued up and out of earshot, Maarcus' bruised legs thumping in time.

Left completely alone, Jilian once again took up exploring in hopes of discovering anything that might help her escape. She had no weapons and nothing that could be turned into one. Nonetheless, she was determined to find something. She peered and probed until they returned.

Maarcus showed no signs of torture; nor any signs of

improvement. They locked him in his cell and opened hers.

'Your turn,' Lyam announced.

'You're back sooner than expected,' she said. 'I thought torture took longer.'

'The prince is a regular model of swiftness, he is,' the guard said, not confirming or denying her charge. 'Let's go.'

Thinking of their casual mistreatment of Maarcus, Jilian went along as instructed.

It could have been easy to forget the dungeon once Jilian entered the house proper. The rooms boasted comfortable chairs adorned in rich brocades and a number of extraordinary hangings.

By comparison, the castle was dismally furnished. Obviously the palace had been stripped to accommodate this secret address. But how had Nikolis managed it?

'Welcome to the private family quarters, sister.' His voice was rough, as if he hadn't used it in a while.

Taking her time and using every bit of aristocracy she possessed, Jilian turned slowly to face him.

And still the sight of him made her gasp. Her brother had aged thirty or forty years. 'Nikolis?'

'You flatter me.'

She moved closer. The man looked very much like Nikolis gone to seed. There were Nik's same square jaw and piercing eyes buried beneath some thirty years and a lifetime of indulgence.

Apparently, he was just as taken aback. As she studied him, he rubbed his jaw and stared blatantly at her. He nodded to himself as if a decision had been made then stepped back to wave his guards through the door.

'You resemble my dear departed older sister. You're

prettier, of course. She had too much of our mother, while you have what, elven blood?'

He made it sound like something perverse. 'So I'm told,' Jilian answered without apology.

'And your brother, the Dragon Prince,' he said with a sneer, 'is he as fine-boned?'

Jilian had never considered herself or Nik as fine-boned, though they ran a little tall for humans and they seemed to age a trifle slower. 'He would not be mistaken for female,' she said.

'Ah, sisterly protectiveness. Unusual in our line, but I approve.' He tsked sadly. 'Too bad there wasn't much of it among Father's first family. Perhaps your mother had the civilizing influence ours lacked.'

'I doubt that,' Jilian said drily, wondering if he had heard the full truth of who her mother was.

'No? Interesting.' He lifted a glass of brandy and took a sip. 'I assume that old, narrow-minded doctor or the humorless magician provided you with our complete lineage. There are a few of the younger brood scattered about. I am Hadrian, of course, King Tabor's fifth child and the only remaining legitimate issue.' Something dark in his tone hinted that perhaps he had been party to the demise of one or more of his siblings, and might be willing to reprise his role.

He came closer. 'You're quite beautiful.' His voice held a slippery quality she didn't like. 'You'd look lovely in one of mother's gowns.'

Jilian didn't bother to hide her disgust. 'I primp for no man and certainly not for my half-brother.'

'Oh, don't pretend to be so appalled. You've lived with your brother all your life.'

Apparently he hadn't believed the stories about Nikolis' previous form, not that she could blame him. The rumors were variably extreme in some cases and utterly accurate in others.

'I could show you things you've only dreamt of.' He tried to smile fetchingly, but it only showed off his fleshy jowls.

'Such as rotting in a dungeon?'

'There is that,' he admitted. 'But other . . . things as well. I've lived in this city all my life and have uncovered provocative secrets.'

'Indeed.' She turned her back to him. 'The only provoking I'd engage in may not work to your advantage.'

He came around to face her, his expression nasty as he let her see a glimpse of the other man who lurked just beneath the mask. 'I can be very . . . persuasive.'

'I'm sure.' Jilian's voice held its own steel.

'There is the matter of your traveling companion.'

'Yes, there is,' Jilian said, hoping her concern for Maarcus didn't show.

'Lyam, there's been a change of plans. Give the princess 'Phelia's room.'

The man's eyebrows went up but he said nothing.

'I'll look forward to our next meeting.' Hadrian walked her to the door.

Jilian dipped her head, not trusting herself to speak. Lyam moved down the hall and she followed him, clear in her understanding she was still a prisoner – not ill-treated at present, but a prisoner nonetheless.

Prince Nikolis rode his horse with visible discomfort. He could not walk, plain and simple. However unwelcome it was to be a commander ill-at-ease sitting a horse, it was far worse to be a leader lost among the infantry before the battle was joined.

There'd been precious little time for lessons – or any

sort of preparations. The trolls approached relentlessly. Reports of the random havoc left in their wake had reached every corner of The Cliffs. Panic was rising. He had to confront the trolls now if he expected to have an army willing to fight.

Two weeks ago, he'd hoped to defeat the elfwitch's army. Now he merely strove to slow them down enough that the refugees might flee elsewhere before the trolls ransacked the capital.

Nikolis kept to the outside of the troop, lest he accidently jostle the men. 'Dress up that line,' he called uselessly. Someone had found a wine cellar last night and they'd toasted each other's courage far too many times before the prince discovered it. A good percentage of the men were hung over and not a few were still drunk.

We're doomed, he thought. I've come into power simply to watch men die. He wished he'd been able to convince Wanton Tom to serve as his second. There was hardly one among this rabble who knew which way to thrust his sword.

He took up position at the front of his troops. Prudence might dictate a safer position, but wariness would not get this army past the outside wall of The Cliffs. He raised his arm, sword in hand. Beside him, a man blew a horn and another tapped a drumhead. In slow and jolting pace, they proceeded down through the town and out into the blowing snow.

After a while, Nikolis grew used to the clashing of arms and shouts of dismay. So long as no one was killed, there was no point in checking the squabbling until they reached the battlefield.

It was an odd undertaking, going into Alvaria's territory. Though sworn to do the elves' bidding, Lyda nonetheless felt ill at ease. Exhausted, she bowed her head and put her shoulders to it as if she were walking into a strong wind, though the gusts had dropped away to nothing much to speak of.

Willam and Ceeley followed behind, one bone-weary and the other bouncing as if she'd been introduced to a new game. The girl dodged and parried, or swatted at things that Lyda couldn't be sure were altogether fanciful. She preferred to believe they were part of the child's imagination, but doubted any whimsy existed in this barren land. The few bushes seemed twisted, stunted, and strange in color.

The river seemed to appear from nowhere. It was a welcome relief at first, a more tangible reminder of life. Yet it was odd. What river was this? It should have been Tomar's River, but she knew that it wasn't. Could it be the Elven River? Had they travelled so far? The three instinctively separated and took to exploring the bank.

'Mama-Lyda,' Ceeley called out.

Lyda paused with a cupped hand of water raised to her mouth. 'Yes?'

'Mama-Lyda, what's that floating in the river?'

Lyda thought better of drinking untested water. She let it run through her fingers and splash to the ground. 'I don't know, child. Let me see.' She sidled down to where Celia stood on a low cliff. 'If you fall in from here, you'll be knee-deep in the river.'

'But I won't fall,' the girl answered sensibly. 'I'll stay right here. And the thing is right there,' she added. 'In case you forgot, Mama-Lyda.' She lowered her voice and spoke in a polite whisper. 'Grown-ups sometimes get distracted.'

Lyda followed the line of Ceeley's finger. She squinted to focus on the spot Ceeley pointed out and found nothing unusual. The object was as veiled to Lyda as the creatures the girl had played with for the past hour or two. Hoping to discover whatever Ceeley saw, she shaded her eyes and continued peering out into the current and over to the opposite bank.

'You can't see it, can you?' the child asked in a quiet voice.

'No, I'm afraid not.'

'Do you think I've lost a few pegs? That's what my da used to say about some addle-brained folks. "Lost their pegs!"'

She put an arm around the child. 'Absolutely not. I'd say you have more than your share of pegs. I've seen a few who don't, remember.'

Celia relaxed against her. 'Yes, I guess you have. I wouldn't want to be like that.'

She squeezed the girl closer. 'Don't you worry.'

'We're in for a marvelous sunset,' Willam called from above them. 'Come on up!'

Lyda stood and offered her hand to Ceeley.

'What are you two whispering about?' Willam teased.

'Oh, you know, girl things,' Lyda said, as they ascended. Willam blushed a pale pink. 'Oh, I'm sorry.'

Ceeley giggled. 'Oh, Papa-Willam. Sometimes you are so silly.'

'The girl's right, Willam. We were just talking and looking into the river.' She paused. 'I've missed the river in our travels.'

'Yes,' Willam agreed and there seemed more emotion in the one word than he normally spoke in a hundred. They joined him on the cliff overlooking the water. After a while, he said, 'There's somethin' wrong with that river.'

'It's not as fast as the Queen's River,' Lyda said.

'True, but it's not just that. There's somethin' else.'

Lyda's misgivings grew. First the child, now her husband. Why didn't she feel what they did? Hadn't the elves helped her to see beyond the surface? She took a step backward. Suddenly she knew the elfwitch had led her here – which the elves she had so dutifully obeyed were in league with – 'Willam! Ceeley! Move away from—' She didn't get to finish her sentence. Celia grabbed her foster parents, one per hand, and pulled with surprising strength until all three jumped feet first into the sluggish water.

Remembering Celia's question about the addle-brained, Lyda said a quick prayer to protect the young and the foolish. What had come over the child?

The water was surprisingly warm. It felt like swimming in a shallow lake . . . or blood. Efforts to head for shore were utterly wasted. The river corrected for each stroke and returned them to the central flow. Lyda had no fear of drowning. The water buoyed them as the current carried them where it would.

Willam, who didn't know how to swim, was strangely the calmest of the three by far. He seemed to be smiling as he drifted along.

Ceeley fought the hardest, splashing and thrashing and having no effect whatsoever. Finally, she gave in to it. 'It's no use, is it? We'll go where the elfwitch wants us to.'

'We're bound to see the elfwitch and the realm of transformations,' Willam sang.

Lyda didn't need to see her husband's face to know the expression would be other-worldly. His voice and words made it quite plain he had misplaced a few of his pegs. 'Willam, what's gotten into you?' Lyda asked, not sure she wanted to know.

He floated on his back, totally at ease. He raised his hand from the soup around them and pointed to his chest.

'Me, Lyda dear? Why nothing, nothing at all. I'd say, it's the other way around. What have we gotten into? Not, what's gotten into us.' He swirled away from her.

She put her arm out to grab ahold of him but missed. She could not reach him or Ceeley. She looked from one to the next and felt panic rising in her throat.

Wide-eyed and open-mouthed, Ceeley nodded to Lyda. Suddenly her eyes and mouth closed, and her body went limp.

'Celia! Celia!' Lyda's shouts did not rouse the child. But neither did she sink below the surface.

The river . . . no, the elfwitch, did not want her dead. This was somehow the most terrifying thought yet.

'Not to worry, not to worry, lovely Lyda, lovely Lyda,' Willam sang.

He hadn't called her that since the early years of their marriage. It did not comfort her to hear those words now in this unnatural sing-song voice.

'Oh, Willam.'

'Oh, Willam. Oh, Willam,' he echoed. 'Lyda, Willam, Ceeley, floating out to sea-ea, floating out to sea.'

I should hope not. She was afraid to speak the thought aloud for fear he would tell her something else she couldn't bear to hear just now.

Lyda's tears slid down her cheek and mixed with the blood-warm river. The three swirled in their separate eddies, each unable to influence the others.

It was a disaster from the start. The instant Tom touched the wall, he felt eyes on his back. Strange fears such as he hadn't felt since his maiden battle threatened to consume him. 'We have to turn back, reconnoiter. They know we're here,' he whispered to Grosik.

'And give them that much more time to prepare their defenses?'

The dragon was right. It was now or never. Maybe this was just a general warding, not directly set against Wanton Tom the mercenary. Then he might yet have a slim chance. He reached the top of the wall and quickly took in the surroundings. The huts were arranged in concentric rings as he'd been told. Ginni would be in one of the inner circles for best protection. He lowered himself to the ground.

Suddenly the irrational fears ceased. He breathed a sigh of relief even though he felt worse. They had something special planned for him, he was sure of it.

Despite the hour and the cold, Ginni sat in the courtyard as pretty as you please. She was humming quietly to herself and knitting.

Humming maybe, but knitting? This was not a good sign. Still, he'd know his daughter's face anywhere.

'Ginni?' he whispered.

She looked up at the sound. Gone was the fearsome glare he knew as Roslin's. In its place was something even more frightening, a complete lack of recognition.

Her eyes widened as he stepped closer and her mouth opened to scream. He rushed forward to cover her mouth, then stopped in mid-stride when he realized there was no need. She seemed unable to speak.

A woman stepped out from behind the silent girl. Something tickled the back of his brain. They'd met before, many years back. Was this Roslin's nemesis who'd plotted her dismissal? Outraged at Ginni's condition, Tom lost all fear. 'What have you done to my daughter?' he demanded.

'No more than she asked for.'

'I doubt that.'

The witch shrugged, unconcerned with what he thought. 'She was troubled by her mother. This is no longer the case.'

'I'll bet.'

Through it all Ginni's expression merely went back to its former placidity as she returned to her knitting.

Suddenly it all went confusing. An unexpected wind from Grosik's great, beating wings scattered dead leaves and twigs as he landed and roared a challenge.

Tom realized the dragon must have decided no sign was as much a signal as the proper one. The mercenary tried to turn so that he could snatch Ginni and flee, but found that he could not. His legs seemed rooted in place. All sound swirled inside a bell-jar.

'Ginni, it's Wanton Tom. Run to Grosik. Run to the dragon, Ginni! Run!'

She only looked at him.

The total absence of understanding broke his heart.

'It's useless, Grosik!' he shouted, not knowing whether Grosik could hear him. 'They have us. Save yourself!'

Grosik's wings flapped fruitlessly. He moved as if his wings were pinned in a myriad of different places all up and down their length. For the moment Tom forgot all about his plight and focused his will on the dragon. If wishes alone . . . He almost laughed at the old saying, which ended, 'Then dragons would fly.'

The witches must have underestimated the dragon's claws. He struck at the unseen bonds with his back feet. Lightening flashed in the darkened sky when claws met the arcane magic. Again and again, the dragon reached out until one wing sprang free. After that it was inevitable. The witches could not hold him. In a moment, the second wing fluttered loose and Grosik was off the ground.

He glanced once toward the place where Ginni and

Tom remained captive. With a mournful sound, he rose into the air.

He'll be back, Tom thought, with reinforcements. But who would the solitary dragon find when his only two companions were beyond his reach?

Outwardly impassive, the Revered Novice watched the entire strange episode. Inwardly she felt like a cauldron of turmoil. She was sure she owed these witches her life, but a small part of her argued this assertion was nonsense. The man who tried to save her had sacrificed himself on her behalf, yet she couldn't fathom why. Still he seemed to know her, even if she didn't know him.

The dragon was an even bigger puzzle. She almost thought she might have played with a dragon long, long ago, but this seemed as improbable as the possibility that she had ever lived anywhere but here among the Forty-nine Towers.

The man stared and stared at her. Disappointment stronger than any she had ever known shadowed his face. It changed to complete outrage when he faced Revered Mother.

Ginni found him fascinating. She couldn't remember having ever felt such strong emotions toward anyone or anything and she wondered if this was true of all women. Were only men this excitable? What a nuisance it must be. She'd have to ask the Mother later when all the fervor died down.

Only when they took him away did she feel a twinge of regret. He seemed so sincere that it would be a shame if they hurt him. As nice as they were to Revered Novice herself, she knew they could harden themselves when they felt threatened. It was the way of all mothers.

Revered Novice supposed she herself would have to learn the trait one day.

But for now, she had knitting to tend to. She bent back to her task.

Nikolis understood the trolls better than any of his men, but what could he tell them? That only so much could be ascribed to intelligence was no comfort when everyone knew how few people survived whenever the beasts attacked.

He had hoped he might win by organizing the assault, because he didn't think the beserkers were capable of ambush. He didn't expect humans to lead the trolls' onslaught.

He was wrong.

He was wrong on all counts, wrong on everything that mattered.

Archers caught the troops well before they reached the scouts' reported sightings of the trolls. His front line was down and bleeding in the snow. His men fought but he needed two of his own for every one of the trolls. The changeling beasts were slow and stupid, but they'd been created to destroy.

It was almost worse when a soldier succeeded in killing one. The battlefield was littered with steaming bodies collapsing in on themselves. The obvious magic unnerved the men, distracted them from their duty. Not a few simply ran away.

Reeling from the weight of his looming failure, Nikolis rallied his men and urged them forward. No use. The trolls were on them before they could gather a defense. Fire burned all around them. He shouted orders, but he might as well have been standing inside a glass jar.

Quickly, Nikolis called retreat. The handful of men

followed him, crouching or crawling to stay under the smoke. He covered the horse's nose, but she balked and fought. When she stepped on one of the men, he let go of her rein and wished her Sisters' speed.

A wall of fire appeared from nowhere and nearly blocked escape. Nikolis threw down his cloak and kicked dirt to smother the flames. Others jumped up to join in once they could see what was happening. Together they managed to clear a space and dive through.

Safe for the moment, Nikolis called a halt. Mumbling dispiritedly, the men straggled to a stop.

The prince squared his shoulders and surveyed the remaining soldiers. He was utterly dismayed as he counted up the casualties. The elfwitch had taken well more than half his troops and completely demoralized what was left.

He winced inwardly as he thought back to the day on the parapet. Where that earlier bunch had been boisterous and invigorated, this one was subdued and beaten down. Here were men who could barely gather the courage to look past the ends of their swords for fear a troll stood ready to rend them limb from limb.

Nikolis didn't know what he planned to say, only that he needed to stop this leeching of their wills. 'You've done a good job, men.'

'Don't have very high standards, do you, sire?' muttered one of the men.

'My standards are higher than you'd expect. We won't beat her this way, but we can slow her down.'

'Slow death, there's an honorable way to go.'

'There is nothing honorable about this war,' Nikolis said. 'The elfwitch doesn't know honor. We'll have to find a way to remain honorable while fighting dishonor.'

'Bugger honor and dishonor both!' someone shouted.
'Here, here!' another joined in.

This isn't going to inspire them, Nik thought. He
cleared his throat and dry-swallowed. 'I don't have to
tell you it's going badly. We all suspected the odds
were less than even.' He exaggerated a shrug. 'So now
we know the odds. But we're not here to place bets.'
Nikolis felt an old anger surge within. He nurtured it
and let it inspire all who heard him.

'We are here because we are men and this is a just
cause. We are here because your brothers and fathers,
sisters and daughters have been treated worse than yesterday's refuse. They have been twisted into a form
abhorrent to human and dwarf, to a form many elves
themselves would not sanction. The elfwitch will have
us all bent into trolls, a form no beast should endure.'
His voice rose as he spoke, so that by the end the booming
volume seemed augmented by magical means.

'This must not stand. Evil cannot be allowed to exist
unchallenged.'

Nikolis stopped to take a breath and found he had
nothing more to say. He faced his men and was shocked
to see each and every one standing at attention, his once
pitiful soldiers re-formed into a proud army. They were
as prepared to fight as they would ever be with so many
of them already littering the battlefield.

The prince nodded and the men shouted spontaneously.
'Three cheers for the Dragon Prince!'
'Hip, hip, hooray!'
'Hip, hip, hooray!'
They surged back onto the bloody ground and Nikolis
could not have been more honored. They had chosen to
fight the trolls, knowing their chances, knowing who and
what they fought.

The prince's newfound pride was short-lived. An archer caught him unawares, burying an arrow deep into the flesh behind the target's shoulder-blade. Nikolis cried out and fell to the ground.

# Chapter 11

## CAPTIVE AUDIENCE

Maarcus turned away from the scrying bowl in disgust. Quietly and without passion, Walther continued to describe each man's death so that the physician might know the full extent of the battle. 'What was I thinking to agree to this?' he said to Abadan. 'What were you thinking that you would risk your own death to use the forbidden magic? What good is it to know they're being slaughtered while we sit in our soft-cushioned "oversight position."' It came out sounding like a foul word and when the physician thought about it, he decided it deserved to. 'We are cowards!'

'No,' the magician told him, still studying the scene before him. 'No, we are not. In some ways, what we do is much more difficult. We are here to observe and learn. With each of the witch's mutilations and tortures, we learn so that we can prevent the next one.'

Sweat dripped from the dwarf's face. 'By the Sisters, I hope so,' he murmured. 'No fate can be more horrid than this.'

Beside him, Zera's man, Harmon, seemed in shock. His eyes were wide and his face was leached of color. Stiff hands gripped the edge of the table.

'But we live!' shouted Maarcus. 'How can you be so callous?'

Abadan shook his head and looked up at the physician. His expression was full of pain and regret. There was no anger in it, only resolve. 'We do what we must. We could not have prevented this massacre in any case, not without more time. We live, yes, but we live to stop the evil.' He paused and licked his lips in an uncharacteristic gesture of unease. 'And we live knowing we have watched men die in this war just as we watched them die in the last.'

That was exactly it, Maarcus thought. He had seen enough dying. He'd never had a taste for it and had only barely managed to stomach King Tomar's campaigns by hovering close to the king himself and considering most of the deaths as nameless body counts. He assuaged what guilt he allowed himself to feel by declaring himself a physician, a healer. He'd saved very few lives in that war and it seemed he would rescue even fewer in this one. 'I am too old for this,' Maarcus spoke aloud without meaning too.

'We will always be too old for this,' Abadan told him. 'Yet we are here because others are too young. They deserve their fates even less than we deserve ours.' He moved back to the scrying bowl and whispered a few inscrutable words.

Maarcus watched Abadan watching men die. Was he a coward for standing back from the front lines? Or was he a coward because he'd rather die than stand by while others did? His hip, injured in the war so long ago, ached worse and worse these days. It seemed to mark the final hours of the One Land, for they fought not just the superstitious inborn hatred of another people from realms near or far; they battled an evil that made the other seem petty and insignificant.

The physician forced himself to face the devastation without flinching. If he could not bear the battle from a distance, how could he expect the soldiers to bear it first-hand?

He did not need Walther's mumbled description to know the scene was familiar to any who have witnessed war – blood spurted from wounds the injured barely acknowledged, as they themselves fought to protect their fellows and battle the enemy. The trolls would be a dreadful sight – big, relentless, devastating. But as he imagined their faces, he slowly came to realize they too held the humanity, the elfness or dwarfness of their forebears. They too might be swayed by strong moral argument if they could be released from the witch's spell, if it could be managed without further slaughter. So many ifs, so little hope.

At long last, Nikolis was flying. He soared over the destruction from a great height. The wings he'd yearned to stretch held him aloft. Wonder was tainted by horror, yet he did not return to the ground. He could not bear to give up the splendor of flight.

His men were dying.

Nik looked away. He could glimpse the sea from here. The palace was an insignificant dot within The Cliffs; the city a tiny grain against the shore of the One Land.

Something rocked his shoulder. He twisted to see – and pain overtook him. He plummeted like the wingless man he was.

'Come on, prince, it's all over. Nobody left but you and me, the cowards of the bunch.'

Nikolis forced his eyes open. 'Watch how you speak to your prince, soldier. No one calls me a coward.' He sounded weak and unconvincing, even to himself.

The man nodded. 'As you wish, sire. I won't tell if you won't.'

The prince sat up, wincing as he put weight on his right arm. 'Tell what?'

'This is rich. First I save you. Now I gotta tell you what you missed.' He frowned, plainly skeptical of the prince's ignorance. He shrugged. 'Have it your way. A trifling little arrow wound knocked you so far gone the rest of your troops got ground up into troll-bait while you were nappin".'

'Uh huh. And what about you?'

'Why, I dragged you out of the line of fire and saved your princely rump.'

'Just as likely you're the one who shot that trifling little arrow.'

'Think what you like. It'll just be you and me returning to The Cliffs with a long list of dead men.' He smiled, enjoying the prince's predicament.

'Not if one of us dies along the way,' Nikolis snarled. This man stunk of rank opportunism, if not the elfwitch herself.

'Won't be me. I'm the one with the weapons.' He held up Jilian's knife along with Nik's short-sword. 'I'm just thinking of you. These blades are dangerous for one not skilled in their use.'

'What do you want?' Nikolis asked through clenched teeth.

'Nothin' much. Full provisions and a place for me and my friends that's not crowded with vermin of every stripe.'

'Everyone receives the same rations.'

'But I'll bet some portions are bigger than others.' He slapped Nik's shoulder in a falsely hearty guffaw. 'Isn't that so, prince.'

The prince bit his lip to keep from shouting. 'I wish it were. I'll see what I can do about your living-quarters. There must be an apartment somewhere.'

'I hear there's extra space at the castle.'

He's maneuvering me, Nik thought. Still, we might be able to keep an eye on him there.

'You can announce I'm to be knighted for saving you from certain death.'

'A knighthood! Next you'll want . . .' He let the thought go unspoken. Why borrow more trouble?

'Could be I'll want that too,' the mercenary agreed, as if he knew what the prince was thinking.

'Let's go,' Nikolis said. 'It's a long walk.'

'Not to worry, sire. I've got your horse right over there. You won't mind sharing, will you?'

The prince remained silent as he followed the man to a horse that by all rights should have been dead.

He casually strolled a route intended to take Nikolis through the worst of the aftermath. Corpses and the occasional steaming troll littered the battlefield. Blood still flowed from many of his men's wounds. How long had he been out?

'Too bad we won't be able to take care of the bodies,' said his despicable guide. 'Ah well. I'm sure the elfwitch will put the buggers to good use.'

With heavy heart, he closed his mind to the dead. He had to protect the living now. 'What happened to the trolls?'

'Don't remember that either, huh? I guess you wouldn't. They're gone.'

'Gone where? Headed for The Cliffs?'

He shook his head. 'Don't think so. Maybe the elfwitch called them back.'

This was more disquieting than their defeat. 'But why, when they're so close to . . .' The prince couldn't bear to voice the possibilities.

As they mounted his horse, Nikolis told himself over and over that the battle would have happened just this way whether or not he'd let himself ascend to the skies. She'd planned it from the first.

Try as he might, he didn't believe himself for an instant.


Lyam took Jilian to a well-appointed chamber. He nodded politely and bid her a formal 'good night, princess' as he closed the door behind him.

She might have been visiting distant relatives if not for the lock bolted from the outside.

Relieved that at least Nik hadn't betrayed her after all, Jilian collapsed onto an over-stuffed chair. How could she have ever thought him capable of such heinousness, and why hadn't she paid more attention to Maarcus's repeated questions about the prince?

It all came back to the elfwitch. Alvaria could twist whomever she chose, using more fear than magic. Jilian was no less susceptible than the fleeing refugees. When she thought about it, she realized the elfwitch only needed to remind the princess of her lifetime of treachery and death in order to render her powerless. This was one of the many inner battles Jilian must win if she expected to defeat Alvaria.

Jilian paced, exhausted but unable to sleep. She couldn't help but be struck by the comparison to her stay with Zera. She'd thought herself trapped in the elf's elegant home because of what the elf had expected of her, but in the end she had been free to choose what she would do.

Here she was truly caged, whether in one of her half-brother's dank cells or in more tolerable surroundings. The best treatment she could hope for would be as a perverted plaything. Intolerable as that was, she knew it would be no more than a way-station between here and something more dreadful.

A basin and pitcher sat atop a wash-stand next to the chair. Hating herself for taking advantage of any comforts while Maarcus remained in worse conditions, she couldn't resist the compulsion to cleanse the stench of the past days. She poured water into the pan and dipped in a nearby cloth. The water was surprisingly warm and scented with roses. How did he . . . ? Never mind. Jilian didn't want to know.

She scrubbed the grime from face and neck with misgivings. Hadrian may have temporarily changed his tactics. Just the same, he hadn't given up wanting something from her and he didn't appear to be a man who was often denied.

She pulled off her boots. Fully clothed, she lay down atop the covers. There might well be a nightshirt hung in the wardrobe, but she was repulsed by the thought of wearing it. Hadrian would surely have dressed another hapless woman in it and Jilian didn't want to come within spitting distance of anything he'd touched.

Several hours later, Princess Jilian finally drifted to sleep. She dreamed of dead men. Men who died in battle, men who died at the hands of assassins, men who died of old age. Men she'd known well, men she hadn't known at all. She struggled, tossed, and turned against the tide of bodies. It seemed there was no escaping from the endless swirl of blood.

She awoke with the taste of iron thick on her tongue, but it was not the nightmare that had awakened her. Years of protecting royals from assassinations had taught her to note any slight flux in the air. Sound asleep or wide awake she could focus all her attention on the change as though an alarm tolled in her ears.

She wasn't surprised the door was quietly swinging open. A shape in the doorway smelled of leather and sweat and expensive wine. Overlaying it all was a perfumed musk – applied, no doubt, to mask the others scents.

Hadrian.

He closed the door behind him.

Jilian silently sat up with her back against the headboard, leaving a lump of blankets in her place. She had been without a weapon since the ruffian captured her, but she was not defenseless.

The prince sat down on the bed and leaned over to where he expected her to be. Finding her not there, he began vigorously patting the blankets. 'She couldn't have escaped . . .' he muttered, the words understandable despite the alcoholic slur.

Though she was tempted to let him continue searching, she didn't want to risk raising his anger further. 'Looking for someone?'

'Huh?' He turned in the direction of her voice.

In the near darkness, Jilian caught a shadow shift as his face widened into a smile.

'So you like to frolic. Good.' The words came from deep in his throat. 'I enjoy spirited carousing.'

This was not what she intended. 'I don't engage in such diversions,' she told him matter-of-factly. 'I was merely protecting my skin from those who would do me harm.'

'Rest assured, lady. No harm will come to you –

or your skin – so long as I have something to say about it.' He paused dramatically. When Hadrian spoke again, he sounded much harsher, nastier – and more comfortable as his true self. 'That is, so long as you co-operate.'

'All depends,' Jilian said easily. Contrary to her interest in copulation, she was expert at word play.

'On what?' Hadrian snapped.

'Circumstances.'

'Such as?'

'Whether I'd be inclined to fornicate without coercion.'

'And would you?'

Jilian considered her answer carefully. He was close enough to straddle her if he chose and she'd be hard pressed to get out from underneath his bulk. Finally, she let her voice get throaty. 'It's difficult to say. We've just met.'

'You seem to misunderstand who controls the reins here.' He was losing patience.

The princess kept her silence.

Her half-brother leaned forward. 'I always get what I want,' he whispered. 'It's the one true privilege of royalty.'

'I've found patience is often its own reward.'

He licked his lips. 'I admit anticipation sometimes makes the getting more enjoyable.' He reached out to snatch her arm. 'But this is not one of those times.'

Jilian belatedly wished she'd worn her boots to bed. 'I'm a girl who prefers to see what's going on,' she said, her voice unnaturally husky. She reached out with her free arm, pretending to light a bedside oil-lamp, and swung her leg hard.

He whoofed in pain as she hit him squarely in the groin with her foot. He let go of her and curled into a fetal ball.

Jilian slid off the bed and put her back to the wall. 'It's polite to ask a lady's permission.'

'I ask no one's permission,' he said through clenched teeth. 'Consider this. Maarcus will pay for your effrontery.'

Thinking of Maarcus made Jilian go limp against the wall. There was nothing she could say that would help him.

'Next time, princess, you will yield to me. I won't be nearly as gentle as I have been today.' He sat up on the bed. 'Ivan!' he called.

The door opened again and her jailor entered the room.

'We've been too kind. Take her to join that flaccid excuse for a Shoreman.'

The guard nodded at Prince Hadrian and roughly took her arm. 'Come along, princess.'

Jilian didn't struggle. At least she could see how Maarcus was faring. Together they would find a way free of this misery.

'Oh, Ivan.'

The man stopped instantly and turned back to the prince. 'Sire?'

'You know how much I hate sharing. She's mine. Do you understand?'

Jilian couldn't read the man's expression as he replied in a monotone, 'Yes, sire. I understand.'

As she descended the stairs, Jilian couldn't decide whether the prince had warned Ivan away from raping her – or invited him to take his pleasure.

Celia Sailclan knew the river they floated in was wholly unnatural. Nowhere in these hills could there exist water so warm in the depth of winter. The dwarf had learned to swim in the cold mountain rivers near her home, where the water was as much snowmelt as river. Even in high summer, the children didn't take much coaxing to be called onto the sun-warmed banks.

In contrast, this water caressed and embraced her like her mama and pa as they told her bedtime stories – but underneath was something decayed. It was like the rotting wood in her uncle's beautiful but ill-kept boat.

As proud of her origins as any Sailclan could be, Ceeley couldn't help hating this river. It took over. It filled her with a fear that blocked out all else.

She reminded herself over and over that she was a strong dwarf. She thought she spoke aloud, but it was hard to know. No one answered her call. No one.

Mama-Lyda and Papa-Willam floated in their own swirls, but they could not help her. They were in thrall to the elfwitch. She wanted to save Mama-Lyda and Papa-Wil, she really did, but what could a child do? They would die just as her real parents had because Ceeley couldn't think of the right thing to do. She couldn't think of anything at all.

. . . Ceeley's birthday had started so merry. Today she turned six and nearly the entire village would help her celebrate – or so it seemed.

They started the morning with a game of Bucket Brigade. Instead of water, the buckets were filled with bright streamers. Each person added one to the bucket as they passed it on to the next one. Each placed a small gift among the ribbons. By the time it reached Ceeley, the wood bucket was overflowing with birthday ribbons. Her parents were the last to get it before her.

She clapped her hands and jumped up and down, then dug into the bucket to find her gifts. 'Oh, Mama, Da, they're so wonderful.'

Da tossled her hair. 'Happy Birthday, Celia.'

But her mother was not smiling. She was open-mouthed and staring at something beyond her. 'Trolls! Trolls!' she shrieked.

Her da snatched up Ceeley and her best friend, Rea, and ran. He yanked up a bush and pulled on a trap-door apparently hidden here for just this reason. 'Don't come out,' he told her. 'No matter what!' He stuffed them in, closed the door, and fled.

She heard the screaming. She heard the torture. She wanted to help, but her da had told her to stay where she was. He was always right, wasn't he?

Rea wouldn't wait. She had to see. She had to know. She left Ceeley behind in the dark.

But as the day wore on and the screaming lessened, Ceeley wasn't so sure she could obey her father's rule. Finally, hunger and thirst drove her out into the dead silence. She could not find her family. She could not find Rea. She found only bodies, and . . . pieces.

Except down by the river.

Down by the river, they were put in cages. In minutes that stretched for all time, she saw living, breathing dwarves changed into dead things. It seemed like their very breath was sucked out of them.

More scared than she'd ever thought she could be, she stood rooted like a tree and watched her family die.

In a strange unexpected way, Willam thought the blood river saved them. On the bank, the cold was settling in. Frostbite would have become a problem soon. He'd seen frostbit skin blackened and flaking off in hunks. He'd known an old man who'd lost several fingers and toes when he'd been caught unprotected in a storm.

Willam worried what would become of the three of

them, but he felt his resolve cracking. He'd managed to withstand the human mage, Roslin, easily enough. Then again, the elfwitch made her seem like a bright autumn day that only hinted at the harsh winter to come.

He was surrounded by true evil, like the kind behind the elves' visit to him back when Lyda walked out on him. They'd led him to believe she'd died – simply to torture him. Now for the first time since she'd found him, he wondered if that would have been better than suffer this unknown slow death.

The river took him then. He remembered no more than the warmth of fluid harkening back to the months before birth.

. . . A young Willam tapped on the flimsy door of the witch's hut.

'Come,' whispered the old hag, so quietly that he thought he might have imagined it.

The fading daylight leaked through chinks between the boards. There was no lamp inside and he could barely see. He let his eyes adjust to the dimness and took a cautious step toward the bundle of rags sitting in the corner.

'Yes, what is it?' Her voice seemed much louder than it had from the door.

'I've been told—'

'I don't care what you've been told. What do you want?'

He tried again. 'My wife, she wants to 'ave a child.'

'And what do you want?' the witch repeated.

'I . . . I'd like her to be happy.'

'I don't deal in happiness. Go away.'

'But they said you could . . .'

'I can do many things, but I can't make someone happy. Your wife's got to do that for herself.'

'The baby, we've tried so 'ard. Please.' His voice

broke. He thought he would cry if she turned him away. 'You're our last hope. Please.'

'Closer.' A bony hand poked out of the heap of cloth and motioned him forward.

He approached the hand until he stood next to her. She smelled of rotten fish, which made his stomach roll.

'You said "we." Do you or do you not want a child?'

This time he knew better than to hesitate. 'Yes, I do.'

'Why?'

Willam desperately tried to find the words she wanted to hear, but he couldn't imagine what they might be. Finally he just told her the truth, something he'd never even admitted to himself. ''S difficult to explain,' he began. 'You see, my Lyda sort of 'ad to talk me into it. I wasn't sure I'd know what to do with 'im when he cried and . . .' He trailed off and looked down at the witch's face.

She gave no sign of whether she heard him, but neither did she stop him.

He continued. 'After a time, I began to get all fired up inside. It wasn't just the, um, you know. It was the planning, the feeling that maybe something was bigger than just us two. I was as 'appy as she was when she got with child. And then . . . then she lost the baby.'

And now Willam did cry. He could feel the tears rolling down his cheeks, but he did not wipe them away. Nor did he look to see if the witch listened or not. It no longer seemed important.

'We tried again and again, but each time the same thing. My Lyda was so brave to keep goin', but it was wearin' her out. We thought per'aps the Sisters didn't want us to . . .' He trailed off, not sure what he'd been about to say.

'What if the Sisters have other plans for you?'

'We'll abide it. We'll have to.' What else could he say to a witch who surely must have a more familiar tie to the Sisters than he did.

'You'll abide it, but you won't like it.'

'Now I didn't say that 'xactly.'

'You didn't have to.' The witch rose off her stool. She was shorter than he'd expected.

She moved from her pile of refuse to a low table he hadn't noticed earlier. She kept her back to him as she clattered bottles and muttered under her breath. 'There's no rule that says you've got to like what the Sisters decide. You just have to bear it.' She turned around and thrust a large bottle at him. 'Give your wife one good swallow's worth as soon as the child quickens. Do it every morning until the vessel's empty.'

He took the bottle. 'Thank you.'

She scowled and shook her head. 'Do not thank me. If the Sisters wish it, your child will live.'

Her voice stopped him at the door. 'One final warning. Follow my instructions exactly. Tell no one of this potion. Especially your wife.'

'But how do I get her to take it?'

'Not my concern. One more thing. Do not ever come back here.' Her expression made sure he would not want to.

Lyda did conceive again and Willam devised all manner of ways to sneak the fluid into her each and every day. He hovered and worried and watched, but he said nothing. To her questions, he merely answered that he wanted her to be happy.

Her time drew nearer and nearer and he began to actually hope. The delivery was long and hard, but not unduly so for a first child. Laughing and crying, he began loud words of thanks to the Sisters . . .

They died on his lips when he saw the midwife.

'I'm very sorry,' she said. 'The child . . .' She shook her head.

He felt as if all the air had been forced from his chest. 'And Lyda?' he asked, afraid to hear.

'Your wife will recover.'

He managed to force out enough air to ask, 'What happened?'

The midwife looked truly befuddled. 'The child was perfect. He simply would not breathe.' She shook her head. 'Sometimes it's just the Sisters' will.'

The midwife's words, so close to what the witch had said, hit him like a smith's hammer. The Sisters had measured him and found him wanting.

It nearly broke his heart to see Lyda. She was so lovely and so sad, so unbelieving, staring down at their stillborn son.

'I'm sorry, Lyda, so very, very sorry.'

'As am I, Willam. As am I.'

He held his wife and they cried together long and long.

Railing against the Sisters did no good, but he never asked for anything again. The world was a harsh and unforgiving place. He would simply have to accept it . . .

Lyda rebelled from the first – no matter that the warmth should have been welcome relief from the cold. She recognized it for the deception it was. She thrashed and tried to catch Ceeley to get them both to shore. No amount of swimming did any good. The river had its own purpose and wasn't interested in hers. When she fought it, it pulled her under to inhale the foul blood then spat her into the icy air. When she eased up, it allowed her to float atop and breathe effortlessly.

She could hear Celia's screams and worried that her actions might cause the child anguish, though she knew by now the river would not do them physical damage. They would not drown – as much as she might prefer it.

Unable to bear Celia's screams, she gave in to the river and let it carry her where it would.

Later, she woke in a world of red. Her thoughts were of blood and death. She was aswamp in them just as she had been immersed when she visited the village of ashes.

Willam sang a nonsense song that sent chills down her spine. Ceeley stared glassy-eyed and did not cry out, not once. The silence was more horrible than her heart-wrenching sobs had been.

'Drown me, oh sweet Sisters, drown me,' she prayed. But the Sisters could not hear her underneath so much death. They abandoned her to her past.

. . . Lyda entered the old woman's cabin. Everything seemed too bright. Candles were lit everywhere, exposing her failure and her shame. The witch was young, vibrant, the very essence of fertility. It was all Lyda could do not to claw out the woman's eyes.

The place was decked out like a bordello, heavy with red, black, and white, and too much lace.

'I know what you seek,' she said in a husky voice, before Lyda could speak. 'And if I do this for you how do you intend to pay for my services?'

Normally a woman who understood the value of coin, Lyda stared dumbfounded at the woman. She had not expected this bluntness. Everyone told her she would need to haggle. She knew how to haggle, but this?

'I would give you whatever is in my power,' she said, even as she realized she'd already given up her bargaining position.

'There is a bracelet in your possession. You know the one.'

Magic draws to magic, but still Lyda was surprised the witch knew of the bracelet given into Willam's care. 'I'm sorry, I don't know—'

'Do not lie to me,' she spat.

'—that I will be able to give you that,' Lyda finished lamely. 'It would be my husband's death.' And hardly worth begetting a child only to raise it fatherless.

'Never mind. There is a man who waits for me. You will go in my stead and do as he says. If you please him, your child will be healthy.'

'Won't he know me?'

'He'll see only me.'

Lyda had no illusions as to the nature of the meeting. The alternative was worse. She bowed her head, 'How long?'

'A few hours at most.'

'What will I tell my husband?'

'Whatever you like.' The witch muttered some words and knocked on a door. She let Lyda into the adjoining room.

Indeed he did not know her, but Lyda knew him. And indeed he seemed wholly satisfied.

Lyda hoped it might end there.

She never had to repeat her humiliation, but the man took to shopping frequently in their store, buying trinkets for his 'girls' as he called them. With each visit, her sin was born anew and she could not tell a soul.

She was almost not surprised when the baby was stillborn. Anger and betrayal were as commonplace now as the wretched man's visits.

There was no way to avenge herself on the witch or

the elves who had forced the bracelet into their care. No way to do anything at all . . .

Goatboy ran in the frozen wilderness, nearly starving, nearly freezing but somehow not quite doing either. Elves called him, directing him across the Dunavs.

He collapsed in the high passes and lay shivering as the sweat of his labors dried. He could not remember why he needed to continue struggling.

He forgot the frozen trail beneath him, as the goatboy who was and was not Notti found himself transported back to the clearing behind the altar.

This goatboy knew he wouldn't be able to abide the One much longer. She hoped to make him party to her loathsome acts, but he would not. This goatboy had no choice but to step in and stop the torture. Step in and die.

A strange ethereal elf seemed to watch over this goatboy. In a glance, he understood the boy's predicament. 'We all grieve,' the elf said, 'and we do what we can. Soon you will make your escape.' And then the elf was gone.

Goatboy blinked. Wasn't he high atop a mountain? Perhaps he had imagined the entire episode in a frozen delirium.

Goatboy blinked again and returned to the elfwitch's side. The ceremony proved to be more horrible than his worst imaginings. He saw for the first time what his clan had already seen of the dragon prince's excruciating transformation. It was horror itself . . . but ultimately Notti knew the conversion was meant to be. Human was the dragon's proper form.

Not this. This was indecent and vile.

First the elfwitch gathered a small group around her,

leaving most of the camp to go about their daily tasks in subdued and fearful silence. When he realized he had been granted a 'privilege' that his own pious father and stepmother had not, he tried to trade his place for theirs. The elfqueen insisted he must see what happened to those who mistreated him and thereby opposed her.

Goatboy chewed at the skin around his thumb-nail, the nail itself having already been destroyed. The witch slapped his hand out of his mouth. 'Are you not preparing for your manhood celebration? Did I not agree to the lessons? Consider today a preliminary ceremony to that.' She leaned into his face. 'One cannot become a man without learning to embrace the harsh aspects of life. Do not stand there like a frightened boy. Attend!'

The witch was so near and her warning so vivid, yet he could hardly bring himself to watch. He did not want to know more than he must about an achievement so evil as this.

Through unfocused eyes he watched her prepare. Bottles unstoppered, foul-smelling liquids and strange, dried bits of stuff – animal or plant, he didn't know which – flowed into her scrying bowl. The tent smelled of evil, of death, of carrion left too long in the summer sun.

Goatboy swallowed his bile.

'Good,' she whispered. 'Very good.'

He did not know if she spoke to him or her magicks. He kept his silence.

The elfwitch waved her hand and a dwarf was brought forward. He looked underfed. His clothes hung on him. His cheeks were sunken, his skin grey. His eyes said he knew his fate and accepted it perhaps as relief to his mistreatment, perhaps simply because he was too weak to fight.

To the elf's untutored eyes, the dwarf seemed no

older than Goatboy himself, but he knew dwarves aged differently. He might be older. He might be younger. The elf's stomach twisted at the thought. To never reach a manhood ceremony; to meet such a fate. He turned away from the dwarf before he gave in to the impulse to rescue the poor lad. He's really older than he looks, he told himself.

Alone in the deserted mountain pass, the unconscious Notti shouted, 'No, that's not how it happened! There was no dwarf.' His cries echoed down the hillside and no one answered him.

Inside the One's tent, Tabor and Theron, eyes taped wide, were bound and gagged in a corner.

The elfwitch muttered quiet words that rang harsh in Goatboy's ears. He gritted his teeth and reminded himself he had already failed to escape.

She slit the dwarf's throat without seeming to notice the falling body as she caught the thin blood in a basin.

Goatboy watched the life drain from the dwarf's face and felt a part of himself waning too. How could he simply stand by? Behind him, the brothers let out muffled screams.

The witch ignored them all as she told one of her sentinels, 'Clean up the dwarf. Be sure the bones are scrubbed free of all flesh. Whoever did the last ones left strings of meat attached.'

'Yes, mistress. It will not happen again.'

'No, it won't.'

The assistant cleared away the body, his own face nearly as grey as the dwarf's had been.

Goatboy's stomach lurched again, but still he remained rooted to his spot. He was achingly aware of everything that went on around him, including the large motionless elf who stood at the entrance with his sword drawn.

No one would leave without the elfqueen's permission.

This, too, was all wrong. The ceremony had been outside for everyone to see.

She waved her hand again and Tabor and Theron were brought forward and dropped at the elfwitch's feet. Unlike the dwarf, they had not been tortured and starved beforehand. It did not matter. The drug drained their will to struggle.

The witch's words grew louder, though they made no sense to Goatboy. She poured the blood in a complicated circular pattern that made him dizzy.

The effect on the elves was nearly immediate. They writhed in pain on the floor. Goatboy stared as they changed shape from the familiar long-boned elves to bulky men-things he barely recognized.

She waited impatiently until the transformation was complete. 'Rise now.'

Intelligence peeked out of their eyes, but confusion dominated their expressions.

'Stand!' the elfwitch shouted.

Too slowly they attempted to reach their feet. The One held out her hand and her guard slapped the handle of a whip into it. She cracked the whip once on the face of each. Blood trickled down the surprised creatures.

'You will find I am not a lenient master.' She raised the whip again. 'Stand.'

This time, they moved more quickly and managed to regain their feet.

She nodded to the guard. 'He will show you what to do.'

The three shambled out.

The elfwitch smiled at Goatboy. 'Never disappoint me.'

The goatboy who was and wasn't Notti nodded. When she said nothing more, he ran from the tent, hand over his mouth. Closer to her than he would have liked he lost control and heaved.

It was a long while before he stopped. He could have sworn he heard the elfwitch laughing through most of it.

Goatboy sat back from the mess and closed his eyes. A steady snick-snick-snick brought him back to the world. Not ten steps away, an elf sat cleaning a large animal.

The man smiled. He tossed a small bone to Goatboy. 'They say these are good luck.'

'Thank you,' the young elf managed to get out through dry lips. He reached to pick up the bone and examine it. A stray bit of meat reminded him of the elfwitch's words. In horror he dropped the thing. 'Th-that's a f-finger!'

'Was indeed not too long ago.' He pointed his knife at the bone on the ground. 'Go on, take it. You look like you could use some good luck.'

Goatboy tried to stall. 'W-won't th-the One be angry wh-when she f-finds out?'

The man spat into the tall grass beside him. 'Ah, the One won't know. She's not keeping tally. 'Sides, she's got plenty of the little ones.'

Goatboy's empty stomach gave another lurch. 'H-how many?'

'Fingers, toes, ribs, spines?' He shrugged. 'Don't know. I just clean 'em. I don't count 'em.'

'D-don't you m-mind?'

'Mind what, boy?'

'Y-you know.'

The elf stopped his work. He held up the partially-skinned bone in one hand and the knife in the other. 'No different from cleaning fish – or goats. Once they're dead, there's nothing I can do to bring 'em back.' He returned to his chore.

Each snick of the knife as it scraped away flesh seemed a small stab in Goatboy's gut. 'Well, no, b-but . . .'

'First time, huh, kid?'

The elf assumed he meant observing a transformation. 'N-no, n-not exactly.'

'No?' He looked up in surprise, then understanding dawned. 'Oh, you mean that furry creature she turned into a man a while back. Sisters' truth, that don't amount to the same thing.' He laughed, dismissing the dragon. 'He wasn't no elf. Come to think of it, neither was this guy.' He took up his scraping once again.

'Listen here,' he said into the remains but addressing the boy. The man's voice held no rancor. 'You've got to forget about it. Sometimes it's hard when you knew the guy, but—' He shrugged again. 'Getting upset isn't going to change a thing. She's more powerful than all of us joined together, so might as well learn to do her bidding and enjoy it. Better that than . . .' He let the thought trail away.

Goatboy didn't need a reminder of the options. He'd seen most of them first-hand . . .

Far away, a frostbitten boy raved at his nightmare vision, 'But that never happened! I was already gone. I swear by the Seven I had nothing to do with that dwarf!'

Wanton Tom had a strange dream that night. He dreamed of a time he couldn't have seen, but somehow knew in his bones . . .

Ginni was birthed harsh and cold with no one to attend Roslin – whether by Roslin's choice he didn't know. The labor was long and hard. The mage seemed to resent every moment of it. She had no tolerance for weaknesses in anyone, including herself, and this seemed the ultimate betrayal of her body.

The delivery would have shaken Tom by itself. There were some things men weren't meant to see. Bloody death they understood, but not bloody birth. Birth should be clean and easy, not a struggle more dangerous than war.

But the delivery was only part of the dream. After Roslin wrapped the child in a sacred cloth, the vision took a darker turn back to the cave where Ginni had found the bones. The infant child was crawling through the refuse, playing with the hallowed bones and transforming slowly from one creature to another. She was herself; she was a stableboy; a barmaid. She was Roslin, an elf, a dwarf, a troll, a dragon . . .

It was the last which woke him in a cold sweat. She held to some semblance of her true shape with all the others, but the dragon resembled a human not at all.

Tom sat up, gasping for air. He stared wildly around him, looking for Grosik. He couldn't find the dragon.

He peered into the gloom, wishing for Ginni's fire. Finally he remembered the events of the day. He and Grosik had tried to rescue Ginni and failed. The dragon had barely escaped and was likely injured.

No Ginni, no Grosik. Wanton Tom was as useless as a dancing-girl's veil without them. Might as well light his own funeral pyre.

Deflated and disheartened, he lay back down and sunk into sleep. As horrible as his dream had been, it was easier to face a legion of them than the onrushing hours at the mercy of the Forty-nine.

# Chapter 12

## COERCION

Sir Maarcus stumbled, then slammed into the table hard enough to jostle Abadan's scrying bowl.

'Maarcus, find a chair and use it! I nearly had something, but now I'll have to start all over if I'm to trust what I see.'

'Sorry,' Maarcus muttered. He looked about the room and chose a straight-backed chair as far from the worktable and Abadan's two apprentices as he could get. Why had he let Abadan talk him into waiting inside the chamber in the first place? For that matter, why had the magician insisted on his presence when he knew how the place sent chills down his spine?

Abadan poured off the liquid and began again. A dwarf held out a small bottle. The magician accepted it and added a single drop. 'We'll need more of that serviceberry soon,' he muttered. 'Going through this stuff faster than the refugees are using up the food-stores.' He leaned forward and peered into the bowl.

From his position, Maarcus could see nothing. In spite of himself, he leaned forward and willed Abadan to find them. That was it. He remembered now. Abadan was helping him discover his grandson's whereabouts.

'Ah, there he is.' The magician sounded wholly satisfied.

'Yes?' Maarcus asked.

'I've found your grandson.'

The physician walked around the apprentices and came to stand next to Abadan. He was immune to magic and wouldn't see anything, but it made him feel better. 'And?'

'He's here.'

'Here, in the palace? Isn't the boy a bit old for hide-and-sneak? He must be at least eighteen or so by now.'

'More like double that,' Abadan said slowly.

'What's that?' Maarcus asked him. 'I don't take your meaning.'

'Never mind,' said the magician. 'He's here in The Cliffs.'

'But why? What about that girl he's been seeing . . . Julianne, was it?'

The magician turned to face his friend. 'He's being held captive.' He shook his head. 'I don't know about Jilian. She wasn't with him. If she had been, I doubt I could have found him.'

Maarcus squared his jaw. 'Who would have thought. Does he look well?'

Abadan stared back into the bowl. He didn't look up as he said, 'He's been better, but I think he's all right.'

'Are you sure?'

'No, Maarcus, I am not sure. I—'

'What?'

'He's been beaten and he's chained to a wall.'

The physician didn't know what to say. All his maneuvering had not protected the boy.

For a rare moment, Abadan lost his brashness. 'I'm sorry, Maarcus.'

The physician nodded his appreciation, afraid to try to speak.

'I think he's going to need help.'

Maarcus nodded again.

'We'll need to talk to the prince.'

'Isn't that dangerous? Wouldn't we do well to talk to the king?'

'Maarcus,' Abadan spoke gently. 'The king is dead, remember?'

The air rushed from his lungs as if he'd been punched. Yes, yes, he'd known that, but the knowledge felt like a fresh wound. 'Of course,' he said. 'But surely you wouldn't trust my grandson to any of Tomar's abhorrent children?'

'No, not the ones you speak of. The Dragon Prince, Nikolis.'

Nikolis? Maarcus couldn't recall any prince by that name. He couldn't remember so many things these days. He thought he might ask Abadan for clarification, but reconsidered. The magician was lost to the vision in his bowl.

In her dreams, Ginni struggled against the witches. They marched through her mind, peering at every secret, inspecting Roslin's work and finding every bit of it wanting.

What was the point of all this? Ginni would have told them anything they wanted to know. Hadn't she come to them freely?

Invasion was their point. They sought to control her and she resisted; they would break her or kill her in the attempt.

She might have been able to withstand one, for even the powerful Revered Mother Caronn must rest. She could not oppose all three.

They took turns in a never-ending swirl of opening mental doors and slamming them shut. 'Enough!' she cried, exhausted. 'Take whatever you want.'

'We have what we want,' said Revered Mother. 'You. But it is well that you yielded to us now. Your mother continues to harm you every moment you waste attempting to repel us.'

'It is as you suggest,' Ginni answered, very nearly believing them.

She woke to familiar surroundings, but . . . not.

She probed her memories, finding them laced with gaps as obvious as a missing tooth. Bits and pieces of information were no longer locked away. They were simply gone. Stolen.

She picked at the new layers as if pulling away freshly formed scabs, but there was nothing underneath. The wound went all the way through to . . .

Nothing.

Her mind was just a hollow tree with the wind whistling through the recesses.


Roslin once told Wanton Tom that he was closer than any man ever came to one of the Forty-nine – and so he thought he knew what to expect. Instead, he found the activities of the witches within the Tower to be a bizarre mix of the exotic and the routine. Worse by far, he had underestimated their cunning.

He anticipated dreadful torture when they lashed him to

a stiff bed and left the room. But rather than Roslin's harsh and unforgiving treatment, they tried a subtler approach he would not have considered possible.

It began when they sent in a lovely young novice. She was a pretty thing, seemingly innocent. Tom almost fell for her. Her swirling skirts and unaffected smile tickled the mercenary's old, carefree bones.

Strapped down as he was, he had almost no choice but to watch her. She loosened her bodice just enough to show a deep cleavage which promised more. Her fingers lightly brushed his face and neck while she whispered tantalizing nothings. The girl climbed atop him and nibbled on his earlobe.

Tom closed his eyes and prepared to let happen whatever would happen. If they wanted to arouse him, he could be seduced without telling them anything just as easily as he could be tortured without telling them anything. Either method would be equally likely to serve their goals, because their magic was stronger than his defenses.

Straddling him now, she cleverly worked her way around the restraints to unbutton his shirt. He kept his eyes closed and did not watch. He wasn't sure he wanted to see her face or to guess at her thoughts.

The girl laughed at his foolishness. 'Can't bear to watch the dirty work, eh?'

He jolted against the rope and twisted to see her face, hidden by the hair which had somehow come undone. 'Dirty work' was just a turn of phrase. It couldn't be Ginni.

He could not lift his head, let alone shoulders, arms or legs. It didn't matter. He had lost all lust for this girl. If she weren't actually Ginni – something of which he was suddenly no longer sure – she could well have been. Age, height, poise all so like Ginni.

He thought of Roslin's similar use of Ginni. She had shown no qualms at the risk to her own daughter as she sent her to tease men in hopes of gathering information. To be abuse this girl thus made Tom all the angrier.

He did know Roslin. Perhaps he did know these mages as well.

'Get out,' he told her through clenched teeth.

She pulled back from him, surprise and confusion showing in the wide eyes and wrinkled brow. 'But don't you like . . .' she started to ask and trailed off.

'No, I don't like.'

She hung there over him. 'Please don't send me away. Revered Mother will be very angry with me.'

'The Mother can go fall in a dark pit.'

She tossed her head back and forth, hair flying. 'No, no, don't say that. She took me in when no one wanted me.'

'Get down at least.'

'You're sure?'

He nodded. 'I haven't been this sure of anything since I promised to watch over my daughter.'

'I have many talents.' Her face brightened. 'I could be your daughter.'

He grimaced. 'Not my cup of serviceberry, thanks. Trust me. There isn't a thing you can do to interest me.'

Slowly, with many sidelong glances, she backed off. She looked at the door and Tom thought he saw real fear in her eyes, the fear of the slave who has displeased his master.

'You don't 'ave to leave right away if you don't want.'

'I can't release you,' she said hurriedly, making sure he didn't get any ideas.

He shrugged under his bonds. 'Didn't think you could. Just thought you might like to wait a spell before returning to wherever you've got to return.'

'I don't do magic.' She wrapped her arms around herself in a defensive posture.

'Good.'

Her big eyes went bigger with disbelief. 'Really?'

In this one matter it was easy to be sincere. 'Haven't had too many run-ins with magic that I didn't come out with the short stick.' Ginni excepted, he thought.

'Then why did you offer to "wait a spell"?'

Was this girl missing a few pegs or just left too long in the cold? 'Figure o' speech,' he explained.

She gave him another puzzled look.

'A way of saying something. I meant, you can stay here a while if you'd like.'

Understanding flared alight. 'Oh, I see. Revered Mother always says exactly what she means.'

He doubted that but he didn't comment.

'I thought you wanted me to perform some sort of magic,' she explained. 'You know, "wait a spell"?'

He lifted one eyebrow and squelched laughter. 'Right, sorry.' Could the girl truly be this naive? Then Tom remembered Ginni's look of utter shock. Yes, she could be, either by nature or magic.

'Revered Mother will know I've failed.' Her voice was barely above a whisper. 'Revered Mother always knows.'

'I'm very sorry about that.'

Silent tears ran down her cheeks.

'I really am. You just remind me of someone else, is all. I couldn't . . . Well, you know . . .'

'Do I, honestly? Remind me you of someone, I mean?'

'Sure do.'

'Is she pretty?'

'Very.'

'Revered Mother says I can be pretty when I try. I try very hard.'

'The Mother's got it half right. I'd say you'd be pretty no matter what.'

'Even now?' The tears stopped and a quivering lip took its place.

Wanton Tom couldn't help but wonder if this was yet another ploy. 'Es – even now.' He'd almost said 'especially now' but thought better of it. No need to give her more of an opening than he already had.

They sat quietly for a twin-minute. Normally a master at out-waiting, Tom finally said, 'Why don't you tell me about yourself. How you came here, that sort of thing.'

She blushed and looked down at her hands. They seemed almost alien to the rest of her, unable to be still, plucking at her dress, pulling on her hair. 'I was very young. I don't remember much. Revered Mother took me in, taught me everything I know. I'm terribly grateful to her.'

This last seemed added, as if she wanted someone to hear it.

No doubt she did.

'What about you? How did you end up here? It's a rather strange place for a man.' She spoke as if he'd come by choice, as if he weren't trussed up like a holiday pig.

'I was looking for someone,' he answered simply.

'The same someone I remind you of?'

So, she wasn't completely without a brain. 'Uh huh.'

'I hope you find her.'

'Oh, I found her.'

'And?'

'She doesn't remember me.' He watched her face for a reaction but there wasn't a twitch.

'That's very sad.' She didn't sound sad, more like she struggled to preserve a new-found monotone.

'Yeah, it is.'

'I'd better go.' Suddenly she was eager to leave. She jumped off him and ran out the door before he could respond.

'Score one,' Tom said to the air. 'Now we're gettin' somewhere.' He smiled. 'Not sure where, but somewhere.'


Jilian was almost relieved when they took her back to the dungeon and settled her in the cell next to Maarcus. Prisons were all pretty much the same: cold, dank, heavy brick, and high barred windows (windows optional). She knew the hazards. Here she never doubted that everything was her enemy. The cold damp that settled into lungs, the chains and shackles that rubbed great wounds, the rats that gnawed at the wounds – these were only the outward extensions of the true danger. Here she would not be lulled into false security by Hadrian or his men.

Only Maarcus could be trusted now . . . if he lived.

To see a hostage tortured is terrible. To know the victim is agony.

Maarcus hung from the wrist-irons. Delirious, he yelled out now and again. Each time he did so, Lyam or Ivan stepped inside his cell and landed a body blow. He had no strength to protect himself.

A third man entered. He released the Shoreman's irons and gently lowered him to the ground where he coaxed Maarcus to drink. It made no sense to Jilian until she realized the fluid was drugged. Hadrian was too much of a coward. He wouldn't hesitate to persecute the weak or defenseless, but he would not risk letting Maarcus come fully awake.

She spat on the ground. 'That's for you, Hadrian. You and your cowardice!'

To Jilian's surprise Maarcus seemed to revive after the man left. 'We must stop meeting in such grisly places,' he joked through his pain.

'I'm doing my best,' Jilian answered, and bit her lip to keep from crying.

'Not the elfwitch then?' Maarcus asked.

'Not yet anyway.'

'Quiet!' shouted their jailor. 'You been behavin' this long. You can manage a mite longer.'

Jilian gripped the bars of her cell. First she would bend the bars and then she'd rip the man limb from limb.

'Easy,' he whispered. 'We'll be okay.'

She stared at Maarcus. It was just too much, seeing him this way after Hadrian's attempt to force himself on her. To her this was anguish, plain and simple, and she didn't take kindly to it.

Jilian would make them pay, oh how she'd make them pay.

'Who?' Maarcus mouthed.

'None of that either,' bellowed Ivan inches from Jilian's ear. 'I'll be nice and give you a hint, Sir Maarcus the Seventh.' Each part of the Shoreman's title was spoken with growing sarcasm. 'Let's see. Who's the rightful heir to the throne? Can't be you, Princess Jilian. Can't be him. He's not even close.' He pointed at each one in turn. 'Can't be that half-son of a man, Nikolis.'

'Hadrian!' Maarcus hissed. 'How dare he?'

'Oh, I see you know of him.'

Jilian snuck a glance at Maarcus. 'But I thought—' the princess started, unable to contain herself.

'Thought they were all dead,' Ivan finished for her. 'The rest of 'em are. All but Hadrian. He's a lot smarter than he lets on.'

Unlike a certain cretin, Jilian thought. No she hadn't thought they were all dead. She'd been well briefed on Prince Hadrian. But the senior Maarcus and Abadan had seemed quite sure he held no interest in the throne. Perhaps he's only feigned lack of interest in order to keep his head, she thought, not that she could entirely blame him on that count. Regardless, he'd clearly made a change in his plans.

'Why, princess,' said Ivan in mock surprise. 'Where's your cuff? The prince will be most displeased with me.' He spun on his heel and returned in moments with chain and ankle-cuffs. He held them up, considering the bonds and the prisoners. 'I guess this can wait until Lyam comes with your grub.'

They were generous at first, fastening only one foot to the wall and leaving that loose enough to slip out of if she wished. She gathered up the chain and looked at it. It seemed to be ordinary metal links without any additional magic surrounding it. She let the chain play out as far as it would allow while examining her quarters. She could reach the barred door on the far side of the post securing her, and all but one corner closest to Maarcus.

She studied the farthest corner. The bricks seemed to match the rest of the wall. The bars seemed identical to their kind as well. Still she sensed something wrong. Jilian pulled the chain as far as she could.

And felt the trap.

If curiosity compelled her to find out what lay hidden in the one unreachable corner or if fear for Maarcus drove her to him, she would then have to slip completely free of the bond. But if she did so, she would surely set off some sort of alarm somewhere.

Jilian backed away from the forbidden spot and immediately felt the coercion weaken. Fine, Jilian thought, two can play this game. She looked down at Maarcus to explain the snare, but he'd passed out again.

She was almost insulted that they felt she could be so easily duped, before it set her mind to thinking. What would have been the consequences, and why did they bother trying to trick her when she was already at their mercy? Was detecting the bait as bad as not? Either way, they would know something about her she didn't want them to know.

Why would Prince Hadrian care if she could detect magic when she didn't know how to use it against him?

Unless he had joined the elfwitch.

Full dark and a moonless night reigned over the city when Prince Nikolis returned with one nearly dead horse and one much too lively companion. Weary and sick at heart, he felt grateful no one had waited up to pass on the word of their failure. They dismounted and headed toward the guard tower.

His guide-captor put a hand on Nikolis' arm. 'Wait, I know another, better way in,' the soldier said quietly.

'Where I'll be gutted and robbed. No, thank you.'

'You do me a disservice, sire. 'Sides, I could've done that hours ago,' he whispered in his ear. 'Listen now. Why rush to proclaim your disaster? It will be just as ugly by daylight but less horrifying for others. Let them have one last night of peace.'

'If there's one man, woman or child who sleeps well tonight, then such a person has no soul. No, I will wake the guard and face this as a prince and a man.' He took a step forward.

'Hasn't it struck you that they already know? News of misfortune travels faster than a dragon. Per'aps they're hiding.'

The man was right. They must know by now. Nikolis spoke over his shoulder. 'Perhaps they are mourning.' The horse whinnied. 'In any event, all the more reason to formally announce my return.'

'Suit yourself, Sir Prince. I'll just wait back here.'

'I thought you sought a room for the night.'

'That's as may be, but I don't think I'd want it known that I saved your life until their ire is worn down. I like my skin where it is.'

Prince Nikolis rubbed the sides of his horse's face and considered. No question the man was a brigand, but he was also a survivor. Perhaps the prince would do better not to leave his life so throughly in the hands of the Seven while it was still deepdark. Nikolis could assemble the bereaved in the morning and likely few would genuinely mind. 'All right,' he said. 'We'll do it your way.'

'You'll thank me later.'

I doubt it, Nikolis thought. Nonetheless, he allowed the man to lead him around to one of the many places where the city wall had collapsed from age and warfare. They picked their way through the rubble and came out very near the palace. Too near. 'I need to get someone over here to mend this,' Nikolis mumbled.

'What's that, Sir Prince?'

'Nothing important.'

He looked at Nikolis a long moment, measuring. 'You'll give me safe passage into the castle, of course.'

'I give you my word.'

'You'll give more than that if you betray me,' the man said.

What am I doing with this disreputable cretin? Nikolis asked himself yet again. 'I insist we enter the castle by way of more traditional doors.'

The man smiled. 'I wouldn't have it any other way.'

Nikolis left him to his smug expression. He thinks being seen with me grants him higher regard among my men. He doesn't realize that most of my reliable troops just died in battle.

The prince led the final steps to the guard's checkpoint. He nodded to the chief sentry. 'We're home. Alert Sir Maarcus and Master Abadan. I'll be in my study.'

'Yes, sire.'

'I'm impressed, Sir Prince. You've got them trained so well they didn't even question your failure.'

The man was baiting him. Nikolis counted slowly backward from seven. He had to repeat the routine several times before he could walk beside the self-proclaimed soldier without the distraction of inventing various clever means to kill him.

Nik's attendant caught up with him not far from his study. 'Take this man to the east wing,' the prince said, 'and show him every comfort. He is my personal guest.'

The attendant nodded. He did not need to comment on the prince's unusual phrasing or the fact that he never had personal guests. He led the man away and would post a discreet guard to observe him while he saw to the man's more ordinary needs.

There's one rat caged for the next few hours, Nikolis thought. 'I don't want to be disturbed,' Nikolis told the guard outside his office.

Holding his characteristic brandy, Abadan waited inside

.with his back to the fireplace. Walther was crouched trying to stir warmth out of the dead flames.

'Never mind that, Walther. We haven't enough wood to make it worth the trouble. Come sit, both of you.'

The three settled into chairs arranged to take advantage of the now cold fire.

'Where's the physician?'

'He's not well, Nik.'

'Hasn't been for months. Is he worse?'

'I'd say so, yes,' Abadan answered. 'It didn't seem worth disturbing him since he seems to have forgotten who you are.'

Nikolis winced, thinking of their last meeting. 'He needs an attendant.'

'Harmon is with him.'

'Good.' The prince paused, reluctant to move on to more unsolvable problems.

'Let me make it easier,' Abadan said. 'I actually have a bit of good news.'

Nikolis leaned forward in his seat. 'You found Jilian! Wonderful, excellent—'

'No, not Jilian, but . . .'

Nik's heart sunk. He had to find her. 'Well, keep searching. You're my best hope.'

'Nikolis, listen to me,' Abadan said impatiently. 'I'm trying to tell you I've found Maarcus. He's here in The Cliffs.'

'Whatever in the world is he doing? Hiding—'

'Nikolis!' the magician spoke sharply. 'By the holy Seven, quit jumping to conclusions and listen to me! Maarcus is being held captive by your half-brother, Hadrian. I have every reason to believe he has Jilian as well.'

'Ah, I see. What are the ransom demands?'

'None. I don't believe Hadrian is aware we've discovered him.'

'If he wants this rotten throne, he can have it. After today, there's not enough left to save.'

'Who knows what the man wants?' Abadan said. 'He was always very clever at concealing his true ambitions.'

'Obviously.' Nikolis scowled at him. 'You gave us the impression he had no interest in anything beyond a warm little house where he could practise his perversions . . . Jilian!' The prince covered his face with his hands. 'We can't leave her with that lecher.'

'We won't, Nikolis. But one thing at a time. First, you must tell me of your battle.'

'What's to tell? I led them to a slaughter and watched them all die. I am responsible.'

'Nikolis, this is not what I mean. We know the outcome. We saw much of it with Walther's help. He's quite talented you know.'

The dwarf gave Nik a weak smile.

'Yes, I know. For all the good that talent does any of us. No offense, Walther.'

'None taken.'

Abadan took the last sip of brandy and set down the glass. 'Nik, you need to tell me everything you remember. It's important.'

The prince looked from the magician to his apprentice. Both waited, expectant. He supposed recounting the horror couldn't be any worse than going to bed and dreaming it. 'All right.' And he began.

Walther remained solemn and quiet throughout. Abadan was uncommonly silent himself, interrupting only to ask a question or two.

'And where's this man who claims to have saved your life?' Abadan asked when Nikolis had finished.

'He's in the East Wing with a guard. He'll keep a while.'

'What do you think?' Abadan asked the dwarf.

Walther face reddened, embarrassed no doubt to be asked his opinion in such a critical discussion. 'He is clearly the Dragon Prince. Everything he says points to the papers I've studied these last days.'

'I agree,' Abadan said.

Nikolis drummed his fingers on the chair-arm. 'So I've been addressed from the moment I was transformed. It seemed only natural given my earlier shape as well as our family coat of arms. Are you saying there's more?'

'Yes,' Abadan said.

'What?'

Walther spoke up. 'That is the difficulty. I've read and read these past few days in hopes of finding a way to defeat the elfwitch, to undo her dreadful spell-casting. Apparently what little written information that exists was stolen long ago, either by Alvaria herself or someone who thought to protect others from the knowledge. Therefore, I ran across few references to shed light on what we already know about the troll transformations. However, each and every time I did, without fail it was accompanied by text on the Dragon Prince. My best understanding of him would be to describe him as a man transfigured and orphaned and transfigured again – all against his will.'

'Interesting,' Nik said, 'but I don't think it helps us much.'

'It can,' Walther insisted. 'The true Dragon Prince can learn to direct his shape-changing.'

The prince stared at Walther dumbfounded. 'Are you saying I actually was a living, breathing, flying dragon?'

Abadan answered for the dwarf. 'Nikolis, you can master a forgotten art. Walther and I will help you.'

'No,' the prince said. 'I cannot do it without Jilian.'

'That's nonsense, Nik. Admirable of you, but war doesn't always allow for such sentiments. You've already proven you can do it.'

The prince jumped out of his chair and began to pace. 'I'm serious, Abadan,' he said, earnest now. 'Jilian is more than my twin. We've always worked as if we knew one another's intent. It's how we've survived. With her, I have a chance, a real chance.' He stopped in mid-stride and stared into the cold fire. 'But without her we're doomed to failure as devastating as everything else we've attempted since we began working separately.' He spun about to face his companions. 'We've got to rescue her from Hadrian – for her sake, and for that of the One Land.'

Notti woke surprisingly warm and in high spirits. Despite his frostbitten fingers and nose, he felt only contentment.

They absolved me, he thought. I must be dead and gone to the land of the Sisters.

A quick look around dispelled that notion. He couldn't imagine that the Sisters would have need of wooden huts. They seemed much too earthly.

He opened the door and peeked out.

His heart sank. He'd been returned to his home camp. He was worse than dead: he was troll-makings.

He stood unthinking, unseeing for a long moment before he realized he didn't know these elves. They were not his clan.

They were smiling.

Smiling?

Several children lay on their backs, making snow Sisters. Their laughter rang across the clearing.

Adults went about their chores with the efficiency

of most adults everywhere, but these elves were singing.

Singing?

The children stopped. Laughter ceased.

The One!

No. The elves were staring at Notti.

'He's awake!' shouted a boy.'Uncle Jedrek, the goatboy is awake.'

Did he reek of goats even now?

'His name is Notti,' said a woman.

No one here could know the nickname but for . . .

'M-mother?' he asked tentatively. 'Please, please . . .'
He wasn't even sure he knew what he was asking.

'Notti, come out, child. Meet your new family.'

'F-family?'

'You're home now. Safe.'

'But how?' he asked, not daring to believe. He leaned against the hut's doorway for support. This was one of Queen Alvaria's cruel jokes.

A beautiful woman squatted down next to him. 'All things are possible with the Sisters' help. Jedrek's been watching out for you.' She hugged him hard. 'Oh, Notti, I'm so sorry for leaving you. If I'd had any choice . . .' Her voice broke.

'Sh,' he whispered, comforting her. 'I've kn-known all al-long that y-you had n-no choice. B-better th-that you l-lived in ex-exile than d-died at h-her hand.' Or worse, he thought, unable to speak the terror of the trolls aloud.

She straightened up and smoothed out her dress. 'Foolish of me to treat you like a child. You're almost a man now. I know about the trolls,' she continued, and from her somber tone, he could tell she knew about the trolls and maybe worse still. 'But I couldn't be sure you knew. You were so young then.' She gave him another quick hug. 'Have they treated you well? They promised me they would.'

Notti's mouth opened but no sound came out at first. They had abused him time and again, but what use would it be to have her fretting over the past? Then again, she should know they had lied. 'I s-survived it,' he said, after a long pause.

Her brow creased in worry, but she respected him enough not to push him further. 'Come. I want you to meet the others.' She wrapped her arm around him and began a lengthy list of introductions.

He greeted them one by one with a quiet smile and a stuttered, 'H-hello.' In turn, they welcomed him by patting his back and kissing his cheeks. Children tossed snowballs at his feet while they sang a festive song.

Each person had a function, a place within the group. It was all so neat, so organized. It reminded him briefly of the camp he'd fled, and this was not a comfortable thought. At least he'd had a purpose there, as unappreciated as it was. He couldn't imagine what his role would be here.

But were they not all elves? Had he not endured? Had he not survived the deadly trek through the mountains in deep winter?

Notti relaxed. He was home.

# Chapter 13

## BLACK SHEEP

The river finally spat up the three travellers onto the shore. The water was as cold as ice and just as clear. Lyda saw not a trace of the deep red she remembered. It was as if that other river of blood had never existed.

Almost.

The journey left the distrust of old wounds in its wake. Lyda thought she should fight the ghosts of false pain, yet they tugged so insistently at her mind and soul.

She looked warily at Willam and Ceeley.

Willam seemed much the worse for his ordeal. He still babbled under his breath, but the words had taken on an eerie cast. She couldn't make out everything as his voice rose and fell, but he kept repeating 'babies' and 'promises.' Each time, she felt the accusation and her shame redoubled.

She clenched her fists, ready to . . . what? No good. She searched the ground for a jagged rock with a sharp point. There at Ceeley's feet was the perfect weapon. She picked it up and up and up until it was over her head set to strike.

She'd have to kill Willam if she couldn't silence his scorn any other way.

She opened her hand and dropped the stone. Such a casual thought of murder horrified her, yet there it was. She couldn't deny it.

Lyda turned to Ceeley, hoping the delight of a living child would distract her from base speculations and her dead past. 'Celia? Celia, are you all right?'

The girl looked out through haunted eyes. She started to speak but only managed a squeak before rushing up the embankment, throwing herself in the grass, and sobbing.

Lyda shivered. They were so cold and so alone in the elfwitch's territory. She dragged herself out of the freezing river. With barely a backward glance at Willam, she wrapped herself around the girl.

'I tried,' the dwarf said. 'I tried, but I couldn't help. And they screamed. Oh, they screamed and screamed.' She put her hands over her ears as if to block out the sound. Her eyes went from possessed to feverish. 'And the elfwitch has taken all the strong ones, all of them.'

Lyda held the girl tighter, fighting her own impulse to shove her away in disgust. 'It'll be all right now. It'll be all right,' she whispered through chattering teeth.

But it wouldn't. Her elves had not guided her to this place. Somehow, the elfwitch had found them and brought them here. Nothing would ever be all right ever again.

'Our baby!' Willam wailed. 'You killed our baby!'

'No!' Ceeley shouted back. 'It wasn't me. I tried to save her. She wouldn't listen. Oh, she wouldn't listen.'

Lyda knew Willam addressed Lyda herself rather than

the child, but how could she break through Ceeley's panic to explain it to her?

'No, sweetheart. It wasn't you,' she whispered. She rocked Ceeley and hummed a traditional lullaby to drown out her husband.

'Maybe it wasn't any of us.'

Maybe it was Willam.

Only the Sisters knew what Hadrian was doing to Maarcus, but he was ingenious in his torture. He had spent years learning to uncover a victim's frailties and brought all of his knowledge to bear on Jilian. For the next several days – or maybe it was hours, who knew?—he did his best to disorient the princess.

Jilian's anger drained away too suddenly, leaving her feeling sluggish and sleepy. Each time she roused herself, she awoke in a different corner of her cell. Once she was in a different cell altogether. He could only have managed it through toxins or magic.

Her chamberpot was emptied without pattern. Either it was filled to the brim rendering it worthless or the porcelain was scrubbed so clean that she'd swear on her foster-mother's grave that it had never been used.

The guards took to delivering the food in undependable portions at unpredictable hours. A large feast sitting heavy in her stomach might well be trailed by another. Unsure when her next meal might arrive, Jilian ate as much as she dared, only to realize the chamberpot remained full and foul-smelling. The following hours brought stale bread and no fluid to wash it down. The princess resolved to fast rather than succumb to Hadrian's manipulations, and immediately felt better.

When Hadrian discovered his half-sister's small measure of control, he became furious and instantly chose a different route. 'You'll learn not to thwart me,' he warned her. 'I know your weaknesses. Maarcus is yours and you are his. I'm going to enjoy this.'

Against their will, the captives quickly proved him correct. Maarcus and Jilian sat huddled in their new joint cell after Prince Hadrian's most recent session. The potions hidden in the princess's drink had backfired more than not. It was clear through her delirium she had irritated the prince by prattling on about Ceeley. This was a man who had no use for children.

Hadrian hadn't won yet, but they were still imprisoned – and Maarcus was growing weaker and weaker. His head hung heavy and low, his chin against his chest. They were both shivering like frightened children – and maybe that was what they'd been reduced to. The lashmarks on Maarcus' back and arms were not healing well, and Jilian suspected their captors of lacing the straps of the leather whip with poison to keep the wounds festering.

Still shaky herself, Jilian gently probed around the cuts but there wasn't much she could do without fresh water. Woundwort would help a great deal, but she might as well wish for their freedom.

All the while, she whispered into his unconscious ears. 'Maarcus, we've got to escape. Come on, you can do it. We've got to survive for the One Land.'

Over and over, she murmured to him but got no response. Finally she tried invoking the names of those he loved and had hoped to protect. 'For Zera, Maarcus. Don't let her death go unpunished. For Ceeley, Maarcus. For little girls who survive against the odds. Un-cle Ma-arcs,' she sang in a child's voice, using the girl's pet-name for him.

He roused slightly but did not come to full consciousness.

'All right, Maarcus, all right,' she said, too disheartened to keep at him. 'Don't you worry. We'll get out of this somehow.' She hugged him tightly trying to warm him, attempting to comfort them both.

'How touching,' growled Ivan.

'He needs a physician.' Jilian tried to keep the anger out of her voice.

'I'm sure you've got just the one. Grandfather Maarcus, perhaps?' The guard sneered, clearly enjoying himself.

'At least bring fresh water to let me clean the cuts.'

The guard hitched up his pants in a show of virility. 'The prince said not to, but I don't guess that can hurt. What'll you do for me?'

Jilian swallowed her first retort. If she could get him to open the gate wide enough . . . 'Ah, well, let's have the water first,' she said, with a coquettish smile.

He echoed her smile, then stepped back to his station.

'It won't be long now,' Jilian whispered to Maarcus. 'You've got to be ready.'

The guard returned carrying a pitcher. He made as if to unlock the door then swung the other arm, dousing Jilian and Maarcus with cold water.

Jilian gasped. Maarcus grunted awake.

The guard laughed at her. 'You must think me an idiot. I serve my master. You would do well to remember that.'

Prince Nikolis took breakfast in his study. He invited Abadan to join him, along with whomever he wished. Still Nik hoped to keep the session sane, and his heart sank when the magician arrived with an odd entourage. There was Abadan himself, of course, and Walther, as well as Sir Maarcus and the physician's keeper, Harmon.

Nik waved them forward and went back to picking at

his food. He couldn't force himself to exclude Maarcus; neither could he look forward to involving the failing physician as he had earlier. More than anything, the prince simply lacked the energy to deal with the man just now.

'I've lost him again,' Abadan announced.

Nikolis swore. 'Does nothing go right in this cursed town?'

'What does that mean?' Maarcus asked. His eyes were wild and his hair seemed to have escaped combing since Nikolis had last seen him. Harmon hovered behind him as if he had the power to hold the man together.

By the Sisters, the prince thought, please don't make us explain it all again.

The magician continued with only a slight nod to the physician's request for an explanation. 'Either your grandson is back with Jilian, which is very good news indeed, or he's . . . not, which could mean . . .' This once, even the acerbic magician stopped short of pointing out the obvious.

'Never mind,' Maarcus said evenly. 'Some visions don't require magic to be seen.'

Nikolis silently let out a sigh. The stubborn expression on Maarcus's face told him that the old physician was alert today and had chosen not to speculate on the worst possibilities until forced. Nik didn't blame him. It was far better to assume that his weasely half-brother had placed Jilian and Maarcus together for some reason, rather than that he'd killed them.

It should have been a comforting thought, but the Dragon Prince didn't find much solace in the unknown these days. He felt sure the physician agreed, being the sort of man who enjoyed being able to explain all the details of a problem.

'My grandson can't wait much longer,' Sir Maarcus added.

'He's right,' Walther spoke quietly.

The dwarf seldom spoke without a need. 'Is there something I should know?' Prince Nikolis asked.

Walther blushed, still uncomfortable when singled out. 'Not that I can put in so many words,' he answered. 'Only that we would do well to act.'

'I just said that, young man,' snapped Maarcus.

Terrific, Nik thought. Whatever Walther was thinking, he'll be too intimidated to voice it now.

Nikolis fingered the dragon coin in his pocket like a lucky talisman. The token led him to considering the talents of true dragons and ultimately to the mercenary and his dragon. 'What about Wanton Tom and Grosik? They should be back from their mission by now.'

'No one's heard from them since they left here, sire.'

'Probably stepping back from the front,' the prince offered. He turned to Abadan. 'Can't you raise him with your box?'

'I can try.' His voice made it clear what he thought of the odds of success.

'Please do. In the meanwhile, we have other problems to tend to.'

'You would dismiss your sister and my grandson so easily?' the physician accused.

'Sir Maarcus,' Nikolis hissed.

Harmon moved between them – as if the prince would have punched the old man.

'Sir Maarcus,' he repeated in normal tones. 'I assure you I do not take your grandson's situation lightly, all the more because my sister is with him. Nonetheless, let me remind you that we are battling the elfwitch. All else,

273

including my sister—' He coughed and paused to regain control. 'All else must yield to that.'

The physician glared at him. 'Be careful that Alvaria does not wriggle past your defenses and steal these two while you focus on your nose.'

The words carried the heavy weight of truth and settled like stones in the prince's stomach. Hadn't he said as much himself hours ago? Still he refused to admit he agreed with the old man, but instead argued, 'We must deal with the families of the men slain in battle.'

'There is nothing you can do,' Maarcus said. 'The men are frozen corpses.'

'The men are dead, but their families live!' Nikolis responded hotly.

'Not for long.'

Abadan looked at Maarcus as if his long-time friend had suddenly sprouted a third ear. He sipped his morning tea. 'What do you know, Maarcus?'

'The same as every man, woman, and child in The Cliffs. The elfwitch is coming and she is in league with this man!' Maarcus stood and pointed at Nikolis himself.

'Don't be ridiculous,' the prince said.

'I am no more ridiculous than you are.'

'Abadan, get him out of here.'

The magician nodded to Harmon, who placed his hand on Maarcus's elbow.

'It's time we left, sir.'

'I'm not through.'

'Please, sir.'

Maarcus gazed at the others, one by one. He pulled himself up. With great dignity, he said, 'I see the way you pity and patronize me. Perhaps I deserve it. Nonetheless, this does not change the fact that Alvaria is a master of misdirection. She will send her trolls upon you, but not before she has divided us and reduced each of us to cowering fools incapable of defense.' He nodded to Harmon. 'I'm through.'

The room seemed to cool once Maarcus left. The three sat in uncomfortable silence.

'He's right,' Nikolis said. 'He's dead right.'

Abadan let that hang like a noose between them before speaking. 'We need to take care of the soldier who brought you in last night,' he said suddenly. 'He's part of their plan. He'll spread lies dangerous to you and to the One Land.'

'What do you suggest?' Nikolis asked.

'He must be hushed,' Abadan said.

'What do you suggest?' Nikolis repeated.

'We don't have the forces to guard him.'

'What do you suggest?' Nikolis asked for the third time.

The magician hesitated. He studied the younger men with him, men who fought a different war from that he had known with Tomar. 'Kill him,' he said finally.

Nikolis had expected this. He'd never felt more weary in his life. Every muscle taut, he said, 'Tell me when it's done.'

Notti's mother followed him everywhere for hours. At last Elder Jedrek called on her to serve a duty she could not pass along to one of the others. She left him with more goodbye hugs than he'd had altogether in the past ten years.

So much attention would take getting used to. For now, Goatboy was glad of the solitude.

Goatboy watched a squirrel scamper across the ground and up an evergreen to disappear among the upper branches. He stared in wonderment for long minutes after he could discern no movement. This simple sign of life, of a creature doing as the Sisters had meant it to do, restored his own serenity. Whatever the One had asked of him would ultimately have only so much effect on the world. The Sisters would right the balance.

Still he hesitated to step away from the tree. How long had it been since he watched any animal scurry up a tree-trunk? How long had it been since he even ventured to look above the ground?

Twelve, thirteen years ago his mother had delighted in pointing out the vitality of life all around them. Except what he embraced in order to herd the goats, he barely recalled any of it now. No one taught the lore anymore; Alvaria declared it a squander and waste of the most deplorable sort, since they lived in one place and knew all they needed of it.

Notti missed the pull of the forest, the welcome indifference it offered.

The wood did not exist at the pleasure of elves, however much the One wanted them to believe otherwise. It was too big, too vast, too varied and unpredictable. At times too deadly. They might tame a piece of it, might subdue the entirety, but they would never bend it to their will.

The idea strengthened him. Perhaps he had not really been bent to the witch's will either. Perhaps he had merely swayed in the storm winds and could once more straighten and reach to they sky.

Finally, he looked back to the ground. How much more interesting it seemed. Under the packed snow, life waited to bloom again. Not merely goats and elves, but a number of creatures would feed well after the deepsnows melted.

He had been rescued for a purpose. Perhaps he too would thrive come spring.

Abadan moved about the chamber, setting out his usual scrying tools just as he had done every day since Maarcus and Jilian had disappeared. 'Today you join me,' he told Walther.

The dwarf nodded. 'Whatever you think is best, but shouldn't we tell the physician and the Dragon Prince?'

Abadan absent-mindedly shook his head as he studied his bottles and potions. 'It will only worry the old man that we haven't found anything and it isn't likely to comfort—' He stopped in mid-sentence and looked into Walther's eyes. 'What did you call him?'

'The prince.'

'No, no you didn't. You called him the "Dragon Prince." Why is that?'

Walther wrinkled his brow in thought. 'Did I? It seems appropriate, doesn't it?'

'For other people who don't know him as we do, yes, but not us.' Abadan fell silent, looking at Walther as if the dwarf might uncover a valuable secret even though they had discussed the prince's title only hours ago. 'Well,' he said finally, 'let's see what we can turn up.'

The scrying bowl was dark. The magician waved a hand and Walther brought a lamp closer to see. Abadan prepared to add the serviceberry drop by drop when suddenly the fluid cleared.

Abadan looked at Walther, but something in the dwarf's mind batted away the magician.

The scene was of a young magician receiving his confirmation divination. The man kneeled while a blind woman robed in white placed her hand on his head.

'You will advise kings and princes, achieving great

things . . . And succeeding in all that you set out to do.'

The young man smiled and tried to rise, but she pushed down on his head. He winced and settled again.

'But—' her voice rang throughout the small chamber, echoing as if it were a large cavern. 'But,' she repeated, more quietly now, 'you will be overcome in the end. One stronger than you will rise in your place.'

The man's shoulders slumped and the rest of him seemed to follow until the seer's hands pulled him up. 'Rise for the naming, rise and know that you have a great future ahead of you.'

'Except,' the boy's lips seemed to form. 'Except . . .' The rest died there.

'I name you "Abadan".'

When the dwarf came out of his trance, he found the magician staring at him, eyes full of tears. He brushed them away angrily. 'I can see we won't make any progress today. You may go.'

Walther rose silently, leaving his master alone to consider his downfall.


Revered Mother and Revered Sisters, Masha and Dita, gave the Novice the job of tending the man. Mother and her two Daughters explained it to her as she sat in the courtyard idly trying to remember what had brought her out here.

'He'll need someone to tend him,' Mother announced.

'Someone gentle and careful,' Masha said.

'Like me?' Ginni asked in her ten-year-old's voice. She was very flattered to be given such a big responsibility.

Revered Mother Caronn nodded. 'Like you. But mind you, there are risks in dealing with a man. You must take precautions. First, do not listen to what he says. His words are peppered with language unfit for a young lady. We have therefore gagged him. You will never remove this gag.' She stopped and stared at Ginni. 'Understood?'

The girl nodded. 'I understand.'

'Good. Next. Do not speak or sing in his presence. You are much too sweet for his coarse ears and likely to drive him mad should he hear your voice.' Again she paused until Ginni indicated her obedience.

'Finally, never let him touch you. We have bound his hands to ease his temptation. However, he is a man who no doubt has seduced more than one lovely girl. A union with you would be more dreadful than I can bring myself to describe.' And yet she did in terms that the Novice couldn't digest. As she spoke, Revered Mother's face contorted into utter disgust and a shudder shook through her.

The Novice felt a sympathetic spasm. 'But—'

'No, buts!' shouted the Mother.

'I only wanted to ask—'

'You must obey without question.' Her expression did not allow for argument.

Novice looked down at the floor. 'Yes, Revered Mother.'

All seemed well and good until later that day when the cook gave her a tray and told her it was for the man. She took the food where she was directed.

He sat in a chair, hands tied and mouth gagged as the Mother promised. His eyes went wide when he saw her and a smile seemed to stretch around the kerchief.

She returned his smile and offered him the tray.

He could not take it with the bound hands, of course. She stood over him, holding the food. What was she to do with it? At no point could she envision him eating with the gag in place. She could feed him and leave his hands secured. She could let him eat with his mouth like a pig at the trough, but that seemed a violation somehow. Or at the least, it was an indignity a Revered Novice should not force on anyone.

She could both untie and ungag him and let him feed himself properly.

She put the tray on a table next to him and slumped into a nearby chair. Was the goal to feed the man or to scrutinize a young novice? She had tried to ask questions and been staved off. This had to be a test of her loyalty.

She stood suddenly. 'I'm sorry,' she mouthed without voicing the words, then fled from the room.

The Novice ran down the hall and slammed the door to her bedchamber. She had to keep as much distance between herself and the man as she could manage. He would shame her. Revered Mother said so.

But Revered Mother had given her the task of tending him.

The Novice blushed. She was behaving like a fool child. She sat on the room's only chair and chewed her lip.

She snatched up the brush from the dressing-table and began stroking her hair. Revered Sister Masha said she was vain to lavish so much care on her hair. Probably so. Still, the motion calmed her enough to think.

Why did the man seem even the least bit familiar? The Novice knew no men. She'd always been here.

Hadn't she?

The door opened and she leaped up from her chair. 'Revered Mother, I . . .' She broke into sobs. 'I tried. I did. I failed you.'

Revered Mother Caronn smiled and the Novice knew she'd been forgiven. 'Not to worry, child. You've done very well, very well indeed.'

She hugged the Novice and let her cry until there were no tears left.


'By 'uh Sis'ers!' Tom mumbled around his gag, after Ginni slammed the door closed behind her.

In its way, this episode was more bizarre than the attempted seduction. The simple truth was everything smacked of witch-work. Strange though it may have been, Tom found comfort in that one thought because witch-work could always be undone.

Somehow.

Ginni would be back. Next time, he would be ready for her no matter who she seemed to be playing. In the meanwhile, he was hungry enough to eat the food, bewitched or not. He rolled to face the opposite wall where he couldn't see the tray.

Many minutes later, Revered Mother Caronn entered without warning. She did not look as if feeding the prisoners was her foremost concern.

'It was foolish of you to come here.' She paused but didn't seem to expect an answer, which was just as well with the gag in place.

'Ginni came of her own accord. According to our code, she is ours now. We will train her as we see fit. It is not for you, or any man, to interfere.'

Doesn't appear to mind taking my seed, Tom thought. Just like a woman, she only wants the useful bits and throws out the rest.

Abruptly, she pulled a chair next to his, untied the kerchief, and began massaging his jaw. 'But we may yet have a use for you. We have long been interested in dragon lore. You are the only man in living memory reported to have forged a relationship with a dragon. Your instruction as to how this came about would be invaluable to us.'

'I'll bet,' Tom said. Even if he could tell her anything useful, he wouldn't betray his friend.

'It could mean your freedom.'

'That's nothing without Ginni's as well.'

She fidgeted with the heavy ring on her finger. 'That could be arranged.'

'I want her whole, intact, body and brains back the way they were.'

The hag laughed. 'I doubt even the Seven could manage that.'

'Then no deal,' said Tom.

'You misunderstand your options here. I do not make false bargains. We might be convinced to return her to you, but only she can restore the balance in her mind.'

Tom frowned. 'You've just been helping her find her way.'

'Well, yes, to a degree.' She smiled. 'From a certain point of view.'

'Point of view,' he echoed. 'Right.'

'One way or another, we will discover what you know.'

'Okay,' Tom said. 'I give. You want it so bad, it's yours. A gentleman's show of good faith.'

She snorted. 'I have known gentlemen. You, sir, are no gentleman.'

'Maybe not,' Tom said easily, as if he controlled the situation. 'Chances are a more reserved fellow wouldn't spend twenty years seeing the terrain from a dragon's back. Anyway, this is the entire secret. A sociable dragon and an unsocial human prefer each other's company to that of their own kind. History's full of such partnerships, from elves and their goats to men and their dogs. Just so happens my beast can talk.'

Revered Mother roughly retied the gag and stood to

leave. 'I can get tavern wisdom from any barkeep. Let me know when you decide to be more forthcoming.'

Yes, but sometimes barkeeps have more sense than witches, Tom thought, but he made no effort to speak around the kerchief. What could he tell her? How could he invent knowledge that would satisfy her when he'd never been able to puzzle it out himself?

Revered Mother stopped at the open doorway. 'Some notion of where the dragon roosts at this moment would be well received. Remember I speak true when I tell you I will find a way to learn what I wish to know. You can have your daughter or your dragon. You cannot have both. Think hard on your choice before you end up with neither.'

She slammed the door behind her without waiting for a reply.

Where was Grosik? Tom thought. I couldn't point to his whereabouts if she dosed me with all the serviceberry tea in the One Land.

As it happened, Revered Mother's suggestion turned out to have a powerful effect. When the mercenary considered it, he realized maybe he did know where the dragon had gone. Home for Grosik was a cave not far from Tom's first battle.

Not far from the Tower of the Hags.

Maarcus retired to his private chambers after his humiliation in front of the young prince. Harmon, ever-present these days, sat with him in a discreet corner.

'Well,' the physician said when Abadan came to visit, 'come to laugh at the senile old man?'

'Certainly not,' Abadan snapped. 'If not for the grace of the Sisters . . .'

Maarcus jumped out of his chair. 'So you do think I'm

slipping,' he accused, half afraid to hear it confirmed, half relieved to be able to stop pretending.

The magician was not so easily cornered. 'You must admit you've not been acting yourself these last weeks.'

Maarcus slumped back into his seat. 'No, I haven't and I don't know what's come over me. Enough chitchat. What brings you here?'

'You.'

'Me and what else?'

'I can't raise Wanton Tom.'

'Why tell me?' Maarcus said bitterly. 'Tell the prince.'

'I thought you'd want to know.'

Maarcus shook his head. 'This will be our failure, and after we've come so far—'

'We have not failed yet,' the magician interrupted. 'We still have the prince.'

'How long do you except that to last? He won't be able to refrain from going himself to save Jilian, now that he knows she's so close.'

'We need to keep him busy with confronting Alvaria. She must be planning to bring the trolls here.' Abadan spoke as if the choices were clear-cut.

'Ignoring, of course, that our best sources of intelligence never came close to gathering anything useful.'

'No,' said the magician. 'Even now, as prisoners, they are being useful. They can't help but pick up information about Hadrian while they're there. It is simply that we would rather put them to a better and safer use.'

Maarcus stared at his friend. 'No wonder magicians never marry. What woman could bear children for such uncaring beasts?'

'No need to get personal, Maarcus, especially since you've had such good fortune with women.'

'At least my wife bore me a son.'

'A man of fine character, too.'

'Of finer virtue than someone I—' The physician halted himself in mid-insult. They hadn't squabbled with such malicious intent since they'd been enemies vying for the king's ear. It was childish then, and it was ridiculous in men of their advanced age.

'We haven't really addressed the other problem,' Abadan said, as if the argument had never happened.

'Yes, I know.'

But the magician wouldn't let it rest. As always, he had to voice it. 'We greatly underestimated Hadrian. He could easily decide this is the best chance he's had in years to claim the throne. Most of the pretenders have murdered each other, and the common people are too distracted by the elfwitch's coming onslaught to protest his rise to power.'

'Yes, I said I knew,' Maarcus repeated. 'I am not deaf or daft.' Abadan might as well have stabbed him between the ribs while he slept. Suddenly he realized that was just how he felt. Executioners had already slipped in and about the castle, searching for Nikolis or any who might be loyal to him. They hadn't succeeded in killing the prince yet, but they would . . . eventually. 'So you think Hadrian is behind the earlier assassination attempts?'

'I should hope so.'

'You hope so!'

'If not, our problem is even bigger than it currently appears.'

Grosik took the inconspicuous approach, flying high and with reserve.

The air stank of dragon dung, though not a one was in sight. Doubtless he reeked of the humans and likely their magic as well.

Dragons do not banish their kind outright. They are too few in number and breed too seldom. But like any community, however loosely tied, they have rules of behavior and means of enforcing them. So returning home felt odd to the outcast dragon – not that he'd been gone such a long time. Thirty or forty human years measured only a few moments in the lives of his own kind. The strangeness was more a matter of the dragon's circumstance – his uncommon departure, and his extremely unusual use of time in the past fifteen years. It would be many more years before Grosik would be widely welcomed here.

'Away for an eye-blink and no more sense than to arrive swathed with the stench of our lessers. Could you not take your punishment without disgracing yourself?'

Each word flowed into his mind, sharpened with barbs that were almost physically painful. There was no proper response, so Grosik did not offer one. Strictly speaking it was not even necessary to greet another dragon after an absence, but it was a courtesy granted to companions and nest-mates.

'Hello,' Grosik spoke into the other's mind, casually, pleasantly, and without rancor.

His brother responded with the horror of having been addressed by an outcast. Too shaken to make an appropriate retort, he flew beyond easy contact range.

'Anything to avoid the appearance of sanctioning a renegade,' Grosik said to his back. 'Parasites are all the same, regardless of species.'

The interchange left a sour taste in his mouth, like the raw meat left too long in the sun and that was considered everyday fare here. He'd foolishly hoped for a few serene breaths, where he might enjoy the surroundings before his first unpleasant encounter.

On second thought, Grosik decided it was just as well that he was reminded of his place among his own. His brother would not have welcomed him in any case; and Grosik had not come to seek out cowards.

He relaxed. He did not expect another challenge for some while yet. Most would prefer his brother's course of avoiding him.

The dragon did not search out anyone he knew to be of his blood-line. Instead he went looking for the female who laid his children. She had not treated him any better than the rest when he left, but she alone had consented to letting him fertilize her eggs. She alone had once thought him worthy of continuing his line.

He made no effort to announce himself or to rush. The former was accomplished the instant he reached the border, and the latter only on the direst occasions.

The terrain was all cliffs of red sandstone and millennia-old rock formations. Slowly the wind wore down the rock, but not so slowly that the oldest dragons couldn't remember when boulders toppled or the sculptures reshaped themselves.

It took hours to unearth his one-time mate. Barik's taste for sunny outcrops had not changed – but her interest in companionship had.

Family as the two-legged beasts knew it was not relevant here. As soon as Grosik could fly, his mother had left him just as her mother had done. There was no danger. Dragons ruled this realm more thoroughly than any other creature claimed its den. Only the great beasts of the sea had as much freedom.

He found her accompanied by two young adults. Men of any two-legged race would find this an unremarkable, small group. In traditional dragon terms, she was utterly encircled. No dragon volunteered for such a position.

None that Grosik knew, anyway.

His instincts had guided him to her and now a plan began to take shape.

# Chapter 14

# TORTURE

The servant set down the bowl of warm stew and took away the cold dish the prince had barely touched that morning. Nikolis nodded his thanks, and the man left him to his isolation.

He speared a piece of meat and examined it. It turned his stomach just to look at it. 'Too bad the old goat gave up her life for me,' he said to his fork. 'Poisoned or not, I can't swallow it.' He wondered if the current cook had met another mishap or whether there simply was no other food to serve. He'd have to see that his rations were sent to the refugees. Someone should benefit from them.

He might as well work off the food he didn't eat. Maybe a little swordplay would loosen his foul humor.

No good. He needed Maarcus – either of them. The younger was unreachable and the elder might as well be. He couldn't trust anyone else in the castle not to run him through.

Nikolis decided he was just looking for something to

gnaw at and worry over. He fretted for Jilian, first and foremost. Maarcus concerned him as well – a talented man, but too soft of heart for this business.

Then there was Ceeley, who'd become as dear to him as she had to the others. That she had been compelled to leave was bad enough. That she could slip away and out of The Cliffs without their knowledge was worse still, and not just because it pinpointed the glaring weaknesses in their security. Imagining her safe did little to salve the guilt.

The dwarf girl inevitably reminded Nik of the goatboy. He longed to know the fate of the elf who had nursed him when he was still a malformed dragon, who had risked himself when the elfwitch closed in. Nikolis hoped she hadn't killed the boy, that she had found a use for him. But even this was cold comfort. Being useful to Alvaria hardly seemed a fitting way for such a fine elf to live.

Nikolis would have to rescue the boy if he could find him. The old Mut never would have become attached. Personal crusades were foolish and often deadly in the midst of battle. But there it was, one more person to fret over.

The prince rubbed his thumb across the dragon coin in his pocket. The elfwitch had drawn them together. Nikolis could not leave the boy's fate in her hands. Sisters help him, he just couldn't.

Any more than he could ignore Ginni's fate in the grip of the Forty-nine mages.

'A knock would have been appreciated,' Nikolis said to Abadan as the magician silently closed the door behind him.

'I didn't want to alert anyone in the hall to my presence.'

'Not even the guard?'

'He seems to have deserted his post.'

'Ah.' Nikolis studied his lunch, thinking, It's just as well I have no appetite. 'You're back so soon. You have news, I take it? Then get on with it.' Nikolis felt a rare fit of temper growing on him. He seemed completely unable to affect anything that mattered.

'The man who brought you back from the battle-field—'

'Is dead?' He tried to feel sorry for him and couldn't. The soldier, if indeed he was one, was of the lowest sort.

'No, sire. He's missing.'

Nikolis braced his arms against his desk and pulled himself up as slowly as an old man. He opened a drawer, searching for something his mind had yet to inform him about. The drawer was empty. Jilian's knife was gone. Naturally. The man had stolen it from Nik yesterday.

Abadan waited for the prince to acknowledge him. The prince did not.

'Sire?'

Nikolis bit his lip so hard that it bled. 'You're still here?'

'Sire, there's more.'

'Later.'

'Now, sire.' Abadan stood his ground.

Nikolis would have to remove him bodily. 'Guard!'

No one came. The prince would have to throw out the magician himself. He couldn't picture himself lifting the man up – or rather the vision it created was absurd. Nikolis laughed aloud. 'It seems you win. Tell me.'

To his credit Abadan did not smile. 'Rumors have begun. A tale goes around that you sacrificed your army to the elfwitch in order to save yourself.'

'How bad is it?'

'Few believe, but many will become convinced if you can't find a way to quell their fears.'

Nikolis stormed across the room and stopped within inches of Abadan's face. In that moment, he seemed to tower over him. 'Unless I can find a way! What exactly do you expect me to do?'

'Sire, the One Land will crumble to nothing if you . . . Everything we've worked for . . .'

'Correction, Abadan. Everything you have worked for. By the Sisters, I was just an infant manipulated and reshaped into someone's image of a liberator!' He pulled the dragon coin from his pocket. 'This is what I think of my heritage and of you!' He flung the token into the blazing fire. He stared into the flames, keeping his back to Abadan.

'You can't deny it, Nikolis, any of it. It is who you are, whether made by man or the Sisters. You can choose to lead or follow, but you can not choose to leave it behind.' The magician stepped across the wood floor and closed the door behind him with more force than was necessary.

Nikolis waited many minutes before he turned to be sure Abadan had gone. On impulse, he bent and snatched the dragon coin from the flames. As he'd expected, it remained undamaged.

Though he held the fiery metal in the palm of his hand, he felt no pain. The skin remained pink and intact.

Abadan was more right than he knew. It was not simply impossible for Nikolis to ignore his fate. He would have to decide to lead or it would force him to.

Goatboy hated the audiences with the One. Though he knew in his heart she was evil, still he tried to please her, still he was proud when he seemed to succeed and downcast when he did not. He knew himself for a fool and yet he couldn't stop himself.

Alvaria's dreadful grin chilled him to the bone. When she smiled at him, he knew the worst was coming. A day or a week, later, she would degrade him or make abhorrent demands that would twist his insides and fill him with self-loathing as he performed the task.

And he would always carry it through.

This was her true talent – twisting others to wickedness by making them behave so abominably that they come to believe their actions were justified, rather than admit they themselves were villainous.

Those who resisted her met exile, torture, death.

She broke many. The few who had the strength to rebel outright met her most cunning fate. They were transformed into the troll slaves who wreaked such havoc against their own.

Goatboy felt sure he was destined for such an end. The warmth and comfort were part of a darker plan. He would not accept her gifts.

He would reject her.

Notti woke, beneath a mound of blankets. He tossed them off. If the quilts came from Alvaria, he would rather sleep naked on the cold ground.

A woman entered carrying a bowl of broth. 'Notti, you'll catch your death.' She pulled up the covers. 'Here, sit up.'

She was not the One, but his mother.

She had denied the One.

He allowed her to spoon in the rich broth. Belly full, he drifted back to sleep while she stood guard.

He felt her hovering and tending, jumping at each sign of movement from him. He kicked off the blankets only to have them instantly replaced.

It was nurturing to the point of stifling. He was not accustomed to so much attention. He felt like a starving man being force-fed a banquet and choking on the heaps of food. He could swallow only so much, no matter how these elves meant well.

With a great effort, he shoved the entire pile of bedding to the floor. He looked up to see his mother rising from her chair in alarm. 'It's all r-right,' he told her. 'I'm n-not used to s-such s-s-soff-tness. F-forgive me.' He arranged the blankets on the floor, curled into the mound, and pulled up exactly one to cover himself.

She settled back on her seat.

He gave her a reassuring smile, and closed his eyes so as not to see her hurt expression. He wasn't being altogether honest with her. He would have enjoyed the bed if not for the constant attention.

Finally, he lay still long enough that she relaxed her vigilance. Notti in turn let his body unwind. Warm, fed, and protected as he hadn't been in as long as he could remember, he fell into a sleep that was more trance than sleep.

Voices swirled above him. He was not sure if he should stir or not.

'I never expected him to get this far,' said a high voice, heavy with the lilt of hope and music. His mother?

'No. Nor I.' This one was deeper, more pessimistic.

'But it's good that he has, yes?'

'Perhaps, perhaps not.'

'How can it be not,' she asked, a hint of anger daring to creep in.

'Perhaps Alvaria sent him to us. Certainly she seeks to exploit our every weakness. How better than to encumber us with a burden which we can't abandon.'

'But he's no trouble at all.'

'That's not the onus of which I speak,' the voice said softly. 'but rather the responsibility of decision. Chances are we should send him back—'

'Or kill him.'

The voice seemed different, but Notti couldn't be sure if the same person spoke . . . or whether anyone had. His imagination was mired with confusion.

He tossed and rolled. He could not wake.

A cool hand felt his forehead and his cheeks. 'Rest. You're safe here.' She seemed to believe her words.

But did he?


Ceeley sat on the bank watching the blood river. She no longer thought of evil as something foreign to her. Like the river phlegm dripping from her clothes, it enveloped her. It wormed its way into her skin and made her itch.

She knew this itch. Scratching made it worse, gave her a rash like she got sometimes when she rubbed against poison oak. The thing to do was ignore it until it went away.

Two human grown-ups were washed up on the sand. A man raved like maybe he was a lunatic. The woman had tried to hug Ceeley when they first emerged from the water, but now she merely pinched her ugly face in disapproval of the world. They both reminded her of someone she'd known once, or maybe met in a dream.

She had very interesting dreams.

Ceeley shrugged the people off. They weren't her responsibility. She was just a little dwarf kid.

Elves were waiting on the bank for her to come to them. She eagerly scrambled over the rocks to the grass above.

Above the river the land was desolate. Snow lay in patches, but the ground was cracked and hungry underneath. With the top-soil blown away, the wan, yellowish earth reminded Celia of a fever dwarves could catch from river insects.

A bitter wind blew and she shivered. The elves paid no notice. They didn't offer a blanket or dry clothes and she was too proud to ask. They waved her forward and took up a position on either side.

Four more elves hung back, sticking around for the humans to reach them.

The silence was spooky. It wasn't so much quiet as an absence of sound. (Absence was a new word she'd learned and she felt pleased to find a use for it.)

The pressure on her ears wrapped her in a bubble of not-sound; but she feared the elves would leave her behind with the crazy man if she paused to try to clear them.

Maybe noise got lost here.

The dwarf concentrated hard to pick up sound some other way and noticed the ground was shaking. Something was coming. Something big.

Or did she imagine a sound to fill the empty hole?

Ceeley's clothing dried stiff with river rubbish as the three walked toward camp. She could no longer see the river – would have forgotten it existed but for the reek of her tunic. To her right and left were misshapen men and women of all races – or no races she knew – laboring at mysterious tasks. Could they be foreigners from distant lands?

An elf's whip slapped the air and suddenly the sound came rushing in. Mournful cries and the pounding of machinery broke through first, but other, fainter noises followed. A baby whimpered nearby. Fire crackled far off.

She realized she was warm again without a coat.

Thick greasy smoke billowed up, coating her nose and throat. She tried to cough only to discover an open mouth gave her a stronger taste of the putrid smell.

Behind her, a woman sobbed, deep heart-wrenching wails. Ceeley hurried to get away from her.

What was the matter with that woman – and with all these people? Didn't they understand life was a crude series of let-downs great and small? Didn't they know this was all they could hope for, unless they served the One well enough that she might ease their way into the hands of the Sisters?

And then they could join their parents. For Ceeley no day could be finer than the one on which she saw her ma and da again. She looked back at the crazy man and the frowny-faced woman. Maybe those two grown-ups had forgotten their parents were waiting.

Maybe they didn't have any parents.

She didn't know why she thought so, but it seemed it must be true for them to be so upset. Ceeley felt a little bad for them then. It's a sad thing not to have parents, a very sad thing.

Hadrian delighted in giving Jilian the report of the battle and its aftermath. He swaggered into the dungeon, stopping first to joke with the guards in a loud voice.

'Won't be long now before they crown me, boys. That princeling led the soldiers into a fool battle and couldn't stomach the carnage. The bugger passed out. Can you imagine?'

Ivan and Lyam let out loud guffaws for the prince's benefit.

'I hear he ran from the worst of it,' Hadrian continued. 'He returned just long enough for the clean-up and to put a few of the wounded out of their misery.'

'Too bad we don't have him here, sire,' Lyam said. 'We could show him the meaning of bloodshed.' The guard grunted as if stabbed.

Jilian sat with her knees pulled up to her chest and her arms wrapped tight around them. Nikolis was no coward. If he'd left the battlefield, there was a greater need elsewhere. Or perhaps he'd never left it at all. Perhaps it was all a rumor spread by Hadrian's men. In order to shut out the present ridicule she tried to focus on worrying over what Hadrian had done with Maarcus.

But she had dreamed of the dead men.

'No survivors but the prince himself. Isn't that fine?' Hadrian broke through Jilian's best efforts to ignore him.

'I'm sure you had a hand in that.' The corpses would be undeniable, if not the cause.

His face showed surprise, then pride. 'Anything to aid my homeland.'

Jilian turned her back to him, but he remedied that by entering the cell next to hers. He stood as close as he dared, just beyond her reach. 'I have waited since before you were born for this and I will have it.'

'You're more than welcome to what's left.'

'Care to put that in writing?'

Jilian cursed. 'I'd rather be transformed into a troll.'

He frowned, his eyebrows forming a black and grey vee across his forehead. 'Ah well. Still simmering I see. We'll have to bring you to a full boil if we expect you to see our way of thinking. Fortunately there's no shortage of water in The Cliffs.'

The princess could only wonder what he'd done to the water.

Changing tacks, Hadrian breathed warm moist air on her neck. 'You're quite lovely,' he whispered.

Jilian swallowed a grimace and said nothing.

298

'It's appropriate for a lady to thank a gentleman when paid a compliment. I suppose your foster-parents must have been lacking in social graces.'

'Thank you,' she said, not rising to the bait.

'Or perhaps it is your mother who lacks.'

What could she say to that? The usual defense did not apply.

'Is she as ruthless as they say?'

Jilian kept her silence, and waited to see where he led the twisted path of conversation.

'Speaking for myself, I'm doubtful she's behind the trolls. Women simply don't have the fortitude for battle. Wouldn't you agree?'

Jilian did not answer.

'Look at me,' he ordered. Jilian turned to face him but kept her eyes fixed over his shoulder.

His hand reached through the bars and gripped her chin. He yanked her head sharply up and down. 'Don't you agree?'

'Many say so,' she answered, unsure of his intent.

'Women prefer much more devious routes. For instance, I've found the best assassins are female. What do you say to that?'

'I wouldn't question your experience.'

He tilted his head sideways as if he were deciding whether she insulted him. Apparently concluding she hadn't, he let go of her chin and backed away.

'You won't profit by resisting me.'

'Oh?' she asked.

'No, it only prolongs your friend's agony.'

It was the first time Hadrian had mentioned Maarcus since he'd taken him away. Jilian yearned for more information, but kept her silence. Prince Hadrian would tell her only what he wanted her to know.

'He's strong, as I expected,' he continued. 'But he's wasting his time. I will break him . . . even if I have to go through you to get there.' Hadrian rose and left the cell.

'I'm through here, Lyam. It's time the princess found a permanent home.'

After the disastrous battle against the elfwitch, Walther took to spending his time in the magician's chamber. He read the scrolls or practiced simple healing with Harmon. Occasionally, Abadan stole a moment to comment on Walther's progress.

More and more, the dwarf suffered visions.

He lay on his back still breathing hard from the most recent episode. Not as ghastly as some, it left him exhausted nonetheless.

Slowly Walther rose and slid onto what had become his stool. He held out his hand, willing the tremors to cease. When he was sure he could control his own flesh, he dipped the quill into the ink and began writing.

'We stood on the edge of the world. The Green was behind us under feet of snow, but we knew it was there. Life lay beneath the apparently fallow soil.

'Sometime, perhaps in high summer, we might have enjoyed the vastness. On this cold, lonely morning, we felt smaller and more unwelcome than we've ever felt in our lives. Evergreens did not grow here; most trees were no more than barren branches. Ahead was a huge brown plain, arid, windy, and wholly uninviting.

'If the elfwitch sends her storms to rage here, nothing will hamper them until they reach the far side.'

Walther fixed on the vision of the elfwitch astride such a frenzied squall, and shuddered. She seemed unstoppable already.

The Novice followed Revered Mother's detailed instructions for tending the garden. As she dug in the rich soil and weeded out the unwanted plants, she found herself staring at leaves, petals, and stems trying to divine their ultimate use in poultices or tonic. Something tickled at a memory too distant to pull up. There were herbs hidden among the vegetables . . . Just like in that other garden, common plants disguised forbidden twins.

She let her fingers sift the soil, smelled the comfortable smell of another garden, another time, a younger child. The greenhouse was only a windowsill back then. It was not this greenhouse, but she was that child.

The sun beat through the panes and warmed her, despite the cold and wind and snow. Here she was protected, cared for. She had not been safe watching over the other herbs.

She idly drew the shape of a dragon in the dirt. The beast seemed almost human, almost familiar. She stared and stared at the image before wiping the surface clean.

Revered Novice wanted to smell the blooms. Blossoms in deepwinter! How remarkable . . . and not possible in the old garden. The light or heat was wrong. She'd had to mix them with different plants that didn't work as well as her lady wished.

The lady who made her kiss a man, many men . . .

A man! But that was impossible . . .

They always fell to the ground after.

She'd killed someone! Had she been an assassin?

Revered Novice plucked the leaves from the plant and sniffed.

No, that wasn't it. She'd straightened him out, checked for a pulse, and left him sleeping.

Only sleeping.

The Novice looked up at the sound of heavy footsteps. Too heavy.

It must be the man.

Her stomach tightened. Another test. But why? They'd given her no new directions. She'd done as they commanded.

'Ginni?' His voice was soft and surprised.

She looked up from her work and held herself erect. She nodded an acknowledgment, neither smiling nor frowning.

'I didn't know you'd be here. Why am I here?' He rubbed his hand across his face.

So they had untied his hands.

She shrugged her shoulders and bent back to the soil. He was not her problem.

'Can I help?'

Staring into the dirt, she shook her head 'no.'

'I once knew a woman who used to plant these in little boxes set by the window. Funny, she never would tell me what they were for.'

The Novice glanced up in alarm. That was her memory! He'd stolen her memory. 'How dare you!' she shouted, unable to control her tongue. 'How dare you lay claim to me!'

Shocked and dismayed at her failure to keep quiet, she clapped a hand over her mouth and ran from the room.

Hair flying behind the girl, Ginni reminded Revered Mother of Roslin. The witch sighed. Roslin had been such a promising student.

Her lips tightened into a line. Caronn would not lose the

daughter, who was at least as strong in the Seven Sisters' blessings as the mother. The Forty-nine would take those gifts, then mold and remold them until they were certain of the girl's training. To waste such a valuable resource in her mother's time was a minor blasphemy. To do so in these days was beyond unthinkable.

Revered Mother smiled to her attendants. 'The conditioning seems to be taking very well. If she can't manage to be in the same room with the man for more than a few moments, we are surely succeeding in breaking the bond between them.'

'But, Revered Mother,' Dita asked, 'isn't it possible she's simply afraid of him after all we've told her?'

'Possibly. All the same, she does not recognize him.'

'Yes, but what if he—'

Caronn gave her an icy smile, forestalling further hair-splitting. 'If he what?'

'Forgive me, Revered Mother. I forget myself sometimes.'

'Yes, you do, Sister. See that you work on that.' She continued on down the hall, inviting the others to trail slightly behind her. 'On to more important matters. What shall we do with the man? As you know, we are divided among the Inner Seven. I admit the tidiness of disposing of him appeals to me. However, the Sisters delivered him to us. I will not kill that which has been gifted.'

'He may yet call the dragon,' Dita offered.

Revered Mother frowned at her for speaking out of turn. She would require disciplining once the crisis passed. 'Yes, and what then?'

Masha laughed. 'What is one ordinary man and an injured dragon against the world's Forty-nine most powerful Mages?'

Caronn joined in the laughter. 'A very good point, Sister. Excellent in fact.'

The hags had been harrying Tom in his sleep while they smiled coyly during his waking hours. He knew the smiles were as false as, well, as false as a witch's smile. He laughed ruefully. There was no comfort in meeting the root of a soldier's saying first-hand.

For the inexplicable moment, he had seemingly free rein to wander where he would. Yet wherever he went, the Sisters all reminded him of Ginni.

As for her, what could he think? She was lost in a world of their making. He went short of breath and his chest ached every time he saw her. Too many days like this and he'd damn himself forever, anything to set her free.

Left to himself after his daughter fled the garden, Wanton Tom did the only practical thing. He studied the plants Ginni had been poking and prodding.

He was no expert on greenery. In his opinion, plants were too much trouble whether they were the eatin' kind or decoratin' ones. Still, it didn't take much to figure the old hags weren't likely to grow a few plants just for looks. If anything, they'd pluck out the pretty flowers and leave only the ragged weeds. Besides, Roslin's habits were truer to the Forty-nine than they knew. If she kept one of these around, it had a use.

But what?

Eyeballing it didn't tell him much. He hesitated to touch or sniff it. Poison came in many forms, and Tom had no interest in killing himself, especially now that Ginni seemed to be remembering who she was.

Instead, he walked around the greenhouse, paying no particular attention to anything, just sucking in the overall spirit of the place. There seemed to be no foodstuffs here, only medicinals and their kin.

He couldn't help but wonder what the hags ate during the winter. There were no towns close by. Who would brave the weather to sell them food? On the other hand, who would dare refuse them?

Stranger and stranger.

And what good did any of it do him or Ginni?

'We have decided on your use,' said a woman from behind him.

Tom went rigid with attention. There was no way this could be good news. 'Yes?'

'You will bed your daughter until you beget a grand-daughter.'

'That's vile. You'll have to kill me first.'

She came closer and held a sharp point to his back. 'There's no need to kill you when we can kill Ginni.'

He held his calm against the urge to punch her. 'What's the point? She's the powerful one. I'm just a man.'

The Revered Sister smiled. 'I'm delighted you understand your position. However,' she let it hang as she performed a lengthy inspection of the plants. 'However,' the Sister repeated, 'she is not the only option, merely the most elegant.'

Tom hated to consider what 'elegant' might mean to such women as these.

'Once the girl is born . . .' She stopped, seeming to think better of what she'd been about to say.

'Once the girl is born, what?' he pressed.

'You are a man. They will be none of your concern.'

'Says you.'

'You are wasting my time. The girl will be ready when she comes to you tonight. You are to do as

you are told or your daughter won't see the next sun-
rise.'

'I will not.'

'Oh, but you will.' Her eyes held a callousness Tom
had seen in few men. 'By the Seven Sisters, you will.'

# Chapter 15

## EXPENDABLE

Elder Jedrek didn't relax after finally flushing out the rebels. If anything, he grew more nervous worrying about the traitors he hadn't yet identified. He sat behind his desk, the same desk where he'd been when they rushed him, the same desk he'd had since Alvaria had exiled him.

The desk itself was an absurdity. She'd forced it on him and he'd kept it to remind himself what he gave up. Yet, how could he expect his clan to honor the traditional ways with this heavy reminder of the other? It was more likely to cause jealousy among the weak-willed than serve as a ward against the past.

His finger traced the patterns dug deep into the wood, those which followed the grain and those which ran counter to it. Only a few had ever divined the secret power of those designs and half of them were imprisoned.

The desk reminded him that there were too many

structures in their lives. They weighed down Jedrek and his people. He needed to rid himself of the load, and yet he was as guilty as the most spineless among them for relying on the artificial nature of elf-made things.

How did they differ from Alvaria herself, when they had been known to mislead others in order to provide for themselves? Some argued they deserved their physical and mental comfort, that it was only fitting given their deprived circumstances. Jedrek had once agreed with them, but now knew it to be no more than self-delusion and justification for their own selfishness.

Jedrek looked around him. Virtually all their wealth had ended up in this room. For safe-keeping at first, but ultimately through lethargy of a newly established tradition. Cushions, hangings, carpets. They'd been allowed whatever they could carry, and as a group they'd managed to carry more than one might imagine. Alvaria had laughed at their struggle and now he understood the full extent of her amusement. She had won several times over while they had shouldered unnecessary burdens.

The robes of office he wore – what nonsense! What office? He was no more fit than any of the others. He had simply protested the loudest. Here he sat years later, still a loud voice swallowed up by the din and still no closer to his goal of redressing the balance.

Their exile should have been a pilgrimage, an opening to eye, heart, and soul. Instead, it was just another excuse to squabble, dicker, and form yet another unproductive alliance.

A soft knock at the door brought him to himself.

'My mother said you wanted to see me, sir.'

'Ah, Notti. Come in, my boy.' News of the child's arrival lifted Jedrek's spirits in a way nothing had since the betrayal. The boy had stayed behind and learned more of endurance than their exile came close to teaching during those same years. The child could inspire them all.

'What news do you bring of the outside world?' Jedrek asked, as he rose and motioned the child to be seated.

The boy took a while before speaking. 'I d-don't b-bring much. I was the g-goatboy of my village and so I g-gathered very l-little in worldly g-goods or s-sp-spiritual ones.'

Jedrek settled beside Notti rather than returning to his accustomed place behind the desk. 'You collected more than you know.'

The elf sat and waited. He had extraordinary patience for one so young. Finally, Notti said in a quiet voice, 'Sir Jedrek?

'Yes?'

'Well, s-sir, I know I've b-been here only a v-very short while and I h-hate to impose on you so s-soon after arriving, b-but—'

'Yes,' encouraged Jedrek.

The boy watched his feet as he thumped his heels against the floor. 'Alvaria – Th-the One?'

Jedrek couldn't imagine what Alvaria had promised the boy. He braced himself for the terrible disappointment of another soul wasted.

Notti cleared his throat and began again. 'Alvaria once told me I was old enough for my m-manhood c-ceremony,' he managed almost without stuttering. 'I w-was w-wondering if she was sp-speaking the tr-truth.'

Jedrek looked at him, trying to gauge his age. With so many years away from children, he'd lost the knack for it. 'How old are you?'

'Thirteen or f-fourteen s-summers.'

'I'm puzzled. You must know the answer to your question as well as I.'

Notti flushed. 'I'm v-very s-sorry, s-sir. I h-hate to t-take up your t-time when I'm p-plainly unw-worthy.'

'No, no,' Jedrek said in a soothing voice. 'I meant nothing of the kind. I am genuinely befuddled.'

'The v-village k-kept any knowledge from m-me that they d-didn't w-want me to h-have,' the boy explained.

Jedrek patted Notti's back. 'No, I should apologize to you. I should have realized.'

'Well?' asked the boy expectantly. 'Is it t-time?'

The elder smiled, genuinely delighted, and he had not been truly pleased in a very long time. 'It is indeed. We'll begin the instruction today. In fact, we'll begin right this moment. Make yourself comfortable.'

Notti placed his feet flat on the floor and perched on the edge of his chair.

'Relax, my boy. This could take some time.' He smiled, half sad, half delighted at old memories. 'When I was your age, this was considered the most important work any adult elf could perform. Only the most trusted members of the clan would be so honored to instruct young ones in the proper ways. It's not just a drilling of the Principals. It's also an understanding of why we have lived this way for so many generations despite large temptations to do otherwise.'

Notti nodded and looked wise beyond his years – as he no doubt was. 'I'm ready.'

'Who created the earth?'

The younger elf looked puzzled. 'I'm not sure. The S-sisters care for it, but I don't th-think they created it. Because if they did, who created th-them?'

The boy's thoughtful answer surprised Jedrek. 'You've observed more than I'd hoped. We don't believe the

Sisters created the world, but rather that they guide in knowing right from wrong, which includes our dealings with this mortal realm.'

Notti's brow tightened as he considered this. 'Then who created the S-sisters?'

'We don't know. We can only see the Sisters' influence and know that whoever created them must have been a supreme force for good.'

Notti squirmed on his seat.

'An uncomfortable thought, not to know for certain, don't you think?'

The boy nodded.

'But far better to admit our ignorance than purport to know that which is uncertain, and to behave with the arrogance of false knowledge.'

Notti smiled. He had no trouble with this concept, having already weathered that which the elder warned against.

'What do we know of the Sisters?'

'They c-control the f-four elements and the three r-races.'

'Close but not quite. Guide, they guide the elements and the races. We always have freedom to choose to turn away.'

'Then Alvaria chose to d-defy the S-sisters?' the boy asked in a whisper, as if he expected her to strike him dead.

Jedrek answered him without hesitation. 'We believe she did.'

'But why w-would she do it?'

'You might as well ask why there is evil in the world. There will always be those who fight to be above others simply because they are more talented or bigger or older or younger or stronger. Just as there will always be those who seek to use their gifts – and often the very same gifts – to help their fellow mortals.'

Notti chewed the skin around his thumbnail in silence, but his eyes were far away.

'I think that's enough to absorb for one day.'

The boy jumped up from his chair. 'Yes, sir, thank you, sir.' He opened the door to find his mother on the other side.

'You are here. Good,' she said, but she was addressing Jedrek.

His few moments of tranquility vanished in that instant. 'What is it?'

'We've received word that Lady Lyda has been captured.'

Jedrek froze at the news. It had not been his goal to see her harmed, though this was always the risk. One set the pieces into motion with benevolent purpose, and one hoped. There wasn't always a difference between the results of good and bad intentions. People bled. People died.

He'd aimed to train the human to confront Alvaria. Perhaps the witch had divined his plan and twisted it to her own ends. Perhaps . . .

'It's not your fault,' she said.

'I will always bear the responsibility for my requests. Beyond that, I have learned to let the Sisters work as they will. It is a difficult thing.'

'Yes, it is,' she said.

Mother and son shared identical expressions, as if to say they both knew exactly how difficult.

Maarcus refused to join Abadan in his magical chamber. If the old stuffed hat needed him, he could bloody well come to him.

Instead, he sat transfixed by the fireplace while Harmon kept brewed tea at the ready.

The physician dreamed of the death of his son. The dream was familiar; indeed, for some years it had visited him nightly. Time passed and eventually other nightmares took its place, but he'd always known it would return one day.

It began and ended with his son. At sixteen, the junior Maarcus was an active boy with no patience for the sedentary studies of his regal age-mates. He didn't need fine weather or taunting for an excuse to sidestep his lessons. Nothing seemed to matter to him but the pleasures of the moment.

Maarcus the Sixth repeatedly apologized to his deceased wife. She'd given her life in birthing their only child, trusting her husband to carry on. Instead, too distraught over losing her, he'd done a very poor job rearing their son.

Arguments and accusations from father to son were constant and endless. 'What will become of you? How can you hold up your head in the King's Court?' met scowls and foul language.

Finally, his son pointed out the obvious. 'How can you hold me to a standard higher than that of the Great King himself?'

'Your lack of respect for His Majesty is appalling! How dare you speak of him so? He made the One Land what it is today. He made us what we are.'

Chin outthrust in a face rouged in the current frivolous fashion, the young man said, 'His children will undo the Land and us both. We may as well enjoy our downfall.' The boy stomped from the room, lace ruffles swaying behind at every movement of arm and leg.

Maarcus did not call him back. He didn't have the stomach.

It wasn't long after that he made two decisions. The first was to see his boy married to someone who might civilize him, and the second was to speak with the hated magician Abadan regarding the dying king's heirs.

The latter had turned out well enough, but the former he still wondered over. For even here his son had pre-empted him by finding an unsuitable girl. A pretty thing to look at, she was as poorly reared as the worst-mannered children at court. The girl was as easily swayed as a young seedling and with no more thought to the consequences. His son haughtily confirmed he had been seeing her for some months, and that in fact she carried the next Maarcus.

'How can you be sure the child is yours and no other's?' he'd asked.

'Simple,' the other had answered in a harsh tone the father had never heard him use before. 'Otherwise, I will kill both her and the baby – and she knows it.'

Such savagery did not reflect well on their lineage, but this too was something the king's physician was reluctantly learning to accept.

The wedding was a quieter affair than Maarcus the Sixth had initially hoped for. Now, he simply wanted his son and this girl wed before the rumors became jokes.

When the child was born, Maarcus was at least relieved to discover there was no question as to the boy's parentage. As he grew, he looked every inch a Maarcus. He smiled their lopsided grin. He even had the inconvenient immunity to magical ability.

He would make a good physician, Maarcus thought. But by the time the boy was three or four, he realized this would not be. Marriage and parenting had no effect on his son, just as it seemed to completely bypass the girl he married. When Maarcus suggested apprenticing the youngest Maarcus into a clan of elves, his father made no objections. He seemed not to notice his absence at all.

The physician's daughter-in-law yielded, but the loss of daily contact with her child seemed to drain her. She grew mournful, dropping away from her friends and refusing to eat. Her son's brief visits home revived her for a time, but she eventually chose poison.

Where she came by such a fast-acting potion, Maarcus would never discover. He knew only that her last act was an attempt to poison the physician himself.

His son, too impatient to wait for his own wine to be served, had snatched his father's glass.

'Live by the sword, die by the sword,' Abadan had commented much later. Maarcus had wanted to argue. To his great shame he could not.

Maarcus groaned in his sleep. He despised the dream, itemizing all his failures brought to bear in so short a time. That he had done well with his grandson was no more comforting than a cold fireplace, especially now that the young man's fate also seemed beyond the elder's reach.

Harmon shook Maarcus awake. 'Sir, sir, are you all right? Are you hurt?'

'An old wound, Harmon, very old.'

'Can I get you something?'

Maarcus shooed him away. 'I'm fine.' He did not tell the elf of the vision that always hung in his mind upon waking from that dream. He couldn't bear to speak aloud of his son curled tight in convulsions, dead of a poison meant for himself because he could not let well enough alone.

As proud as he was of his grandson, to this day Maarcus could not decide if he would choose the same had he the chance. To lose one's only child is a hard thing for a man, a very hard thing.

\*　　\*　　\*

Nikolis barely rid himself of Abadan when Maarcus came limping through his door. 'I'm very busy,' he told the man, hoping to put off another frustrating and meaningless exchange.

The physician looked determined as he raised his hand. 'I know what you are.'

The prince gripped the still-warm coin. 'And what is that?' he asked, against his better judgment.

Maarcus stumbled forward as if he were making his last steps. 'You are perfection, but you are only half of a whole. Without your sister, you are not human. Please,' he begged, 'please rescue your sister.'

'What of your grandson?'

Maarcus sank into a chair. 'I have thought of him constantly since he left. I have dreamed of his father's death. I fear the Sisters are trying to prepare me for my grandson's demise.' He smiled in a ghost of his former grin. 'I wouldn't know. It's common knowledge that I have no talent for magic and I've no desire to acquire it now.'

Nikolis worried about the old man in spite of himself. While Nik had spent carefree years, the physician had put all his energy into rescuing a faltering country. He knelt down beside his chair. 'Can I get you anything?'

Maarcus shook his head. His chest heaved in labored breaths. 'Maybe it's my own death the Sisters were warning me of.' He raised a hand and let it drop. 'Promise me,' he whispered urgently, 'promise me on your father's grave that you won't let everything he did be for nothing.'

'I won't,' the prince said. 'By the Sisters and by the Great King, I won't let you down.'

'Thank you,' Maarcus said. 'Thank you.' He took in a deep breath and closed his eyes.

'Sir Maarcus?'

The physician didn't stir.

The prince shook his arm. 'Sir Maarcus!' The man was as motionless as a corpse. 'Guard! Guard!' Nikolis shouted. 'Someone get the magician.'

The hallway was quiet. No one came. 'Of course,' the prince muttered under his breath. 'They've all deserted me.'

He took the man's wrist to check for a pulse and felt nothing.

Suddenly, the door slammed open and Harmon ran in. 'I've been looking everywhere for him,' the elf explained. 'He left his chambers when I went to the privy.' He approached Maarcus. 'He's as white as the snow. Is he all right?'

'No, he's not. Go fetch Abadan quickly.'

Each time they dragged Maarcus out of the cell, Jilian made her own escape by turning inward. She heard the water dripping and the rats scurrying, but they were no longer part of her world.

The princess sensed someone seeking her talent. Tendrils pulled at her, trying to touch her. She recognized the feel from her earliest years. Sometimes they'd entered her nightmares or found her in desperate moments such as this.

Instinctively she had always pushed them away. No good could come of a magician clawing at her dreams.

It was an easy thing to do it now, but she half-wished she had the courage to invite the intruder in. Perhaps it was Master Abadan or Walther.

Perhaps it was another of her half-brother's tricks.

Perhaps it was her true mother, the elfwitch.

Jilian's entire body spasmed in revulsion. No, there

was no choice. Better to turn away her allies than risk welcoming the enemy.

Once Hadrian's elixir got Jilian thinking morose thoughts, she couldn't stop. She twisted away from the probe only to find herself caught in another subconscious quagmire, Celia Sailclan. She missed the dwarf's chubby hand in hers and her bouncing, boundless energy.

She would never wish for Ceeley to share her own current predicament. It was just that she wanted to do right by the child. She'd all but adopted Ceeley, then left her to fend for herself when she had other obligations. She had failed Ceeley.

Ceeley, Nikolis, Maarcus, her parents . . . Everyone . . .

The bars clanged open. Lyam dumped Maarcus into the puddle left from the overflowing chamberpot. 'Filthy troll-bait,' he said, when he saw what he'd stepped in, and kicked him once for good measure.

Maarcus grunted once and lay still.

Lyam slammed the iron door. 'Won't be much longer now, Princess Jilian. Just long enough for Ivan to have a quick twist and roll.'

Jilian ignored the guard. Already on the floor beside Maarcus, she lifted his head off the dank stone. His face was the pasty white of a dead man. His breathing was fast and shallow. She had to get him out of here before they came back for a final session. Her only option seemed to be facing that which she feared most.

No time for cowardice, she told herself. She took a deep breath and called out to the unknown. Whoever had been looking for her couldn't be that far away. 'Please, please, by the Seven Sisters, let it be Abadan.'

A light pulsed on the wall just above where she'd been shackled. Jilian stared at it, knowing the cold touch of Alvaria.

She shook Maarcus to wake him. 'Maarcus, help me. What do we do?' she whispered. 'Maarcus.'

He was too sick. His head rolled on his shoulders and flopped back. His eyes fluttered open and closed.

She hugged him tightly. If she took him to the elfwitch, he would probably die. If they stayed here, he would definitely die and likely very soon.

She had survived Alvaria before. Maarcus could too.

All right, Mother, she thought, have it your way. She didn't need to speak the words aloud for Alvaria to hear her.

A hole appeared in the wall. Jilian knew the tunnel would lead to wherever Alvaria chose. Yet it was away from here.

The tunnel light called to her medallion and made her wonder how she'd kept it away from Hadrian all this time, even considering its bespelled nature. Clearly her mother knew she carried it.

Jilian hesitated, weighing their odds.

Suddenly Maarcus gasped and began to spit up blood. Whether or not Alvaria had engineered his current condition, there was still no choice. The princess might well be carrying him from the cooking pit into the flames, but there remained a slight chance she could leap past the fire to freedom.

She had to try.


Abadan's chamber did not protect Walther from the truth. Stone and mortar, brick and board didn't keep him from knowing when the riot began.

Most of the servants spent the hours beforehand deserting the castle. Walther wasn't one to expect exalted treatment, but he found the empty hallways eerie. He tried to stop a man now and again to determine precisely why the servants were fleeing. They looked at him – some with pity in their eyes, others with contempt – but none heeded his requests for details.

After checking the other common rooms, he stationed himself in the main hall. He planned to snatch the next person who ran by and refuse to let go until he got answers.

The first to race past was a young boy. Walther let him go. The second was a man big enough to shrug away the dwarf as if he hadn't been touched.

Walther waited and was finally rewarded by two washerwomen walking as quickly as the old women could go. Rather than ask directly, he impulsively backed into the shadows and listened.

'They say he eats a special diet while the rest of us starve,' said one.

The other shook her head. 'Plain out sad, I tell you. 'e seemed like such a nice young man.'

'Not like the rest of the Great King's other brood, true,' agreed the other. 'You can't deny it, though. Not a single soldier came back but 'im.'

''ow could he sacrifice 'em to the trolls like that? Can you imagine?'

'They say there's nothin' more terrifyin'. Still, if you ask me, who needs a prince that'll lie down and let 'em take The Cliffs, the very heart of the One Land?'

Shouting began outside. The crashing of pottery and glass followed.

'We've got to hurry or they'll leave without us.'

The women pushed on out of earshot, carrying bundles the dwarf belatedly realized were not another's clothing but their own.

Walther sighed. The refugees had all sought sanctuary here. Where could they go now?

*   *   *

Locked in her mind, Ginni bounced and bounded from toddler to adult to child. Her mother scolded her for stealing the morning's breakfast, but made no effort to see the girl fed the rest of the day. By late afternoon she knew she would need to 'borrow' – as she thought of it – again. She planned to pay them back when she was bigger.

Her father was more soft-hearted but no use at all in explaining the ways of women. He blushed uncharacteristically when he tried to mumble out a few words of comfort. At least he didn't banish her from the cave or swear at her pathetic moans of female weakness.

Ginni ultimately returned to her mother's care, to take up the chores of Roslin's choosing. In preparation for reconnaissance, she tightened the strings of a snug, low-cut bodice she had been instructed must be worn above a man's leather pants. No, that wasn't it; something was out of sorts. She couldn't remember how to knot the laces.

She didn't belong as she was. She didn't belong as she would be.

In her room within the labyrinth of the Forty-nine Witches, Ginni of the One Land began to dream again. She dreamt of a silly child flirting with men, of a girl disguised as a boy, of a child who flew with dragons. She tried to dismiss them and could not. Her mind repeated the litany again and again, prodding her to realize who she was.

All the while, a woman whispered in her ear and in her dreams to guard well what she knew. Others would steal that which she possessed, the more fleeting the more attractive to such thieves.

Ginni woke, holding her head carefully to balance the many chattering voices. Tears slid down her cheeks. She embraced the voices, for they were all Ginni of the One Land, daughter of Roslin the mage and Wanton Tom the mercenary.

Convinced the hags would drug him to get his co-operation, Tom refused to eat or drink anything after the so-called Revered Sister's visit. His precautions were too late. He felt the tonic taking effect long before he was thirsty enough to be tempted to drink the water brought with his dinner.

They'd probably dosed him hours ago.

'Well, no one ever said a man is worth anything without his fool dragon,' he muttered, not quite knowing where that had come from or what he meant by it.

Still he dug in his bare-footed heels. What had they done with his boots anyway? As sleep overtook him, he stubbornly remained upright in his chair. Perhaps he'd get nothing but a sore neck for his trouble, but it was better than being stiff somewhere else.

Tom woke with the closing of the door. He had not heard her knock. She crossed the room. Everything about her was as lovely as he'd ever seen it. Her smile and movement were tentative, unsure, so very different from her day-to-day bearing as a witch of great repute.

A softness she hid from her sisters, from everyone but him, penetrated every motion.

Tom the Mercenary held open his arms to his beloved and Roslin the Mage grinned wickedly as she came into them.

Willam was lost without the river of warmth. Over and over, he recalled how he'd let down Lyda. The Sisters found him lacking and so punished them both. Now body and soul were exposed to the elements. He stood in the snow and laughed without cause or control.

He ate if someone fed him; went hungry without complaint if they didn't. The food when it came was a greyish gruel that did little to sustain him but quieted his stomach for a while. Whenever he ate, he joined the others seated on tree-stumps and boulders, eating as noisily as they.

Trolls watched over them, eager with a whip to discourage any who might escape. Willam couldn't imagine anyone with the strength or wit to try.

He went where they bid him; he paid no attention to his task except to finish it. Willam wasn't much good working with his hands, but chopping wood and digging pits were simple labors a boy could do.

His sporadic laughter touched no one on the wide, wide plain.

No one at all.


Of the few who survived travel down the elven river sometimes known as Blood River, Lyda held herself together best – and so Alvaria saw that she suffered the most. Lyda remembered who she had been; she remembered rubbing her fingers across her sister's grave-marker; she remembered leading the humbled refugees to a safer place; she remembered Willam.

She recalled her shame.

The elfwitch chose a special punishment for Lyda. They dressed Lyda in a cruel mockery of her coming-out clothes. Like all the rest, she knew it was meant to humiliate her, yet knowing didn't make it more tolerable. If anything it increased the effect, for she knew it was working and blamed herself for succumbing to it.

Blame was the smallest part of the misery.

The first violation was a shock. They couldn't possibly

mean it. Everyone knew elves were repulsed by humans, males and females alike. But that was just it. This was war, and she was theirs to abuse for their own amusement.

She serviced Alvaria's army and her torment was endless. In the moments between episodes, she had a world full of time to contemplate who she had been and how she had disappointed the Seven Sisters.

When Lyda was a young girl before the war, it was still possible to live fairly well in town. Her house was packed in-between others, but the air was clean, and a girl and her sister could bounce a ball down the narrow streets without worry. As she grew older, she came to know the unpredictability of a land where rulers seldom died of natural causes. Even so, the chaos rarely reached her daily habits, nor stole more than a pinch from the bread left in the window to cool.

She was not a beautiful woman, though not displeasing to look on. Her sharp wits kept more men from the door than did her appearance. When she met Willam none of it mattered. They found delight in small things, and she no longer wanted to discuss the weighty issue of the collapsing One Land. But as time wore on and the miscarriages heaped up like so many rotten melons, she began to brood. Her tongue grew sharper and Willam strayed.

All this and more she lamented. Her reunion with Willam seemed only a dim memory in the glaring light of her downfall.

The elves made her cover her face when they came to her. If she was not beautiful by human standards, she was fully ugly by elven measures. The men laughed as they whispered 'sterile troll-trash' and 'whore-bait' in her ears in time to each thrust.

Each soldier increased by sevenfold her guilt and worry

over Willam. It was all the worse not knowing where he was, but hearing his hysterical shrieks echoing without direction through trees and tent walls.

Were they truly Willam's cries? What had the witch done with Ceeley?

Alive but unwell was the best Lyda could hope for – and she feared dead might be best after all.

In her bleakest moment of pure horror Lyda wondered if her stillborn child had been the luckiest of them all. No! She rebelled at the notion. Without life there is no hope of a better future. Awash in death, she could not help but yearn for so many lost possibilities.

Or so she tried to tell herself when the next drunken elf entered the tent and forced himself upon her. They twisted the truths of her life so that she no longer recognized who she had been, and thus she began to believe in their words. She was the barren woman left to pay dues and protect those elves who were full-bodied and fertile.

The voice of the girl who once bounced a ball in the dirt streets of her village was no more than the shrill cry of a bird shot from the air.

Maarcus took a deep breath and coughed. 'No, I'm not dead yet,' he said to the circle of concerned faces. He softened the words with a weak grin, but no one returned the smile. 'Throw some more wood on the fire, would you, Harmon?'

The elf moved to obey. When he realized there were no more logs, he scanned the prince's study for a substitute.

'Use this,' Nikolis said. 'I don't think we'll be needing it.' He broke a leg off the straight-backed chair he'd been sitting on and gave it to Harmon to throw into the flames.

The physician frowned at the demise of the Great

King's furniture. 'Come to that, have we?' He coughed again. 'Never mind there's no time—'

'Maarcus, don't talk like that,' Abadan said.

'Don't light my funeral pyre yet. I don't mean for me, I mean for the rest of you. I might make it, but you surely won't if Jilian and my grandson aren't rescued.'

'I'm on my way to find Walther,' the prince said. 'Together we'll figure out something.'

'You'll do the best you can, but I want you to know everything I know about Hadrian. Something might be useful.'

'Maarcus, I appreciate that, but as you just said, we're very short of time.'

'No, wait, Nik,' Abadan said. 'Maarcus is right. Hadrian is ruthless, and he's likely to know much more about you than you about him. You need any advantage you can get.'

The prince nodded impatiently. 'Well, go on, quickly.'

'There was an odd thing about Hadrian's mother,' Maarcus began.

Nikolis frowned at him, but let him continue.

'I don't know why this is important, but I think it is,' Maarcus explained. 'She was a weaver and a seamstress. No matter what she made, the patterns always came unraveled. It was as if she always came close, but somehow fell short of the art or the skill to perform the vital stitch. She never knew of her shortcoming, for she dispensed the clothing as presents and no one would tell her how the seams and the knitting came undone.' The physician stopped to catch his breath.

'Maarcus, please don't strain yourself. We'll—'

He held up his hand to silence the prince. 'It was as if the weaving and sewing was the outward sign for all that she did. All her plans inevitably faltered. She did not know

326

how and would never learn how to think a thing through. She would confuse the forest with the trees, think them one and the same, and therefore miss the beasts that lived in the forest, the birds that lived in the trees. She raised Hadrian,' he said.

Nikolis paused to consider. Maarcus searched desperately for the right words, the perfect morsel of information.

'It made Hadrian angry that his mother was whispered about behind her back. Her blamed her for his ultimate status as an outcast rather than king-in-waiting, and he saw to it that his older siblings died one by one.'

Maarcus was hurrying now, trying to get it all in before he lost the energy. 'I once heard him remark, "The useless wretch has seen her just reward if indeed the king genuinely fathered other children – and on an elf, no less!" Certainly he showed no remorse over her death from a slow-acting and ugly poison.'

'He killed his own mother?' Nikolis asked, appalled.

'No, that's another story for another time,' Abadan cut in, and Maarcus was grateful for the chance to rest. 'At least, we don't believe he had a hand in the actual killing, but we're sure he eventually would have if given the chance. And now there's your sister, his half-sister,' the magician continued, seeming to realize where Maarcus was headed though he couldn't have said himself. 'She's strong-willed and attractive . . . after a fashion.'

Nikolis glared at him.

'It's important for you to understand his thinking,' Abadan said without apology. 'He's likely to be drawn to Jilian. She won't yield, of course. He'll be repulsed and fascinated simultaneously. People have submitted to his whims all his life. Any who didn't became enemies – and most of them died.

'He'll try to make Jilian into an ally. The only way he can do that is to show her how weak you are, how weak Maarcus is. He'll have to break you and Maarcus both.'

'And he'll enjoy doing it,' the physician whispered, nearly spent.

'He was behind the massacre, wasn't he?' Nikolis asked.

'Probably,' Abadan said.

'And the rumors of my presumed treachery.' Nikolis looked angry now.

'Yes, but keep in mind, he couldn't have done it without Alvaria. He does not control the trolls,' Maarcus said. He reached out his arm to the prince. 'Beware. Save my grandson if you can, but you must rescue Jilian.'

Nikolis winced. 'Don't worry. I'll free them both or die trying.'

'No, Nikolis. You and your sister are the fruit of prophecy. Maarcus is . . .' The physician closed his eyes, letting the sentence suspend unfinished. He had lost his son. Now he was doing what he knew he must, offering to sacrifice his only grandson to the One Land. But not even the threat of the wrath of the Seven Sisters could make him speak the word 'expendable' aloud.

# Chapter 16

## FALSE ESCAPE

He stood on the edge, on the precipice, looking down, looking up until up became down.

Walther thought boats were bad, but now the ground itself threatened to pitch him over the brink – whether side-walls existed or not.

The castle promontory jutted into the sea. Violent waves crashed against the shore, against the heavy grey stones. Walther saw a dragon flying overhead and he could not tell the vision from reality. Here, an instant from drowning, anything might happen.

The dragon floated where the world was quiet and uncluttered. Sounds traveled differently there. They moved just as quickly, but man's noises did not exist. Man's cares and chatter were unrelated to clouds and rain.

Walther fell up until he joined the dragon; felt his vision split into separate bird's eyes' views. He noted the mountain jammed so tight against the sea, the peak crowded with men come to join the dragon's fight. He watched the actual now as rioters stormed the castle. In everywhen, people scurried, preparing for battle – preparing to die.

From here there seemed no distance at all between the rocks which gave The Cliffs its name and the murderous, booming ocean – no time at all between this moment and war.


Notti left his mother to confer with Elder Jedrek while he went exploring the village. Oddly, the structures were all much more stable, more permanent than the tents in his old camp.

Did these elves not migrate either?

Despite their stated beliefs, they appeared to harbor their own version of deception. It made Notti feel disappointed and old.

Without realizing he needed tangible distance between himself and his newfound clan, he wandered past the outbuildings and up the trails winding through the mountains above. He'd been hiking some minutes before he glimpsed the camp. The sight took him completely by surprise. He didn't know what he'd expected, having missed this view on his way in, but it wasn't this pristine clearing. The quiet, empty place amidst the trees caught him unawares. If he hadn't known elves lived here, he would never have guessed.

He watched, waiting, trying to figure how they managed it. Finally, he caught the white moving against white, people going about their business in ones and twos and threes. Notti tried to count but kept losing them in their winter camouflage. His best guess came to a Sisters' dozen, plenty to keep a colony alive and barely fewer than his own village.

'Notti? Notti!' shouted his mother, 'come down from there.'

'What's the m-matter? What's h-happened?'

'Never mind. Just come down. Hurry.'

He rushed to obey, feeling like a child nowhere near ready for his manhood ceremony.

She stood at the foot of the trail, anxiously chewing the skin on her thumb. Miraculously, the village had become solid and substantial once more.

'Y-yes? Are y-you all r-right?' he asked, out of breath from running down the steep trail.

She hugged him with relief. 'I'm fine. I was worried about you. Sometimes newcomers stray away from the camp and never find it again.' She tilted her head at him. 'But you saw us, didn't you?'

'It t-took s-s-some ef-f-fort,' he admitted.

She embraced him again. 'I'm so glad you're here.' She let go and stepped back. 'Notti,' she said, excitedly. 'Jedrek and I were talking. He's decided to hasten your lessons. He'd like you to return to continue your session.'

Notti smiled. Perhaps he did have a place among these people.

Jedrek began as soon as Notti reached the threshold of the elder's private quarters. 'Your training is not simply a matter of recitation and endurance. You must seek understanding behind the words and strength beneath the exercises. Now, keep your eyes open, but attend my voice.'

He nodded, doing his best to ignore the luxury of the man's room, forbidden to commoners and so much like Alvaria's tent.

'Who are the three Great Sisters?'

'Barik, Ezrek, and Nadik,' said Notti without a trace of his stutter, sure of this answer at least.

'And why are they great?'

'Because they represent the three great races.'

'And do the Great Sisters quarrel amongst themselves?'

Notti paused. 'I d-don't know,' he said finally. 'It would n-not s-surprise me if they d-did.'

'Why not?'

He scrunched his brows in thought. 'Each h-h-has a w-w-will of her own. Is it not p-p-possible that these are n-n-n-ot alw-w-ways in agreement?' he whispered slowly, fearing he'd spoken blasphemy.

'It is.'

Notti went loose with relief, then recovered himself immediately to resume his former alert posture.

'But . . .' Jedrek let the word hang a long time. 'But, as in all things, we do not think less of them for this, nor question their motives, nor assume them to be other than divine.' His voice was stern to be sure this point was not taken lightly.

'And do the three races fight?'

Notti looked confused at such an obvious question. He hesitated, making sure there was no trick behind it, then answered simply, 'Yes.'

'Should we expect more of ourselves than of the Sisters?'

'Ah.' He understood where Elder Jedrek was headed. 'We can hope to attain p-perfection and p-peace, but we know we will nearly always f-fall short.'

'But do we not try?'

'We do.'

'Always?'

'Always.' Notti showed no signs of doubt.

'Good, very good.' Jedrek brought his hands together once in a loud resounding clap. 'Let's try something more difficult. 'Lift your right leg with the knee high. Hold it here. Good. No, leave your eyes open. Fine. Once more. Who are the three Great Sisters?'

'Barik, Ezrek, and Nadik,' Notti said, as easily as before.

'And their four lesser Sisters?'

This, too, he answered quickly. 'Alpia, Dunavia, Linia, and Zephria.'

'And what do the lesser Sisters govern?'

'Earth, water, fire, and air.' His thigh-muscle was beginning to wear out.

'But do they govern them?' Jedrek asked.

Notti's leg slipped lower and lower until the toe tapped the floor. Embarrassed at his failure, he instantly lifted it high again. 'G-govern, s-sire? Well . . .'

'A difficult question, perhaps. Think of this. Do any of the Sisters govern?'

Here again the boy was puzzled. He chewed his lip and tried to think of what to say.

'Do they guide?'

'Yes, absolutely.'

'There is your answer. You may put your leg down.'

Elder Jedrek circled him, letting his voice rise and fall as he spoke. The exercises were a balm to Notti's soul, easing the pain of his worry over so many things he had done for Alvaria. His mother came and went several times, but he was too absorbed to note more than that.

When the drilling was through, Notti rested contentedly in the warmest corner of Jedrek's workroom, studying the fresh herb leaves the Elder had set out. One by one the boy marked the shape and color in their present form. He picked up each from its place on the drying-rack and sniffed its scent. Primarily they smelled of dirt and growing things, yet they did differ. The first was bitter; the second sweet; the third seemed to have no aroma at all, but rather absorbed those around it.

A man suddenly stormed into the room without asking

333

permission and Notti looked up at the commotion. The elf standing before Jedrek was big. Though he clearly owed allegiance to the Elder, his air of command filled the room.

'My lord,' he began then stopped when his eyes met Notti's. 'My apologies. I interrupted.'

'Not necessary, Paly,' Jedrek said. 'Please continue.'

The man took a last glance at the boy then squarely faced the Elder. 'The three have escaped, vanished from their cell despite all precautions. I don't know how it could have happened. They were guarded day and night despite how few we are. I . . . I have failed you.' The man's words wound down and his energy with them.

The Elder let out a sigh. 'It was fated to happen. Alvaria had to call back her own. Else they would be useless to her. How did you discover them missing?'

'We checked at the change of shift and all was as it should be, but when my man entered to bring them their next meal, the tent was empty.'

Jedrek nodded. 'At least your guards will be allowed some sleep.'

'But my lord, shouldn't we send out a search party?'

'And put more lives at the mercy of Alvaria? I think not.'

'Better we had put them to death when we discovered their treachery.' Paly clapped a hand across his mouth. 'I beg your pardon. I had no right.'

The Elder waved away the transgression. 'You only speak to me what others mutter behind my back. I understand the impulse, have considered it many times in fact. But I will not sink to Alvaria's form of leading through terror.'

'What would you have me do?' His voice was subdued now, bowing to his leader's will.

'Do? As I said, let your men get some sleep.'

The man nodded. 'Anything else?' he asked. He seemed to need some task to begin to make amends for his failure.

'There is one thing.'

'Yes?'

'Do not let anyone into the tent where they were held until I examine it. We may yet be able to learn something.'

'As you wish.' He turned to go.

'And Paly?'

The man snapped back to attention. 'Sir.'

'You did well. I had hoped the three might be persuaded otherwise, but their betrayal was fated from the moment twenty years ago when she planted them in our midst.'

The guard's eyes grew wide, but he offered only a crisp 'sir' and left the room.

Notti returned to his herbs, but had lost all ability to concentrate.

'Well, Notti, what do you think?'

He was almost afraid to voice his thought aloud, but Elder Jedrek's eyes were on him. 'I th-think, I th-think it is not h-happens-stance that their d-departure comes s-so s-soon after m-my arr-rival.'

The Elder gave him a wry smile. 'Indeed. I wish I disagreed.'


Wanton Tom spat out the leaf the harlot had stuck in his mouth when he'd tried to kiss her. 'That's disgustin'. What're you tryin' to do, choke me to death?'

She waved the leaf at him. 'What are you trying to do, Uncle? Seduce me?'

Wanton Tom was as tired as a soldier on forced-march.

After his time among the hags, he'd never be able to look at a barmaid the same way again and that made him mad. Something about this one seemed familiar. Great, he thought, they're coming back for seconds. He let his eyelids fall closed, and rolled away from the approaching female. 'I'm not your uncle.'

'Wanton Tom,' the girl whispered fiercely, 'Tom! Get up!'

'That's a cruel trick, soundin' like Ginni,' he growled. 'Go 'way. I'm all spent.'

'No, you're not. Come on, Father.' The woman shook his shoulder.

'I already told you. I'm not your fat—' He twisted back to face her and cautiously opened both eyes. There stood Ginni before him as clear-eyed as he'd ever seen her. Tom sat up in bed, fully awake now. He wanted to believe it was truly her, but how could he trust anyone here – most of all his daughter? 'How do I know this isn't a trick?'

Ginni's face went blank and mysteriously transformed into that of an innocent child's. 'I found something today, you might find of interest, Wanton Tom sir.' She opened her hand and a tiny flame sprouted from inside her palm. Next to it was the undamaged leaf he'd spat out.

'Did that piece of greenery bring me to my senses?'

'Partly,' she answered, in the voice of an adolescent boy. 'The rest will take a while to tell and we're in a hurry just now.'

It was Ginni all right, using one of the many guises she'd devised to greet him secretly when they were on the road. He wrapped his arms around her and gave her a loud kiss on the cheek. 'Glad to have you back. Let's go!'

'Shh! You'll bring down half the tower.'

'Right, sorry.' He threw back the covers with unrestrained delight and headed past her for the door. 'Time to hit the snowy trail.'

'Uncle, aren't you forgetting something?'

Again Ginni used his old nickname, yet she sounded strangely subdued. Tom's heart sank. Half expecting her to be holding a knife at his back, the mercenary turned around with painstaking care.

His daughter held his pants high enough to block her sight of him in his long underwear.

'Yeah, well, thanks.' He snatched them from her outstretched hand, unsure which of them was the more embarrassed. In his hurry to get them on, his foot snagged in the folds. He lost his balance, but Ginni caught him before he fell to the floor.

'Thanks, Gin, but why the face? You've seen me in my drawers before.'

'Not in a long time, Uncle. You've gotten—'

'What? Old!' He angrily yanked up his pants and fastened them at the waist.

'No, not old. Thin.' Her voice was full of remorse and her eyes filled with tears. 'I'm sorry, Uncle. I didn't . . . I couldn't . . .'

He cupped her chin in his hand. 'I know you didn't and you couldn't. There's nothing to be done about it now.' He gave her his best boisterous smile. 'Don't you worry. My beer-gut'll be back as soon as we get to a civilized tavern.'

'Your boots, Uncle?'

'Boots, right.' He was so glad to see her and so anxious to be finally leaving that he wasn't thinking clearly. 'Boots. I always put them next to my pants.' He searched the small room. 'Okay. Not by the chair. Not under the bed. Not in the corner.'

Ginni closed the bottom bureau drawer and straightened up. 'No luck here.'

'Do you s'pose they took my boots?'

She bit her lip. 'Could be.'

'We'll have to shove off without 'em then.'

'But you'll get frostbite.'

'Prob'ly.' Tom looked down at his stockinged feet and wiggled his toes. He liked those ugly buggers. 'Been nice knowin' you fellas.'

Ginni glanced down, then back up again. She nodded. 'Okay.'

'Okay.' He rested his hand on the catch. 'Ready?'

'Uncle, I have never been so ready in my life.'

That was his Ginni, all right. No one else could be as pleased as he was to escape this place. He opened the door slowly, stepped out of the room, and nearly tripped over the body slumped against the wall.

He didn't honestly care if the Severe Sister breathed or not, but an exhalation of breath confirmed his suspicion that she did. As always, they would not kill unless they must – partly because it felt right, but in this case common sense told them not to anger the witches any more than they must. 'Nice job,' he signalled, and she acknowledged with another brief tip of her head.

The hallway was dark but for a sputtering torch at the bend some ways down. Still deepnight then. He suddenly realized how disoriented he'd become. No time for that now. He shrugged it off and waved Ginni forward. 'Which way?' he whispered.

'Around that corner, down a flight of stairs, left at the bottom.' She stopped. 'This is silly. May I?'

Tom smiled. This was not the Ginni who had led them into madness attempting to rescue the prince, nor the one who retired to a cave and singed Grosik's tail. This was the practical, clear-headed daughter he knew and adored beyond reason. He mock bowed. 'Please do, m'lady.'

Without another word, his daughter tiptoed quietly down the hall and Tom slid after in his stockinged feet.

Maarcus already knew he was dying. The dream unsettled him all the more because of it. He hadn't dreamed of Zera in a generation.

He had spoken with her and worked by her side at times. He had grieved at her passing, but he had not dreamed of her since their mutual decision to end their liaison.

He'd sometimes wondered whether they had both agreed. He thought he must have chosen on his own to let Zera go, because he'd never been susceptible to magic of any sort. Still, she was female, and women could always find ways to influence men. It was born into the make-up of all animals, not the least elf, dwarf, and human.

In the dream Zera was a young woman, younger than she had been when he met her. In truth, he was a small boy when she reached adulthood, but she befriended him nonetheless. She chatted with him as he skipped shells on the beach protected by the cliff-side and castle walls above it.

In those days, elves and humans were merely different sides of a coin, their conversations no cause for comment. But she sought him out, just as she had later when he was a middle-aged human and his son newly dead.

In the dream he wondered if he knew her from some-where – a reception for the king perhaps, a celebration of their triumph in joining the realms of the One Land.

Her eyes changed color with the ocean, grey to green to deep blue when the storms rolled in. She spoke softly of preparing for the future, of aiding the Great King in all his endeavors, and of sometimes seeing just a bit farther than the king in order to convince him of the proper action. She spoke as if she knew the king personally, though this seemed unlikely to the young Maarcus for she herself appeared barely of age. In the end, he didn't understand what she required of him. Frustrated unto tears, he would have granted her anything if only he'd known what she asked.

Maarcus the Sixth woke an old man who felt every battle wound ever inflicted. He thought of Zera, who should have lived much longer than he if not for a daughter who was as evil as her mother was good.

As a young man, he had not put much store in dreams; he had believed in the observable sciences. He had learned better, but the learning gave no comfort. His king had still died and the kingdom had still fallen to ruin and war.

The physician had done all he could, but it was not enough to save his king or his country. With tears running down his cheeks, Maarcus let out a long sigh and did not breathe in again.

Maarcus the Seventh began to mend quickly once they left the prince's dungeon. Jilian told herself that the new healthy pink skin replacing the lash-marks on his back was a sign she had chosen well.

No amount of lying to herself could convince her of the truth. The tunnel led them somewhere other than where they wished to go. They had traded a stationary dungeon for a mobile one. She kept her thoughts to herself, so as not to worry Maarcus – even while she continued to brood over the nature of his cure.

The ground and walls were as uneven and formless as smoke. So far, her fingers and feet met firmness; and when she stumbled, bottom and sides always met her as any cave floor would. But she kept expecting to poke through to nothing if she pushed just a little harder.

The longer they walked, the more Jilian felt the elfwitch permeating the air, the dirt, her thoughts. No one else could maintain such powerful magic. With growing certainty came growing dread that they should have confronted death at her half-brother's hand, rather than accept life under Alvaria's.

She grabbed Maarcus' arm and attempted to pull him back the way they'd come.

He looked at her wearily. 'There is no return, Jilian.'

'What?'

'Look behind you. There is simply nothing there.'

She spun about. The world was as black as the depths of a bottomless pit. She reached out and met frozen nothingness, as if the world ceased one step behind them.

'Why didn't you tell me?'

In the grey half-light, she saw him shrug. 'You could not have changed it. I thought you deserved a few calm moments.'

Jilian choked down panicked laughter. 'And I didn't voice my fears to you for the same reason. See where our restraint's got us.'

'Exactly where we would have been regardless.' He took a step closer and folded his arms around her. 'Jilian, I would have died there. The elfwitch might have us, but as long as we're alive we can fight her. If we die, she wins.'

The darkness closed in tight around them. Cold wound through their bodies until their bones ached.

Jilian's dragon coin, all but forgotten, grew warm against her chest. Alvaria was calling to her. The princess nodded, as much to herself as to Maarcus. 'All right, let's go.'

Maarcus and Jilian linked hands and resumed their trudge into the strange wilderness.

The cave was smaller than Grosik remembered, though he'd seen it only a moment ago as a dragon registers time. Maybe he wasn't giving enough credit to how quickly four dragons can overflow a space formerly occupied by one dragon and two average-sized humans.

'This place is ghastly,' his son Nadik said.

'You notice it now because you are young. Never forget that such places mean us no good. We do this because we must,' said Barik.

'Your mother and I will go first. Nadik, watch after your sister.'

'I can take care of myself,' Ezrek strutted.

Barik glared at the children until they quietly fell in behind her. 'We are agreed,' she said, in a voice that left no room for argument.

Grosik led the way to the back of the cave. His skin prickled with magic run rabid. The cave narrowed quickly and the two adult dragons could no longer walk side by side. Grosik started to pull in front and thought better of it. Likely his bulk in such crowded confines would keep Barik from seeing the bones. He stepped back. 'You can feel it's only a length or so ahead.'

'Yes, I know.' She let out something like a sigh.

'Cousins warned me against days like this when I took up flying with you.'

Grosik stifled a laugh to keep from vibrating the ceiling down onto their heads. 'It sounds like you've spent your share of days among humans.'

Barik looked up. Her ear-flaps were flat against her head in alarm. 'You will never repeat that.'

'You're right. I will never repeat that,' Grosik agreed readily. He needed her help. He would have enjoyed the companionship of knowing he wasn't the only admitted pervert who enjoyed the company of the lesser races; but there was no gain here in forcing her to confess something she preferred to hide.

She waited, measuring his sincerity. 'Very well, Grosik. To our purpose here.' She moved forward, slowly and deliberately. The cave echoed with her steps.

Grosik could no longer hear his son and daughter at the cave mouth. He hoped it was because they had fallen silent of their own accord.

Barik hissed and her tail slapped the ground hard enough to send stray rocks a-tumbling.'You bring me all this way to observe dust?'

'They were bones when we first saw them. The girl-mage disturbed them.'

'Then she has seen to it that no one can know their intent.'

'It was a transformation spell. Elf and human.'

'Why am I here? Why did you not tell me this before?'

Grosik didn't answer. His motivations were complicated . . . and not. He wanted to rescue friends, human friends. He thought these bones would help. 'I was compelled to return,' he said finally. 'Though I warned the humans away from them, I knew I would return.'

'And you drag us into your compulsion?'

'You came of your own accord.'

'Did I?'

Grosik fought to return to the subject. 'What of the bones?'

'There's nothing left to observe. I take your word for it that they were ever more than they are now.' She bordered on calling him a liar.

Grosik chose to ignore the insult. 'I would see the dust before we leave.'

'Let me by then.'

Grosik backed up until there was space for her to pass. Once she'd given him more than enough room, he moved forward to where he'd stood the day Tom and Ginni had first found the bones. He gritted his teeth and ran his forepaw through the pile. As Barik had said, there was nothing but a very fine dust now. It had not deteriorated naturally. Had the dragon prince done this? Did the dragon prince even know of it?

At the cave mouth one of the three raised its voice in deadly challenge. Grosik hurried to the front.

The youngsters were scuffling despite all common sense to the contrary.

'Mother, he did it.'

'No, she did it.'

'Ezrek, Nadik! Quiet, the both of you!' Grosik roared. 'Hatchlings have more sense than this.'

'It's the bones,' Barik said. 'Or what's left of them.'

'I agree,' said Grosik. 'Let's get some fresh—'

Barik and their children were airborne before he could finish the thought.

'I admit you've got my curiosity up.' She paused. With something like affection in her voice, she added, 'You always could.'

Grosik knew better than to push his luck this time and kept his teasing to himself. Having Barik around was like carrying Tom and Ginni. After a while, he'd got used to the way they irked him and he missed the irritation. 'From things Ginni said before she ran off to the Forty-nine Hags—'

'Stop now, Grosik. Do not tell me we are headed for the Witches' Tower.' She hovered in mid-air, plainly not moving forward a single wing-span until he answered her.

'I've been there once. It wasn't so bad.'

'We're going to see the Ha-ags. We're going to see the Ha-ags,' sang the children.

'We are not going to see the Hags,' hissed Barik. 'Grosik, how could you put me in such danger? And your own offspring?'

Definitely not the usual dragon family, he thought. But then he'd known that the minute he'd discovered Barik shared her name with one of the manling's Great Sisters. They hadn't been able to resist naming their hatchlings after the other two. It never would have occurred to Grosik's mother to notice such things, any more than she or most dragon parents would worry over what perils their offspring might fly into. If they couldn't learn to face danger as hatchlings, they'd never survive to engender their own.

'I'm sorry,' he told Barik, genuinely contrite. 'There's something about that girl and her father that matters. To me and to their whole world. I couldn't ignore it. I wouldn't ask any of you to attack them. I was hoping you might just back me up if I get caught again.'

'Again! You've already been there and failed. And now you want reinforcements.'

'Yes, I've been there. But Barik, I lived and I'm none the worse for wear. I've had less pleasant days digging for food in the aftermath of a border skirmish.'

'I don't want to know about it,' she said primly.

'From what Ginni—'

'The girl-mage?' asked Ezrek.

'Yes, the girl-mage,' answered Barik impatiently.

She seemed eager to hear the story in spite of herself. Without commenting, she resumed flying forward.

'Ginni believed the bones were meant for the Dragon Prince – the one transformed from a furry beast his sister unknowingly called a dragon.'

'Told you that story was true,' Ezrek nagged her brother. She flapped a gust of wind at him.

Grosik ignored the bickering. 'Perhaps the bones crumbled to dust once the spell was unraveled.'

'Makes sense,' Barik said, thoughtfully.

'So are we going, Mother? Are we?' asked Ezrek and Nadik.

'Yes, I think we are.'

Brother and sister spun delightedly in circles, cawing their joy to the skies.

'But first, some rules. You stay behind us.'

'Ah, we want to see the witches.'

'I want to see you stay alive.'

Grosik had known he'd done the right thing in coming to Barik. For all the world, she sounded like Tom protecting Ginni. He chuckled despite himself and turned it into a cough before the younger ones caught on.

Willam had ditch detail when the elves snatched him away from the trolls. He was coming to like the poor beasts – they reminded him of a sweet-natured dimwit he'd once befriended – and he hated to disappoint them by abandoning his duty.

The elves laughed at him as he tried to explain. Maybe he wasn't speaking clearly?

His second attempt got him whacked on the head with a shovel. When he rose from the ground, he didn't chance a third.

They led him to a tent set apart from the others and indicated he should stand guard while they were inside.

He smiled to let them know he understood, and made

no comment about the goat-dung at the spot where they directed him. If these men thought it important for him to genuflect in a pile of manure, he'd learned better than to question them. Shovels made very good teachers that way.

The wind picked up after they'd been gone some time. He smelled dead things and dinner, possibly one and the same. He heard the laughter from within the tent and wondered idly what amused them.

Kneeling with his back to the tent, he recognized what the rhythmic thumping and grunting defined, and he didn't want to know more than that.

He concentrated on the smell of goat-waste to keep his mind off the elves. It worked until the shouting started.

'Stay still, you troll-trash.' A hand smacked loudly against flesh.

A woman cried out.

'Not my 'ffair,' Willam told himself. Affair, good joke, he thought. Shrill laughter bubbled up from a terrified place in his back-brain and exploded across the camp.

'You out there, shut up!'

'What'd you bring him for anyway?' said the other elf inside the tent.

'Oh, I have my reasons,' the first said. 'Isn't that right, troll-trash?'

From the moment Willam had fallen in the river, fear and regret had overlaid his righteous anger. He lived and breathed in a bubble pierced only by order and obedience. The elves' laughter at the woman's anguished cries changed that. Their cruelty stabbed him to the core, and his rage crashed to the surface.

Suddenly aware of more than his immediate surroundings, though still not entirely himself, he pulled himself erect and scooted back from the refuse. Willam focused on the woman's voice to decide where to direct his next move. Thinking he needed to cover his abrupt shift in mood, he continued to let out an occasional shriek of laughter.

Willam needn't have worried. The elves paid him no attention. He was just another pawn doing as he was ordered.

The two came out and walked away without dismissing him from his post. They returned with three others, who took their own turns inside the tent. Willam kept his face blank, and tried not to think how they might well have tried all going at once if the canvas could have stretched to hold them.

The woman's sobs were squelched by another blow. Willam wondered despite himself whether she still lived.

He was trembling from cold and anger by the time they finally left, snickering and chuckling at the 'idiot human.' 'Wouldn't she make him a lovely bride?' they asked.

He waited, counting slow sets of seven sevens and another seven sevens again before he rose from the filth and entered the tent himself.

She did not so much as moan when he let the flap drop behind him and cinched it tight. Maybe she was afraid – as he had been – or perhaps she hadn't heard him.

The poor woman was a ruin. He began with her face, tearing a rag from his shirt and wetting it with his own spit to clean away the worst of the dried blood. He found a puddle of snowmelt and packed it on her swelling eye.

The good eye opened and went wide with alarm.

'Shh, it'll be all right, lady. We'll fix you up. Don't you worry. I always keep my promises.'

The woman relaxed and drifted off to sleep. How very like Lyda she was, trusting him even in the face of utter wickedness.

He felt her limbs and belly for broken bones and hidden bleeding. Arms and legs were intact under the bruises, but she had a broken rib. As he tore another strip from his tattered tunic and wrapped it around her, he realized he knew this woman, had known her all his adult life.

Gently Willam finished the task he'd started.

Quietly he sank down on the floor, put his head next to hers and wept.

# Chapter 17

## ROYAL RIOT

Walther Shortdwarf tried to shed the dragon skin to no avail. The One Land was aflame and he was fated to watch, frustrated and worthless.

Princess Jilian led the great magic confrontation against the elfwitch. Prince Nikolis stood at her side as much a part of her as she was of him. Maarcus the Seventh defended them both. Walther almost missed himself, so short behind the humans.

Where were Abadan and the elder Maarcus? He beheld only a greyness where they should have been, a greyness Walther had never experienced and had never heard spoken of in the many tales of the storytellers.

The dwarf felt the greyness pulling him into its maw. He fought and struggled to return to full consciousness, but fell into its absence.

Ah, there was Abadan. A single candle-flame pinpointed the lesson the magician had been trying to teach Walther for the past two weeks. They had been interrupted so frequently that he finally gave up in disgust.

Walther focused on the drawing of a triangle surrounding a square. 'Think of the Greater Sisters as forming a triangle equal on all sides. The Lesser Sisters make up a square around it, shielding the triangle, protecting their Greater Sisters. Just as we defend the royal house.'

Walther shook his head. 'But don't the Great Sisters look after the races of humanity while the Lesser watch over the elements? Can't elves, dwarves, and humans safeguard earth, air, water, and fire more readily than the reverse?'

'I've never tutored a dwarf before,' Abadan said. 'I suspect you view the world in such proportions because you are closer to the earth than humans.'

'But no nearer than the elves and humans once were,' Walther argued. 'Perhaps the religion has been corrupted, reversed in a way. What if it was not the square's work to protect the triangle but the reverse?' He made his own drawings.

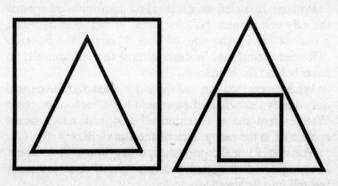

'Maybe there is a kinship among the Seven Sisters that has been forgotten,' Walther insisted. 'Can one leg of the triangle change places with one side of the square and maintain the balance?' He stopped. 'Can the twins remain propped up without a third or fourth limb?' he asked quietly.

This last was not a question he had considered when speaking with Abadan, but it jolted him from his vision with unexpected force.

'Nikolis! I've got to find him.' He roused himself from the dusty corner where he'd collapsed when the sight overtook him, and ran toward the magician's chamber.

Furniture had been smashed to kindling everywhere. Bits of food trailed through the hallways and dripped from the walls. Walther offered a quick thanks to the Sisters for protecting him during the mêlée, then instantly turned to worry over what they would eat now that their stores had been sacked.

'No time,' he told himself. 'No time. Have to find Nikolis.'

The door to Abadan's magic chamber hung open. His magicks were so much bubbling stew thrown to the counter and floor. Walther hurried into the smoke-filled room, shouting, 'Master Abadan!'

No one answered.

They've killed him, he thought. But no, there were no bodies hidden in the bespelled haze.

Outside the door, a man yelled, 'Down with the Dragon Prince. Long live the rightful king.'

Walther scooted back into the smoky shadows, holding his breath to keep from inhaling deadly fumes all the while.

A mob of rioters carrying Prince Hadrian marched behind the man. 'Long live the king!'

The dwarf let them pass around a corner then rushed the other way in search of Abadan.

He finally found the magician in the Dragon Prince's study—

Keening over the body of Sir Maarcus.

So that was why the physician was missing from the vision. No time, no time, he thought. He put his hand on the magician's shoulder. 'Abadan, where's Nikolis?'

Lost to his mourning, the man didn't answer.

'Harmon, where is the prince?'

The elf managed a red-eyed shake of his head.

No time, no time, he thought. At last, Walther bellowed, 'Abadan, where is the King!'

Completely confused, the magician twisted to look at the dwarf. 'What king, you idiot? We have no king!'

'Nikolis! Where is Nikolis?'

His mouth hung open in a perfect 'o' before words finally escaped. 'He was looking for you.'


The rioters broke into the castle much quicker than Nikolis expected. From cracked pottery to battering-ram took less time than a trip to the privy.

Hadrian, all Hadrian. He would kill the man if he ever came within a knife's reach.

Nikolis ran the wide halls, searching for Walther. If he didn't come across him soon, he'd have to go alone. Jilian couldn't wait for reinforcements.

In his haste, he swung wide around a corner and nearly ran down a man old enough to be his father. 'Your pardon,' he said without thinking.

'Not bloody likely,' the other returned. A sharp note in the man's voice suggested he might have the authority to do more than pardon if he wished.

Against good sense, Nikolis stopped to stare at the man. He seemed frighteningly familiar. He might have challenged the man another time, but Jilian needed him now. The prince attempted to sidestep the man.

'I was hoping to happen upon you,' he said while

blocking Nik's way. 'It makes things so much more efficient.'

Only then did the Dragon Prince realize the other had drawn his sword while he moved to box him in.

'Do you prefer I run you through or do you want to defend yourself? Your highness.' The honorific oozed disdain.

Nikolis slowly pulled his own sword from the scabbard, eyeing his opponent. 'Have we met?' he asked cautiously, as he circled slowly around the other.

The man laughed. 'Unlikely. I haven't been welcome here since you were a child.'

Nikolis looked harder. The features might have been his own twisted by time and decay, or a different mother. 'If you've harmed my sister . . .' Nikolis swung wildly.

Hadrian easily dodged. 'Pity, I was hoping for a better challenge.'

Nikolis composed himself, concentrating on where he could most wound the man without killing him.

'You know your sister is quite lovely,' Hadrian taunted. 'Clean her up and she would be well worth bedding. Given a little more time I could teach her to appreciate you almost as well as she does me.'

Nikolis saw white. Vision simply did not exist. His ears roared with the sound of the ocean. He smelled the stink of the other's sweat close up against him. He tasted the blade-tip against his lips.

Sight and sound returned as quickly as they had fled. His half-brother held a knife at his throat while he wrapped Nik's wrists in rope. Then he bent to hobble his captive's ankles.

All that time wasted on sword lessons, Nik thought wryly despite the grim situation. I'd've done better to spend my time with Abadan – and suddenly he knew it was true. His future lay in learning about his mother's legacy, not his father's.

'This way,' Hadrian said with false politeness. 'I have my own special entrance.' He shoved Nikolis down the hall a few steps only to stop abruptly and make a sharp left. Hadrian pushed a brick and then another. The wall angled open to reveal a passage.

'I haven't been here since I was a child myself.' He sounded almost wistful. 'Unless you count just this morning.'

So this was how his betrayer escaped.

Hadrian peered inside. 'A little dark but you won't mind. You'll get used to the dark . . . Just as our sister did.'

Nikolis spat at the man he couldn't see in the pitch-black. 'You leave my sister out of this.'

'Ah, you've got as much venom as she did. That'll make breaking you so much more fun.' In the next breath, he added, 'Don't ever do that again.'

Nikolis smiled at his back. I guess I got him, he thought.

They stumbled along in the dark. Hadrian halted occasionally, perhaps to get his bearings, catch his breath, or needle Nikolis with threats of, 'You'll see what it's like to live on the slop you've left to us. You'll know what it's like to live in obscurity.'

As if any of that mattered to Nik.

They finally came out inside a well-appointed house. A very well-appointed house.

Outside, the starving exiles still raged, looting what they could and smashing what they couldn't.

This is Hadrian's home, Nik realized. Jilian is here somewhere.

'Lyam!' the man called. 'Lyam, upstairs now!'

No one came.

'Foul, no-good . . .' Hadrian muttered. He looked skeptically at Nikolis. 'I know you're a better swordsman than you pretend. I've got reliable accounts.'

The Dragon Prince said nothing as he surreptitiously eyed his surroundings.

'You wanted to see your sister. I'm happy to oblige. Let's take a tour, shall we?' He paused. 'Ivan! Lyam!'

Still no answer.

Hadrian appeared unconcerned, but Nikolis knew better. Something had gone wrong. He hope Jilian and Maarcus had escaped first.

'I could show you the bedchamber your sister stayed in.' He stopped and considered. 'On second thought, I don't think you're ready for that just yet.' His words exuded confidence; but he was distracted as he spoke – as if he was becoming truly bothered by the whereabouts of his absent men.

Nikolis proved a co-operative prisoner as they descended the stairs to the dungeon beneath the house. Hadrian's yells of 'Lyam' and 'Ivan' echoed off the stone walls but never brought an answer. By the time they reached the prison, Hadrian had given up all pretense of nonchalance.

'I'll have their heads if those two are gone. I'll have—' He didn't finish as Nikolis stepped past the carnage to give him a better view.

'I'd say someone's already got their heads,' Nikolis joked.

Two misshapen heads on the floor. Arms, legs, and internal bits scattered everywhere.

Hadrian didn't seem to notice when Nikolis stepped away to examine the cells. Empty, all empty.

The Dragon Prince let out a half-held breath. She was still alive at least.

357

Hadrian cried out. Nikolis couldn't help but look. The elfwitch stood at the foot of the stairs. She held up something bloody. Hadrian's hand?

'I'm sure you can rule your little seaside resort one-handed.'

White-faced with shock and lips tightened into a line, the speechless Hadrian stared at the bloody stump of his arm and fell to the stone floor.

'I told you to bring them to me,' she said to his unconscious body.

The elfwitch faced Nikolis. Without a single move-ment, his rope and shackles fell away. 'There.' She pointed toward a vacant cell and a tunnel entrance spread wide. She walked forward to grasp his arm harder than Hadrian ever could have and dragged him into the abyss.

Escape wasn't as easy as the early moments would've suggested. Ginni knew the Revered Mother would leave guards in unexpected places. She'd known about the obvious ones outside her own room and Wanton Tom's. It was the roaming women who served as Revered Mother's eyes and ears she had to fear. These were not wholly within their own control and therefore more difficult to predict . . . or disable.

She rounded a corner and sprinted down the last stretch to the outside door. She could feel Tom a few steps behind her. Here they were most exposed. Anyone could come down the hallway and see them from a distance.

Ginni leaned on the door, but it wouldn't budge. She motioned Tom closer. Anxiously they shoved together until the door opened.

Another body lay on the ground. This Revered Sister didn't seem to have fared as well as the others. Blood pooled underneath her head. But how?

They stepped out the door and Ginni bent down to examine the woman more closely. She found claw marks slashed across the victim's neck. 'Grosik? Has he been here all along?'

'Don't see how he could've managed that without finding himself back in their net,' Tom whispered.

'I haven't,' Grosik boomed. 'Just long enough.'

Ginni hugged the big beast's neck. 'How'd you know tonight was the night?'

'Not me. Barik.'

'Who?' Ginni asked.

'His mate,' Tom said. 'She—'

'Later,' Grosik interrupted. 'It's quite a long t—'

'No!' Revered Mother shouted from behind them. 'The girl is mine!'

'Quickly,' Grosik roared. 'I've seen more of the Hag's snares than I care to.'

Ginni and Tom needed no more urging to scramble upon the dragon's back. The three rose into the air. Only once Caronn's screams had faded behind them did Ginni relax enough to glance around her. The three dragons trailing Grosik startled her at first until she noticed he was humming like a mother cat.

'What have you been up to, you sly old grouch?'

'Later,' Grosik whispered. 'Much later.'

The grey morass spat Jilian and Maarcus into the waiting arms of Alvaria's trolls. Shocked by the sudden return to the world they knew, the two didn't have a Sisters' prayer of escaping the ring of strong-armed creatures.

All across the camp, the princess saw the barren patches and burnt trees caused by the devastating battle months ago. No one had rebuilt or cleared away the refuse and now it served as a reminder of their single defeat.

A small hope caught in Jilian's throat. She didn't welcome torture for Maarcus or herself, but they both knew the risks in confronting the elfwitch. Jilian was stronger now than when she'd last battled with Alvaria. She could steel herself against anything the witch might thrust at her.

Or so she thought.

They were taken to a tent set only paces from Alvaria's own and shackled to the center pole. If they pulled on the irons, the entire tent collapsed on top of them, trapping them underneath and alerting the camp in one move.

'Never let it be said she isn't clever,' Jilian remarked.

'Like mother, like daughter,' Maarcus joked.

She glared at him. 'I suppose I should say I'm glad you're feeling better, but I'm in a foul mood so I won't. What would you know of breeding? You of the line which has bred true unto at least seven generations. If I breed true I'm as likely to produce Alvaria or Hadrian as King Tomar.'

'Or Zera.' His voice was full of longing and pain.

Zera. Maarcus had known her better than Jilian, who shared the blood tie. 'Has that gash on your back reopened?' she asked, trying to change the subject. 'I wish I had my pack.'

'No, it seems thoroughly healed.' He paused, then added, 'I was thinking of my father – the one who was Sir Maarcus the Seventh before me.'

It was Jilian's turn to wince. 'I'm sorry. You said he'd been poisoned. It didn't seem dishonorable considering the short-lived survival of anyone living in the capital.'

'Then why was I given his identical title?'

Jilian flushed. 'I hadn't thought about it. I assumed that was the way the Shoremen do things or perhaps . . .' Her excuse sounded feeble even to her.

'You know that is not the way we do things,' he said. His voice dropped to a sad whisper. 'Nevertheless, it is sometimes the way things are done.'

The princess didn't improve her show of deportment by staring at him with her mouth agape. To think of Maarcus's family hiding dirty linens in their closet gave her cause to reconsider many of her assumptions about the old physician.

Imagine, he was capable of erasing his own son! To be as ruthless with one's own as with those one presumed to lead was a trait she had not thought he possessed. She could not help but wonder how it had shaped the man chained next to her.

What might he do if forced? She tried to sound understanding. 'Better to lance the boil than let it fester, I suppose.'

His face showed horrified disbelief. 'You think Grandfather would poison his own son!'

'I'm sorry,' she said softly. 'It seemed to be what you were telling me. He was poisoned and you were endowed with his name.'

'Oh, yes, I see.' The brows unknit slightly. 'I only meant my own father was not as concerned over the fate of the One Land as my grandfather was.' He paused, then added, 'Or as I seem to have turned out to be.'

'How did your father die?' she asked gently.

'I've never told a soul. Better to let others assume he fell to intrigue rather than ineptness and gluttony.'

'I don't understand.'

'My mother poisoned him.'

'Was he so terrible as that?'

Maarcus smiled in spite of himself and their dire circumstances. 'No, it was an accident. She attempted to murder my grandfather because he had sent me away

361

– or perhaps she meant to commit suicide over missing me so.'

'The latter is hardly more comforting.'

Maarcus seemed to approve her sentiment. 'Spoken like a true orphan,' he said, then went on to explain. 'She poisoned the wine. By all accounts, my father refused to wait until a fresh bottle was opened but insisted on drinking that which had already been poured for my grandfather. It killed him in a matter of moments. Seeing what had happened, my mother swore once at my grandfather then finished the tainted wine.'

'Oh, Maarcus. I'm sorry.'

'You've said that already, but I appreciate it.'

They slid down to the floor, sitting side by side in an awkward silence, not looking at each other, not touching.

They were still sitting there when a young dwarf girl brought them a tray of food.

The child had a remarkable resemblance to Celia Sailclan.

Jilian rubbed her eyes and watched as the dwarf set the tray next to them. 'Ceeley?' she whispered. 'Ceeley, is that you?'

The girl continued puttering at her task, doing nothing useful that the princess could see.

'Celia Sailclan, it's us, Aunt Jilly and Uncle Maarcs.'

The dwarf looked up then.

When she saw the child full in the face, the princess gave an involuntary gasp. 'Oh, Ceeley.'

The girl was indeed Celia Sailclan, but her eyes held a dead expression. Before this, Jilian had seen Ceeley hide herself in sleep to escape from her terrors, but she had always come back to herself when she awoke. The child would have no need of sleep now, for Ceeley didn't know who or where she was or why she would require escape.

Maarcus was speechlessly reaching out to her. Tears poured down his cheeks.

Jilian tried again. She spoke as if everything were perfectly normal. 'Hello, Ceeley. It's good to see you. We were all a bit wor—' Her voice broke. They had had good reason to be worried after all. 'Wondering, that is. We were wondering how your travels with Lyda and Willam had gone.'

'Lyda,' she said. 'Willam?' A flash of confusion crossed her face and was gone. She stared past Jilian as if she heard something in the distance, then turned to acknowledge the princess for the first time. 'My mistress bids you eat.' Her tone was as flat as a corpse's.

She curtseyed so precisely that it wrenched Jilian's heart worse than all the rest. The last time the princess had seen it so perfectly performed was the dwarf's first introduction to Nikolis not so many weeks ago. Jilian squeezed her eyes shut to block the tears. When she opened them – intending to thank the child, to try again to bring her back from wherever the witch held her – the girl was gone.

Little chattering Ceeley, gone without a sound.

Lyda had no illusions when Alvaria released her from her burden of servicing the soldiers, and left Willam free to keep her company. This would transform into a new atrocity soon enough.

Hardly a few hours passed before her suspicions were proven out. The elves entered, bearing ceremonial ropes before them as if in offering. Willam squeezed Lyda's hand and held on tight until the elves snatched his arms to tie his wrists behind his back.

She recognized the elf who had backhanded her and split her lip. He labored under the elfwitch's bidding, blind to his task, and did not notice her at all.

Her right eye was swollen shut, but it didn't take two eyes to see where they were going. The bloodstained dais was plain as plain could be from this distance, just as it had been when they first installed her in her tent of misery.

They were pushed past the restless, angry mob. Here was not only the pitch of evil, but also the tone of desperation and deprivation. Alvaria spared no one in her march of destruction.

Despite the horror, Lyda felt serenity settle on her like a dusting of clean snow. She was not really ready to die, but she had done all she could. She had done her best to rescue those who could be rescued. She whispered a prayer that the Sisters might watch over Ceeley. Lastly, she forgave herself and forgave Willam.

She hardly noticed as they strapped her to the stone altars, though she heard Willam struggle against his captors. 'Peace, Willam,' she said softly. 'Alvaria might win our bodies but she will not win our souls.'

Her husband calmed.

'Quiet,' hissed an elf hovering nearby, but he dared say no more to the captives without the elfwitch's sanction.

Lyda lay still and waited.

Jilian felt her mother's presence before Alvaria raised the tent flap. 'She comes,' she murmured to Maarcus.

The elfwitch wrapped herself in white upon white, invisible as a snow-leopard in winter. She stood as imperious as ever, true to herself at least, Jilian thought.

'Take him.'

Two trolls hurried forward to unshackle Maarcus from

his place next to Jilian. They gripped him firmly under each arm. If he challenged them, bones would break.

The elf overseer cleared his throat. 'May I ask . . . ?'

'Just don't kill him yet. I will have a use later.'

The elf bowed and signalled the trolls, who hauled the Shoreman away.

Jilian was still staring at Maarcus's newly-healed back when the elfwitch said conversationally, 'You waste precious resources in fighting me. Because you are of my blood, I have been able to overlook your obstinacy.' She smiled. 'The trait seems to run in the family.'

The princess kept her silence. Somewhere she felt her brother, but knew no more about him than that he lived.

Alvaria's voice went as cold and hard as steel. 'This third chance will be your last – or by the Sisters, Great and Lesser, I will torture you as no one has ever been tortured in all the histories of the Seven Realms.'

Jilian's tongue moved quicker than her brain. 'How comforting to know I will hold such a special place among your prey.'

Alvaria backhanded her across the face.

Jilian expected it – saw the arm swing ever so slowly toward her – but she couldn't ward off the blow with her hands bound behind her back.

'You cannot manipulate me into doing something reckless,' the elfwitch said. 'My every move is well considered and known beforehand.'

Jilian thought about her own temperament and knew this to be true. Even her fits of seemingly impulsive pique were within what she expected of herself. Like mother, like daughter.

Wind whipped at the tent, but no cold outside could match the iciness within. The elfwitch's voice swelled to fill the entire tent. 'Consider well your future these next few days. Consider too the fate of those you would protect.'

Jilian locked eyes with the elf. Somehow the princess would defeat this woman.

Alvaria broke the gaze and casually waved forward another guard.

He unlocked her restraints, released her from the tent-pole, and fastened the shackles once again.

Alvaria led Jilian out into the chanting crowd and up beside her on the dais.

'You have seen my mother's death,' Alvaria proclaimed.

'We have,' they answered.

'Many of you shared in her demise.'

'We did.'

'Know that this is my daughter,' she shouted. 'She has yet to make a choice.' She raised Jilian's bound arms. 'Should she choose well, these fall away and she becomes my noble daughter, to be heeded in all things.'

The crowd recited in a monotone, 'Long live the Queen. Long live the princess.'

'But—' That one word silenced them all in an instant. 'Should she choose poorly, she is no more than the two before us. Less than they, she will be a lowly half-breed, destined to be reshaped to my will.'

They cheered, as if this mention of the transformation were a reward for their own suffering.

Jilian tore her gaze away from the savage mob to look at the altars where three lay lashed to stone. The dwarf was a stranger, but Jilian knew the two humans. Lyda and Willam lay as if entranced.

Lyda and Willam, blessed by the Sisters themselves.

Or so it had seemed.

Beside her Alvaria began a litany of the sins of the

rulers of the One Land – the sins of Jilian's father, King Tomar.

Mesmerized by the horror, Jilian did not see Alvaria's knife until it sliced the throat of the first victim. The dwarf's blood drained into a painted goat-hide.

As the elfwitch held the knife aloft to the crowd's chanting, the princess recognized it. For how could she not? It was her own, given to her brother less than two weeks ago.

The knife plunged, but this time it pierced not human skin but goat skin. The warm blood splashed across the faces of husband and wife. Together they screamed an agony beyond anything Jilian had ever known.

She could not shut out the sound. She could only add her howls to their torment.

# Chapter 18

## BREAKTHROUGH

Ceeley liked it in her cocoon. It was warm and quiet, as comforting as a bear-hug. That Aunt Jilly person had ruined everything. She had singled Ceeley out and now the elfwitch would punish her.

It would hurt, really hurt.

Already she could hear the shouts of the ritual. Soon she would be part of that same ceremony. Ceeley didn't think she would like that.

Unless she could stay safe in her cocoon. Unless she could pretend everything was just as it had been. She would have to make-believe well enough to convince the elfwitch.

The child carried her tray back to the elf's tent. The guard would not let her pass. He called her 'troll-bait' and said that no one was there. He told her to bother somebody else.

Where to go now? The cries were getting louder and tearing great gaps in her cocoon.

A shadow passed across the ground. She looked up to see what manner of beast could cause such a shape.

There was a dragon . . . two . . . no, four dragons! Four dragons flying overhead, and one of them carried people on its back.

This was too wondrous to miss!

Ceeley stepped out of her safe wrapping—

And the misery rushed in to engulf her.

She tried to run back inside, to hide, but it was too late.

Jedrek enjoyed teaching the boy. A quick study, he reminded the Elder of the joy he had forgotten, of the pleasure of greeting another day. He called Notti back and kept him longer than was fair for one so recently through the Dunavs.

Together they repeated the litany and examined its implications. Together they poked at roots and leaves, finding the hidden remedies. Together they felt Alvaria pull at the life-force of the One Land.

Notti opened his eyes in alarm. 'She's done it again. Pity the poor souls.'

'Yes,' Jedrek echoed, as if he were the student and Notti the master. 'Yes.'

'We must help,' Notti urged. 'It could be the Dragon Prince.'

Jedrek shook his head. 'You know it is not. Someone precious, someone pure, but not the Dragon Prince.'

Notti's face twisted in the anguish of those fated to stand by while others suffer. 'Please.'

In his battle to overcome Alvaria, Jedrek had forgotten how it felt to care for the injured. It took a small boy to remind him why he had fought to begin with. 'Not yet.' He swallowed hard. 'But soon, Notti. I promise, very soon.'

Together they bowed their heads. The elves added their petitions to the many offered all over the One Land, by exiles who could not fathom why they stopped in mid-flight to pray for another's miracle – but were compelled nonetheless to hope these new victims might withstand Alvaria.

Walther tried everything he could conjure up. Abadan would not be moved. His sorrow for Maarcus consumed him for hours.

It felt like days.

Finally, when the magician stepped back from the corpse now hidden in a secret tomb beneath the castle, Walther could stand it no more.

'Master Abadan, Sir Maarcus was a great man. He lived a full life and yet he died too soon.' He shook the magician's arm. 'But Master, there are greater men than he and they will surely die too young if we don't help.'

Abadan looked into Walther's eyes. 'Let them,' he said. 'I'm too tired to care.'

Staring into the grieving man's eyes, the dwarf instantly understood Abadan's naming ceremony. This was the moment the seeress had predicted.

'Abadan, Harmon can watch over him now. We must go,' Walther said. 'I know you are weakened by your distress, but lend me what strength you have left. There is no more time. She has them both. You know that she does.'

The magician glared at the dwarf as if he had gone mad. The minute stretched, and still the man did not move.

Was he too remembering the prophecy of his downfall?

The magician raised his arms and spoke a word, summoning power from a place Walther hardly knew existed.

Abruptly they were sucked into a grey nothingness, cold and harsh and deadly. Just as suddenly, the greyness spat them onto a battlefield of carnage.

Alvaria did not bother to hide Nikolis in a tent. He had shown himself capable of escaping such flimsy prisons before. She lashed him to the tree herself, and assigned enough archers to ring the entire trunk.

Nikolis ignored the elves. They were not his concern. For all he cared, they could put each other's eyes out with so many raised and notched bows. He would not be here to suffer the arrows.

He would be among the captives on the dais.

Their wailing rose above the crowd's dirge. Nikolis did not let it distract him. He thought about the itch in his shoulders. He pictured himself flying above the mob as he had done at the massacre only a few days past.

He was the Dragon Prince.

He would become the dragon.

Nothing happened.

But whose shadows were those flying high overhead, diving for the dais? What dragons travelled in packs? What single dragon willingly attacked an elf-mage? Did Nikolis imagine himself among them?

No, he was not looking down on the horror from a great height. He still felt the rope which bound him to the tree, smelled the sap dripping from the bark which scratched against his bare skin, heard the cries of pain, saw the archers aiming as one at this new target.

'Now,' he begged silently. 'By the Sisters, let them waste all their arrows now.'

Wanton Tom would've bet he'd never risk his butt against the elfwitch once, never mind twice. This time, he could have flown away perfectly safe and left the battle to the younger and the stronger. Instead, this time, he led the onslaught to protect the younger and the stronger. Not simply his own who chose for herself, but for all those who couldn't.

Grosik took point and his family followed.

It was not a fair fight.

Trolls don't have much hope against one dragon . . . or four.

Tom hacked his way past the elves to the dais. The elfwitch was not there.

Two creatures, half human, lay covered in blood, but breathing still.

The mercenary raised his sword to end their misery, but Ginni stayed his hand. 'No, there is hope for them yet.'

Tom glanced at the hideous forms. 'But honey, they're in so much pain,' he said to his daughter.

'Father, to live is painful.'

He lowered his sword and used the edge to slice their ropes. The two huddled together, and it seemed they knew who and what they were.

Ginni stepped closer to examine them.

Tom could not bear to stare into the eyes of such bald-faced pain. 'Where is she?' he asked his daughter.

Ginni pointed without looking up from her task.

Across the meadow, Alvaria led two struggling humans, a man and a woman, brother and sister.

'She's got the royal twins! Grosik, stop her!'

The great beast shook off the desperate trolls climbing his back. He flapped his wings twice and was there in front of the witch.

Alvaria had other plans.

A mist covered the meadow that not even Grosik could penetrate. He snorted and the mist cleared.

No one was there. No Alvaria. No Jilian. No Nikolis.

Grosik looked this way and that and rose into the air. 'I'll find her, Tom. I swear by the Seven, I will.'

In the midst of battle, Ginni was afraid to use her magic. After examining the half-humans on the dais, she decided there was too much magic run amuck here. She couldn't be sure her own newly tamed talent wouldn't make matters worse.

Thank the Sisters Tom had insisted on old-fashioned sword lessons, if only to pass the long winter nights. He'd always claimed she'd need the know-how some day.

But what she really needed right then was an extra pair of arms to help parry the attacking elf's manic thrusts.

All at once, a loud boom sounded and the world shuddered as though something large crashed to the earth. The opposing elf's eyes went wide and the fight suddenly drained out of him. He stood with sword arm raised, but made no effort to use it.

Sure, I can appreciate a breather too, Ginni thought, but this is stranger than a dog in a cat-house. She held her own sword ready but closed in to investigate her opponent. Not surprisingly, he was breathing hard. The odd thing was that his attention was riveted across the meadow – as was that of most of the other combatants on the field.

Cautiously, Ginni circled around the elf so that she could get a better view.

Grosik lay on his side coughing such as she'd never heard him. Now that she noticed it, she couldn't believe she hadn't felt the ground trembling as the dragon heaved and hacked.

'Alvaria will pay!' Grosik swore in a voice so loud the trees shook. 'My heirs will visit yours in the underworld.' He choked once more and lay still.

The air hung thick with the smell of blood and the sound of silence.

Ginni and Tom converged on the motionless dragon.

'What?' she asked, as she knelt down by the great beast's head.

'The elfwitch was escaping with the royal twins,' Tom explained. 'Check that. Did escape. Grosik vowed to find them and gave chase. The next instant he came crashing back down.'

She put her ear against his chest. 'He hasn't quite given up on breathing,' Ginni whispered. 'But what do we do?'

'Leave him to us,' said an unfamiliar voice.

'I'd sooner revisit the Tower of the Forty-nine,' Ginni hissed, without looking up. 'No one drags him away to be pecked over.'

'Gin, it's the other dragons, the ones who helped us,' Tom said.

'Uncle, I don't care if it's the first dragon ever hatched. I won't send him back to those who revile him.'

'He will be tended,' the beast assured her. 'If Grosik can be made well, I am the only one who can do it.'

Ginni thought about that for a long minute.

'She's right,' Tom said. 'We don't know the first thing about this kind of injury.'

'Am I not a mage?' she asked with a hint of her mother's imperiousness.

'Am I not your father?' Tom snapped back. 'Is he not my best friend? Can you swear to me you have the know-how to get him back in the air? If so, get to it. If not, please give us a hand moving this behemoth somewhere safer.'

Ginni looked at the dragon hovering overhead. Two smaller ones fluttered not far away, hoping to stir up more action. She peered at her father, greying and wrinkling. He wouldn't be able to fight this way indefinitely.

He was letting her decide. She sighed. 'All right, Uncle. Let's get him out of here.'

'We'll need a carrier,' the female dragon said. 'I can take it from there.'

'Let's tear down one of the bigger tents,' Ginni suggested. 'Tom, all right if I do that while you guard him?'

Her father nodded. 'But hurry.'

Ginni dashed across the meadow, dodging half-hearted attempts to engage her sword and jumping over the now-routine sight of dead trolls collapsing in on themselves. She ignored Alvaria's tent though it was the largest, and headed for another one nearby.

'Anyone in here?' she asked. 'Come out now before it all tumbles down on your head.'

No one answered.

'You were warned!' she called. She did not take the time to check inside before pulling up stakes.

The tent sagged to one side.

A child shrieked.

'Hey,' an angry man shouted in an educated human accent. 'Haven't you people put this girl through enough?'

Ginni ran to find the tent-flap amidst the folds of embroidered fabric. 'Out,' she said frantically, holding the entrance open. 'Quickly.'

A man and dwarf child emerged.

'Sorry,' she said, waving them out. 'Need this. If you can help, we're over there.' She pointed to the fallen dragon and urgently finished dismantling the tent.

Walther and Abadan arrived on the edge of the clearing. Steaming bodies littered the battlefield in front of them. Blood and refuse filled the air.

'It's all over but the funerals,' Abadan said, without his usual sense of irony. 'Even the great Grosik can't win against her.'

Walther followed the magician's gaze to where several people struggled to get the beast onto a giant canvas. 'They could use our help,' the dwarf admonished, and hastened to the scene.

'Uncle Walther!' Ceeley exclaimed.

'Ceeley? Celia Sailclan? Is that really you.'

She gave him her most indignant smile. 'Of course, it's me. Uncle Maarcs saved me. Now come over here and help pull.'

Walther happily moved to her side. 'I finally get to meet a dragon,' she whispered, 'and he's sick. Actually, he's hurt, really bad. We're trying to rescue him.'

At last Abadan made his way to the spot. 'Is he dead?' he asked bluntly.

'Not yet,' the mercenary answered.

'Will be soon if you keep tossing him around like that.'

'Thank you, Honorable Master Abadan,' said the girl Walther realized must be Ginni. 'However, since we are currently short on time and pulleys, this is the best we can—'

'Why don't you lift him up and slide the tent under?'

He asked the question honestly, but left the rest flabbergasted. Walther supposed this was what came of a man who lived among servants for all his adult life.

'Most of the handy help is putrefying at present.'

'The magician is correct,' said another voice. Walther glanced up and was amazed to see not one but three more dragons. 'Even a claw's height off the ground would be sufficient to have my younglings slip the cloth beneath him.'

Silently, she called the smaller dragons to her. Each took a corner of the tent and prepared to yank the rest as soon as their mother gave the signal.

'Walther, Ginni, come here.' Abadan motioned them to him. He raised his arms in preparation for a powerful spell. 'I had never thought to do this again . . .' He trailed off. 'This will not be comfortable for you, but better this than letting Alvaria complete her work.' He placed a hand atop each of their heads.

Walther closed his eyes to help empty his thoughts and open his mind to whatever his master intended. Pain lanced behind his eyes and the dwarf fell to his knees. He struggled to rise and finally settled for sitting upright. A giant wind blew bits of dirt in his face and he ignored it.

Slowly the agony dulled to an ache. He opened his eyes. The dragons were already aloft. The female clutched the four corners of the tent in her talons while Grosik hung like a dead weight. The younglings circled, flying guard.

'Goodbye, dragons!' Ceeley called. 'Good luck!'

Seated on the ground next to him, Ginni whispered, 'The very best of the Sisters' luck, you old grouch.'

'We've got to help Mama-Lyda and Papa-Wil now,' Ceeley said. 'I know they're here somewhere.'

The group looked at each other and away. Only Ginni would meet the little girl's big eyes. 'I'll go,' she said. She struggled to rise, but couldn't gather the strength.

'Rest,' Walther said, unable to imagine why she would want such a dreadful task. 'I'll go. I owe her this much.'

'Come on, Uncle Maarcs. We should go too.'

'No, honey,' he said, his voice full of sorrow. 'Uncle Walther will tell us where they are.'

Walther stood and walked as far as he could get away from Ceeley before he slowly began checking the corpses. Everywhere steaming piles of flesh dissolved to reveal the people beneath. He tried to be comforted in knowing that they would no longer serve the elfwitch, and merely found himself growing angrier and angrier.

The dwarf fought not to remember earlier sites of devastation, not to remember the families gone, dead, or worse. Just as he had in the aftermath of every battle, Walther sifted through the refuse, sorting details without realizing it. It was his nature to do so and he could not stop even in the wake of so much death.

He entered Alvaria's tent. Miraculously it was intact. Her magicks remained on her work-table as if she might reappear any moment.

Feeling only slightly like a thief, Walther culled her items, left the more common leaves and roots as they were, pocketed her supply of serviceberry. As he picked up the vials, the value of the parchment below became unmistakable. His hands shook as he lifted off the rest of the jars and used his forearms to hold the scroll's edges.

It was a map of the One Land, a map such as he had never seen.

Gently, gently he rolled it up. He searched until he discovered a cloth to protect it, and wrapped that around the outside.

Map in hand, he exited the tent and walked toward the one place he hadn't explored, the altar. Walther did not want to encounter Lyda and Willam here.

The humans were lathered in blood, sticky and rank.

He set down the map and inspected the human. He was surprised to find someone had already cut loose their bonds. They must be dead. Again, he had arrived too late.

No, not like so many others, these two still breathed.

'Over here,' Walther called, forgetting about little Ceeley.

The child arrived at the head of the group. 'Mama-Lyda, Papa-Wil. You found them. Oh, thank you, Uncle Walther. Thank you.'

She ran to hug them, stopped, and turned to Walther. 'Ceeley, I'm s—'

To his surprise, she hugged him and said, 'It'll be okay, Uncle Walther.' He stood dumbfounded as she climbed onto the altar.

The creature who had been Lyda slowly sat up. 'Ooh,' she moaned. 'Ooh.' She saw the girl and held her breath in mid-groan.

'Mama-Lyda, you're all right. You're all right!'

'Ceeley, no!' Maarcus shouted, but he was too far away. 'Walther, what were you thinking?' the Shoreman asked.

What was he thinking?

The woman-thing put her arms around the girl. Finally, Walther forced himself to move. 'No, please don't hurt her!'

The woman-thing backed away.

'Uncle, you'll hurt her feelings. Mama-Lyda just looks different on the outside. She's still the same on the inside.'

Walther held her eyes. Though he'd met this woman only a handful of times, he recognized her intelligent gaze. 'Lady Lyda?'

She nodded. 'It's me,' she answered with some difficulty.

'Mama-Lyda,' the girl said sternly, 'we've got to get you washed up. You're disgusting.'

The woman-thing that seemed to be Lyda laughed a sound not made by human throats. 'Yes, I'm sure I am.'

'But how?' Walther asked.

'It's not my blood,' she explained haltingly.

'And Papa-Wil!' Ceeley hopped off the one altar and onto the other, as if they were no more daunting than a child's tree-house. 'Papa-Wil?'

He groaned and painstakingly rose—

While the surrounding adults stared at the three victims, living and dead.

'I found something,' Walther said, still fixed on Ceeley.

'I'll say,' muttered Maarcus.

'Not them,' Walther whispered. 'It's on the ground right here.' He pointed to the base of the central dais.

Ginni stumbled forward to pick up the scroll. 'It was mother's! Wherever did you find this?'

'In the elfwitch's tent along with most of her supplies.'

Out of the corner of his eye, he watched Abadan move closer to study the map. 'We can guess how Alvaria got it from Roslin,' the magician said. 'But how did Roslin come by it?'

'Better not to wonder,' Tom said. 'Roslin was never one to give away secrets.'

Ginni shook her head. 'She never offered explanations for anything she did or owned. By the time this came into her possession, I'd long since learned not to ask.'

'Hmph,' grunted the magician. He hoisted himself up on the dais next to Lyda. 'Do you hurt?' he asked humbly.

'The Sisters provide,' Lyda answered.

'Yes, I guess they do,' Abadan said. 'I guess they do.'


In the cold, grey wasteland, Alvaria held the undisputed throne. Her subjects numbered merely two. They were not elven, but human.

None of this mattered to the elfwitch. She had at long last reclaimed her own. She had won the gamble.

*Or so she believes,* Jilian thought, as she clutched her dragon's head coin. *Even in this mysterious land, we can fight.*

'You won't need that where we're going.' Alvaria plucked it from her, with no more consideration than she gave to speaking in this barren realm where heat seared the throat and noxious fumes clogged the nose.

Jilian reached out, but the token had already disappeared before she could will her arms to move in the soupy air.

'Your father would be proud of both of you,' the elfwitch told them. 'Unfortunately, I never did agree with him on much, least of all the rearing of children.'

*How can she bear to speak in this foul land,* Jilian wondered. *I can hardly breathe without retching.*

*How? Because she does nothing without forethought,*

she answered herself. She knows this place as well as Mut and I knew the lands where we grew up.

Nikolis, she thought desperately, Oh, Nik! This was all planned, all of it!

I know, he answered, without speaking aloud.

Jilian jumped at the voice in her head. She hadn't expected him to hear her, never mind respond. Is that really you?

I hope so.

What if she can hear us?

She probably can.

A few steps ahead, Alvaria trudged on across the cracked plain. She made no move to silence them or hurry them along. Together they traipsed behind her.

Count on it, Nik amended.

We were meant to come here, to this place – wherever it is, Jilian told him. Whether our mother or the Sisters served as the vehicle is unimportant. What's important is what we learn here, because the answer to everything we seek is here. Right here.

Why must you refer to her as our mother? Nik asked, distracted by his disgust into missing the greater point. She did no more than give birth to us.

That's it, Jilian thought. That's it! We are an unalterable part of her in a way that no other creatures can be. Since we live she can never nullify us. She can kill us, but she will never be able to go forward as if she had not known wc lived. We rule her as much as she rules us.

Like mother, like daughter, Jilian said to Nikolis, unable to keep the laughter out of her thought.

He glanced at her in alarm.

Jilian put her finger to her lips, motioning him to keep quiet. She could feel the doubt in his mind, but he honored her request.

'Hey, Nikolis,' she said aloud. 'I think I'm getting to like this place.'

The prince grimaced and continued on.

Alvaria turned and smiled. 'I knew you'd come to understand things my way.'

'Absolutely,' Jilian answered. Completely at ease now, she opened herself to her mother and welcomed the flood of desires the elfwitch poured in.